I0641364

# WORLD'S ABYSS

## A JOURNEY OF EXUVIATION AND REBIRTH

KIKI YAW SARPONG

Copyright © 2024 by Kiki Yaw Sarpong

All rights reserved.

No part of this publication may be reproduced, distributed, or transmitted in any form or by any means, including photocopying, recording, or other electronic or mechanical methods, without the prior written permission of the publisher, except as permitted by U.S. copyright law. For permission requests, contact Kiki Yaw Sarpong.

The story, all names, characters, and incidents portrayed in this production are fictitious. No identification with actual persons (living or deceased), places, buildings, and products is intended or should be inferred.

Book Cover by Martin Lugwarha Kalere

First edition 2024

To my mother, my present, and my future family.

# CONTENTS

# PREFACE

I am a creator of worlds and a conqueror of my imaginations. I am a seeker of truth in all its forms, and I won't deny that I express heavy disappointment when the truth I seek alters from my fantasized idea of the world. I'm an adventurer of the mind, though I'm still trying to get better at my adventure in nature. I am in awe at the beauty of the world and ache at its inequities. I know of balance, and the unchangeable flaws of people, but I still selfishly hope everything about the world was all-good. Can it ever be? Or is our objective idea of "all-good" flawed? I would understand in all honesty because I myself am flawed. A flawed man, a hopeful man, a black man. I write my stories hoping to create the fantasized ideas of the world I build in my head. I create the characters with a love I didn't even know I could have for scribbled words on a piece of paper. Love for the ones you may deem objectively good or objectively bad; each one I put careful thought into, to craft their dreams and their desires. I apologize in advance however, because even in my fantasized world, I couldn't make everything "all-good". I found my idea of that was also flawed.

I'm a creator of worlds and a conqueror of my imagin... hmmm, I wonder if my imaginations rather conquered me?

To all those who helped me get here. The list might be too long to write but know that you'll always be appreciated in my heart.

## CHAPTER ONE

# INTO THE WORLD'S ABYSS

*"Breathe ... Let the wind guide your hands and focus on your target."*

The string weighed tense on her fingers and the fletching steadied as the breeze kissed her cheek. Her father's words echoed in her ears. The point of her arrow gazed at her opponent, its golden skin bathed in sunlight unbeknownst to the perils that lay hidden. With her fingers firmly nocked, it raised its eyes, meeting her gaze; two little dark voids each bordered by fur white as clouds. It stood unmoving, oblivious to its fate though its eyes still begged for mercy. Naemi stared back, doubt filling her heart, she let go.

*"Hahaha — I knew she couldn't kill it, father!"* Her brother uttered, springing out of the bushes. Naemi reached out to knock his head, but he ran.

*"You can't even hold a bow well, you doodle,"* she fired back. The doe was long gone by now. Fast as lightning it scattered, maybe faster. An

arrow whizzing past its ears was as good an indication as any to find new feeding grounds.

"*I'm sorry father,*" said Naemi. Eyes lowered, unable to glance at her father.

"*You'll get it next time, we already caught three rabbits today. Let's head home so I can make my famous rabbit stew you like so much.*" he responded. An answer that lightened his eldest child's face. He noticed the uncertainty in her eyes as she drew her arrow toward the doe, and regretted asking her to do it even though he thought it necessary. Hunting was a great skill to have and he was eager to teach his children one of the basic foundations of survival. Naemi was a great archer, confirmed by the numerous times he'd watched her hit the center of her mark on tree targets during her "secret" practices. Weirdly, she seemed to always miss an actual target. It wasn't until their third hunting trip that he observed her arrows consistently shooting past the prey's ears. Close enough to signal danger but far enough not to hurt it. A couple of similar experiences followed and he kept trying, hoping that one of these days she would take the next step, but it was all for naught. At least these misses seemed to amuse her brother who was always eager to mock her afterwards.

"*Hmph.*" Ozai let out a sigh. Another failed attempt.

He initially wanted to hunt the doe himself but thought this might be a wonderful teaching experience, and a great story at that. Unfortunately, he now had neither the story nor the doe, and was just grateful he had caught the three rabbits earlier.

Naemi was now in full pursuit of her brother. Arrows hopping in their quiver as she chased after him. She was fast, but Dakai was faster. A boy of three and ten, three years younger than his sister; svelte and of medium height. He dashed past the trees, springing over branches, barks and stems with no effort. His braided black hair bounced around his head as if in excitement for his triumph in evading his sister. Naemi slowly came to a halt. Her mistake was letting him get a head-start. A mistake she never learned from. He was truly elusive.

The walk back home was as calm as it could be. *Rabbit stew,* she thought. A smile plastered across her face again. It had been a while since she'd had some, and just the thought made her salivate. It could be argued her father was one of the best cooks of rabbit stew in their entire town. He was not as good at cooking other food, but for rabbit stew, he had a sorcerer's touch. He never divulged his recipe even after the countless times she'd asked. She once guessed the secret ingredient to be ground Séte leaves in her attempt to replicate, and ended up cooking the worst stew she'd ever tasted. She remembered her father trying his best to ingest it with a pleasant face while her brother dramatically spit his scoop out of his mouth with visible displeasure.

"*Are you trying to poison us?*" he blurted out. This was the day Dakai came up with her infamous "Poison princess" nickname.

She hated it.

Admittedly, she was never a good cook and nor was her father, apart from his specialty. This much she knew. Dakai was the one with the sorcerer's touch in this aspect. He made meals that made her taste buds dance with excitement. Of course she never acknowledged his delightful cooking, and always retorted with, "*It's a decent meal,*" anytime their father gave him praise, but deep down it was one of his qualities she adored him for.

Speaking of her brother, she realized an opportunity to sneak up on him while he admired some plants ahead and burst off.

———————◦———————

The sun inched closer to rest. Its rays dimmed and the clouds scrambled in the sky as they lost their golden shrouds. The forest air smelled of green and tranquility, and the tree leaves swayed with every pulse of a breeze. The night-dwellers were on the verge of awakening and the day-wanderers made preparations for slumber. Sounds of playful teens and rustling branches rippled off trees and forest floor into the forest void.

The town wasn't too far now. Fenced by the forest of Anul and the mountains of Lua, it boasted a sizable population, vibrant and peaceful.

Ozai walked well behind his children. Their playful antics had sped their return home, and he felt no similar burst of energy to keep pace. No matter, he loved the quiet — or not entirely quiet walk home after a somewhat successful hunt. The forest was peaceful and he could reminisce about old glory days as much as he wanted. He rarely spoke of those days with his children, for the emotions that surfaced with some of the words were sometimes too hard to bear, and he despised showing any emotions of sadness in the presence of his "gems" as he called them.

"*Our gems,*" his wife would always correct him mockingly. "*I did most of the work.*" She'd add.

And of course she did. Naemi's birth happened in the middle of one of the worst storms to hit Soros in five summers. She came days ahead of what the birth-mother predicted and took till night to be birthed. He remembered running to the farmer and his wife the next house over to seek help because there was no way to get to the birth-mother, and Shaye was screaming so much, he thought she'd die. Night fell and amidst the rain, a brown-eyed baby girl was born, with curled hair as black as midnight, and skin brown and shiny, it reflected the light from the candle flames. She didn't cry, not once. Just stared in his eyes as he held her, rainstorm be damned. "*Naemi ... That should be her name,*" Shaye said, bloodied and exhausted.

"*Through the storm,*" Ozai reiterated in approval. Tears in his eyes and a smile across his face, he gazed at his first child in admiration.

Dakai was another story. Came out screaming like his hair was on fire. Half the town could hear him the moment he popped out. A single tear streamed down Ozai's face and trickled along his cheek.

Ozai smiled. — Oh how he missed Shaye.

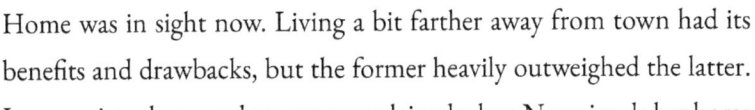

Home was in sight now. Living a bit farther away from town had its benefits and drawbacks, but the former heavily outweighed the latter. It was quieter here, and no one complained when Naemi rode her horse as fast as she could. "*Who's that standing in the middle of our yard?*" Naemi asked.

"*Can you not recognize Aunt Rema? You truly are blind,*" Dakai responded, walking by her side. Enough running had tired them both and a truce was called.

"*I'm not blind, you just see too well with those eyes,*" Naemi fired back.

"*Whatever you say poi...*" He stopped himself before he had to deal with the consequence of his name calling.

Truce still intact.

Naemi was going to ignore him just this one time. Chasing after her younger brother was no small feat. She lost most of the time yet never gave up.

"*We lost father,*" Dakai said. A usual occurrence on most of these trips. Ozai used to grumble at the constant departure of his children on the return home but grew used to it in time; even desired his time alone now. He would still appreciate it if they carried the game home once in a while, it would save his shoulders from the weight.

"*Naemi, you want to finish this race home,*" Dakai proposed. Naemi looked back at him with disinterest.

"*Are you not exhausted? And what is that stuck to the bottom of your pants?*" she responded. Dakai looked down and she burst off again. If she lacked the speed against her brother, trickery was going to be her helper.

As Ozai once remarked, "*You're either the fastest or you're not,*" and she most definitely was not.

Rema looked back to see a speeding Dakai and his sister panting and frazzled right behind him. A scene she wasn't a stranger to. Basket in hand, filled with fruits, fresh radish, cabbages, and potatoes from her farm. She and Ozai supported each other after becoming victims of the same dreadful predicament. The widow and the widower, some in town called them though never to their faces. Others guessed they would get married and support each other since they were close and had built deep bonds of friendship. It seemed logical. These opinions however rarely left the privacy of their rooms. Once, the baker's daughter made a comment about Rema acting like Ozai's wife when she was buying bread for him. A comment she paid for with a nasty smack to her face. "*Have you no respect girl?*" she fired.

The truth lay significantly far from the gossip. Close friends before, tragedy brought them closer. They complimented each other and helped as best as they could. From sharing fresh ingredients from her farm and his hunting game, to looking after children, fixing broken tools, cleaning stables and any activity that either of them required help in. Their relationship worked in the most unique way possible but never went any further. It'd been four winters since her husband passed, Ozai's wife passing a season before, and time had barely healed her wounds. Maybe at one time, in a moment of vulnerability, she thought of taking the extra step but what that meant was a question better left unexplored.

Even Naemi fell victim to these gossips, and what followed was a fortnight of tantrums, scoldings and tears from all sides in this endeavor. Except for Dakai, who just went about his day looking for herbs and visiting the town healer. After the fortnight of chaos, tempers calmed and both families had a discussion. Turns out Rema's daughter and her youngest son had similar concerns, and this discussion was indeed needed. Clarity helped a whole lot, and both families grew in their appreciation for each other. Naemi and Rema's daughter bonded even closer and Naemi ended up being one of her flower-hands at her union last summer.

Dakai whizzed past Rema to a halt.

"*Sorry auntie, you seem startled.*" Her reflexes saved her lest she dropped her basket.

"*You almost made me spill the food!*" Rema barked back. Dakai reached out to rid her of her extra weight and she willingly obliged.

"*Where's your father? Leave him again?*" she asked.

"*He just walks too slowly and Naemi was chasing after me every chance she got,*" he responded in defense.

"*You two truly never get tired. Any good game this trip? The butcher's wife mentioned some scarcity in the market today.*" she questioned.

"*Yeah, we had trouble finding anything for a long while but lucked into a nest of fat and juicy rabbits, and a nice-looking doe a bit after but we lost the doe,*" Dakai answered.

"*Let me guess, she missed again, didn't she?*" Rema said with a laugh.

"*Not on purpose Auntie!*" Naemi, who finally reached them, responded amid loss of breath.

"*I am sure it wasn't sweetie ... I'm sure it wasn't,*" Rema echoed sarcastically.

The door to the house creaked open. Always first home, Dakai often had the keys. He picked up the basket and went inside. Aunt Rema followed.

Naemi stayed back to check for any signs of her father. She could have relieved him of at least one of the rabbits, she thought to herself with remorse.

He would have a faster return if she did, and she'd be way closer to some sweet rabbit stew. Next time she won't be consumed with the thought of catching up to her brother; next time she would be the darling daughter and walk beside her snail-paced father carrying all the game.

A trend of her history will call these statements into doubt.

———◄O►———

Night came slow and steady. The season of early summer was fading and the late summers came with longer days and shorter nights. Flickering lights sprouted in different parts of the Zenu home and joined other sporadic flames in brightening Soros from above. Hungry horses neighed from their stable for their dinner, and fireflies buzzed around without regard or ambition.

The door opened and Ozai stood at the threshold. Rabbits in hand, he tossed them to the side with a tremor. "*It's getting quite chilly,*" he remarked.

"*You're getting old Ozai, the children got home long ago,*" Rema interjected.

"*Rema? I didn't know you'd be coming by today. Did Daem leave for the capital already?*" Ozai asked.

"*He left at dawn today but not to the capital. A messenger-bird came to the town's old-guard requesting all army foot-soldiers near the east shore to report to the eastern infantry. Something about pirates or warships or an enhanced, not really sure which it was,*" she answered.

"*An enhanced? That sounds dangerous,*" Ozai responded with concern.

"*I thought so too. However the message was more uncertain, and Daem mentioned a lot of false alarms most times, only known enhanced is part of the queen's royal guard, so I reckon it's false,*" she remarked. And Ozai nodded in slight agreement.

"*Well, I need to get to cooking. Rabbit stew tonight and everyone is quite famished. I was going to get Dakai to bring one of the rabbit's over to you, but you can take one home since you're already here. Want to stay for rabbit stew?*" Ozai asked.

"*Good thing I brought some fresh radishes just in time, and could I ever say no to your rabbit stew? It's fit for the queen,*" Rema responded in excitement.

Dakai descended down the stairs hearing his father's voice. "*Finally! I am starving, father.*" He said in exhalation; as dramatic as only Dakai can.

"*Okay… Okay, I will go get to it then,*" Ozai teased as he left the room. Dakai in close pursuit.

Rema collapsed back on the rocking chair. Arguably her favorite piece of furniture in the Zenu household. Made of Oakenwood and cloaked in a heap of soft sheepskin, this is what she imagined lying on clouds would be like. She loved it so much she asked Aika, one of the most skilled carpenters in Soros to make a replica for her, but the result never felt the same. It rocked too hard or too slow. Or the fur didn't feel as right even after she switched it infinite times. She tried at one time to just ask Ozai for it. A question that startled him but ultimately decided if it meant that much to her, she could have it. Unfortunately, that didn't help either. It creaked so much in her home, she returned it in a sennight.

"*Some things feel right in only one place,*" she remembered Ozai saying satirically. And he was right. A trait he visibly derived pleasure in.

The windows rattled rhythmically as a faint zephyr filled the parlor. The lamp flames danced around occasionally but still held their ground. Rema put some extra logs in the fireplace and the flames roared back in appreciation. More light filled the room with warmth in hand. The bricks adopted the color of the luminescence of the flames, and Ozai's hunting trophies gleamed on the walls with pride. The hide of the famous Irkshire wolf that tormented the town for weeks, a skull of a mountain deer with horns big as tree stems and the white scales of a snowlizaed; as surprising as that is having one this close to Soros.

Admittedly, this shouldn't be possible for a common blacksmith. Even Daem questioned the legitimacy of killing the snowlizaed, citing the best army archers would lose in an encounter with such an imposing creature. Town gossip would have that he just found a dead young snowlizaed and brought it home, and Ozai never argued in defense. Regardless, the town's old-guard relentlessly pursued him in recruitment, an act which he denied time after time. Unknown to most is that Rema saw for herself what was returned from that hunting trip. An accident really, she showed up to the Zenu blacksmith forge in need of fixing some broken knives, and witnessed what she could only describe as parts of an animal she couldn't identify. It had bright white scales and it oozed blood that had lost its hue. Shaye was hunched down over it, axe in hand.

"*Rema?... You startled me,*" Shaye said, slightly flummoxed.

Rema looked back at her quizzically. A little silence followed and Shaye added, "*Oh we caught a shara ... umm a snowlizaed. I didn't even think we had those in these parts, their meat tastes incredible!*" Shaye said with enthusiasm. Rema continued to gaze at her. The words for a response hadn't formed yet or couldn't. Ozai walked in the smithy from behind her.

"*I see you broke another set of knives. I can just make you stronger ones instead of buying from the market you know,*" Ozai joked.

"*Have you seen Naemi and Dakai? We haven't seen them since our return and the snowfall is getting heavier,*" Ozai added.

"*Uh ... Uh I saw Naemi on her horse a while back but haven't seen Dakai,*" Rema responded.

Thud! Shaye hacked into the meat over and over again.

"*You can leave it and I will get Naemi to bring it back when I'm done. Tomorrow evening, perhaps,*" Ozai concluded. She nodded and dropped the knives. Turning around to leave, Shaye stopped her and handed her a pot of meat continuously raving about its good taste. In hindsight, the memory blurred together, and she couldn't tell how long she stood there or when she got home. Her husband filled with disbelief when she accounted what she saw but evidence made it harder to discount. Curiosity got the better of them and they both reluctantly tried out the bepraised offering they'd been given, only to conclude that there hadn't been anything sweeter on the tongue under the Mother's light.

They never mentioned this encounter to anyone, but this wasn't their last time experiencing something unusual in the Zenu home.

A crawling aroma interrupted her thoughts. Dinner was close.

———◆○◆———

Naemi poured more grain into the bucket. The other horses were not even close to finishing but Bellie had finished his with expedience. He looked angry, as angry as a horse could look and huffed repeatedly to signal her to add more. She obliged. She was late to serve their dinner and they did their best to voice their displeasure, Bellie always the loudest and headstrong. She was almost done with cleaning the stables.

*Dinner shouldn't be too long now,* she thought. It was her responsibility to feed the horses and clean the stables. She loved being around and playing with the horses, but not so much the cleaning. Someone had to do it regardless, and she'd rather do this than the forge. Yes, it smelled worse here, but the forge was hot, dark and dusty and made her cough and sneeze till her chest gave out. Better a job for Dakai. At least this way, she could spend more time with Bellie and saddle him at her whim. She picked up a horse-brush and combed his hair. Gray like a gloomy day with brown patches splattered across his head and body, his beauty couldn't be hidden even at night. He was her favorite and he knew it; the other horses did too. He neighed in gratitude with more strokes of the brush. It truly is surprising how fast and strong he had grown. A sickling as a foal, it was by mere chance she encountered the trader who owned him on his way to sell him to the butcher. "*Good meat must not go to waste,*" the trader claimed.

Some bonds are created in the most peculiar of times. However, pleading and tears weren't enough to persuade the trader to let go of his possession for free when he could get a few bronze coins in exchange.

Ozai opened the door to a crying Naemi, a stranger and a small — almost dying horse.

"*Your daughter said you will pay seven silver coins for the horse!*" He barked in a hoarse tone. Ozai looked at his daughter's expression of anguish and knew entirely what had happened. He hesitated still. Not for the fact that a fully grown healthy stallion sells for ten silver coins but because losing Shaye a summer ago tore them in pieces and he feared what another attached loss might do with wounds still bare. Nonetheless, he paid the price to buy his daughter joy; even if it might be brief.

The days that followed came with a lot of unrest and trips to the town-healer. Different concoctions later, the horse's sickness barely budged. At night, the foal would sleep next to Naemi on a small cot Ozai built next to Naemi's bed, and she would always get off her bed to sleep next to him, regardless of how many times Ozai moved her back. He gave up after a couple of tries. Sometimes, he'd squeal in agony at night's peak and she'd hug him and rub his belly in response to dull his pain. The more days that passed, the more Ozai questioned whether he had made the right decision. The foal's health wasn't improving and he continuously searched for answers. On one of these searches, the town-healer proposed a solution. A venturous endeavor. If potions and medications weren't helpful, it could be possible the only means of discovering the issue was exploring inward.

An older woman of seventy and nine, she tended to almost all the health needs of the town, seven assistants under her tutelage, and a high reputation that stretched towns over. "*I want you to know it would be very risky but I'll do my best to help him,*" she said. Naemi obliged as she laid the foal on the wooden table for the procedure. Four of her assistants stood close-by in preparation. The second of the butcher's daughters; Azzie, a woman of thirty from Shoretown in the east; Fael, the one-eyed baker's third son; Lupe, and her youngest assistant, Dakai. In truth, this wasn't a resort she'd normally engage in, especially for animals but beseeching from her assistant had gotten to her. She had at least located the source of the pain; a small region on his underside, close to his hind legs.

The operation wasn't a pleasant one. Blood, bodily fluids and excrement were the least troubling items extracted. The worst had passed, and the wait for possible recovery or inevitable perish was forthcoming. Naemi stayed in the outside room throughout the entire process. Through the low groans and high moans, Ozai stayed right with her. It was almost sundown when they returned home, foal in his arms and his children close behind. The young horse was still breathing, even through all that pain. A fighter through and through. The upcoming days came with brightness for the Zenu family.

"The little thing," as Ozai liked to call it, was showing more signs of life and energy. Undoubtedly a member of the family now, his appetite for grain and bran was nothing to be trifled with. He was walking on his own accord in a fortnight and running in the fields by two. Fully healed at this point, you could almost never know his history if not for a large black scar on his belly-side. Henceforth his name — Bellie.

———◆———

"*It is time for dinnerrrr!*" Dakai yelled into the stables.

"*You don't need to scream it, I'm standing right here!*" Naemi fired back. Her job here was done and she lifted her lamp to leave. A final goodnight pat to the horses who were on the verge of sleeping, and a goodnight hug for Bellie.

"*We aren't going to wait all night for you, princess,*" Dakai budded in as he left with a sheepish smile on his face.

———◆———

Dinner was served.

Ozai looked at his masterpiece; pride filling his lips and his ego growing with every passing scent of aroma. Took a little bit longer than usual but the food was finally here. Rema helped set the table. Four chairs and four hungry mouths tired of waiting. Dakai entered the room with Naemi at his heels.

"*No running in the house! And I don't want to hear any excuses,*" Ozai scolded vehemently.

"*You should be too tired for all that child's play,*" he added.

"*Sorry father,*" they said in unison, and calmly headed to their seats.

With everyone seated, Ozai looked to his daughter for a prayer. "*But I said the prayer last time.*" Naemi defended in a childish tone. A response Ozai countered with a stern look filled with grim. She gave in. Eyes closed, she prayed.

"*We give thanks to the Mother, for unending light and fruit of the land. We give thanks to the sailor, for blessings of the sea and salt from water. We give thanks to the warrior, for devotion and servitude in protection of the Mother and queen. The Mother's light is forever eternal. Xalem.*"

Spoons clashed bowls and food filled throats and bellies. The crickets choired songs in the distance; never sweet enough to be acknowledged or desired. The creatures of the night traversed the Anul forest in search of food, territory, or any other things beasts do in their free time, whilst the streets of Soros ran empty except for an old-guard or two patrolling the roads. The patrols weren't glorious most times but necessary regardless. Once or twice every season, a beast from Anul strayed close and would attack a native in the dawn of morning or peak of night. Worst of those attacks was the mountain bear that attacked two winters ago. Five men sent to the infirmary with cuts and claw marks drawn all over their bodies. Two breathless before Arwa could even set sight on them.

Fire filled the town center, broken sheds filled the roads and roars filled the air. When the smoke cleared and the sun brightened, the damage in view was colossal. The days that followed went slow. Mourning and burials occupied the earlier days. After, the town's people banded in camaraderie and worked to fix what could be fixed. A dozen days later and the new town center buzzed in attraction. Brighter than previous, it boasted a bigger market and better sheds. Another tragedy endured, another entry into the history books.

Back in the Zenu home, dinner continued.

"*So I heard you're leaving for Shoretown tomorrow morning?*" Rema asked.

"*You heard?*" Ozai countered inquisitively.

"*People talk you know,*" She responded with a smirk. "*Ahh the butcher still can't keep his mouth shut,*" Ozai said with a smile. He added, "*He needed some tools fixed, and I don't have the supplies for it. I'm low on materials and work keeps piling up.*"

"*I was wondering when you were going to go this season. Do you mind getting me some Tuscan-fish at the Sea-market? I haven't had some in ages, and they're plentiful around this sun-period,*" Rema replied.

"*Are any of them going with you?*" She asked, looking at his children.

"*It's just two days and I'll be back before nightfall. There's no need to bother them. And of course I can get some fresh Tuscan. Naemi loves those too,*" Ozai answered.

"*But I want to go! I'm the only one who has never visited Shoretown. You never take me anywhere,*" Dakai blurted in frustration. "*You took Naemi with you the last time,*" he appended.

A brief silence ensued with stares and seeping emotions.

"*I will take you when you're older,*" Ozai responded bluntly. An answer Dakai wasn't pleased with, evident by him storming off. Ozai just looked on. This wasn't the first time he'd denied his son of experiencing the world outside Soros and it probably wouldn't be the last. Rema ate the rest of her food in silence. Awkwardness had crept in and she did her best to hold her tongue. Indeed, Ozai had a peculiar strictness with his youngest child. He rarely left him to his whims and freedom, and once scolded him emphatically for engaging with a traveler. She was surprised however that he let Dakai learn under Arwa. Shaye was the one probably liable for that decision. She and Dakai shared a lot of resemblance; he was a copy of her features and exuberance.

"*I haven't seen Raex in a while, he doesn't come by anymore,*" Naemi said, trying to rekindle the smoldered flames of conversation.

"*Oh... he's trying to join the old guard unit and is preparing for the test of warriors. He's following in his older brother's steps. I barely see him except for when he has to eat or sleep.*" Rema answered feigning enthusiasm. Two of her children already residing in the capital and possibilities of her youngest also leaving certainly didn't excite her in the slightest. The younger generation loved adventure, and Soros did little to quench their thirst. A small town caught between the mountains and the forest, it flaunted beautiful scenery and little excitement. The capital on the other hand roared with advancement and jubilation. The tournaments, festivities, banquets, and more opportunities for employment pulled children from parents in their quest for grandeur and better living. Soros did none. Far enough from the capital, it also wasn't significantly close to any larger towns. The closest large towns: Farla, Rune, and Shoretown, were spread across the coast about half a day's ride to the east. Bigger and thriving. Meros, a smaller town lay in between them but shared a lot of similarity in size with Soros. Farther to the west along the road to the capital, more towns lay sporadically and in varying sizes; all under the realm of Primea.

"*Well, I think that's great for him, he always talked about joining the warriors core,*" Naemi concluded.

"*Yea it is,*" Rema dully added.

A couple of similar short conversations passed around the table as night continued but dinner neared its end.

Rema left the Zenu home sometime after dinner ended and the tables cleared. Basket in hand, she made her way home denying an escort from Ozai. "*There's no need to worry, I can make my way home. You need to go rest for your journey,*" she said, and waved goodbye. The night enveloped her as she walked away. One after the other, flames gave out and the family took to slumber. Night was at its peak.

---

Morning came with warm light and incoherent songs. The birds weren't in unison, but still sang to their heart's fulfillment. Naemi rolled in her bed with eyes still closed. The sheep skin felt as soft as ever, and her head sank in her cotton pillow as she stretched to her content. *A little bit more sleep won't hurt,* she thought, and it didn't. She woke sometime later to the clashing of pots and pans, and the scent of fresh bread and wheat. Food was ready. She jumped off the bed, scruffy and disheveled, and raced downstairs to the cookery.

"*You look as wonderful as always, sister.*" Dakai said as he passed her to the dinner table. Naemi ignored him and continued. She popped back out with a bowl in one hand and a big loaf of bread in the other.

"*Did you see when father left?*" She asked.

"*No, he was already gone when I got up,*" Dakai responded, and continued his meal.

What followed was a routine the siblings had indulged in many times over. Chores, cleansing and venturing into the wild. Dakai would go visit the town healer for any new duties, and on free days, would play around with other boys his age, while Naemi would go riding Bellie, practice her shooting or explore more of the forests and mountains with an occasional dip in the gray valley lakes. Today was no different, and the siblings were back home at sundown exhausted and dirty.

Someone knocked on the door and Dakai opened.

"*Hey Dakai,*" Raex greeted with a broadened smile, standing at the entrance with a basket of food. The siblings jumped to hug him, expressing their joy. A boy of one and seven; he was one of their oldest friends.

"*I haven't seen you in ages,*" Naemi said excitedly.

"*Your mother said you were training for the warrior's test? That's amazing!*" Dakai declared.

Raex laughed at their enthusiasm.

"*Mother thought you'd be hungry, so I brought some pig-feet soup and potatoes,*" he replied with a laugh, a response that delighted the siblings more. Conversations persisted as the children shared laughs and stories by the fireplace in the parlor. Not exactly where they should be eating, but who could stop them. The moon was out tonight and it's light out with it. Less torches needed and the darkness spited. The night grew older and the chatter amongst friends showed no signs of deadening. A horse neighed, cutting through their discussion. The banter halted.

*"A bit too late for Bellie or the others to be up to their antics,"* Naemi commented. In a flash, the door creaked and blasted open. A moment before they were all full of laughs and giggles, and now two strange figures stood barring the entrance. The bigger man on the right, held a drawn curved dagger and stepped forward while the other followed. The first had a face full of markings, which continued down his neck disappearing into his cloak with piercings on his lips and nose. The moonlight reflected his lack of hair and his eyes popped bloodshot. The second crept quietly behind, shrouded in the shadow of the first but his teeth peeked with filth. Raex swiftly grabbed the unburned end of log from the fireplace, holding the fiery end out in a sword stance as the children retreated slowly to the edge of the stairs. The door to the cookery at the side of the stairs opened and another man appeared. The back door through the cookery was most definitely not an option for escape. They continued their retreat.

*"You don't have to die tonight young one, but you will if you don't put that down. We are only here for the boy with colored eyes,"* the pierced one engaged in a shrill tone. He put his other hand beneath his cloak and revealed another smaller unbent dagger; reflecting the flames as they burned with indifference. The one behind him cackled in response. His

words pierced them, but this was no time for reactions. The third, who was at the edge of the stairs in slow pursuit, was younger, had a head full of woven brown hair and was deprived of scars, except for the sly grin he wore.

"*So what fate do you choose?*" The younger added, looking at Raex. A brief pause ensued and he lunged toward the siblings. Raex responded with a fiery swing to his face that exploded the fire embers in a puff of smoke cloud. Then the children burst in speed up the stairs. The closest room with a window was Naemi's room. Dakai got there first and kicked the door open with the others close behind. The pierced one anticipated their move and threw his dagger at Raex as they ran. His younger accomplice shrieked in pain on the floor with his hair on fire, and the shrouded one leaped to help.

In the room, they slammed the door and pushed the bed against it. Naemi noticed a trail of blood dripping on her arm and searched to find its source. "*Your...Your back!*" Dakai said in horror as he looked behind Raex, blood dripping. On cue, the pain hit him. Right below where the back of his left arm met his shoulder, the dagger was sunk in. He collapsed to his knees.

"*You need to run,*" Raex said, as the siblings helped raise him to the window. A plea they ignored. The door banged and pushed against the bed. It won't hold for long. Naemi grabbed her bow and quiver by the corner, and they made their way through the window. The door flew open as Naemi jumped last. The stables were right by the side of the house and the horses had already awoken from the frenzy. There were two entrances to the stable, one by the front of the house and the other by the rear. Dakai opened all the doors bounding the horses, and from behind him the two smaller attackers raced from the front door with swords drawn out. Naemi helped Raex get on Bellie and turned to see Dakai caught on the ground with the shrouded one on his back with blades drawn. Call it instinct, or experience from countless days of practice, or a sister's desire to protect her brother. The arrow flowed from the quiver to the bow strings into the ball of the man's right eye in an instant. He was dead before his body hit the ground. The younger one was aghast with terror, and swiftly leaped to the side of the stable just in time to avoid the next arrow. Dakai jumped up to run to his sister.

"*Naemi! Behind you!*" Dakai yelled. And behind her he stood, with a curled sword like a green snake moving on a hot summer's day. He approached the horse with Raex clinging to it; losing blood by the ounce. Bellie raised its forelegs to kick him and he slashed through them, causing the horse to tumble to its side. Raex fell first and Bellie fell right on him, with the weight of the horse pushing the entire dagger right through his chest. Blood from Bellie oozed as water oozes from a fountain, and he neighed in pain wriggling over the corpse that lay under him. Naemi screamed louder than she ever had in her life. No sound came out, but her throat bled with pain. She attempted to get another arrow from her quiver, but the pierced bandit engaged in his same shrill tone.

"*Do you want me to take him too?*" Pointing his sword at Dakai who had a dagger to his throat from the younger attacker. Tears flowed from her eyes as her only answer to her helplessness. She fell to her knees with bow in hand. He walked up to her and gazed down. Raised his sword and slammed the hilt to her head. She dropped unconscious.

"*Tie her up. We are taking this one too,*" he said to his accomplice.

"*What about the body of Xod-de?*" The younger one asked with concern.

"*The dead are of no use to us,*" he answered.

Naemi faded in and out of consciousness, picking up little pieces that flashed her senses. She could feel the blood running down her head, and the pain that pulsed like drums that beat for a dance. Her body bounced as her hair dangled and the air whipped her face. Her hands were bound and she couldn't move her feet. A hand was placed firmly on her back, and she could smell bits of the forest trees. The horses moved fast and their riders held onto their captives as predators do prey. The moonlight clearing their trail.

They couldn't use the main roads for fear of being noticed, and had to settle for the longer return through the woods. This path wasn't going to be smooth and allowed for little breaks in their journey, but their relentlessness never wavered. They'd captured a bounty worth a hundred thousand gold coins with only a half-wit dead. Rawthe smiled, *good riddance anyway,* he thought. He had expected a father to be there as he was told but only a fool will complain about easy work. Nonetheless, they needed to get to the ship before word spread.

Primea was one of the worst places to get caught as a pirate. *Deluded worshipers of the All-Mother,* he thought. Due to their history, murder was amongst their most loathed crimes, and piracy was a close second. Taking a job here wouldn't be worth it in most cases, but this wasn't one of them. His grip tightened on the reins and he kicked the horse harder. The ride continued.

Sunrise came slow and steady, posturing in its beauty for all of Shoretown to gaze a bit longer in admiration. The Sea-market was already buzzing, and ships strung around the market pier with workers moving all over preparing for trade. The market was the prize of Shoretown, and it boosted its economy tenfold. Wooden sheds opened and sellers filled their corners with their goods in anticipation of the chaos. Ships from all over filled the pier with almost everything approved under the queen available for sale. Old-guards strolled around in the dozens to control chaos, which consisted mostly of breaking up quarrels between sellers and buyers. In an hour or two, the market would be filled and overflowing.

A horse and wagon descended down Sea-street and through the crowd with cloaked riders. Rawthe fumed at the traffic, smell, and noise, but his frustration lay with the delays that held them. A stop to disguise his victims in a fruit wagon to pass guard checks, and another to send a messenger bird to his captain delayed him more than he had calculated. It was not a good idea to depend on luck heavily, and he wasn't planning to. He whipped the reins and urged the horse to move faster amidst curses and swears from those offended.

Naemi wiggled in the crate with no effect. She was gagged and shoved into a box at their last stop and her brother in another. He wasn't conscious as they moved him, and all her calls to him fell on deaf ears. Her confinement felt the seeping scorch of the blaring sun, and the weight put on top of it creaked with every movement. It was loud outside; she heard people and screamed into the silence of the cloth that bound her lips. She wiggled herself harder and was finally able to move her head to a tiny vent that poked at the side for air. Through it, she called to the eyes that couldn't see her. One after the other, she passed them by. Each one engaged in their own reality, while hers was full of despair. The caravan stopped. Almost at the ship, a kid tripped and fell in front of the horse, and the child's mother slowly aided her to more infuriation of Rawthe and his younger accomplice.

Naemi looked around helplessly hoping to meet the gaze of a random stranger with inquisition. In her search, she saw a familiar face standing just a reach away. By the Tuscan fish vendor, Ozai stood. She screamed with everything in her, biting on the cloth with all her might. Her throat vibrated as the sounds pushed forth were pushed back.

If blood could substitute the tears that flowed desperately from the eyes, it would. She shook around so hard the wagon moved and Rawthe whipped the horse into a gallop toward the string of ships that lay ahead. Ozai turned to look unto people throwing curses at a fleeing caravan and turned back to buy the fish he'd promised his children and neighbor. It won't be long now before he sets out back home.

The horses slowed as they got close to a shipmaster who stood in front of one of the ships by the pier. Rawthe exchanged glances with him and signaled to the boxes he wanted hidden. It won't be too long now before he meets up with his crew in the open seas.

The ship set sail not long after. Packages on board and a smirk on Rawthe's face. Down below the ship, as she sailed away bound in a box, Naemi had no tears left to cry and no screams left to shout. Her reality had been turned on its head and all that was left of her world was the abyss that lay forthcoming.

## CHAPTER TWO

# A PRAYER TO THE ALL-MOTHER

The sea roared with calmness and the clouds looked on in nonchalance. It was a gloomy day, and the gray clouds dulled with every drop of sand in an hourglass. The trading ship: the Spice Mistress, floated somewhere south with the speed of the wind pushing against its blue sails and white pennant. She glided through the open seas with grace, her rudder splicing the water like knife splices bread. The sea water slapped at her hull repeatedly. She was old, but far – far from broken.

*"A decade's worth of journeys under her name and more to go,"* her shipmaster was known to say. On the main deck, her crew moved around with incessancy, doing one activity after another.

A barrel-man shouted from the crow's nest alerting of a ship in proximity. Rawthe stood up from the barrel in the corner of the ship's hold and stretched with satisfaction. *"Finally!"* He proclaimed. Gorm broke from his nap at the sound of Rawthe's loud stretching.

"*Are they here yet?*" he asked, and Rawthe grunted in response. Keys clanged at the other end of the door and the door flung open. The shipmaster entered with three crew members and signaled them to the two boxes that sat in the middle of the hold by the wooden pillar. Rawthe exited the room with Gorm not far behind.

The two ships anchored shoulder-to-shoulder with a bridge descending from the unknown ship to the Mistress. Rawthe was the first to come up from below. The light hit his eyes harder than expected, and he raised an arm to shield himself.

"*Ahhh, there's my champion!*" A familiar voice hurled with exuberance.

"*Captain!*" Rawthe answered with a smile as the man lunged at him in a forceful hug. Gorm came out after with the other crew holding the boxes behind him, and the captain broke into a maniacal laugh at the glance of him.

"*You finally lost that pretty face and became a man like the rest of us. Whores will pay in gold to fuck you and hear tales of your journeys now,*" he added with enthusiasm. He'd gotten some report of what transpired during their mission, but nothing about his youngest and "*prettiest*" pirate; in his own words, losing the privilege of beauty. Half of Gorm's face looked like he had been shoved in a fire, with faint colors of red drawn by the side of his left eye and down his cheek. The captain did however show remorse for the loss of his poisoner. Xod-de wasn't the brightest, but he liked him and benefited a lot from his skill. Another crew member lost to the seas, but for a worthy price. He drew his attention to the boxes and beckoned to two of his crewmen to carry them over to his ship.

He paced forward toward the ship master and handed him a bag of coins and smiled. "*For your troubles,*" he professed, and walked away. As he got to the edge of the ship; by the foot of the bridge, he turned and said to the ship master, "*I really do hope our little arrangement remains private; I'd hate to send my men to see your little daughters again. They might not be able to control their urges a second time.*"

Ways parted and the Mistress steered onward, hopefully never to cross paths again.

---

A pry bar jammed underneath the nails and loosened the cover of one of the boxes. Once, twice and creaked open on the third try. The crewman kicked the box to the front and Naemi fell out, slamming onto the dirty wooden floors. Her eyes were barely open, and her hands stayed bound to each other behind her back, as did her legs beneath her. Her eyes unfolded slowly, flinching with every light ray that hit it, opening just enough to see the feet of the people who surrounded her. She had lost the essence of time and had no clue how long she'd been concealed. She was famished so much her stomach hurt, as did her arms, legs, thighs, neck, and feet. Another box creaked open and a heavy slam followed. She looked on to her younger brother in a similar predicament. His eyes were still teary, and he groaned through the cloth that bound his lips.

"*Release them and hold them up. I'd like to see my prize.*" The captain said, and the crewmen obliged.

Naemi struggled to find strength in her feet and collapsed to the floor. Hands held her up again as they did Dakai, and the agony lingered. They stood in the middle of a circle with eyes gawking at them from every angle. A man walked toward Dakai, daunting in size. The hand on his right, filled with rings on every finger. And on his left, nothing, just a shiny metal fist that disappeared into his sleeve. His clothes stood out from the company he kept, but the scars on his face rendered him indistinct. Hair as colorful as an orange filled the top of his head, and the hair beneath his chin descended down his neck into knots. When he spoke, his teeth shone with specks of silver behind a voice filled with huskiness. He held Dakai by the chin.

"*Open your eyes boy ... wide!*" He said, and moved his hands to widen Dakai's eyes when Dakai hesitated. He burst into a laughter Naemi recognized earlier.

"*Leave him alone!*"

The words parted Naemi's lips before she could find the strength to shout them. Her lips still felt numb, and she barely felt the sound leave her mouth. He ignored her and continued his act.

"*I said leave him alone.*" She barked again. This time catching his attention. He turned to stare at her, letting go of her brother and moving to engage her instead.

"*Shame you don't have your brother's eyes, I would be twice as rich.*" He remarked in disappointment.

"*What do you want from us?*" She asked.

*"From your brother? Everything. But you ... I'm still wondering what you're worth. You don't have the eyes but any child of the Kaku bloodline will fetch a heavy weight in gold. How heavy will your weight be?"* He answered with a grin, the silver in his teeth in full display. The crewmen echoed his smiles behind him with greed embodied on their faces. Men of varying build with no good intentions. Two women stood at the forecastle looking down the main deck. They didn't seem to be prisoners as she was and wore faces of indifference. Next to them was a man — no, another woman, sharing a similar expression.

The wind started to pick up, and the black sails of the ship flapped in accordance.

*"Take them inside."* The one who was clearly captain commanded.

⸺◆⸺

Their new confinement wasn't glorious but infinitely better than the former. The caged cell the pirates threw them in was filled with stench, but they found solace in being able to finally touch and speak to one another. The siblings hugged with all the strength they could muster and consoled each other in their pain. Whatever their new reality was, they had each other, and for now that was something they could hold on to. Questions however still lay unspoken. Where was their father? What happened after they got kidnapped? Where were they headed? Did anyone have any idea how to find them? For now, it was best to keep those questions buried and focus on their health. They would need strength to survive this journey if they were to survive at all.

Dakai's left wrist was bruised from the bondage and Naemi tore off part of her robe to treat it with his guidance. She held him in her arms as his pain soothed and his eyes closed. Helpless and powerless, she turned to the only one she could.

She was never a believer of the All-Mother. True, she said the prayers when instructed and attended the gatherings when the mothers of light, servants of the All-Mother visited the town on occasion, but most of her effort was bound by curiosity or her father's compelling. The pious were always intriguing to her and their devotion to a non-existent being was more reason for confusion. They claimed that the All-Mother was the bringer of life in all aspects of nature, and the protector of Primea through its darkest times. The stories rage on about countless periods the All-Mother protected Primeans in war, famine and through disease outbreaks; not that she had ever experienced any of those. To her the stories were just that — stories. Tales believers told non-believers to aid conversion.

Her life had never known despair to this day, but despair makes believers of us all. In her hopelessness, she sought from the divine as the powerless often do. If it was ever going to be possible to get back home, she needed all the help she could get. So as Dakai laid on her lap with her hands around him, she prayed to the All-Mother. Her dried eyes had no more tears to shed and her lips moved in silence. This was her sacred plea to the holy; whether anyone was listening or not, she prayed. Offering whatever part of herself she could trade in exchange. Whatever deal could be made, she was willing to make it. In her moment of selflessness, all she desired was her brother's health and safe return home even if that meant in exchange for her. The whispers left her lips and floated on into the void. Whether the All-Mother heard or not, her last hope left with that prayer, and for the first time she was truly hopeless.

------◄O►------

Dakai opened his eyes to fading lights from the small window circles that showed nothing but blue water in excess. The room had only two windows and their cell was at its opposite, next to a heap of barrels, crates and filled sacks. The cell itself was almost empty except for the dirt and pieces of wood that lay scattered. The foul stench stood unswayed and kept the siblings company. Naemi's arms were around Dakai and still. He looked up at her lost in sleep, leaning on parts of a broken barrel. Weirdly enough, he felt content in seeing his sister get some needed rest. The days previous had been unbearable; he barely found any peace to sleep being cramped in a box and reckoned she didn't either. He moved her hands gently and retreated to the other end of the cell to free her of his weight. A moment passed and she switched in her sleep to a position of better comfort.

Dakai sat in silence as darkness greeted them again. Questions paced through his mind running full and overflowing, his emotions swaying with every question. One emotion always stood out however; his feeling of blame. He blamed himself for their predicament. His sister, his father, Raex, Rema, and Bellie. He wondered if their very lives would have changed if it wasn't for him. *What did they do to deserve this?* He thought. And the only answer he came up with was they were associated with him. Blame turned into hate and he cursed himself, cursed his eyes. For whatever reason they needed him, he wished those he loved didn't have to be hurt in return. A memory from three fortnights before their father left for Shoretown replayed in his head.

Word had spread of a circus touring the coast that planned on going only as far in the mainland as Meros. News that excited a lot of the young boys and girls in Soros. Dakai was ecstatic to hear the news and see all the acts he had heard about from the bigger boys. In their words, this was something that happened once in many years and he couldn't miss such an opportunity. Devastation hit him when Ozai slammed the idea shut and forbade him from going. He had never thought much about his father's warnings of strangers and travelers. *Something every father must tell their child*, he assumed, but this was an event he couldn't miss. So the night prior, he mentioned at dinner that Arwa needed a lot of help the next day and once his cover was granted, he snuck on a friend's wagon going to Meros early the next morning.

The circus was glorious. He stood in awe at every act and jumped from station to station, laughing as loud as he could with his friends. Whatever scolding his father would give him if he got caught was worth it. A woman from one of the acts offered him sweetcorn and remarked how beautiful his eyes were.

"*Where are you from young child? I haven't seen eyes like that in a very long time,*" she stated. She stared with a weird intrigue, and a smile that creased her skin as she parted her lips. She was a nice old woman and fed him and his friends free sweetcorn till they were bursting. They talked at length about him and his family, so much that he almost lost track of time to return home. Soros was about a four hour ride away from Meros, and he got home just after nightfall. His ruse was strong and Ozai never saw through the cracks.

The woman from the circus visited Soros surprisingly sometime later, offering him a chance to join their circus on their next voyage outside Primea. An opportunity he wished he could take if not for his family. *Imagine the joy of working with a circus every day, visiting town after town*, he imagined, but ultimately denied her proposal. That was the last he encountered her.

The memory fueled his emotions and he bowed his head in regret.

<hr>

Footsteps came from outside and keys jiggled. The door opened and the person entered with a lamp in hand, walking to secure it on the lampstand by the door. Naemi's eyes adjusted to the light as the bringer of light stood in front of their cell with a tray in hand. It was the third woman from earlier. She bent down, dropping the food and water gently and pushed it toward the metal bars.

"*Leave the bowl out when you're done,*" she said in a stern tone. She was tall, not as tall as her captain but still towered in sight. When she bent, the flame light worshiped the muscles of her arms in yellow highlight. Her hair flowed down into a braid and her face looked like she had never cared for anything in her life. She looked to be in her late twenties, but there was no certainty to that assumption. The siblings lunged at the water. Chugging down one gulp after the other, and next the soup bowls that sat waiting. She walked to the corner of the room behind some barrels and came out with a bucket and cover. She took her keys to open the cell door and paused.

*"If you think of trying anything funny I will cut out your eyes myself."* She mentioned with an emotionless expression while opening the gate. The siblings retreated to the back of the cell in fear. She dropped the bucket and cover inside and locked the cell back up.

*"For when you want to go,"* she said, and left with the same heavy footsteps she came with.

And so was the routine.

She'd come in twice a day with food and little words. A light for the nighttime and occasionally another pirate half her size who walked in a wobble. He smelled of ale and piss, and would come in to give them sea water to cleanse themselves, then empty their bucket while she stood guard. Time flashed by through the window circles, and the lines they marked in the wood to count the days grew longer. Storms would hit infrequently and sea water would seep through the wood drenching them in salt. Naemi suffered the worst at sea. The motion didn't agree with her and sickness flared up constantly. She had lost weight and often pushed out the food she took in.

*"Do you have any kalyps herbs onboard?"* Dakai asked his captor in desperation. She ignored him and continued her daily ritual.

Two days passed and the ship made its first stop. There was little to see through the window, but the siblings finally heard the buzz of a crowd. They stared through the window for hours, switching between shifts in hopes of seeing anyone pop up near the ship, but nothing, just rocks, stone and more water. As time crept close to the end of the day, Dakai prepared to end his shift, then something caught his eye. A smaller boat filled with a couple of boys playing sailor came into sight. Dakai called out to Naemi, and they both instinctively started shouting for help as loud as they could. In hindsight, this was a foolish idea, but desperation is the explorer of all avenues.

Pounding footsteps quickly descended the stairs and the muscled woman entered with the angriest look they'd seen on her. She yanked open the cell and punched Dakai hard in the gut, and next his sister. The siblings tumbled down in pain.

"*They are not going to save you. Nobody is!*" she barked at them.

Naemi coughed in agony.

"*Where ... are you ... taking us?*" Naemi stuttered. She slowly got up from the floor and helped her brother stand.

"*You can't keep us here forever,*" she added.

The woman stared at her and answered, "*You may not believe this, but there is much worse ahead for you and your brother. And no one you call out to will save you.*" Her patterned look of stolidity cracked with slight sadness.

"*Why? We didn't do anything to deserve this.*" Naemi shot back with tears starting to form in her eyes. The woman ignored her as she locked the cell and proceeded to walk out.

"*Please ... If we are going to die, at least tell us why.*" Naemi added, tears flowing recklessly down her face.

The woman hesitated in her walk toward the door. She stared at the door as if in a dilemma, and turned toward a stool at the corner, grabbed it and sat facing the cell.

"*I will answer only three questions.*" She spoke.

The siblings faced her with their faces behind bars. Three questions to know the entirety of their future. They stared at each other, and Dakai nodded to Naemi in approval of her leadership.

"*Why are you interested in my brother's eyes?*" she asked.

The woman looked back at them for a while and started, "*There is a huge bounty on descendants of the Kaku imperial clan, mainly ones with eyes of two colors. No one really knows exactly why, and no one cares as long as the gold is good. You wouldn't be able to walk on any land past the Dalt seas without being targeted and kidnapped.*"

Her words stung, but there was no time to process the pain.

"*Where are we headed?*" Naemi continued.

"*The Zaire region, to the moon city of Ishva. That is where the bounty bidders will be,*" she responded.

Naemi thought hard about her final question and in her search, one thing she always wondered about popped up.

She asked, "*How did you find us?*"

"*A rumor started in the Hayes about a boy with colored eyes somewhere in Primea, and people set out in search. We just happened to find the source of the rumor.*"

As she concluded, she stood up and reached in a bag she came in with and tossed a plant at Dakai's feet.

"*Thank you.*" He said softly as he reached out to grab the kalyps herbs.

She stared at the siblings and added, "*I am not your friend, and I'm never going to be. Remember that,*" and walked out.

Naemi retreated to sit at the back of the cell, trying to process everything she'd heard. Most didn't make sense. She knew neither the places nor the people mentioned except what lay forthcoming. *Much worse ahead? What could be worse than this?* She thought.

"*It was me.*" Dakai said, "*It's all my fault.*" He burst out. Naemi looked at her brother puzzled. "*It's not your fault.*" She responded in consolement.

"*It is ... I lied to father and went to the circus in Meros when he told me not to. I talked to strangers even when he forbade it. I am the reason this happened to us. I am the reason we are going to die.*" Tears streamed from his eyes and his words muffled with depression, repeating words of self-blame over and over. Naemi approached her brother, hugging him harder than she ever had. Dakai fell into her arms filled with devastation. Moments passed and she just held him in a teary embrace.

"*It's not your fault. Nothing that is happening is your fault,*" she comforted.

"*I know you went to the circus. No one else could smell that much like sweetcorn on a regular day,*" she added in a smile.

"*I have lied to father before too and did things he told me not to do, but nobody deserves this. We are not going to die. We can't. We are going to find a way to get back home, find a way to get back to father,*" she continued. Dakai nodded as he looked into his sister's eyes, strengthening his resolve and restraining his tears.

*"I have also been hiding something from you. I saw father in the market in Shoretown while I was locked in the box. I screamed as loud as I could but he didn't hear ... nobody did."* Naemi told her brother.

A glimmer of hope flashed Dakai at the mention of the sight of their father. To him, this was a sign they would be reunited in the future to come.

*"Promise me you'll be with me against whatever stands in our way to get back to father ... to get back home."* Naemi proposed.

Dakai stared back at his sister's solemnity and answered, *"I promise."*

The siblings continued their conversations throughout the latter part of the day and into the night. Putting together everything they had heard and worked to make sense of what lay ahead. On occasion, a memory would be shared with laughter not far behind. Grim circumstances created the strongest bonds, and the siblings continued to be shaped by the invisible hands that forged destinies. The night passed and the sun rose with tides of hopefulness. The siblings woke up to the ship back at sea; on to the next destination.

---

The following days after they left came with different routines. The muscled woman came with more words and some help. She got the short man with the wobble to clean their cage and occasionally added some Alma berries to their food. They caught her name in passing when the short man spoke it, and she warned them against calling her by name. Her threats were always extremely vicious; however, their integrity had loosened over time though they still never decided to explore it. "*Beara,*" she was called, and they weren't entirely certain it was her true name. The ship made two more stops, staying only briefly and moving on. Naemi's sickness was long gone and her body had adjusted to the sea. Their next stops according to Beara were the Quarter Dome port in the lands of Nine, Sailor city in Qarva and then finally Zaire.

They reached the Quarter Dome port two days after, a few hours past sunset. Beara entered with their evening meal with an unusual happiness. Naemi poked in inquisition and Beara spilled with little hesitancy. She was going to see someone she had missed for a long time in the city, and was filled with delight. Apparently Quarter Dome was a favorite stop for pirates. Most of the crew had lovers to meet, whores to seek, and ale to get piss-drunk on. Even the captain who journeys with two of his "ladies" as he loved to call them reveled at the joys the city provided. Dinner went by fast and she was gone in a jiff, leaving the siblings to the company of flame lights and barrels as was the norm. Light from torches and lamps painted circles in the dark like fireflies do in the open. The city view through the window circles was bright and up to no good. The light brightened as the darkness grew, and the siblings sat side by side guessing what nature of people lived there. Were they mostly good, mostly bad or both? A game they came up with to pass the time and quell boredom.

It was past the peak of night and eyes started to weigh heavy. The door rattled. No footsteps or jiggle of keys acted as a precursor. Naemi tapped Dakai and signaled him to the irregular movement of the door and the siblings retreated to the back of the cell in fear. An instant later, it slid open quietly with two figures doing their best to remain secret. They closed the door gently behind them then walked to the front of the cell meeting the eyes of the siblings.

"*Ohh you're still awake,*" the first one said with a silly grin on his face, the other just giggled in whispers. They looked at Naemi like how men unbound by laws or morals look at little girls.

"*Your guard isn't here to save you today.*" The first added, wearing a bigger grin now than he did earlier. His teeth were filled with dirt and gaps, and his nose was so big, it covered most of his face. He was shorter than the second man, and more round. Dakai grabbed the bucket in defense and stood in front of his sister. The first pulled out a dagger from his sheath, "*Open it,*" he signed to the other. The second man moved swiftly to the cell door and started fiddling with pins and locks. Every sound of a click raising the siblings' heartbeat faster. The lock opened at about five clicks and the door swung open.

The shorter one entered first and Dakai lunged at him with the bucket. He dodged with little effort, held Dakai by the arms and slammed him into the bars. He fell instantly with blood gushing from his forehead. The second jumped on Dakai's back, placing his blade on Dakai's throat; almost slicing.

"*Shhhhh ... I will have you next,*" he voiced into his ear and giggled some more.

Naemi hurled at the shorter one and he slapped her so hard in return, she fell to the ground.

*"I heard the Kaku were kings once ... I have never fucked a girl with kings-blood before. Be quiet and we won't hurt your brother more."* Naemi kicked him as hard as she could in the loins, and he groaned and punched her in the face. The punch was strong, and her sight started to blur while her body refused to move as she told it to. She could feel strong hands pin her down with his weight slowly crushing her.

A scream let out. It wasn't hers.

She could hardly see and the sounds around her were barely audible. The weight was no longer on her, and all she could hear were muffled slams and the feeling of vibrating floor-boards beneath her body. Dakai ran to his sister and called her in her daze. He pulled her with all the strength he could summon to the corner, away from the onslaught that was happening near the cell door.

Beara was furious and the sound of her fists hitting a face shook the bars. Blood splattered all over, dripping from her fists as she pummeled him. The remaining teeth the shorter man had flew across the room scattered. His accomplice lay on the floor rolling in agony with a dagger jammed in his thigh.

*"You vermin!"* Bam. Bam. Bam.

*"You worm!"* Bam. Bam. Bam.

*"I'm going to kill you!"* Beara repeated in fury, fist after fist.

*"You can't kill a fellow crewman. You know the rules. Unless you want to go back to being hunted,"* the taller of the two squealed from the floor, screaming through his pain.

*"You have nowhere else to go if you leave this crew. Everyone else wants your head,"* he added.

The slams stopped and Beara's fists refused to move. She stared at the man beneath her and wished so much she could keep hitting him over and over until his skull cracked, but she couldn't. Her hands were covered red and sprinkles of blood were all over her body. She moved off him and his acquaintance limped over to help him off the floor. Blood trailed them as they fled as fast as they could. Beara knelt in front of the siblings with Dakai caressing Naemi's head to provide comfort. The blood on Dakai's forehead trickled down his face and he wiped it continuously with his arm. The right side of Naemi's cheek was swollen and bruised.

Beara stood and left the room in haste and came back moments later with a bucket of water and rags. She cleaned her hands with some and cared for the siblings with the others, staying with them through the night.

A loud banging sound woke Naemi up and a headache hit her the same time consciousness did. She opened her eyes to a face she detested with all her being. The killer of Raex and Bellie stood outside the cells banging on the bar. He was looking at someone sitting in the corner of the cell — Beara.

"*Captain wants a word,*" he said in that shrill tone.

Beara looked over at Naemi, "*Someone finally opened their eyes,*" she said with a smile and got up to leave. The cell gate was open throughout the night and Rawthe asked for the keys when she stepped out. She handed it over and he locked the gate to the cell, then followed her out, locking the door too.

"*How are you feeling?*" Dakai asked from where he was sitting next to his sister. Naemi barely noticed him before and grunted in response. It hurt to move her mouth and a grunt was the best she could manage.

"*Wha – happnd?*" She said slowly through her teeth, and her brother recounted the events of the past night to her. She remembered some parts and not others. The rest of the day went by steadily and Beara never returned. At sun's peak, footsteps were heard and someone entered the hold. It was him again, with the same facial markings and face that triggered dreadful memories for the siblings. He dropped the food as it spilled on the floor and left as quickly as he came. The siblings didn't attempt to eat, and he never came back to recover the bowls or provide dinner.

———————◆———————

The ship left the Quarter Dome a day after the incident. The siblings' new guard had no love for them, and the feeling was very well reciprocated. Less food and water came, and no wobbling man came to empty their buckets. It was about three days since they left, and the little energy they had drained with every passing day. Naemi's headaches had stopped and Dakai's cut wasn't bleeding anymore, but that was the only good thing the siblings had going for them.

On the sixth day no food came, and they went to bed on empty stomachs.

———————◆———————

Boom! The ship shook.

The siblings jumped up in unison just in time before the next hit. The ship swayed and they rolled to hit the cell's metal bars. More followed and Naemi helped Dakai up to the cell gate to help stabilize their balance. Dakai was the first to notice the seeping water coming from beneath the wooden floors. The siblings started screaming for help loudly, shaking the bars with all their strength. Clashes of steel filled the air, drowning their voices. The water rose fast and was as high as their ankles in moments. Rawthe kicked open the door to the hold and moved through the rising water to the cell. He came upon the siblings, with a bloodied sword in hand and moved toward the cell door fidgeting with the keys in haste as he stole quick glances at the exit. He opened the door and grabbed Dakai, pulling him out. Naemi held on to her brother as they both tried to pull away from their captor again. Rawthe raised his sword to slash Naemi and was blocked by another sword.

Beara shoved him back, and he tumbled, losing hold of Dakai. "*It was you. You betrayed us!*" She said, pointing her sword to Rawthe. Naemi pulled her brother behind Beara, next to the wet barrels and sacks, and Rawthe stood up from the ground with his back facing the exit.

"*The captain's dead Beara. He was too old and getting soft with wine and women. I found myself new alliances in the Quarter Dome. I did all the work anyway, why share with these half-wits? You should join me. We can share all the gold from selling the girl, I know you need it.*" He replied with a smirk.

"*You snake!*" Beara bellowed and launched herself in attack.

The duel that followed was a ballad of salt and steel. They moved through the rising sea water, clashing weapons and spitting curses. The tides of the duel rose and fell for each fighter and the siblings held onto each other with all their hopes on their savior. The waves of water building in the ship's lower hold swayed with the ship, and the warriors moved erratically as their foothold shifted underneath them. In a final thrust the end came, and the battle cries stopped. Blood dripped down the sword, dyeing the water below red. Beara's hands firmly on the grip and her blade through Rawthe's chest. His eyes lost their light and he tried to speak words that never parted his lips. Beara withdrew her word and hastened to the siblings.

"*Can you swim?*" She questioned and they nodded in response.

She held Dakai by the arm with Naemi attached and they hurried out the lower hold up the stairs.

The main deck was overrun, and she searched for different routes of escape. A pirate charged at them, and she pushed the children back to engage him. He met his end moments later. The siblings followed her up a second set of stairs into the ballista-deck; the middle section of the ship with large ballista weapons, and she fought off other engaging pirates. On this floor, multiple ballista weapons were arrayed on both sides of the ship, with square openings cut into the sides of the ship to allow the weapons to be fired through. There were more pirates here, and Beara continued to fight more of them. Others were still in heavy battle with the other ship, firing the weapons and reloading the destructive spears and metal balls that served as ammunition. The attacking ship also fired back, wrecking bodies and breaking wood with their firing. Beara protected the siblings the best she could, the three of them rushing through the demolitions and fleeing the decimation.

There were multiple ballista openings at both sides of the ship. One facing the enemy ship, and the other facing the sea on their right. Beara pushed one of the ballista's slightly away from the hole, creating a bigger opening, and took the siblings to the edge.

"The land of *Qarva is close-by. Swim straight that way to shore and go deep into the mainland.*" She said, pointing in the direction of the sea.

Voices echoed up the stairs and footsteps grew louder.

"*Cover your brother's eyes always and trust no one. You're a world away from home and you both have to be strong to survive,*" she added.

"*Will you come with us?*" Naemi asked, as the siblings looked up at her, teary-eyed.

"*I'll be right behind you,*" she replied through a smile and pushed them both out the opening.


The fall felt like eternity and the water felt like ice. Naemi had barely any energy and moved on will alone. A couple of thrusts down and she pushed herself to the surface. Dakai popped out an instant after. Naemi looked to the opening they fell through for any signs of their savior, but nothing came, just songs of steel and battle cries that filled the air. Someone noticed them from atop the main deck and shouted in attention. The siblings hurriedly turned to the shadow of land in the distance and began their swim. The journey was endless with every stroke of movement draining them harder. Naemi stole quick glances behind her and hoped to see Beara in pursuit. The moon shone its light without bias but the tides showed favor. They washed on the rocky shores battered and aching. They could barely stand, and walking was difficult. The shores sloped upward, covered with dense vegetation into a hill with a heavy cluster of trees guarding the peak. Shrubs, green plants and seaweed blanketed the rocks all over. Fire rose from the ship that once held them captive, and it aided in brightening the seas. Specks of small boats could be seen rowing toward land. Resting wasn't an option.

The siblings climbed the rocky slope carefully. Finding footholds on the rocks that poked out in the moonlight. They scurried into the trees and disappeared behind leaves and tree stems, their legs struggling at first to maintain their speed due to weeks of immobility.

The terrain in the woods wasn't favorable, but familiarity with forests and mountains proved to be helpful beyond measure. They moved past trees, rocks and jumped over dried wood logs with whatever little energy they could squeeze into their limbs. Their feet were cold, and small stones and twigs pierced their soles through the light grass as they ran. Regardless, they moved forward. Even without the sight of a pursuer, the presence of one lingered.

Dakai slipped and fell. The dirt covered his arms staining it darker, with pieces of dried leaves plastered over him. They had run for so long they could barely see the sea through the trees and were surrounded only by darkness and wood. Sounds of night creatures filled the forests, and they knew not what direction they had run from or to.

Naemi tried to help her brother stand.

"*Are you okay? We have to keep moving,*" she said through her exhaustion. He fell back down. His left leg couldn't support his weight and stung. Naemi examined his ankle and he winced in pain, grinding his teeth so as not to let out a scream. A swell was already growing. She helped him up again, this time supporting his weight on her shoulder and her arm holding him.

"*Just a little bit more,*" she repeated softly.

And little it was. The pain was unbearable, making him collapse to the ground.

"*It hurts so much,*" he said in a silent cry. Naemi glanced around for shelter. Trees surrounded them with giant roots that spread in and out of the dirt covered in green foliage. Close by stood a tree as big as a dozen ship masts. Its roots danced around it like children do their mother, and had an opening enshrouded under its roots. A peek into the orifice revealed an enclosure bounded by roots, darker and warmer than outside. Naemi ran back to Dakai.

"*We are almost there,*" Naemi encouraged. One last push through the pain and grinding of teeth and they made it under the tree.

The small cave under the tree was a blessing in the sea of demise that had flooded the siblings. It was just big enough for comfort and did its best to warm their chilled bodies. Dakai's swell blossomed into a bulge on his foot, and he rested it to quell the pain. The opening to their enclosure was still concerning and Naemi went outside, breaking off branches with full leaves and retreated back, closing their exit as she crawled backwards. Light fled, leaving only a little that seeped through the branches and roots. The siblings held each other in embrace for warmth and security. One journey completed and another began.

In the vast Bashu wilderness in the eastern side of Qarva, eyes searched near the shore for targets that were long gone. The tides slapped the rocks as they had many times over in an endless battle for dominance. The breeze flowed by the trees carrying the cold and smell of sea only to be devoured by the scent of the forest. Morning will come soon, and its problems with it, but until then, the siblings rested in solace and recuperation.

Arrhythmic melodies choired atop trees echoing through Bashu in harmony.

Wood Sparrows, Nightingales, and Blackbirds vied in their quest to outdo one another as their voices rippled through the morning rays. Flowers blossomed from their sleep with grace, stretching out their petals in warm embrace of the sunlight. Their colors adding to the palette of beauty Bashu wore with pride. Plants washed themselves with morning dew and the grass was soft and moist. The air moving past the trees was glorious, a mixture of pleasure and satisfaction. From above, Bashu looked like paradise; paradise to those who could withstand its trials. Naemi opened her eyes to echoes and the morning sun. Dakai had shifted a bit to the side in his sleep and his foot looked no different than before. Her body growled. A body starved of food and water can only do so much. She nudged her brother awake and he stretched instinctively, knocking his swollen foot against a root. A shriek followed.

"*Ow, I'm sorry I should have expected you'd do that,*" Naemi apologized. Dakai held his foot in pain.

"*I think it got worse,*" he replied.

"*What can I do to help?*" Naemi asked.

"*Arwa usually wraps them in hawthorn leaves; not sure if we will find any hawthorn around here. I need to rest it and hope the swelling goes down,*" Dakai answered, still wincing in pain.

"*I need to go search for food and water. You can't recover with no energy,*" his sister suggested.

"*You're leaving? We need to stay together,*" Dakai answered with concern.

"*We need to eat something or at least get water. You can't heal if you don't eat. We can't stay here forever. I promise I won't go far,*" she reassured him.

Dakai obliged reluctantly. Naemi peeked through the leaves before pushing out the cover to their hideout, and disappeared into the unknown.

The day was bright and blooming. The sun's warmth filtered through the tree branches and glistened on her skin with kindness. Leaving the safety of their hideout was worrying, but she had to take the chance lest they die of thirst and hunger. An unknown environment presented many problems though the most dire would be to lose her way back to her brother. The tree with their hideout stood huge and tall in its magnificence, there was no way she could miss it. She picked up a flattened stone off the ground and drew an "x" shape large enough to be visible with its edges. Her plan was to add one every few paces she took to another tree. More meant she was straying farther and less meant she was getting closer back. If she took a turn, she'd add an arrow to the sign guiding her return. It wasn't an entirely strong strategy but the best she could manufacture nonetheless.

The exploration was long and took her close to the peak of the sun but luckily she heard rushing water and ran toward it. The waterfall was loud, and water rushed down into a small lake and downwards in a river. She rushed under the giant rocks that towered as big as a small mountain and the water fell all over her, wetting her hair soft and pushing her more into the lake. She jumped around with a childlike satisfaction in exhilaration of her discovery. The river flowed down endlessly and tasted better than any water she'd tasted in half a dozen full moons. The water from the waterfall cloaked the rocks behind it which were filled with cave openings. She drank to her content, looking around to find anything she could use to hold water for transport. A couple of bushes lay around the banks filled with berries of different colors. She scampered over, grabbing a few berries, and also found a couple of leaves large enough that they bent over toward the ground. The berries tasted like honey, and she stuffed her mouth full. She folded the leaves into a large cone, pinching the bottom hard while she scooped water. Still the water drained slightly, and she hurried back to her brother.

The return was fast. Partly because the water drained incessantly, although in little drips. A fifth of it was gone when she got back to their hideout but she rejoiced still. With her hands full, she called out to her brother and he crawled out slowly meeting her smile. He gulped down the water with excitement and finished off the berries, sometimes swallowing them whole.

The clouds frowned down with imminent chances of rain, and the siblings retreated back to their zone of safety. It rained the rest of the day and far into the night. They'd stick their heads out to catch some droplets when thirsty, but tried to avoid getting their cloaks wet more due to the falling humidity. The day came and went along with the rain, and Naemi set out again for food the next day. The waterfall was flowing harder than the day before and the lake had grown larger. The sun rays warmed the water and she took off her clothes to bathe. It had been too long and the opportunity was calling. With her clothes on the water bank, she jumped in and splattered joyously. She'd twist, float and splash around in her serenity, never getting enough. "*Dakai will be so jealous,*" she thought.

Eyes stared at her from behind with no good intentions. A twig snapped behind her and she turned to see who it was or in this case what it was.

Its prey looking back at it didn't faze it in the slightest. It had her cornered and it knew it. It dipped one claw in the water, eyes still fixed on her.

Naemi looked back in horror. What it was, she couldn't tell or had ever seen before, but its gnarls and gnashing teeth told her everything she needed to know. It was enormous. How something that big snuck up on her, she would never know. Its head was bright red with teeth poking out its mouth even when closed. It had one leg in the water and the other moved slowly next with claws as big as razors. A tail curled up from behind it to the top of its head like a snake was attached, and fur black as coal covered all over. Its green eyes looked at nothing else other than her and moved with a deadly instinct. Naemi moved back gently pushing against the flowing water. The rocks from the waterfall blocked her from the back and the bank at the other side was not close enough to get to.

*Can I even outrun it? No, no I can't.* Questions raced down her mind.

Half its body was in the water now and it continued its patient advance.

Naemi was almost beneath the waterfall and she remembered the caves cloaked behind the veil of water behind her. She sprung in escape, and the predator sprung in chase.

She ran with all her might, her legs scurrying past rocks and stone going deeper into the cave. The light faded with every step and the cave got darker, but the low growls behind her pushed her forward even faster. She knew not where she was going, and it mattered little.

She launched into another step, but her feet never touched stone. She tumbled down hitting rock after rock as she fell into a hole. Her body slammed onto the bottom so hard, she felt her bones crack. Without thought, she continued crawling forward fervently, deeper toward the blackness at the bottom, but death was near. Its eyes seeing through the dark, the little light that existed being from a dimly radiating white ahead. The beast gazed at its wounded prey with excitement.

The growls got louder and Naemi's fear peaked. She reached out toward the little light she could see in desperation, and touched nothing but stone. Something shot through her, more fear most likely. She turned to face her death in her last moments, looking toward the glowing green eyes that stood out in the darkness as the growls got louder. Naemi stared at her death and thought of her family. Her mother, father, and brother. She never thought she'd die so young, and her heart ached most for her brother. *I'm so sorry, Dakai.*

And in a flash, the beast lunged at her with jaws wide open.

Blood splattered everywhere and wailing followed. Her body was covered red all over and more blood dripped on the floor. The animal wailed in pain with its jaws fractured and hanging. All its teeth were broken, scattered, and blood gushed from inside its mouth repeatedly. It howled in agony, blood oozing from it as it staggered around until eventually collapsing to its death.

Naemi lay still. Not because she couldn't move at will, but because she lacked the intent to or was unable to process the reality that she could. She assumed it was a dream. An illusion to make it easier for her to accept death, but the truth lay there right before her; with a dead body and a cracked head. She tried to move and her body responded. She checked her body for holes, bite marks, pain and there was nothing, just blood. She didn't feel any cracked bones, or any pain at all, except for an anxious heart.

Something stood behind her and she startled backwards. It wasn't a person, or a beast this time, just stone. It was glowing white, and it floated a few steps off the ground. It was as tall as a man and as wide as two arms' length of one. Unknown markings drew all over it and it drifted toward her, gliding on air as she retreated. She could make sense of nothing that happened but for some reason she felt indebted to it. She reached out her hands to touch it and as she did, it vanished.

Naked and covered in blood, she tried to find her way out. She could barely walk properly. The ground felt like it was cracking under her feet. She could feel herself become heavy in one step and light as air right after. On one of her steps, she got shot off the ground and came back down in a slam. Her mind was heavily disoriented, and she tried as much as she could to calm her body down. Slow breathing helped calm her mind from her panic and she could walk slightly better after.

Light guided her path, leading her to the bottom of the hole she fell through. The rocks felt soft when she touched them, and she grappled her fingers through them as she climbed. Most of her movements were mindless. In truth, she was still in a trance and had no idea half of what she was doing. The lights grew in intensity and the sound of rushing water got louder. It was as if no time had passed and her life hadn't been at its end moments ago. At the cave threshold, she stepped under the waterfall into the water. The stream of water descended down as it always had, washing her of the blood that covered her body and the person she was before.

She would never remember anymore parts of what happened in that cave this day. The memory fleeted, exiting into the void of the unknown as easily as she exited the cave. But one thing remains true — the girl

Naemi was before died there, and what rose was someone entirely different.

## CHAPTER THREE

# WINGS OF ROYALTY

The echoes of drums, trumpets and horns rattled past streets and alleyways fueling the enthusiasm of the rich and poor alike. The impoverished searched for their last pennies, the wealthy dug into their gold-plated chests and the deplorable moved with sleight of hand, taking what couldn't be noticed with an eye out for the kingsmen.

The last quarter of summer was at hand and soon the sun would disappear releasing the cold to ravage through the Thrun kingdom. Regardless, this wasn't a time for somber thoughts of winter and dull bodies. Today was a celebration, a day of broken blades and blood showers. Where challengers battled till there was nothing left but the strongest wills. Today was the festival of Broken Sun.

Red powder filled the air and little children ran the streets with wooden swords clashing at one another. Hands dipped into baskets of

blood-sand and threw them in the air as offerings to the Sun-god —
Raja.

Smiles, laughter and elation traced through alleys as crowds headed
to the Arena. Kingsmen lined the entrances in droves but that did
little to control the crowd. Entrances for common folk filled with men,
women and children counting coins to get decent seats and those for
the wealthy, throwing gold to watch from the exclusive towers.

Everyone wanted in, but the Arena was already bursting. The cheers
from outside could drown a man, and the ones from inside could
drown two. Completed over two decades ago, the Arena of the Yellow
Warrior was one of the largest buildings in all of Thrun. Shaped like a
bowl with its edges surrounded by soaring cylindrical towers in support;
it was almost as tall as the Sun-god's temple, a remarkable feat of architecture across known realms and past the Salem seas. The half-witted
would argue it could touch the clouds, but that is a debate best avoided.

The tournament lasted five days and today was the last. Today boasted a special event of sorts. According to the king's crows, there was
going to be a duel between Dions; enhanced individuals who survived
the journey through the White Rift and came back gods amongst men.
Both fighting against the crown prince of Thrun; the only true born
Dion, pure of blood and name.

The news spread faster than the red-pox with no one loving it more
than the bettors and gamblers. Their coffers overflowing with coins
from those looking to dance with luck and make easy gains. The flame
priest of Duran, or the monstrous hybrid of man and beast of Myr
versus one of the greatest warriors ever known to Thrun history. Who

prevails? An easy answer to some, and not so easy to others. Flames and claws will always make for good bets, but not in the presence of the beloved one. Nonetheless, some continued to stake heavy prices on the chance of an upset. *"Heavy gains require the heart for heavy losses,"* one said in passing. No doubt a statement from someone who has never suffered heavy losses.

The chance to see a clash between Dions was a rare one, lest one of royalty. As forces only unleashed in battle, their magnificence was only heard of in their victories and expansion of the Thrun empire; bringing all heretics and infidels under the glory of Raja. An opportunity to witness them today was a cause for further glory. Celebrations cloaked all of the main city of Cratos, and the entire kingdom bathed in joy and jubilation. Ale flowed heavily. The drunk gulped the taverns dry and the pleasurable, pleasured themselves in sin.

The bells tolled for the peak of day and the crowd roared in response. The main event was here.

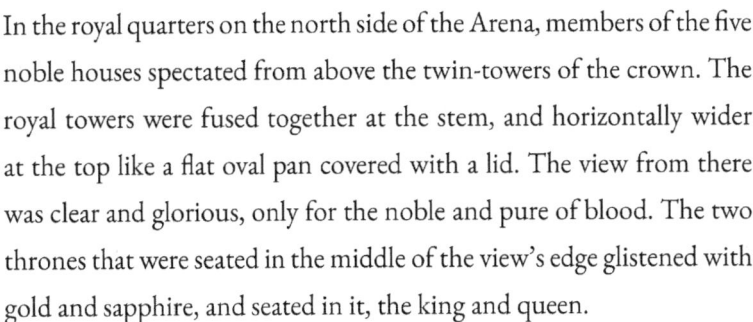

In the royal quarters on the north side of the Arena, members of the five noble houses spectated from above the twin-towers of the crown. The royal towers were fused together at the stem, and horizontally wider at the top like a flat oval pan covered with a lid. The view from there was clear and glorious, only for the noble and pure of blood. The two thrones that were seated in the middle of the view's edge glistened with gold and sapphire, and seated in it, the king and queen.

*"I told you it would be a success, the crown bank will be full by night-time,"* Urgus Taus said to a pinguid man who sat at his side. The man's face was absent of hair, and his neck struggled to hold all the jewelry around it. He wore a robe of blue silk with golden linen dangling over his left shoulder and scoffed dismissively in response.

*"People have seen warriors fight for years, but getting men made gods in heated battle is a true tribute to the Sun-god,"* Urgus added.

The man in question finished his wine glass in calm, beckoning a servant for a refill.

*"And I'm sure ridding the house of Myr and Duran of their Dions had nothing to do with it? We both know how this will end."* He responded with hints of contempt.

*"Everything I do is in service of Thrun, Lord of Mines. An attempt at treason is still treason. At least this way, they make the crown some money before going out."* Urgus affirmed.

*"And when did we start sentencing citizens to death without a court appearance?"* Puid of house Myr replied irritably.

*"They chose their own fate, and the king himself judged them. Do you wish to confront the king about it? He's right there."* Urgus said mockingly, pointing in the king's direction.

*"I know you think yourself a smart man Urgus, but you dance with wolves while oblivious to the wool on your own skin,"* he concluded, and left Urgus's company in search of other groups of elites.

Puid's words lingered even after he was gone. As head of the family of Taus, Urgus's obligation was to always strengthen their position in the state, yet, his list of enemies grew longer and his alliances wavered.

Newly appointed as advisor to the king after the untimely demise of his predecessor, he thought it smart to tread carefully lest he meet the same fate. His ambition festered still. So close to the ultimate power he could almost taste it. Puid's words still rang true — smarter men had tried and had failed. Snakes lay under the boards in waiting; the path to the throne needed something more.

The five noble families of Thrun have circulated the royal throne since its dawn.

Duran, Taus, Myr, Reis and Wuhn.

There are rumors there was once a sixth, but either the scroll masters forgot to add that to the history scrolls or it's just another story wenches and drunks make up to pass time. Not much is known about how a new king is chosen, but in the event a reigning king is rendered incompetent due to sickness or other factors, dies without an heir, or if said heir doesn't demonstrate qualities associated and accepted for kingship, a tribunal of elder nobles is called. Such is stated in the Sun-laws.

———————◆———————

The long balcony to the tower filled with nobles standing with their spyglasses in wait for the event to start. Whispers moved around in gossip only overshadowed by their fine silk garments and feathered robes drenched in majestic fragrance.

One person stood on the fighting stage, the priest of Duran. Pacing in the sands with two long razor chains doused in oil; one in each hand,

and wore nothing but a skirt of chainmail. As a survivor of the Rift, self-proclaimed to be blessed by the Sun-god, his divine ability was to inflame whatever part of his body he desired. Pledging himself to the faith under house Duran, the pious loved him, and he loved the offerings they made to him.

The next came up from the dens through the lower gates, Tuluk, or as most referred to him, "*man-beast.*" Emerging from the journey into the White Rift as the only survivor from a party of a hundred about two decades ago, he was one of the most famous Dions in all of Thrun.

Rumors claimed he was under the service of house Myr but there were doubts his alliances were with the Wuhn family. He never verbally proclaimed to either, unlike his flamed counterpart. He looked as big as an oak tree, tall as two men put together and his arms bulged in the steel pieces that were tied together by leather strings to hold his rerebrace. He wore pieces of armor that were specially made, and fur poked out of his vambraces and greaves. He was barefoot with exposed feet that held claws as big as stone, and his gauntlets were covered in spikes going as far down to the back of his palms. He had no weapons and needed none; the black claws on his hands alone broke swords like sticks.

The crowd cheered as he entered and he gave no response to their love. Children remarked at his horns that parted his head like branches, and parents regretted not betting on him at the sight of his size and ferocity alone.

Seats were empty and people stood on their toes just to get a better look. The short fumed and the tall filled with glee at their unobstructed views. The crowd stood marveling at the fighters in waiting, and a scream was heard around the west end of the arena, so distinct even cheers were overshadowed. On second hearing, it sounded more of an exult. Eyes followed the view of the elderly woman who cried a third time into the sky, above the towers and silhouetted by clouds.

There he stood.

The sun reflected off his armor and he shone like Raja himself had anointed him god of the skies. His wings, steadying him gracefully while he looked down at the opponents below him. Moments passed and praises were lauded up to him in prayer. Women professed their love, and some men too. Even nobles looked to him in glory while others loathed him behind smiles. He dove down, moving as air itself and stopped a few yards off the floor to louder chants from the crowd.

"*You treat our lives as entertainment? Is this the justice the king promised?*" Tuluk bellowed, but even his immense voice could not break past the chants.

"*He promised you justice, and this is the justice you deserve. You can walk out of Thrun a free man into exile if you're victorious,*" Selius answered, descending into the sands to higher roars.

"*We were brothers in battle, please listen. The accusations against us are false. We never conspired against the crown!*" The priest shouted in defense.

"*I didn't pass judgment; your pleas to me are futile.*" He replied sternly.

"*No you didn't. You're just the executioner.*"

"*Yes ... Yes I am.*"

The king raised his hand in signal and horns blared to begin the battle.

Fire exploded in a burst of light and the folks seated closest to the duel shrieked at the sudden wave of heat that came in their direction. The priest was drowned in flames and so were the whips he held. He stood a few yards to the side of the beast and they both glanced at each other in silent agreement; the only path to victory was in collaboration.

Selius stood opposite them, a few paces close to the north end. His armor gleamed white with strikes of gold tracing all over it in patterns, and he bore the crest of house Reis on his breastplate. His wings were shielded likewise, although a separate armor created from the toughest leather with blades edged at the tips. Made exclusively by the highest ranked Mages in the Mage Order, it was a marvel only to those who weren't at the receiving end of his attacks.

Through his helmet, he stared at his enemies as they prepared for their assault. He steadied his weapon in a fighting stance — a partizan, made out of blackened steel and a blade of Fermelstone — and pondered on their plan of attack. Tuluk will most likely rush him head on while the priest lurked in support, striking through opportunity. Their best bet would be to work together and his would be to rid himself of one early. As battled warriors with years of experience, it would be wise to strike fast and decisively, and with that thought, he burst forward with speed.

A puff of sand went up in smoke as a charging Selius barreled toward the priest. He was swift and glided through the air with ease. Tuluk jumped at him to intersect, claws bare and ready for a strike but the prince quickly redirected, pushing off the air and moving to the side and burst forward again quickly. Tuluk had always been awed at the prince's speed but experiencing it didn't prompt the same emotions. The inflamed priest, exposed to the formidability of the prince, whipped his fiery chains in defense and launched a series of attacks at him. He deflected them with his wings and blade, and spun away from a hurling Tuluk behind him.

Now in their desired formation, Tuluk charged forth. Slashing at Selius, but hitting nothing but air. His attacks were ferocious and every one sent the crowd into a gasp. The priest trailed Tuluk, maneuvering around Tuluk's occlusion of the prince's sights and waiting for opportunity. When the priest finally saw an opening, he launched to strike at the prince as Selius avoided another slash from Tuluk. In retrospect, this wasn't a good move. Selius was expecting the priest's attack and as his fiery chains launched, he struck at Tuluk's side in a whirlwind, pushing the beast into the direction of the oncoming chained attack.

A blow to Tuluk's side and an inflamed spiked chain to his back, Tuluk's armor held strong though the force from Selius's kick still sent him tumbling. What happened next, happened in a blink. With one spiked chain caught behind an ally's back and his right side unprotected, the flame priest barely had time to think before Selius struck. The priest whipped his other spiked chain violently to protect his exposed side, but the prince was already too close and deflected the spiked chain again with his blade, spun around him and blew a heap of sand into his flaming body. His head parted next, rolling in the air as the flames withered from his eyes. The flame priest was no more.

The sounds were deafening, so much that they felt silent. Tuluk got back up to witness the priest's body hit the sand. Blood spewing out his headless remains in spurts. Selius stood to the side of the dead with eyes fixed on Tuluk. Familiarity meant he knew all their weaknesses and intended to exploit them. Shinra was always brash and quick to action and now he lay dead. Thoughts raced Tuluk's mind on how victory could be possible. His enemy was quicker and moved with more eloquence. Ferocity without a target would just drain him of energy faster.

*Is this going to be my end too? No,* he couldn't think of such thoughts just yet. A mental defeat will just hasten his perish.

Selius gave him no time to continue his thoughts and hurled at him for a strike. Fermelstone clashed steel gauntlets in one attack after the next. Sparks flew as metal scraped metal and the collisions played a lullaby famous to blacksmiths. The prince wasn't as avoidant of Tuluk's attacks as earlier and every swipe of his claw met the blade of his partizan. Selius jabbed at the edges of Tuluk's pauldrons and rerebraces, and thrust his blade so hard into the thick steel plate on Tuluk's chest that it almost broke. In another strike from his weapon, Tuluk rolled to the side and in motion swatted at the prince's chest with his hind claws.

A surprising move that almost got Selius's head if not for his quick instincts, yet Selius didn't completely avoid the blow; a trail of claw marks drew diagonal on his breastplate and he fumed. Wagerers and fans alike exchanged altering cheers with faint hope of an upset strengthening. Tuluk retreated a few yards to catch his breath. His armor was painted with scars, his left rerebrace had fallen off and a crack ran up his left pauldron. No matter, if he was to survive, he'd have to rely completely on surprise attacks. With that thought, he ran at Selius, roaring with rejuvenated vigor; this time he will be on the offensive.

The attacks were loud and the warriors danced with claw to metal.

Tuluk jumped for another strike and Selius evaded to the side but as the beast turned to strike again, the prince gyrated, extending his wings in full, and the blades at the edge of his wings sliced part of Tuluk's face and horns.

Blood gushed from the top of his eyes rendering him sightless, as his enemy responded with his own flurry of attacks. Blinded and bedazzled. If there was a point he thought he would be victorious, it was long gone by now. A sharp sting struck above the pauldron on his left shoulder just below his neck. His legs struggled to hold his weight and gave out, kissing his knees to the ground. Blood dripped down his shoulder, covering most of his left side red and his vision waned. People celebrated from afar at his demise, though he felt no pain, just a fading existence. His body fell forward into a pool of blood and sand, but his soul had already left him.

Selius stared at the body of the man who once trained him in combat with barely any remorse surfacing his emotions. He had done as he was instructed and cared not for their innocence or guilt. Blood coated his blade and dripped, darkening the red shade of Fermelstone. He looked up to the tower of nobles, to his father's smiles contrasted by the stolidity of his mother. Hails rained all around him, pouring in droves. He extended his wings and burst off the ground in a thrust, disappearing into the skies with adoration trailing his path.

Somewhere in the towers, Urgus smiled with a high of deceit lacing his lips. Two problems resolved and two less Dions to contend with. He would worry about other consequences later but today brought tidings for celebration. He exited his company of royalty to find others more fitting of his mood and desires as the final parts of the tournament concluded. Soon the streets will be twice full, and the merrymaking will continue into the night.

—◆○◆—

Another page in the history of Thrun filled and sealed. As the sun's rays faded and the clouds darkened, gossip still floated people's lips about what was witnessed. It was somewhat of a surprise that the Dions were also in a battle to the death; most assumed it would be more of a fight of surrender. Some theories were thrown around by the overly curious though the thought didn't linger for long. Thrun had the most Dions in all the realms known to man, as well as staggering wealth and power. Two slayed Dions sacrificed in thanks to Raja was but nothing. The talk that lingered was all in laudation of the beloved one. In the outer zone of Cratos, down the street of bards to the lovers' inn, men and women argued, drank, cursed and fought each other in the name of the prince. Their confidence brimmed harder than the smell of cheap rum that filled the air.

*"Tennn gold pieces I bet. Almoost made ten timesss that if not ... for ... for that flying birddd of a man,"* one drunk said as he drowned himself in ale.

*"You fool! You wish you had ten gold pieces, maybe then you could get clothes without holes in them. If you call Prince Selius a bird again, I will slap you twice as hard next time."* A woman who shared his same predicament said with fierceness.

*"Yourrr ... hands are softtt and ... and smeeell like titsssssss ... hees a bir..."* A slap hit him so hard, he tumbled off his chair flying into the ground. Ale spilled into the floors and the jug rolled around bouncing as randoms celebrated the brutality with cheers.

*"I told you,"* she said with a bright grin and chugged down more ale.

The inn was full and lively, a famous stop amongst the lower class of the outer zone.

*"Filth like you should appreciate your betters more,"* she added, laughing.

*"I heard he killed a hundred men and over five enemy Dions in the battle of Roem, is that true?"* A voice shot from a table over. A man of slender weight sitting in the company of five. His company stared back with interest.

*"Ooh of course it's true; my neighbor's son was in that battle. Came back with a scar from his shoulder to his balls. He's the best warrior ever known to Thrun,"* she answered.

"*Who do you think assassinated the entire royal family of the Guyan kingdom?*" She continued in a loud whisper.

"*You shouldn't spread false rumors about the crown prince, Falaea. There's no truth to that. Guyan fell by their own demise and greed,*" said the barkeep from a distance. A rugged man with rugged looks, his voice betrayed his stature.

"*Ooh and I guess we conquered Guyan and now have control of all their Fermelstone mines because we asked nicely huh?*" Falaea retorted.

"*Don't fall for her stories with her many neighbors you lot, she has a different one every day,*" he responded.

The men didn't heed his advice or plan to alter their attention from Falaea. More ears tuned to her stories. Gossip brings together multitudes. She sat upright beckoning to the server girl for more drinks as she engaged her audience.

"*I spoke to a trader from Guyan some summers ago. He mentioned how on that night, fire rose brighter than moonlight. Smoke filled the air, connecting into the clouds and the people watched from below the hills in the city; the royal castle drenched in flames. Barely anything was seen that night, except for a guard who swore he saw a shadow of large wings disappear into the skies,*" she chattered.

"*But that happened six year-cycles ago. Isn't the prince nineteen now? You think a boy-child brought down one of our strongest rival nations in one night?*" A man from the initial company asked.

"*He has always been strong, even since birth. People say Raja saw pity on the queen after years of barren womb and gave her a god-child as a gift for all her years of sacrifice. The Taus family was furious for they thought they would be next in succession. Raja thought different."* Falaea answered.

*"What does he look like?"* asked a woman from the back of the audience. Cutting through the pause that followed Falaea's words. The barkeep just shook his head in disgust as her spectators grew.

*"Oooh, you never got to see him without his armor, eh? Picture a man with long hair that flows like brown silk, his face makes your bosom pump up in excitement. His eyes, nose and cheeks sculpted to perfection. Skin so fair, whores in all the realms get jealous at the sight. Crafted muscles carved on him and fit for royalty — not as bulky as him,"* she said as she pointed to the barkeep.

*"He's everything you'd want a man to be. Even when he was a young boy, my heart melted when I first saw him, and as a man now, it melts still. Shame he's to be betrothed to that whore princess of Mraahb. Why marry into that kingdom when we could just conquer them too?"* Sneering as she ended her rant. More questions followed and answers hence. Her audience engaged her like she had all the knowledge in the world. Might as well have been a gold-starred Mage of the Order, the way they took her words as gospel.

Most of them being sailors and travelers in town for the festival, she basked in her new role, delivering one story after the next, adding little touches and removing others. They curtsied by paying for her numerous drinks and she thanked them with more indulgences.

Shadows of night grew and lamplights grew in proportion. The classed zones of Cratos lit up in shades of beauty and wealth. The city was large and built with intent, with most of the praise attributed to the Wuhn family. As one of the founding families of great Thrun, their ancestors were healers and builders. It is said that when the royal families migrated to the lands now known as Thrun, the Wuhns built and designed all the structures that housed them. The common folk say that when a Wuhn is born, the world of knowledge is passed down to them; a saying that has been proven true over time as almost a quarter of the gold-starred Mages are Wuhns.

The expansion of Thrun was making the work of the Wuhns more noteworthy. With more people from the outer parts of Thrun, conquered kingdoms and far realms moving closer to the city, housing and city growth was among some of the most pressing matters for the ruling family. The higher inner zone, inner zone and outer zone all needed to be extended without compromising safety, security and the region of nobles; where the founding families and ruling family lived. The outer zone was the fastest growing, mostly made up of the lower middle class and below, the zone bordered the sea and extended the sides of the city into the mainland in a spread. The inner zone was next, bordered by high walls and thick brick; it covered the inner front half of the city after the outer zone with some slight difference in size. The higher inner zone followed, just past the center of the city. It was bigger than the preceding zone, even though it hosted less people and filled with smaller hills and valleys lying sporadically.

The region of nobles was the final and fourth section of the Thrun city covering most of the rear of the city extending into the small forest areas and cut through by the river Tames. In the middle of the region, stood the royal fortress; a mesh of giant towers connecting together in stone with lawned gaps sprinkled around for beauty, surrounded by trees and green vegetation that smelled like they were doused in daily fragrance. Sculptures of old kings and their tales laced the walls with gallantry, telling tales that would be passed down generations.

The stone walls glistened in the night, aging as does fine wine but its strength wavered not. If they could talk, their secrets would bring down empires and topple armies, but for tonight, they continued their eternal vow of silence. Halls stretched far, chambers sparkled with magnificence and the rooms were many. Too many to count or occupy. Even accounting for the quarters of the royal guards and servants, more than a dozen rooms lay bare on just the south quadrant of the castle.

The castle towers rose high, with stairs spiraling long into the above that one would lose breath on a long ascent. The highest tower stood at around the north-east corner, slightly separated from the other towers of the castle in distance and age. Built less than a decade ago, it rose up into the skies and opened up like a flower extending into a circular balcony bordered by a balustrade of fine stone and marble. A large room stood in the middle with openings at all sides which were covered in a veil of thin yellow drapery that danced to the tune of the wind. Servants will infamously refer to this tower as the Nest, as it was the tower of the crown prince. The room however had no traces of him tonight, nor did the skies around. Only remnants of quiet and whistles of the wind remained.

———————◆◇◆———————

The night continued unrelenting. Down in the main castle, two crown-guards stood guarding the king's chambers covered in silver armor. Two doors of heavy brown wood and dark metal braces that snaked in swirls stood behind them. Noises seeped through the doors and filled their ears and they did their best to ignore, the little echoes bounced down the walls and down the stairs to the LongHall and into non-existence. The tones weren't of flattery or bliss, but of fury.

"*You let that little snake manipulate you while you turn a blind eye. The crown prince should not be carrying out duties of a mere headsman. What if that attack caught his head? Is that how low you value your son? Your only heir?*" The queen claimed furiously. She'd been irate the whole day and finally had the king to herself to loosen her tongue.

"*You speak as if he's a child Gyai. You seem to forget he's among Thrun's best warriors, and as a warrior, he will do as his king commands, as I command!*" he responded sharply.

"*Selius handing down judgment shows strength in our rule. I too hear about all the silly ploys and wormings that some of the nobles whisper in their castles. Whatever talk of treachery and treason that is going on needs to be struck down with force.*" Adding in a bit calmer manner this time, as he resumed his focus on parchments that flooded his table of work, his wife staring at him from the bedside by the corner.

"*Who cares what those brainless fogs think about our rule? Your heir shouldn't be seen as an executioner by the people he's meant to rule. You see strength and others see a blood thirsty prince. And worse, that worm Urgus made you think it's a good idea. Same way he made you think marrying OUR SON to the Mraahbs is a good idea,*" barking back at Olius.

"*So that's what this is about?*" he said with a sigh.

"*Selius will marry the princess Morlain and that is final. I know you don't approve but the alliance with them is crucial to our expansion.*"

"*And it will take a lot of executions before the people ever see Selius as bloodthirsty. Isn't the whole point of the festival to spill blood?*" he added with a slight laugh.

The comment was not well received, and he could feel the fumes emanating from atop his wife's head. She let out a yell of frustration; something she did when she lost reasoning with her husband and disappeared into the second chamber of the room with heavy steps. The noise disappeared with her exit and Olius went back to his inks and papers. Today would not be the end of her opposition toward his decision, but the break of rebuttal was appreciated.

Olius continued his work on the orders that needed his approval. Another stamp and seal, and the lamplight flickered again, brightening the red ink that formed the crest of house Reis; three swords crossed in a triangle on a round shield.

———————————◆O◆———————————

This warrior faction of the noble houses came into power five generations ago after the ruling Queen Dumona Duran set herself, her consort and her three daughters on fire in a bizarre attempt to appeal to the Sun-god to save Thrun from a ravaging plague.

Six hundred dead in a fortnight, with bodies filled with red spots all over. The disease cared little for age or nobility, and in a month, the dead were growing in the thousands. It spread faster than could be noticed and the Mages in the Order scrambled around helplessly for cures that lay absent. A disease this potent during a time of famine doubled Thrun's woes by the hundreds. Hunger killed the poor and the red-pox killed the wealthy, the latter only showing symptoms just mere hours before death. It started with a light itch that grew stronger over time, then a burning sensation on the skin, heavy feverishness, then incessant sweating leading to an eventual slow decline to death.

In time, people started killing others at the mere mention of an itch even though no one truly knew the method of transfer. At eight thousand dead, it showed no signs of slowing. The pious confessed their sins, the strong barred themselves in their houses, and the weak waited for their passing; some indulging in sin as they enjoyed the last pleasures of the world.

The leader of the faith — Queen Dumona prayed unendingly in cries for Raja to spare his hand of whatever punishment Thrun was being given. On the eleventh month of the year-cycle **241-WT**, on the highest stair of the old temple of sun, Dumona set her family on fire by ordering her guards to pour oil on them as they prayed. Accounts from the royal guards say she prayed as her family burned and doused herself in oil with a torch in hand.

The five crown-guards were imprisoned for treason to be executed, but all fell victim to the pox just two days after. Miraculously, the gold-star Mage Jura Wuhn discovered a cure for the red-pox a sennight later to hails and adoration. After four months of turmoil and anguish, twenty-seven thousand dead and Thrun in complete disarray, the red-pox disappeared with the same mystery it emerged with.

It wasn't all doom however; food was plentiful with fewer mouths to feed, and resources of the dead were shared between those in need and the greedy. People took to the streets with little regard for the cold, some in celebration of survival and others in mourning of loved ones. A census was taken days later and the history books note that almost a quarter of Thrun citizens died from the red-pox. The surviving tribunal of elder nobles debated heavily on the next ruler, and the name that seemed to gain favor was the savior of Thrun — Jura of the Wuhn family. His lovable nature, intelligence and status propelled his publicity, but when word reached that an army from Astor was staging an attack due to their weakened state, the elders reconsidered, thinking it was best to find a leader with experience in war. A decision that led to the hasty coronation of the brawny and tactical Perolius Reis.

The Reis family got the worst of the pox, losing more than half of its nobles over the span. The Duran family was next with more emphasis on the death of the ruling family as well as their overall image as pious zealots. The Taus and Myr family suffered sizable losses with the Wuhn family experiencing the least loss. People claim Raja kept most of them safe in hopes they found a cure, and others have more sinister claims.

Nonetheless, this began the current rule of House Reis.

———————◆○◆———————

The early years of the rule of Perolius Reis started magnificently. Thrun withstood a flurry of attacks from Astor solely due to his remarkable battle tactics and wit. Perolius ushered in a new age of Thrun amid its previous grievances, and provided a sense of protection that was vital to the state's rejuvenation. His uncanny obsession though, was a small region past the twin mountains into the drylands. A forest area with a mist of white fog that stood dense no matter the season. Little was known about the area except for gossip speaking of foul creatures and disfigured men that escaped its confines on occasion. It was unknown the reason for his obsession, but when soldiers started to leave on assignments with an exclusive group of the Mage Order and never return with them, word started to spread. Kidnappings also got more rampant with men, women and children disappearing into oblivion.

On the third year after Perolius's coronation, on the thirteenth day of the sixth month of summer, four Thrun soldiers entered Astor in the dead of night and the Astor city fell hours later. The history books don't go into much detail about what transpired before or during this time, but on this night, the first mention of Dions appear in what will be known down generations as the Expansion.

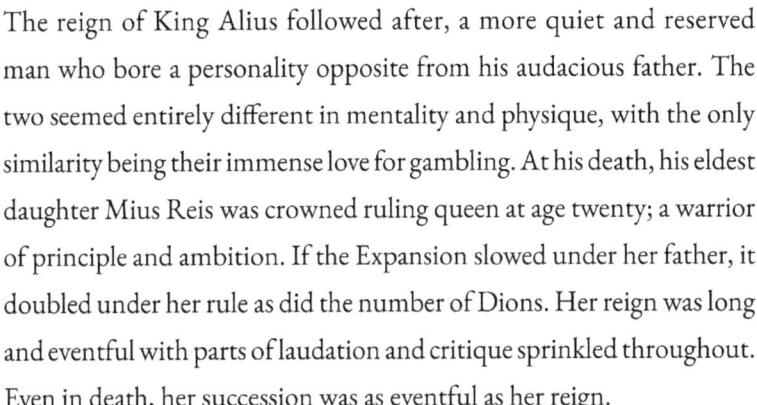

The reign of King Alius followed after, a more quiet and reserved man who bore a personality opposite from his audacious father. The two seemed entirely different in mentality and physique, with the only similarity being their immense love for gambling. At his death, his eldest daughter Mius Reis was crowned ruling queen at age twenty; a warrior of principle and ambition. If the Expansion slowed under her father, it doubled under her rule as did the number of Dions. Her reign was long and eventful with parts of laudation and critique sprinkled throughout. Even in death, her succession was as eventful as her reign.

Days before her eldest son Romulius was to be crowned, he took a secret adventure with five of his closest friends; names found to be Rezus Parchey of the house of white stone, Dona Fry — third daughter of the famed songstress Eona Fry, Dredfud Duran — the plump only son of Dufas Duran, Mosai Lait — the handsome and boisterous son of Fana Lait, chair of house Lait and the commoner known as Bramu the bold; an ironic name given by his friends for his cowardice.

Romulius traveled past the twin mountains and into the drylands with one goal in mind, to walk into the White Rift with his friends and come out a Dion to be crowned king with his Dion friends. *"A moronic decision by a man-child who never grew out of his childhood fascinations,"* one Mage noted in the history books.

At their destination, the friends decided the order they were going to step into the Rift in hopes of getting their enhancements — the king-to-be, his closest friend Mosai, then Dona, Rezus, Dredfud and last Bramu. The last never took his step. Maybe out of fear or a grand realization of the stupidity of their plan. He waited and waited, and his friends never came out. In his account, after he was found by a scout, he defended that the pressure of his friends pushed him to follow but his words fell on the deaf ears of doleful nobles who needed someone to take blame. His head rolled days later.

The tribunal of elders gathered again to choose the next ruler among Mius's children. Her second child — a man of thirty and eight was a drunk, gullible and filled with gluttony; her third — a weakly and smallish woman who shied in the midst of people; her fourth — a boy of twenty and two, slender of build with a keen interest for strategy similar to his mother and great grandfather. He had an adorable kindness about him which made him a favorite among servants, but also shared a contrasting ruthlessness in combat that made his trainers shower him with praise.

Olius, he was called. Mius's last children, both of eighteen, shared no defining traits and were overshadowed by the former. So in the year-cycle **366-SM**, after the death of Queen Mius, Olius Reis was crowned king of Thrun.

———◆◇◆———

Olius's reign was but a faint replica of his mother's. Not as intense, he had a calmer method of governing while still displaying a sense of leadership that drew people to follow him. He was a fine warrior and led Thrun to many battles in pursuit of growth. A year into his rule, he married the jewel daughter of the merchant Bain Craux and a wedding the size of no other followed. A week of celebrations filled the castles and Thrun rejoiced. More years continued and talks of an heir festered. There were no signs of child bearing, and rumors of all types swirled from the crevices of hidden conversations. In such a delicate monarchy, heirs were of the highest importance to the ruling family, and their absence meant a transition was imminent.

According to the Sun-laws, a ruling king or queen cannot remarry under any condition, and any child born out of wedlock is to be exiled immediately at birth. Not that Olius ever intended to, Gyai at age forty and four was still the most beautiful woman he could ever dream of. He'd loved her through all the healers that visited from far and wide, the potions that were claimed to contain miraculous enchantments, the countless prayers of the faith, and her cries that poured at night from exhaustion. Throughout all those, he loved her still. He had come to terms with the absence of an heir long ago but his wife never relented. She was unyielding in her resolve, and searched for any avenue that provided the slightest promise.

———————◆○◆———————

In the spring of the year of **392-SG**, at a dawn of heavy rain and thunder, fifteen nurses stood surrounding the queen in her bed chamber as the child in her enlarged belly sought release of its confinement. Time passed and her screams rang loud past the halls with maids running in and out the chamber with fresh water and cloth. An hour into the exhaustive wait, a head finally showed signs of coming out. Another giant push through her pain and the body slid from under her into the hands of the nurse covered in blood and fluids.

The rest of the nurses exploded with cheers, hastening to help the recovering mother, then someone shrieked. The look of horror drawn over the nurse holding the prince as she stared at feathers protruding out of the back of the child into two wings. Similar shrieks and looks followed as the others realized. The gasps broke Gyai out of her weariness and she opened her eyes to horrified faces in the direction of her child. "*We should cut it off,*" one nurse said, grabbing a knife. A statement that flung Gyai into a frenzy. She leaped at the nurse holding her child and snatched the baby, startling her. An action that finally made the child cry and start moving its limbs. Blood oozed from under her with the cord still attached.

"*Get out! All of you, Get out!*" She screamed repeatedly with curses, wrath filling her eyes. The nurses scurried out the room running. In their absence, she locked the door behind them, blood dripping down her legs as she returned to the bed. She sat in the middle, rocking her baby while singing a lullaby. A boy it was; she smiled with tears filling her eyes staring at the child who wouldn't stop crying.

As dawn broke, the sun welcomed the prince with rays of warmth. His skin soaked the heat with the white now gleaming yellow. Green were his eyes and his hair curled down in strands of brown. Two wings of a light brown hue sprouted from his back with spots of black at the ends. He stretched and stretched some more, his cries dying down to soothing music. Gyai was lost in her trance and failed to notice the keys that jiggled outside the chamber. The door opened slightly and Olius slid from behind, signaling the guards not to follow.

Seeing his wife with child surfaced joys he'd never before experienced, smiling so hard it alerted her of his presence. She looked up, meeting his excitement, *"He's so beautiful ... More than anything I ever imagined,"* she claimed to her husband as he came closer to meet his son.

He already knew what to expect, the price paid for an heir was worth whatever they sacrificed and more.

*"He has your eyes,"* Gyai added, as the two new parents sat on the bed. Olius noticed the pool of blood under her and begged to get a nurse until she agreed. Just one nurse she agreed to, and forbade the nurse from touching her child. Similar experiences followed as months passed. The mother and son were inseparable, for not even nurses or maids came close unless Olius pleaded. Years passed and the child grew into a fine boy with incredible talents. Starting battle training at age six against fully grown warriors, he exhibited strength, skill and a fighting prowess way above his age and physique. His instincts were almost animalistic, and his senses were tenfold better. He excelled in everything fit for a prince. Mages marveled at his intellect and interest in history, combing through books and scrolls of old kings and starred Mages. In time, his notoriety spread like wildfire, *"The Dion prince who would build the Thrun Empire,"* the people said, elevating his excellence more.

In reality, many seldom knew Selius truly. A boy of what could only be described as a peculiar personality. His different sides shifted per his company, wearing characters like robes for an outing. As a child, he made an insightful discovery that went forth in shaping his ideals,

*"Status and Power meant everything in the world, and he had both."*

What people saw as the adorable, charming prince and what existed behind the veil were totally separate beings. Every now and then though, a slight break would occur, a small chink in a hardened armor seeping out dread and malice. His mother would refer to these as, *"Childhood tendencies of a child that knows no better,"* to Olius when the breaks happened. Of course the king knew better, but even in the face of truth, denial was a cherished companion.

Gyai did well to hide these occurrences however, so well even rumor was hard to find. Dead men told no tales, only whispers of silence. The incidents piled up and his mother protected him as every mother would. At age three, a kitchen cook's daughter went missing playing around with Selius in the Celestial gardens by the west lawn, triggering a search that lasted days.

The guards on duty would claim the children were playing around with a small wooden horse a moment ago, and in a blink only Selius remained with the wood carving. Her body was found in the forest area half a dozen days after, near a bank of the River Tames smashed to the ground as if a large rock fell on her, or she was dropped from the skies. At age five, he sliced off a servant's limb for pricking him while being helped with his garment, spurting out blood till the poor boy died moments later.

The incident at the Sumulan village — a territory of Thrun a couple of leagues away from the Cratos — was probably the second time Gyai ever felt genuine uneasiness in her son's actions. Nonetheless, she kept on, a mother's love had to be undying and her love was. The story amongst the people would be that rogue raiders were responsible for the massacre of the entire native hamlet, and not a whiff of anything else.

The first time Gyai ever felt dread from her son happened five days after he turned thirteen. It wasn't an entirely joyous celebration due to the state of Thrun. It was a time of war against the formidable nation of Guyan; the first nation so far to oppose Thrun with its own Dions and the only nation to be in possession of Fermelstone; the strongest metal known in all realms. Both sides had won battles, but the tide of the war swayed back and forth without either emerging victorious.

The Guyans were unyielding and fought with ceaseless resolve. For the first time in over a century, Thrun entertained talks of signing a peace treaty or worse, losing outright. Selius pleaded with his father to join the war many times and he forbade it twice as many. Even with all his skill, he was still a boy and a prince at that. He would fume as a child does and disappear amid his mother's consolement. On this day, he was nowhere to be seen, as was the case some days before.

Gyai hated when he did that; he'd disappear into the skies to a nest somewhere she knew not, to sulk as a child does. It's hard to keep track of a child who flies, and even harder to catch him. She sent scouts to known areas he frequented hoping to at least get word he was okay. The day had passed fast, and the existing battles continued. Olius returned to his chambers from his war council close to the dead of night, and slipped into bed near his wife to slumber. The skies were dark, and the moon hid from prying eyes, a breeze flowed into the King's chambers with cold and the scent of swaying trees. Gyai felt wetness by her feet under the covers and unconsciously moved her legs in avoidance. The uncomfortable feeling grew and she broke out of sleep.

The scream she let out only exited as a whispered squeal, enough to jolt her husband out of bed. His reaction was a sharp flinch before realization of his son. Selius stared back with eyes fixed on his father, crouching on the wooden footboard at the rear of the bed with wings extended. His clothes were dirtied, wet, stained red with cuts and tears all around.

On the bed lay five heads; two with crowns on their heads and a pool of blood spreading. Shock is an ill description for the emotions Olius was experiencing, and petrification was likely a better substitute. Lying at his feet was the entire monarchy of Guyan; the king, queen, their two daughters and two year old son.

## CHAPTER FOUR

# USHURA SIEM FUELIM DÄ

The pain stung more as he shifted himself upright and he ground his teeth, wincing. Every movement jolted a touch of agony, but he fought through with defying resistance. The swell was now a bulge on his foot and lacking the right treatment, it lingered and grew. Not that any of that mattered to Dakai at the moment, even the piercing sensation in his belly that yearned for food was but an afterthought. Half a day had passed since Naemi returned from her trip to get berries and water, yet he hadn't laid eyes on his sister, only her mumbling words from outside and a stern warning not to exit the hideout.

Initially, he thought this a jest, a silly joke unsurprising of his sister's character, but that thought fleeted fast. She answered his questions with slurring speech except for when he insisted to come outside, for that she was obstinate.

"*Don't come near me! Don't come out!*" The last clear words he heard from her and with such vehemence, it chilled him.

Confused and in pain, he questioned Naemi multiple times, but her responses were either inaudible or incoherent. In perplexity, he waited while hours passed and his worry grew; all that marked her presence were the low moans and odd sounds that seeped from outside. At worry's peak, he crawled to the entrance, inching forward through heavy discomfort, intent on discovering what was wrong with his sister.

———◆○◆———

Darkness cloaked the area with little spots of light escaping through the cluster of leaves and branches above, only to be devoured into more obscurity. As good as Dakai's eyes were, even he couldn't see through the black that lay encompassing his surroundings. Faint sounds came from ahead and he called to her to no response. The forest was quiet tonight — too quiet — and all he heard were her slow breaths. He inched closer as if called to a beacon, toward the base of a tree stem some feet from him until her silhouette was visible.

She lay on her side, coiled by the base with bent knees. Dakai called out to her, from a soft touch to a harder shove but she never awoke. No bodily injuries appeared present and that soothed his heart temporarily, however she smelled bad, a scent that triggered a memory of his visit to the butcher's shop once, and her skin felt covered in something — something smeary. Still, he was perplexed what her previous reactions meant and why won't she wake. Was she in deep sleep or was this something else? What could he even do now with night at full rage and every tug of his leg jolting pain? The only conclusion to these queries was to wait for morning's light to investigate further. Maybe she was in deep slumber and would wake at dawn, stretching loud as ever, though part of him felt the faux in his words and unease loomed behind his optimism.

Leaning on the smaller tree with Naemi's head resting on him, his mind lay bare, exhausted and his body hungry, itching with fatigue. He couldn't think and didn't want to, he just wanted to forget and dream, a request his mind willingly obliged, fading out his consciousness to memories of happier days.

———————◆O◆———————

A touch interrupted his utopia and light blinded him as he woke. As his eyes adjusted to the morning rays, his first sight was a face looking back at him; he flinched and jumped back instinctively only to be held in place by the tree base behind him.

The figure was human though it was covered in green and brown, blending into the trees. Long black hair flowed down its neck past its shoulders, and brown eyes peeked through the wooden mask it wore filled with strange markings. It was hunched over his foot, seemingly inspecting his leg and moved closer when he opened his eyes. It paused for a moment, staring harder at Dakai and then over to the girl resting on his lap. It moved forward more, putting its hands on Dakai's face, pulling and pressing as it explored him further.

A voice finally escaped its lips, soft and feminine, but it was words he couldn't understand. Dakai, now a bit frustrated with the tugging of his face, pushed off its hands in defense and it moved back in surprise, realizing the action wasn't appreciated. Someone else spoke, this time from above in the trees. A voice not as soft as its predecessor, and not as feminine either. Dakai's eyes searched the treetops, the cluster of heavy branches above that extended and saw no one.

The stranger touched his swell and pain shot through his body, making him groan painfully. The figure quickly retreated some paces back at his expression of discomfort. It approached Dakai again slowly, beckoning for his approval. Dakai was ridden with puzzlement and anxiety, though he didn't feel any dangerous intent from the stranger. He nodded slowly in approval, and the stranger started to smear what looked like red mud over his ankle from a bag made of dried leaf strings woven into a pouch. Its palms coarse as rock, he felt as though touched by the rugged edges of sandpaper. Dakai winced and it paused again.

"*Shisui ... shisui*," it said, so gentle it could be considered an apology. It stretched its left hand covered in paste to him and pointed at his swollen ankle signaling for permission to continue. Dakai gazed back with unset emotions; the stranger didn't appear to be foe but he still wasn't sure to consider it friend. Regardless, help was needed, and he and his sister would take whatever was provided, so with a deep breath, he nodded again in approval.

The smear stung and felt cold on his skin. He watched as the stranger treated him, its skin covered in what he could only conclude as green dye, wearing only parts of clothes made out of dried furry skin and plant fibers covering its torso and lower waist regions. The thought of the figure being a woman came late to him despite all the clear signs.

When she finished, she reached out her hand to examine Naemi and Dakai grabbed it reflexively — another unappreciated gesture, but this time he was the one to apologize for the rudeness of it. He had hoped she'd be awake by now, wouldn't that have been so easy? A conscious sister and a healthy ankle, was that too much to ask for? Seemed their journey got harder by the day, and now he couldn't even find comfort in his partner in tragedy.

The voice from above came again with words of incomprehension.

The masked woman looked over at Naemi and back at him with the same expression drawn on the mask. She reached into her bag and brought out a flower; purple in color with lines of red and extended the flower to Dakai's nose. Dakai didn't understand the gesture but reached out to take the gift as a sign of acknowledgment. The scent was strong and the effects hit him almost instantly. His senses began to dull, and his vision blurred in bits, his last image being of more figures emerging behind tree-stems into the light. The smell of the plant filled his head like a dense cloud and consciousness waned till empty. As morning's light blossomed and the sun rose in all its glory, the next journey entrenched in the siblings' destiny was already in motion.

———————◆○◆———————

The jungles of Bashu are known to many and explored by few. Even fewer ventured inward with intent, except for those with years of familiarity. Natives from a couple small villages surrounding the jungle were the bulk of its visitors, but even so, caution was heavy lest they get swallowed by its enormity or its inhabitants. The forest gave them gifts of food, water and medicine and they returned their thankfulness with respect.

A simple pact that had been honored down generations, balancing the existence of two bodies in cohesion. In some instances down their history, the pact was dishonored by the latter, and the consequences were colossal. Lessons were learned overtime, lessons the villagers benefited heavily from. Grandparents told parents, and parents told children in the endless cycle of teaching, and stories passed down family trees through the filters of word-of-mouth. Tales told by the fire differed in recollection as time passed, but the premise never changed; wandering deep into Bashu was dangerous and forbidden.

Even so, curiosity is an itch for the bold. Some from the villages and far away, tested their temerity by embarking on quests to slay beasts of folklore, for glory, honor, or whatever else men base their illogical decisions on. These one-sided adventures rarely turned out victorious for the visitors, but strangely, the more people disappeared into the woods, the more its mystique grew, emboldening others to prove they had luck's charm to be worthy.

Only three people have been known to come back from a voyage into the depths of Bashu in recent history. A knight from Sailor City who returned after two dozen days, bloodied, with his armor ripped and partly crushed into his arm, dangling on his side as he limped. A native hunter was first to encounter him and when he was found, he spoke no words, just shivered endlessly. He died from his wounds days later.

Next was a learned man; particularly recognizable with his head wrapped in dark cloth and his enthusiastic personality that made the people of the Ashu village gather to his stories. He claimed to be a Mage from great lands in the east past the Salem seas and into the lands of a famed empire. He spoke of exploration and hoped to be the first man to explore the mysteries of the forest for the advancement of knowledge.

On the day of his venture, the Ashu people amassed for a sendoff with many continuing to try and deter him, but his desire was too strong to crack. He left with his party of five, disappearing behind the thick branches and leaves onward into the soul of the jungle. At sunset of the seventh day after his departure, a man was seen walking out of Bashu into the Ashu village covered completely in a black liquid that was dripping as he walked. He had no eyes, only empty holes in his head, and parts of cloth dangling from atop his head while repeating the same words, "*Raja save me.*"

Locals gathered as he walked mindlessly, his skin covered in black and blisters all over, and as the black dripped, it seemed his skin dripped with it. Gasps and screams shot out from around him, but never from him; his mind was but an empty echo and his body a shell. He paced onward and onward slowly like that was the only purpose he had left in the world. Reports say he trekked for about three leagues before collapsing to his death while others claim he did for about five. Regardless, whatever the learned man learned brought him only death.

The last was an incident from Damu, a settlement a few leagues north of Ashu. Three children wandered too far into the forest and two frenzied parents pursued their children upon realization, with a group of locals helping. A few moments into their search, two of the kids were seen running back in haste with a look of utter terror drawn on their faces.

Exhaustion filled their lungs, and they could barely answer any of the questions thrown at them, but one thing was clear, the youngest of five wasn't fast enough to escape whatever they were running from. The search continued for hours until the natives feared moving any further. This wasn't the first time overly inquisitive children strayed too far and lost their way, and unfortunately the reality was they were never found. The two children jittering partly with gibberish and exaggeration would claim a creature with a face made of giant snakes grabbed their sibling, but fear makes people see many things and another creature got added to the folklore. Tears rolled and mourning happened in the following days, and even though time passed, scars never healed.

Two summers after the disappearance of the child, on a warm morning with blue skies, a family of four woke up to a seven year old boy standing by their bed. His skin was covered in a green smear and he held a mask with strange markings. His mother drowned with joy, and his father hailed the village to see a miracle. When the crowd gathered, shock rippled through their faces and mouths lay agape. How a boy of five survived in Bashu for two years, no one will ever know. When he was asked, he spoke in a tongue people couldn't understand and made foreign signs that held no meaning. Memories will fade with growth, and even as he got older, he would never truly remember what happened to him during his time in Bashu. But occasionally, fragments of his memory seeped out into the open, and faces would come into his mind of the hidden society living in the depths of the jungle.

———◄O►———

Sounds from muffled voices poked at his ears and his skin felt the touch of many hands. The pain in his head rang high and his eyes unrolled slowly. The children ran out screaming when Dakai awoke, shouting out words in unison. He sat up sluggishly, wincing at the pain that shot through his head, letting out a low groan. Parts of his skin were covered in the same green dye he saw earlier, with marks of little fingers, and a bowl by his side on the floor filled with green slime. The upper part of his clothes were off and his left leg was covered in a red coating; noticeably less swollen than earlier.

The inside of the shelter was warm and the light inside was dim. The room was shaped round from the inside with a veiled opening at the front, and foliage filled the floors. Dakai retraced his thoughts to how he ended up in his present situation but his memories failed him, leaving only gaps and confusion.

*Naemi!* He thought, and rushed to his feet only to collapse back down to the ground. Even with treatment, he was nowhere close to walking yet. Someone brushed open the veil brightening the room for an instant. The voice that followed bore recognition and the dark flowing hair bore resemblance. She held two bowls in both hands and stopped when she saw Dakai on the ground. She laid them on the ground quickly and rushed toward him, helping him back onto the bed. Dakai refused the gesture, asking intently for his sister in response.

The struggle between the helper and the helped continued for a moment until she gave in to her opponent's calls for his sister in defeat. Even without understanding each other's words, certain actions spoke clearly as day and she retreated back outside, returning with a thick wooden stick as tall as her. The second gesture, Dakai accepted gratefully as she presented the token to him. He held onto it for support and stood up a second time with much sturdiness. The smell of soup pulled his attention to the food below for his hunger intensified with every pass of time, yet he continued his defiance and focused solely on finding his sister.

He exited the shelter with eyes peeking into the skies at the blue hue, through the giant green leaves and heavy branches of trees that lay spreading. The scenery came all at once and the sight dazzled him in the moment. As his eyes turned from above downwards, the full view of the colony came into sight.

Dakai froze in place, a seemingly subconscious reaction of awe at what he was seeing. As if every beautiful thing he'd ever seen paled in comparison. The ground covered green in short, moist grass with flowers of colors he'd never seen sprouting below and on trees in patterns of delight. Round shelters were built into trees like bird nests; some big, some small and others chained together between trees in a web, hanging in the air. It was an explosion of color and nature unifying in blissful harmony. Faces stared back at him ironically in similar expressions. They all blended into the forest as the strange young woman did but this time their faces bore no masks. Women and men kept their distance, but the children expressed their curiosity openly; poking and pulling at him with inquisition and running back when he looked their way. They ran up into the trees with ease, scaling up its barks as smoothly as a fish swims upward a stream. His eyes drew the most dramatic responses when it met theirs, the red and blue looked like the sun and moon staring back at them, and they broke into loud whispers.

The dark-haired woman interrupted his thoughts with a touch and Dakai broke from his gaze. For the first time he saw her face clearly, eyes more hazel than brown with light bumps on her cheeks and a nose made perfectly in place. Her hair glimmered in the shade, flowing down with little curly waves — long and black. She smiled and spoke again, but her smile overshadowed her words and Dakai just nodded absentmindedly. The walk wasn't long and they came up on a hut built like a dome with dark branches, covered in leaves and more flowers. Inside, Naemi lay on a foliage bed on the left corner and smoke rose from inside a pot next to her. Dakai rushed to his sister and called out to her many times but no answer came. Her skin was hot and her breath was faint. He turned to the woman, hurling many questions but she just replied with blank stares.

"*Alie uj giin mau fi,*" came a voice shadowed in the back.

"*Diei fi,*" the woman answered and left the dome.

The source of the voice emerged with slow steps, an old man wearing a heavy cloak of plant fiber as long as a gown. His white hair, thin and loose on his head, and more flailing around his chin in abundance. He differed from the previous people Dakai had encountered in many ways, and one of his eyes appeared lost behind its patch. Dakai darted his questions at the peculiar man as he came into sight, emotions swelling up inside him at the state of his sister.

"*She needs help ... she needs ... Can you understand me? I need help for my sister ... sh ... she boils from a fever.*" Speaking with a breaking voice and calling out to Naemi through light shoving.

"*Mmm, yes I understand you child,*" he answered subtly with a croaky voice.

Dakai's face lit up briefly, "*My sister is sick and needs help ... some wolfsbane or elderflower can bring down her fever.*"

"*You won't find any of those in these parts, and I already know about her fever,*" he walked closer to the pot that burned with smoke and added more herbs.

"*Those won't even help if you could find them, she's not awake to be able to drink their contents, though she still breathes. The only way to give her healing is through her nose. The smoke from this burning Riya will cool her soon enough. It will be an unpleasant smell for us both however.*"

"*Her energy is faint and her mind seems adrift. What happened to her?*" the man added, retreating to the back of the room.

"*I ... I don't know. She was fine a day ago. She left to find food and water, then was unawake next time I saw her.*"

"*Hmmm,*" he grunted, "*Her body is weakened, I have done everything in my power to revive her, but she doesn't respond to anything, I fear all you can do now is wait,*" he concluded, amounting to the disarray his words carried.

"*There has to be more you can do ... is there nothing else?*" Dakai pleaded.

"*I'm sorry child.*"

Many thoughts flooded Dakai's head, none taking precedence just altering emotions. Thoughts of confusion, fear, hope and hopelessness, moving in circles. The dark-haired woman came in sometime later after the old man departed, with gifts of food for the brother. Dakai didn't notice her presence as he sat next to his sister in deep thought. The aroma caught his nose again but his appetite was far gone from him, leaving only emptiness.

The young woman sat next to both of them quietly, just staring at the strange siblings as one sat and the other slept. The churning in Dakai's stomach got louder and she continued to signal him to eat over and over again until it was tiring to deny. The food melted in his mouth, soft and doughy, and his senses felt a tingle they had been denied for a long time. It tasted sweet, honey-like with a slight sour after-taste that lasted long enough to be pleasant. The soup was slimy and soothed his throat so well he finished it in one go.

The young woman smiled as he finally ate, noticing the extent of his hunger. She left and came back with more food and water which suffered the same fate. Dakai's efforts at conversation fell short to her words and foreign signs, however, simpler gestures were clearer to her and he thanked her as best he could. The day came to an end with Dakai sleeping by his sister with his hand locked in hers. Another night in strange company for the lost siblings.

———————◆○◆———————

The next day came with little changes for Naemi; the aged man covered her in medicinal leaves to assist in bringing down her fever. Her body looked shrunk and feeble from lack of good food and water, both of their bodies did. Dakai worried more, because throughout their new reality all they had was each other, and seeing his sister in this state made his heart sink deeper. The veil to the dome brushed against each other and three men entered. Double edged wooden spears filled their hands and they stood in waiting. The aged man spoke from across the back where he sat,

*"You have been summoned by the leaders of the tribe. The 'Gouzadu' people are not too fond of outsiders and the leaders need to judge whether you both stay or are exiled."*

The words didn't utterly surprise Dakai; the gazes from before and the uniqueness of the place didn't feel particularly welcoming to strangers.

*"What about my sister?"* he asked.

*"She will be fine here till judgment is passed."*

The warriors guided his path down past more trees and prying eyes toward a large gathering. In the center, five trees connected in a half-circle with roots intertwined. In the stem of every tree was a seat carved into it and five figures occupying. The crowd that stood in witness were loud, and the murmuring got louder by the moment. Their gazes shadowed his every move, and he failed to understand the emotions behind their looks.

The men with spears stopped him at the middle edge of the half-circle and retreated. A man from the five stood up and the crowd silenced; he was short and his bent back pushed him down farther. A face full of heavy wrinkles cracking his skin into contours only known to dry barren lands. He spoke and the people listened; his voice was squeaky, but still loud enough to be heard. The rest of the leaders were all similar in age except for one. A boy, closer in age to Dakai sat in the middle seat.

———————◄O►———————

The trial started and seven tribesmen stepped up from the crowd; the dark-haired woman amongst them. Dakai thought about how he and his sister's present fate rested in the hands of other people, and he felt a growing disdain of the repetition of their reality. His leg was still far from healed and how could he carry Naemi in her current state?

Whatever happened to her in the wild was a sign that the forest wasn't safe to be alone in, and how could they even find their way through this maze of a place? The witnesses spoke one after the other as questions were thrown at them, the frustration of incomprehension building up in Dakai. Someone else stepped up from the crowd, the aged man who was treating Naemi. They continued their interrogation as Dakai stood still, disregarded, grasping onto the stick for support. There was still some pain in his foot and occasionally a sharp sting traveled up his leg.

Feeling ignored and overwhelmed, Dakai spoke out,

*"We mean no harm to you. We were taken from our home and are lost in these lands. We just want to be able to go home, but my sister is sick and I can't walk well, if you forsake us we won't survive the forest."*

His plea caused a pause in the deliberation, drawing their attention. The aged man spoke next, translating Dakai's words to the perplexed. A woman from the five spoke after and the aged man translated her words,

*"Our people say they followed great destruction in the forest that led to you and your kin. Were you responsible for this?"*

*Great destruction? What could be meant by that?* he thought.

*"No, we were not responsible. My sister left in search of water. Whatever caused such destruction might have caused her illness too,"* answering with resolve bracing his words.

Further contemplations were prompted from his response and the next question came,

*"How did you come to be lost in the forest, and where is this home you talk about?"* The man's voice wavered in pitch as he asked, and the silent crowd were eager for interpretation.

*"We were kidnapped from Soros in Primea, and escaped from the trafficker ship when it got attacked. We swam to shore and ran as far into the forest as we could until I hurt my leg. My sister cared for me until now."*

Murmuring echoed through as the words were translated, the reason for such gasps weren't entirely clear however. Whether it was the explanation of what a Primea was, or that of a trafficker ship, or the ordeal of the siblings, the words triggered reactions that rippled through the crowd. More questions followed and Dakai answered as best he could. At the end, the leaders concluded that the siblings could stay until they were healed enough to journey home. They would be provided with whatever support they needed, and in return would have to live within the culture of the tribe.

Relief embraced Dakai hearing their words; he showered endless thanks toward them as they stood to leave. The warriors from before approached him, directing him back to the dome through the crowd. As he left, the gazes never wavered; they looked at him with endless curiosity, some stretching to touch his skin and hair as he passed and others keeping their distance.

The dome came into sight and the freckled woman stood by its veil with a face as gleeful as ever, the warriors will leave as he entered, exchanging words with the woman in quick conversation.

The inside was better lit today; a fire flamed in a hole dug about a foot into the ground and parts of sunlight breached through the wall of branches. Food sat on a stone slab close to the fire while Dakai sat by his sister. She was a lot warmer now, but that was about the only change she had. The sound of brushing leaf strings caught his ear and he turned expecting the young woman only to meet eye with the old man. It was surprising how he got anywhere with how slow he walked.

Dakai looked up at him. "*You're not from here are you?*" he asked; the man let out a slight grunt and kept walking to the back; a favorite spot of his with a wood log as a seat and a bigger one carved higher into a stand. Herbs of different types lay on it in addition to small bowls, wooden grinders and flat stones. In a way it reminded him of Arwa's work area and how meticulous she kept it.

"*How did you end up here?*" Dakai pursued as the man sat, exhaling out his exhaustion from walking.

"*Is it that obvious?*" he said sarcastically, laughing and coughing simultaneously.

"*You chose to stay here? Were you also lost?*" Dakai continued.

"*You could say I was always lost until I got here, my life wasn't worth much before ...*" he paused briefly and continued. "*Yes, I chose to stay here.*"

"*Why did you stay?*"

"*I found meaning,*" he answered, smiling through his words.

"*Where are you from? How did you end up here?*" Dakai kept on his path of inquisition.

"*You ask a lot of questions, child,*" the man rebutted, pulling his attention back to his work.

"*I apologize, that was rude of me ... Since we got here, you've been the only person I can talk to, and the only one able to give me any answers on how to find my way back home.*" Dakai's words held hints of pain, and the man sympathized; to be children lost in the world was a horrifying thought.

"*I was born in a small town in the Fernlands, a far ... far place from these areas. My life in the outer world was filled with pain, grimness, and disappointment. In my past life, I entered these forests as a dutiful soldier to an undeserving master, and almost died for it. But on death's door, I was saved by my future. We sometimes find meaning in the worst of times. I wouldn't be alive if it wasn't for her kindness and mastery in healing, I never knew love in my life before, and when I found it, I desired nothing else but her. She was as beautiful as a summer sky, and her heart even more so. I knew there was nothing left for me back in the outer world after. I found a new life here ... and purpose.*" A light smile brushed his lips like the thought of her brought brightness to his soul.

"*So you stayed for love?*" Dakai pried.

"*Yes. And it was wonderful.*"

"*Was?*"

"*She died some time ago, as did my son. Only my granddaughter Ishi remains.*" The man replied as his earlier joyous expressions depleted.

Ishi entered on cue, her dark hair brushing past the strings, and her skin losing its glisten from the sunlight outside; golden caramel to dark amber; the light played its role in her rebirth.

A brief silence ensued; she felt the presence of her interruption. When awkwardness crept in, she engaged.

Dakai stared curiously at her movements, her words; the tribe's way of communication was most peculiar. Words and hand signs in union, never had he seen or heard anything similar. Understanding came slow to him but for some words, he felt he could infer meaning.

"fi" he thought meant *"yes"* and *"dä"* was used in general reference to a person, in most cases him. Still, this was merely speculation and he guessed the meaning of words changed with certain signs. Regardless, he was nowhere close to understanding the conversation and his attention drifted, a brief distraction before his reality set in again.

Thoughts flooded Dakai's mind like rushing water displacing a void, moving away calm to the fiery sounds of erratic turbulence. Questions without answers, whether the answers didn't exist or he didn't want them to.

Despair was now a shadow that trailed him since the day he was stolen from his home. Hopelessness is a bitter feeling; it swallows and drowns, and all that's left is the weight of one's insignificance and a shattering being of melancholy.

The fire crackled and spat little specks of spark that drifted off, eventually fading into oblivion. Its light reflecting off Naemi's dark skin like a sunset glistens off the surface of a lake. Her protruding cheekbones like hills shading the valleys of her nose that slanted up to a curved point. Her cheeks had sunk slightly, highlighting her chin that dropped like the ends of a heart, and her expression was filled with tranquility in her endless slumber. The second day continued its journey to completion and her trance persisted, another day void of food or water, just breathing that slowed with every passing. She hadn't moved, not once.

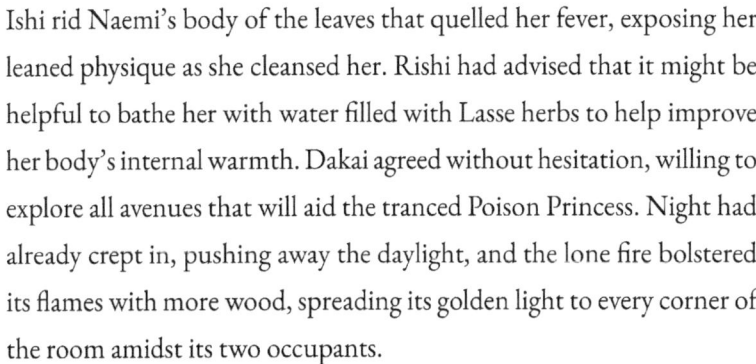

Ishi rid Naemi's body of the leaves that quelled her fever, exposing her leaned physique as she cleansed her. Rishi had advised that it might be helpful to bathe her with water filled with Lasse herbs to help improve her body's internal warmth. Dakai agreed without hesitation, willing to explore all avenues that will aid the tranced Poison Princess. Night had already crept in, pushing away the daylight, and the lone fire bolstered its flames with more wood, spreading its golden light to every corner of the room amidst its two occupants.

Ishi dipped the sponge again into the water, it was cold and discolored red from its contents. She brushed the stranger's left arm, moving slowly as if to make every touch count. Her body was weak, too weak; almost lifeless and her breaths were as silent as the night. Ishi caught herself staring at the girl; just a little older than Naemi, but she looked different in so many ways but for the black hue they both shared in their hair, and that was all that stood.

Similar to the first time she saw them; their uniqueness fascinated her and she wondered how many other different people existed in the outside world. She would always bother Rishi for stories, but he spared little and denied festering her curiosity. It was a shame about the state of this outsider; such frailty, surely she couldn't be responsible for the wreckage. Broken giant trees and cracked land all clearing in a straight path, nothing any of the beasts in the forest were capable of, unless ... unless another one had been created.

They called it *"Fuelim"* — the creator, a mythical being born of the forest or so was the myth among the tribe. She birthed many children to protect her lands, creatures of different forms that roamed through the dense vegetation defending the forest from outsiders. Even the first two *"Gouzadu"* are believed to be the children of *"Fuelim"*, but her other children got jealous of her love for the *"Gouzadu"* and sought to kill them. To protect her beloved children, she gave them the sacred green *"Tounya"* plant to smear its sap as repellant to the other children, and a home within the forest away from her envious offsprings. But without her favorite children, she grew sad and lonely, so she carved a mask from the *"Tounya"* tree with abilities to conceal, so her *"Gouzadu"* children could visit her anytime they wanted without her other offsprings realizing.

This story was one that was passed down generations as well as the secrets of the sacred *"Tounya"*. The tribe had survived this long based on their beliefs, their impeccable knowledge of Bashu, and what loomed within it. Though they weren't always exempt from its tragedies.

Dakai stood at the front of the dome entrance, hesitating to step inside. The finality of the action irked him, knowing what emotions that surfaced and the accompanying sentiments that flooded his mind. He hoped to hear her voice; maybe if he stayed a moment longer it would happen. That annoying voice he argued and fought with many times in the past, the one that ate all his food and complained about it being tasteless, the one that always tried to cheat him into doing more chores and would whine to their father whenever he did anything wrong. He longed for so long to hear that voice again.

"*Don't leave me ... Please Naemi ... Don't leave me alone in this place,*" the words escaped his lips in a mumble, leaning on his support stick with both hands and head bowed. If words could cry, they would. He thought back to home, what would be the joy in returning if he returned with a corpse? Where was Ozai now? What could he be doing? Was he searching for them?

*Father. Na ... Naemi is dyi ...* No! He couldn't think of such thoughts. She breathes, she lives. If he lost his resolve, who else would be there for her? He shouldn't, he couldn't.

He felt warmth kiss the left side of his face and turned to notice the rays of the sun spawning in its cursed routine of perpetuity. Time had passed so fast from the early dawn when he had left his shelter. *Was I standing there that long?* At least it was good to know his ankle felt better today. The red mud worked wonders in combination with the medicine Rishi had been giving him. The medication they possessed was far potent than lots of potions even Arwa — who was deemed a maven in healing — possessed. Unfortunately, it was still not good enough.

He looked around a last time before venturing to enter the dome. It was silent outside, but for some reason, he still felt the gaze of eyes all around.

The fire from the night was but ash now, and his eyes adjusted to the dim inside. He knelt near his sister, putting his hand close to her nose and breathing a sigh of relief. Another day void of food or water. He sat next to her. Today, he wouldn't give his mind the power of pessimism. If she was alive, she could still hear him — maybe. He would talk to her, whether she could hear, or even if she couldn't. Tell her to fight whatever this was. Tell her he needed her, Ozai needed her, and they had to get back home together.

And so was the third day.

Rishi came around occasionally to check on her, but her fever was gone and there was nothing more to do than succumb to the mercy of time. Ishi also visited with gifts of food and well wishes as best she could communicate. However, the day came with other surprises. There was a celebration among the tribe of a birth of a new child. It happened around late midday and the jubilation continued henceforth, deep into the night. A new life created at one end and another hanging by a thread at the other.

———————◆○◆———————

Dakai stood to leave, he had been sitting for hours, his knees ached and his legs felt numb. He had said everything and more, and as the day passed, it chipped away his faith. *Maybe tomorrow, maybe tomorrow*, he thought. As he brushed past the veil to outside, looking toward the joy and dancing not so far off from him, he struggled to take another step.

*Tomorrow, hopefully tomorrow.*

He began the journey back to his shelter; a few steps in and heard a gasp. He paused, hoping his mind wasn't playing tricks on him. It was from behind him, inside the dome. Eyes widened, he heard something move, someone was gasping heavily for air.

He ran inside screaming her name without a second thought to the consequences of his steps. Bursting into the room he saw her, struggling for air with mouth wide open and eyes staring above. Her hands wriggled from her chest to her neck, and she choked more. Three more people burst into the dome, with Ishi in front. Dakai's calls for help attracted the help he sought and in a brief moment Naemi was being carried outside into the open.

Outside was of no aid. Dakai tilted her head backward, pulling her tongue forward to clear her breathing, hands moving frantically. He kept calling out to his sister; her eyes were still open and he could see recognition in them but she still struggled to breathe. She wasn't choking on anything. She just couldn't breathe in air.

It all happened so fast. Her hand on his face, the final exhale, the dimness that caught her eyes and the staleness that crept into her body. It happened too fast to process.

Dakai was still calling out to her, repeatedly, "*Naemi! Naemi! Naemi!*" Still tilting her head to help her breathe. A silent crowd formed behind him. Watching as he called out to a corpse. Naemi Zenu was dead.

The sound of his own voice rippled in his ears. He could feel it; the lack of resistance in her body as he shook, the quiet eyes that looked at him open without light. The deafening silence that ensued. He could feel it. His voice drained with the realization and his eyes stayed stagnant.

A tingle formed in the back of his head, then a heavy stinging sensation turning to a pulsing headache behind his eyes. His heart weighed full, and he felt it beat harder than a thousand drums. He retreated from her body with eyes still fixed.

Disbelief, confusion, agony, despair, pain ... pain.

It crept in his heart and felt like it was being ripped out his chest. The aching in his head pounded harder and grew excruciating. It was the most pain he had ever felt in his being. He retreated farther, crawling backwards away from her as though the farther he got, the less real it would be — a trigger to wake from his tortured dream. The throbbing in his head was getting unbearable; at first at the back of his head, then he felt it behind his eyes, then in them. They burned. His screams were loud to the ones that surrounded him but he heard only silence. The people who surrounded the boy reached out helplessly; not that he would have understood them regardless. Ishi held him tight, arms wrapped around his side through his screams, trying her best to calm him. Whether that was the reason he calmed henceforth or not, the screaming simmered down gradually.

In that brief moment of time, where tribesmen were consoling him through his screams, Dakai felt something unexplainable and certainly not brief. An awakening of sorts invoked by experiencing extreme trauma. He was being flooded by memories, memories that weren't his.

Disjointed fragments of people he didn't know but one. Flashes of individual lives, like he was experiencing them through their eyes, through time, hopping from one experience to another helplessly. A child chasing after peers through sunny vegetation, a man hunting in the forest at morning's dawn, a mother giving birth to a child at night. He saw through all of them, parts of their journeys lying bare and exposed, and in everyone he was a person covered in green, a tribesman.

*This can't be real*, Dakai thought. *What delusions were these? A way of coping with Naemi's death? But the pain ... the pain was real.*

A movement caught his eye. Another delusion maybe, *this couldn't be possible*. The echoes from the crowd said otherwise. He wasn't the only one seeing this delusion. Naemi's body was a foot off the ground — floating in place. As if held by imaginary strings from the sky, it rose up. An instinct told his mind to reach out and grab his sister, but his body won't oblige the instruction. The muttering around him rose as did she, still incomprehensible. She was about fifteen feet off the ground now and an awestruck brother frozen with bewilderment. In a split, she got pulled down by nothing; maybe the same strings that raised her up shot her down — fast. She fell back to the ground shaking the ground, cracking it wide. The tribes-people that fell from the quake stood back up just as fast, not intending on missing a second of the marvel. They were awed at the sight. Their words, undecipherable at first, grew in unison and clarity as their voice loudened.

Another gasp from a body that was once cold; a metamorphosis completed. This time air filled her lungs to the brim and she exhaled. Light returned into her eyes and they widened to her first sight — a darkened blue sky bordered at the edges with the branches of trees. Sound returned to her ears, loud and in unison of words she couldn't understand.

"*Ushura siem fuelim dä*"

"*Ushura siem fuelim dä*"

"*Ushura siem fuelim dä*"

Behold the child of the creator!

## CHAPTER FIVE

# REMNANTS OF AN OUTER WORLD

Her ears were clogged with a silence that drained slowly. The voices that reached her mind felt far and muffled. Her eyes opened to the view of the night sky shaded at the sides by something swaying. The blur washed off her eyes, inviting her to see what surrounded her.

The sight frightened her and she crawled backwards, but her hands and feet moved to no ground beneath them. She let out a scream and fell to the ground, just being a few feet above it. The many faces stared at her with bewilderment, chanting words she couldn't fully hear. Her heart raced even more. She was just in Soros a moment ago, walking with her mother to get fresh onions and radish from Rema's farm. The sun's warmth kissing her skin as she skipped about gleefully, her mother's voice full of laughter at the way she moved her legs.

The echoes of her mother's voice rang in her head still. They had spent the whole of yesterday together in the absence of her father, a day that was full of excitement and laughter. Today was supposed to be no different, so why was she now staring into the eyes of strange beings in the midst of foreignness?

*Is this a dream?* Their bodies looked like creatures of myth and they called out words to her in unison. One of the creatures caught her eye from her side, wearing a face of startle. Its eyes glowed with two colors and a resemblance struck her. She knew someone with eyes like those.

*A friend? No, a brother?* As her other senses returned to her, she heard the words of the masses, still unable to decipher its meaning. Her nose filled with the smell of burnt wood and cinnamon, and her sense of touch felt ... different. Her recollections came in a flurry, little things poking her mind till she was fully whole, staring at Dakai in front of her. He hadn't moved since she awoke. The crisis that happened in his mind not allowing him to accept reality.

*She was dead. I know it. Or was I wrong?* he questioned himself to no answers. There was too much happening in too little time, but his focus remained on the miracle he witnessed.

Naemi tried standing from the ground, noticing the unusual formation beneath her. Her body felt uneasy and heavy, her returning memories catching up to her journey. The last thing she could remember clearly was the sound of rushing water and the feeling of light from darkness.

*Something was after me, then it died, then I came out ... How did I get here?*

When she finally stood up, she could feel strong forces pulling her down. She turned to the face she knew, "*Dakai? ... Where are we?*" she asked. Dakai didn't answer, he couldn't, still processing what was happening before him.

After a long pause, all that came out was, "*You died,*" he responded quietly. The people surrounding moved closer to the spectacle. Even with tales of past history, they had never witnessed the birth of the Creator's child before, nonetheless a human one. The chants had died but the murmuring increased with their numbers.

Naemi attempted to walk to her brother, but there was something off with her steps. The ground felt strange to her feet, and she began to panic from the many changes she felt.

"*Calm yourself, child. Breathe gently and steady your heart.*" The voice came from a distance beside her. He was one of them; one of the figures that surrounded her with the odd-looking skin in the night light, even her brother shared that trait. He was older with more hair on his face than skin, and he approached her slowly.

"*What is happening to me?*" Naemi asked the man through a shaky tone. The man approached more, steadying his feet on the deformed land and standing about three feet away from her and replied, "*You have been reborn.*"

Dakai finally summoned the courage to get off the ground and move closer to his sister in slow steps. It wasn't fear that kept him down, more of extreme confusion. The person standing a ways away from him was who he had prayed and cried for to be alive, and when it happened, he was baffled at the occurrence. He moved closer to Rishi's conversation with his sister, the crowd still eagerly engaged.

*"You must be feeling a lot of changes inside yourself; calm your mind lest you lose control over your body. Think of whatever brings you peace and let it steady your heart."*

Naemi listened to the only help she could get, having no other choice available. Her heart still racing and her body acting on its will, she searched her thoughts for inner peace and grabbed the first memory that was prompted, holding onto it with everything she could.

It was of a spring-time evening some weeks before the tragic passing of her mother. They were having a family dinner during the end of a truly joyous day, a day where everything that could go right, did. As she gobbled down her favorite dish to the amusement of her parents and little brother, their laughter filling the room, and their smiles brightening it ever cheerier, she experienced a sensation that could only be described as pure serenity. She had experienced happiness many times before, but this day imprinted on her mind and her soul, defining what true joy meant to her. Steadying her mind and finding calm, she heard Dakai's voice reach out to her, *"I'm here Naemi, I'm here with you."*

Her heart slowed gradually and she opened her eyes to the light, seeing her brother's hand stretched toward her. She was slow to do the same, fighting the fear of harm. When she overcame it, she felt the warmness in his hands and hugged him as softly as she could. Dakai couldn't hold back the tears that flowed with thankfulness. Whatever happened, whatever was happening, he was eternally grateful to have his sister with him.

Rishi spoke to the crowd while Ishi helped lead the two siblings to shelter. She came again later with loads of food without request, and Naemi devoured them to fill the immense hunger that crawled up her senses. No one else visited them throughout the night. Dakai stayed up through most of it, questioning his sister to know more of what happened to her. She slept off a while later after she reassured her brother countless times she would wake up from this slumber. He poked at her occasionally to make sure her body moved in response, and as the night waned deeper, he too slipped into dreams.

———◄O►———

Naemi felt a vicious shoving and sprung awake. Dakai was kneeling by her side and exhaled with relief. "*Dakai! You scared me,*" she said with frustration. Dakai apologized, claiming he got worried when she didn't answer his lighter shoves. She stared back at her brother, the morning light that escaped into their enclosure giving shine to his smooth skin and arrowed chin.

His woven hair lazing down, dangling in lengthy dreadlocks with the dark glow they always had, but his eyes lacked the usual brightness she knew of him. She could see the clear bags under his eyes and the shriveled face that grew from countless worry. She exhaled, letting out her little frustration. "*How's your leg? You said these people helped you? What do they want?*" she questioned.

"*It's getting better; the pain is much less than it used to be. Yeah they helped us, they say they followed a wreckage in the forest and found us. I don't think they want anything, only to help.*"

Naemi pondered over his answers and while she did, Dakai asked more questions.

"*Are you feeling okay? What do you think is happening to you? Do you think it was from the beast animal? What kind of animal was it? How did you escape?*"

Naemi brushed past his questions, having more of her own. "*What did you mean when you said I died? The old man also said I was reborn? Did I really die?*"

Dakai took longer before finally answering; he thought back over and over again to find some lapse in judgment he had in thinking Naemi died, and it made him lose confidence in his answer. "*I don't know anymore. I thought you did, it felt like it. You stopped breathing and your eyes ...*" he paused, "*Your eyes looked empty.*"

His response gave Naemi more food for thought, and when she finally spoke, she denied the idea. "*I didn't die, I couldn't have. I feel fine, I feel like myself. I didn't die.*" She spoke with defense in her tone, as if she was trying to convince herself of the truth.

"*You didn't see how sick you looked for days, I didn't know what I would have done if I lost you,*" Dakai added.

"*But you didn't lose me,*" Naemi interjected to comfort her brother.

"*What if I did? What if you never recovered? I don't know what I would have done,*" Dakai continued with heavy despondency. He could see the loss for words on Naemi's face, doing her best not to entertain the possibility.

"*If I die before we make it home, keep on and make it back for the both of us. Tell father I tried my best to return.*" Dakai said to his sister. It wasn't something he planned to say or even thought to, but in the moment, his feelings formed words and poured out to the only family he had near.

Naemi hugged him, the only expression she had to show comfort and absorb some of her brother's pain. She fought the possibility that they wouldn't make it back home together, and walled off the thoughts that tried to gain attention. "*We will return home together. We will. There's no other way,*" she said softly, forcing a smile to lighten the mood.

Two people entered the shelter as the moment dissolved. Naemi turned to meet the eye of one of them which was contrasted by a dark patch on the other socket. His strained voice spoke to her immediately after. "*How are you feeling, child?*"

"*I feel fine. I don't feel any of the sensations I felt last night. And thank you for the food. It tasted very good.*" Naemi responded to the old man and the younger woman beside him.

The woman returned her smile and the man only responded with a low "*Hmmm.*" He continued, saying, "*You have gifts outside, the people bring you offerings. They say your presence means good tidings and blessings to the land. Don't be alarmed if they touch or speak to you, they think you can provide them with endless favor."*

"*Ummm ... Uhhh okaay,*" Naemi answered puzzled, and turned to look at Dakai who had a frightening blank stare on his face.

"*Dakai?*" she called, snapping him back to reality. "*Are you okay?*"

"*Yes... yes, I'm fine,*" he answered with a lightened expression. A clear lie on his part. He had experienced another flash of memories at the sight of Rishi and Ishi. One that came without pain, just a brief flick in a moment of time then back to nothingness.

He saw memories of fighting in a war, being attacked by another in the rain and blackened mud, his hands reaching into the dirt for a broken sword to brace against the swing of his attacker, then he was a green-skinned child chasing an insect in a bush and being pricked on the arm by a flower thorn. It all happened so quickly that he couldn't fully react to the revelation. The next thought that set in his head being, *these are no delusions at all*.

"*Sir, my brother tells me we have been here for a while, I thank you for all the help you've given us but we will have to continu...*" The man cut her off mid speech.

"*I know, child. This isn't your home and you would like to return. Your brother says you were taken from it, and that truly is sad. You can always leave whenever you're ready, but don't be in a rush to go. Stay for some days to heal, and fatten your bellies, for your journey back will be uneasy, and the outer world is not fair to the lost.*"

Naemi listened to his words and agreed to them; after all Dakai was still hurt and food was plentiful here. This conclusion leading to their extended stay which stretched more than they forethought.

The fortnight that passed was not what they had planned. Even after Dakai had fully healed, they lingered there some more days with an eagerness to continue their journey, and a fear for what lay ahead in their path. There was a warmth here and after the turbulence they had been through the past months, it felt hard to take the steps forward.

The treatment they were being given also played heavy parts in their delay. The gifts they offered the Creator's child and her brother, the different foods that melted their tongues and fired every sense of taste in their mouths. The joy of climbing the trees and sleeping in hanging nests that seemed to float, the beauty of nature that plastered in waves all around, and the intrigue of their peculiar culture. There was a lot of joy here and with everything they had been through, they needed it in abundance.

Naemi experienced no more episodes throughout the rest of their stay, the unknowns of the changes she went through staying unknown. Dakai on the other hand, kept his experiences to himself. After a couple more happenings, he guessed what was being opened to him. Past memories, those stored in the depths of people's minds that only he strangely had the key to unlock. The flashes went on for some days until they stopped abruptly. Whether that was of his doing or not, he finally broke free from the memories that were forced on him.

The siblings were called to the "Gouzadu" another time, a far different tone than they encountered the first time. The elders proposed a marriage proposal of Naemi and one of their youngest members. A boy of one and four. "*We would be honored for the Creator's child to join us and bear divine children,*" Rishi translated.

Naemi rejected the proposal as politely as she could to their disappointment.

Dakai laughed wildly at the idea, teasing her continuously later that evening. He had been in Rishi's Dome learning the old man's way of medicine when they were summoned, and hearing the words made him wheeze till water filled his eyes.

As all things end, their time there did. On the day of their departure, they stuffed as much food as possible in the sling bag Ishi made for them. It was soft and heavy green, woven intricately in a desired mesh. The gifts were too many for a journey on foot and most had to be left. Rishi however offered something of value. A round jeweled gem with a dull blue hue about half a foot in length, crafted in a heavy bracelet. It was ill-refined and lusterless, dirtied as if dug from the ground.

"*This is a remnant of a world I left behind; I hope you get value in this to help you in your journey. In my time, men used to go to wars for pieces of it; maybe there's still some value in it presently in the outer world for you.*"

The siblings thanked him profusely. They had no money and having something of value other than food was of needed importance. As they were guided outside of the village for the first time since entering, their fears of what lay ahead grew along with the sadness for what they left behind.

They walked through the forest with the three men and two women, covered in green and masks as they were, following their every step. When they got close to their destination where the guides could go no farther, they also said their goodbyes. The siblings hugged Ishi hard and long. One who had been a genuine helper and friend to them. She hugged them back gracefully, an act she was unknown to before, now her favorite way of showing her loving expression.

Walking toward the small flowing river that led to the little settlement outside the jungle, they were now outside the space of comfort that housed them and into the glaring embrace of the outer world. The questions of how to get home, what happens if someone recognizes Dakai's eyes again, and how they avoid another capture, all presented itself. The sounds of rushing water came to them; it wouldn't be long before they encountered people again. They needed to avoid unwanted attention and the green on their bodies stood out like a beacon. So as they stepped into the outer world, they changed to its merits, blending henceforth until they found the path that was to lead them home.

# Chapter Six

# SAILOR CITY

Hooves pounded dirt in slow steady trotting, steps syncing over time till they produced a tune akin to a marching battalion. Once in a while, they'd fall out of rhythm, the left horse always the culprit, a signal for Raegu to whip the reins again till the two got back in phase. The other horse whinnied, also voicing his displeasure of suffering for one's ineptitude. The wheels to the trailing wagon creaked behind with disruption, a bit louder than usual.

The effects of the extra load showed proportional to the wheels' cry for help. The farmer ignored the noise or was probably so used to it, he didn't notice the change. "*They got a few more leagues left in them,*" he would say, and he'd said that for months. He had meant to change them a while ago but new mouths called for new allocations, so he allocated the best he could.

The roads were bumpy in this area, and the occasional jounce always prompted a response from his wife. "*I'm sorry honey,*" he repeated, stretching his hands through the front covers of the carriage to comfort his pregnant wife. She knocked his hand away playfully, an act that made their eight year old daughter giggle.

*"I'm fine, stop poking at me,"* she responded feigning discontent. He retreated his focus back to the clear road and sunny skies with a light chuckle. Almost a day and half traveled and still another two full days ahead to reach their destination. They would get there faster if not for the sluggish thoroughbred. She was old and weary; the years' journeys had drained her strong legs till little remained. In her heyday, she and her sister could cut a full day off their trip no matter the load they pulled.

Three times a year, they'd make their voyage to Sailor City to market their farm produce, and three times a year, those two would gallop like the wind to the city and back home. A shame he had to trade her companion for a younger horse, a painful decision but a necessary one. The grief was felt more on her end; he could swear he saw her shed tears once.

*"Horses don't cry,"* his friends laughed out, slapping their bellies and coughing out ale when he told them. But he swears he saw the tears.

Another bump and a subsequent grimace from his wife. *"Don't you dare say it,"* she barked, prompting another giggle from their daughter.

*"You know you could have just stayed home and rested? I could make all the sales on my own,"* the farmer responded.

*"Hahaha ... So you get out-bargained? No way I'm letting that happen again,"* she retorted with a laugh. Her husband was an excellent farmer, nothing to doubt about that, but he lacked severely in getting the full value for his products. It was sometimes comical to experience; he had

no bargaining skills and those who noticed took full advantage of it. She on the other hand could out-bargain bees out of their honey. A skill she learned from her grandfather; knowing the right buttons to pull to get the best price out of a buyer. A match of two made to perfection.

"*It happened just one time*," he muttered under his breath. Referring to the infamous selling of six sacks of berries for a third their worth. In his defense, the man was a sweet talker and negotiated down so much as if testing if he could get them for free; and it would be no surprise if he did. This wasn't his only infraction, he was too sweet and understanding for his own good, and there is no place for kindness in business.

He wished his wife would trust him enough to rest at home with their daughter; that mattered more to him than getting the best price for the sale, but she'd rather give birth mid-voyage than allow that to happen. She was a strong-willed woman and unyielding — oh so unyielding, he would rejoice on days he got to change her mind. Both their natures rippled off each other in a balanced cohesion; a true testament to the attraction of opposites.

---

The road slept with placidity. They hadn't passed any other traders for leagues and didn't expect to meet any for some more until they got to Fardins Cross about a day away.

The trees bordering the road at both ends swayed to the sides echoing a loud breeze, and the skies flirted with rain clouds peeking and disappearing without commitment. Soon they'd be past the rocky tree line to the low-cut vegetation fields and smaller chain of hills that waited ahead. A historically slower part of their journey to be impeded even more. Their loads also significant this time around; the additional weight of more produce and the weight of strangers.

"*The horses will be fine, they're strong horses just need to giv'em more rest, that's all,*" he had responded to his wife when she got concerned of the extra load. This wasn't entirely true. For the younger horse maybe, but it wasn't a certainty for the older. He didn't foresee encountering two teens helplessly journeying in the same direction: one blindfolded and covering blindness. They looked exhausted, walking barefoot with clothes that didn't fit properly, and a green hand-woven bag filled with food. One look at them and he couldn't pass them by without helping.

"*Where are you young lads off to? Mind some help?*"

"*Sailor City,*" and a nod was the response he got.

"*Sailor City? You plan on walking there? Oh no! Come'on with us, that's our heading too,*" his wife interjected, clearing some space in the wagon for the children.

It was a rarity to see people walking to Sailor City from this region. Not that it didn't happen, he'd heard a lot about it from friends encountering other journeymen on foot to Sailor City, and it sounded dreadful. *That has to be more than a week's journey for sure and even though the roads are much safer now, who knows what one might encounter.*

The horses started traversing the first hill still maintaining the steady pace. The left horse was much more agile now, assumingly tired of the right's complaints. The shafts connecting horse and wagon strained and tugged harder fighting against the gravity of the slant. Some of the produce shifted lightly but still held secure within the strappings. The sugarcane and sacks of berries that flooded the back half of the wagon continued its journey to sale. This period had been particularly plentiful and the family couldn't wait to reap the benefits.

Sailor City was a famous wine market with prestigious wineries that held goodwill even past its borders, an opportunity which meant many buyers and great prices in every fruit-farmer's language. The demand was large and even more came from the many merchants who visited its borders.

Merchants from every corner of the world, visiting what was widely known as a universal hub of trade and commerce not only in Qarva but beyond. The city was vast and rich, a booming economy with vibrant streets. Everything that could be sold, was sold here; the good, the bad and the utterly despicable, all under the jurisdiction of the Trading Alliance. The city's existence and commandments all centered around trade. The most prominent commandment,

*"Blessed be the possessions of a soul and the value to which a soul declares them."*

Here, the disciplined and unruly all must abide or be exiled from access to trade, a privilege many didn't take lightly; for the Alliance itself was a merciless organization with deep roots spread in many parts of the world, able to starve nations and cripple cities with an order. Tales of exiled traders who faded into oblivion, and broken cities that are only reminisced now as stories of deterrence trailed its history.

In Qarva, many farmers came from far and wide to profit from the bountiful climate. Sure they could make good income in closer settlements, but the extra journey came with heavy profits and for that, it was worth it. *The city with a thousand ports,* people called it, and it was hard to deny; an exaggeration still, though the topography played into the illusion.

The city was endowed with a natural geography forming a wide lake-like interior into the landscape and fenced from the sea by two giant cliffs from opposite ends that came close enough to form an entry — the great gates of Salem.

A layout most nations would go to war for, and they had tried; attacks from the sea imprinted in Sailor City's chronicles — failures imprinted in others. The gates stood as two enormous portcullises, titan bars of treated metal made to withstand the turbulence of the sea, closing from the sides: one in the front and another in the rear, and a built arch-bridge connecting the two cliffs in overwatch. This wasn't the only remarkable piece of infrastructure in the blessed city, not even close, for their opulence, political power and reach granted them access to the finest resources and finest minds, and they exploited it massively for their flamboyance.

Open air, chained smaller hills shadowed by high mountains, wet tall grass with moist dirt and a view spanning leagues all around. Wild plants running amok through the vegetation, varied in size and hostility. The land frozen in place like a static wave of water contoured with peaks and valleys, curves and sharp edges indicative of a sculpture's work. Shrouds of vegetation spreading as far as the eyes could see with spikes of trees sometimes sparse, other times clustered as were small patches of barren land.

The region spread far and the road spread with it. The road which was a lanky section of dried up land, stripped of its fertility by the constant stamps of the masses that paraded its surface. Longer than could be fully realized, as far as reaching the area where the ground kissed the skies. The air carried hints of euphoria and smelled with a freshness that bathed the insides of impurity. Maybe that was due to the light rain that showered moments ago or it was just an association with the tranquility of the open space. The clouds cleared again but the sun was close to the end of a day's work.

Lear'ra exhaled hard, just before another heavy inhale. It was far from comfortable inside the wagon and the air smelled of dried fruit. Outside felt soothing with a slight chill and pleasurable sensation. "*Are you done yet?*" she asked her daughter, who answered with a nod. Her complaints to pee had been going for a while till she couldn't bear it anymore. Lear'ra didn't enjoy the act of stopping many times on a single journey; nevertheless there was gladness for this one, her legs were a tad wobbly from numbness, and the weight of the baby felt heavier with every passing day. Three month-cycles till she was due, and it wasn't getting any easier. Raegu's voice sounded from beyond the shade of the high shrubs that covered them. She shouted back in response. *He worries too much,* she thought, as they both began their walk back to the road.

Slow paces up the slope till she got back to the wagon. Raegu turned, hearing the steps of his family. "*Is everything okay?*" he asked with his patented look of concern.

"*Yessss father,*" answered his daughter, feigning exaggeration which caused her mother to giggle.

"*Ohh, you're learning your mother's ways, eh,*" as he chased after his daughter. Lear'ra laughed a bit harder; he was right about their daughter mimicking her actions and thought of being more careful henceforth, lest she picked any of her self-stated negative traits. *A break here wouldn't be so bad, the view is great, the skies are clearer, and the horses could use some rest. We can still get to the village of Sabu before nightfall.* Turning her attention from a playful husband and child to the passengers they carried, one outside and the blind one still in the carriage. The girl stood in the front by the horses; feeding them apples and caressing their manes. They neighed in positive response, showing excitement to their new-found friend.

"*They like you,*" Lear'ra commented.

The girl smiled. "*I think they just like my apples, I thought they'd want a little treat for their hard work,*" the girl said, continuing her pampering of the animals.

"*We're sorry for adding more burden to your travels; the horses look drained,*" she added.

"*Oh no worries at all dear, you're no burden. The horses will be fine. We will be in Sabu soon and they can rest all through the night. Does your friend not want some air too? I know how stuffy it can get inside,*" Lear'ra mentioned.

"*I tried convincing him, but he denied coming outside. How far are we from Sailor City?*" she asked.

"*Oh, is it your first time going? We are less than two days away, if the horses keep a good pace tomorrow. Are you two going to meet anyone there?*" Lear'ra replied, her curiosity getting the better of her. The girl was slow to answer, her attention still on the horses.

"*We have a friend expecting us there,*" she said, looking off into the distant roads. The back of her hair showed black, nappy, high above her head and tied into two puffed buns on either side of her shoulder.

"*That's nice. Do you know which part of the city you would like us to take you?*"

"*You don't have to do that, you've done so much already, the edge of the city would be fine,*" she answered with a smile of gratitude which Lear'ra returned, as she agreed, albeit reluctantly.

Lear'ra however discontinued her questioning which bore coats of invasion; she sought to help but could tell her involvement was unsought. A mother's intuition maybe, she sensed untruth, and not knowing how safe the mysterious teens would be in Sailor City bothered her. So much so, Raegu raised concern later at Sabu about her change in mood, which she brushed off as an effect of tiredness.

She'd heard the stories, the vile rumors of underworld dealings, trafficking, layers of corruption and predation that lay under the city like worms under a board of fine wood. Sailor City was a place full of laws yet permeated by the unlawful, its laws strong on the powerless and vague to the puissant.

The teens asked to sleep in the wagon, denying their many offers of getting them a paid room at the inn. From Sabu, Fardins Cross, Naer and even as they reached Sailor City, Lear'ra would pry cautiously, hoping to get some information on their plans, offering help which was turned down continuously; the blind one even more tightlipped, she could feel an uneasiness about him.

As they entered Sailor City past the guarded gates and armored guards, their association of travel came to an end. The teens thanked them endlessly and Lear'ra still couldn't get a feeling out her chest, the one that yearned protection and warned of danger and uncertainty. She gave them the extra food her family had from their journey, slipping in a few bronze coins she had. The girl noticed and Lear'ra pushed her hand back when she tried to return it.

*"We will be here for a few days selling at the Firu market, we will be on the third stall left of the white statue of the Knight with a blue trident; you can't miss it. If you don't find your friend, you can always come help us sell to make some money for the both of you,"* said Lear'ra, holding on to her husband and child.

The family waved as they left, watching as their passengers disappeared into the crowded road that led to the ports. The streets of Sailor City loud and full of bustle, the whiff of a thousand activities melting into the air, giving a distinct sensation only familiar to the location.

Lear'ra and her daughter entered back into the wagon and Raegu back on his seat of authority. The family continued their journey, getting back to their routine activities in Sailor City — roads once parallel now diverged for eternity.

## CHAPTER SEVEN

# A WEDDING OR A WAR

The clouds stretched far, spread in a sea of white and gray. Soft balls of cotton floating gently with the wind. The hues of blue covering the entirety of his sights as he soaked himself in its domain. The air here was thinner, and the breeze was frigid even through the sun's rays.

The day was close to its peak, but the sun was still shy of a full blossom. He turned around to look into the space above, the vastness of it and the appeal that called to him. It was a shame he couldn't fly higher up, and it wasn't for the lack of trying. Even he had his limits. Unchained from the ground but still bound to the world in servitude. It was a stark realization for him the first time he was exposed to his restraints. Not everything can be accomplished with strength, status and power, a lesson he had become very familiar with.

He glided over the soft cushions of fog below him while continuing his admiration of the beyond. He loved the quiet he experienced in this space of comfort. With his wings spread free and his body devoid of armor, he could feel a connection with everything around him and the feeling induced a blissfulness he loved.

He dove down, under the white layers and away from the blue serenity till the next view came in full frame. The long river Tames, extended for leagues and snaking its way through forest and bare land, claiming territory with its waves of water. Smaller lanes branched from it like children seeking independence from their mother, only to still remain tethered to her breasts.

The city of Cratos could be seen from afar; the Aarcabra, the Sun-god's temple and some parts of the royal castle all peeking from their relative locations. Selius dove down more, sweeping past the clear water till it was but a mirror to his features, highlighting his feathers, his bare chest and flowing hair in the wind. This was a ritual he performed on occasion, away from his princely duties that were hurled at him and the stench of political engagements.

He would fly far and high, over mountain summits and mild canyons grazing over the beauty of Thrun. Like a farmer inspecting his crops in detail, or a god examining his inheritance. Soaring above the kingdom's skies, he felt free and affined to the nature that bloomed below. From his throne in the sky, everything seemed right and in place, and if it wasn't, he would take action to correct it.

The queen loathed these disappearances.

"*The crown prince should always be accompanied by the crown-guards,*" she would repeat incessantly, but unless she found a serum for flight, her words would continue to wilt into limbo. Even her suggestions for him to wear armor weren't heeded.

As he got closer to Cratos, he passed the area of outside dwellers and smaller settlements. The sparse farms of wheat and cattle. He could feel the eyes that looked up at him with wonder and hear their faint cries through the wind. He looked toward the sounds, his sharp eyes seeing the source as clear as ever. Three children, none above the age of twelve jumping for joy at the sight of him. They waved and shouted, their bright smiles only opposed by the dirt that covered their skin from their tedious labor with nature. A couple other older workers tended to the farms spread sparsely.

The hails from the children drawing their attention to the skies.

Selius halted mid-flight, turning around and heading toward the children who called. The children paused, realizing the crown prince was heading their way. Jubilation now turned to jittering anxiety. They didn't think he could hear them from that far up, or would even acknowledge them if he did. The other people who saw him approach shared similar emotions.

It was rare for them to encounter a royal; the closest they came was seeing the giant wings of the crown prince above the clouds on the occasion he flew through this area. He was normally too high up and too fast to notice, but not today. The children cowered in place, afraid to move. Selius descended some feet from them. His silky hair flowing slowly to a halt and folding his feathers. His chest and upper body were crafted to distinction, and his lower parts covered in dull white cotton pants. His bare feet grazed the ground walking toward the three in front of him.

Their eyes widened at the sight of him as their emotions continued in a mixture of fear and excitement. They'd heard so much about him and seen little. He wasn't as old as they thought he would be, his lower face was smooth without hair with a defined jawline stealing attention. He was beautiful, as beautiful as only a royal could be, and his green eyes shot directly through them. When he got closer, he smelled like a basket of sweet fruits and gracefulness. He towered over them and knelt on one knee to meet their eyes.

"*You called?*" he said, and smiled lightly. Those that stood sparse converged to catch a glimpse of the beloved jewel of Thrun. The father of the three children hurried toward them, scolding them to kneel before the prince.

"*I apologize Sire, my children know not better,*" he claimed profusely with remorse.

"*It's fine, you can stand, I take no offense to it,*" he responded with assurance.

"*You have very pretty wings,*" the youngest of the three said. A girl of eight, the most excited and least afraid.

Selius thanked her and extended his left wing to full view. "*Do you want to touch it?*" he asked, and the girl nodded happily. The middle-aged boy in the group joined his sister in engagement. Selius smiled more at their joy, the older people staring at them bewildered.

"*Can you take me up?*" the middle child asked.

"*Yess ... yess can you?*" the younger added.

"*Dauk!*" the father shouted in a whisper. Selius giggled at the request, noticing their father's disapproval.

"*Only if your father agrees,*" he finally said, turning to the man. The man fumbled with his words, unable to find the courage to deny a crown prince. He agreed reluctantly and Selius lifted the children into his arms.

A giant thrust of his wings and they were in the sky, the eldest of the three had barely spoken any words, watching from below with the rest as her siblings took flight. The crowd that watched continued their gazes, thinking of how uncertain their stories would be to those who would hear it.

The flight lasted moments till he descended with the joyous children who had just experienced the world from a perspective only few are ever privileged to. As the children touched back to the ground, still in awe of their exposure to the skies, the prince bade farewell to them, drifting in the air until he was back with the clouds. The dust that floated from the wind his wings pushed, finally settled down.

The eyes on the ground followed his trail even long after he couldn't be seen. Voices now confident enough to form audible words spoke in shock of the experience, questioning the younger children of what they saw and felt. The children answered the questions the best they could, even though their answers did little to fully describe their feelings. For what they were experiencing for the first time in their young lives was the feeling of pure bliss.

Gyai stood in front of the swinging yellow drapery, near the curved marble balustrades on the balcony with her eyes toward the skies. *"Mother?"* Selius said from behind her. She let out a startled gasp and her expression returned to her fumed gaze as she walked back into the room.

*"I've been waiting for you for a half hour,"* she said with discontent.

*"Sorry, I went out,"* Selius expressed.

*"I know I can't stop you, but can you at least tell any of your guards or many servants where you go? I worry, you know,"* the queen said to her son.

*"Worry about what? There's nothing to worry about. I'm always around when you need me,"* the prince said a little defensively.

*"There's always something to worry about. I'm a mother; it's my job to worry. People have tried to hurt you before,"* she continued.

*"Yeah, dead people. Only the deranged will ever try something so foolish. You don't need to worry,"* Selius concluded. Gyai let out a sigh and moved closer to her son. Touching his face gently and leveraging her saddened eyes and words of defeat to sway his conclusion. A trick she was very familiar with. The Reis men were headstrong and stubborn, and she knew her ways of convincing them to reason.

*"Okaaayyy ... okayy I will tell someone before I go. Only if I'm going far. But I still won't wear my armor."* Selius spoke out, and she accepted the truce knowing she couldn't always win everything. She noticed the dirt on his lower chest and his darkened pants and inquired about it. Selius brushed her question off with a vague answer, moving behind

covers to clean and change, and asked her if that was everything she came to his tower for.

*"An envoy from the Mhraab province arrived to discuss the wedding proposal. A date has been reached. You will marry Princess Morlain on the earliest spring of the next year-cycle."* Gyai spoke the words without any enthusiasm, and they were received the same.

*"Do I have no say in the matter? Why are we even affirming the plans of the Mhraabs? Their armies are weak and small in number. Is war not an option?"* He questioned with irritation in his tone.

*"War is always an option, but it doesn't have to be one we choose this time. I don't agree with your father, but marrying you to the princess will keep the Mhraabs in line, and is the best way to bring Mhraab under our rule without bloodshed. They may look weak and without a solid army but the Mhraabs are clever and very good at siege. They know how to use their high ground to their advantage. Moving our armies through those dense mountain terrains for war won't be easy; their mountain city is a fortress in its own right. Your father is only thinking of the wisest moves to better our nation. Getting access to their mountain pass would help our armies move up north without obstruction."*

She looked at her son as he emerged from behind the covers, and smiled seeing his relaxing senses that formed to reason.

*"The king is doing all this so you may inherit it all. He's breaking all obstacles that will stand in the way of your future glory. Marry the girl and father children as is your duty, you may grow to love her or maybe not, it doesn't matter. All that matters is you and the glory you bring to our great nation. There isn't only one way to conquer, Selius, you should*

*know that, and wise decisions often come with sacrifices,"* the queen spoke to her son. Selius softened his expressions more, wearing the look that succumbed to his mother's advice.

*"I would have known more of this if I could attend the council meetings of generals; I'm old enough to join the ranks. King Perolius was a war general at eighteen. I excel in everything and yet father still treats me as if I'm only a prince,"* Selius commented to his mother, finally rooting out the main reason for his frustrations.

*"Only a prince?"* Gyai repeated in animated mockery. She laughed harder, the pearls on her neck rattling to her movements as she brushed a loose strand of hair from her face. The rest of her hair still held secure by the interwoven golden strings that showed more than the strands of gray that grew.

*"You know what I mean,"* her son defended.

She took a pause and said, *"You should speak to your father about this, he wants to see you tomorrow. At midday, in the royal hall."*

*"He does?"*

*"Yes. He is going to talk to you about the wedding. You can present all your qualms to him then,"* the queen concluded.

Her son said nothing to this conclusion. She didn't know he felt this way, and her husband most likely didn't either. The relationship between father and son wasn't as strong as theirs. It used to be at a point in the past, but as the boy grew, Olius molded him with a strictness that wasn't always pleasantly received.

The rest of the conversation lasted no longer than half of a half hour; Gyai's last words as she left being complaints of the long staired tower and her hate for the climb and the descent.

*"I'm too old to climb this much just to see my son. I shall get Lama Wuhn to make some new inventions to help my climb up, not all of us have the luxury of flight,"* she joked to her son. Selius offered to fly his mother down but she refused. *"What kind of queen would I be to have my son carry me around?"* A statement that made her son chuckle.

The room returned to the solemnity it usually bore after the departure of its guest. Its only occupant lay on the large cushioned bed, bordered on its four sides by the canopy bed frame that was crafted with such exquisite detail. The markings told stories that were frozen in fine wood, dark secrets that were only known to the craftsman and his grain.

The light from the peaking sun flowed in from all directions and above, and the wind whistled its tune without care. The inside of the room was grand and majestic. Precious metals and shiny coats gleaming with pride.

Drapery of smooth hand-stitched fabric covering the majority of the bare wall leaving no space void of fine taste. On the far-right section next to the cornered wall, Selius's armor stood fitted unto a stand. The white with yellow flashes of gold reflected the rays that bounced off it. The rest of his armor occupied the other empty parts of the section, and his long blade remained silent in its hold.

Selius's mind was far from his abode however, lurking toward tomorrow and whatever conversation he was to have with his father. It had been more than a dozen days since he'd seen him, their last conversation being prior to his departure to the Astor colony. He'd wanted to embark on the trip with the king, a proposal his father denied.

*"You should stay in the capital and support Urgus in ruling in my stead; you can learn a lot from him,"* the king counteracted, his voice stern and unforgiving.

The prince's disappointment wore heavy on his face. He'd looked forward to the crown's symbolic visit to the colonies with his father, not for the joy of the journey or even for the extended exploration of the heartlands. He'd hoped to spend more time with Olius, time exploring the Thrun regions and being introduced to the people and lands he was destined to rule over. But his hopes ended in dissatisfaction.

Selius stood from rest. The quiet in the room and the thoughts in his head struggling to coexist. He needed to get away from it all and only one destination formed in his head. He brushed past the golden veils to outside, and in a thrust was back in the skies.

———————◄◉►———————

Urgus paced mildly through the tones of the LongHall en route to the call of the crown. His giant mustache preceding his presence, shrouding most of his upper lip only to be contrasted by the thin lined beard dropping down his chin.

A prideful man with prideful strides, he moved with the elegance the Taus family were always known for. The king had summoned him again, twice in just mere hours, making him repeat the carriage ride and this long walk through a hall that stretched too far for no known reason. He knew what was happening; a show of power and control.

*He must feel threatened to stoop to actions this childish*, he thought, and a light smirk brushed his lips with satisfaction. Nevertheless this was no victory, not even close.

He continued his walk through the halls, passing the old sculptures of history and carvings of royalty, seeing the many faces of his Taus ancestors. Urgus was pretty agile for his age; a man of thirty and nine, but he still moved with a slow grace not because he couldn't go any faster, but in his own words, "*I will not run like a dog to a master who calls,*" he spat.

His wife scolded him for the comment. "*The air has ears my love,*" she said with her sedate voice.

"*Your tactfulness and patience will be rewarded soon.*" Tafia replied through comfort. She reached out to calm him with a caress but he shunned her. An action he did so much, it felt like instinct now.

The years of childbirth had taken a heavy toll on his wife, twelve pregnancies and nine children, and she didn't bear the panache she was so revered for in her early years. "*Fatty Tatty,*" he once overheard a servant say in reference to his wife, and he went in a rage that ended in a severed tongue and the boy being thrown into the dungeons.

Urgus stopped in front of a sculpture, looking up to meet the stone eyes of the man that stood with such grandeur. Urgus frowned. An expression he repeated earlier today. The sculpture looked onward, its face old and wise. The Statue of Basus Taus, the last king from the Taus bloodline who swayed the council to select Dumona Duran instead of one of his children for the reason that he feared his own children's incompetence to rule.

A decision deemed most selfless by some and extremely selfish by others, switched the crown family to the house of Duran, and ended the longest tenure of a single family's rule in Thrun history. Once the crown title was lost, the family faced a sharp downfall in the hierarchy.

The Taus were mainly known for their leadership traits and pompous demeanor, and as the role of leader was lost, their pride alone couldn't hold their importance in the echelon.

During the length of their rule, as Thrun grew through time and its strength molded, different families claimed and solidified stakes in vital parts of the kingdom. The Duran lead the faith, the Reis lead the military, the Wuhns lead the Nation's architecture and knowledge keeps, and the Myr lead trade and matters of coin.

When their rule ended and they lost the significance of being the crown family, they had nothing left to lead. As time passed, the elder tribunal saw it fit to assign them as lead of ships; an assignment that was mocked by the other families as the Taus had never been known to the water.

Astonishingly, they thrived in their new endeavor, growing Thrun's fleet to the hundreds, full of ships of different sizes and uses. From stylish trade ships to hardened warships, rugged and tough to test every sea across the known realms. Chief among those who pushed the boundaries was Ugus Taus, grandfather of Urgus Taus.

When they began to smell opportunity as the existing Reis ruler struggled to have children, Urgus was part of the selected Taus offsprings who were primed and positioned for crown selection until the unbelievable happened, and the queen birthed a Dion.

Two maids descended the stairs, halting and lowering their heads at the sight of the king's advisor ascending. "*Sire!*" They said asynchronously, the former slightly louder than the latter. Urgus didn't respond and kept on his climb till he reached the end, turning to walk toward the last stretch of his journey and its giant doors ahead.

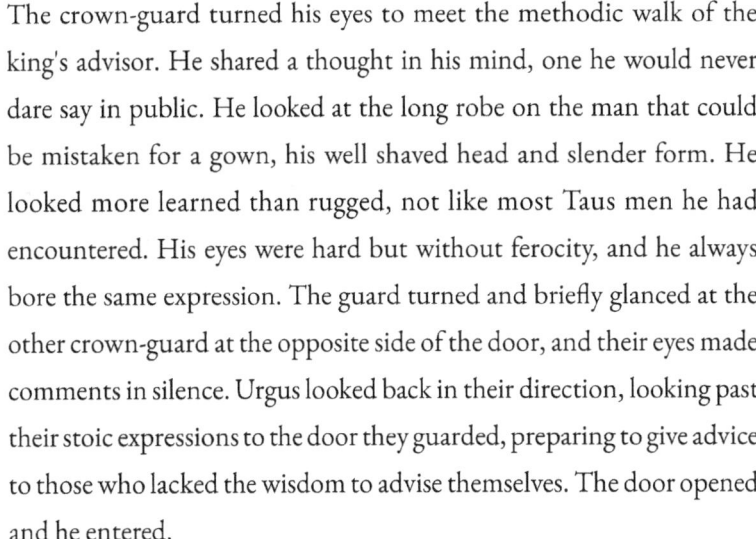

The crown-guard turned his eyes to meet the methodic walk of the king's advisor. He shared a thought in his mind, one he would never dare say in public. He looked at the long robe on the man that could be mistaken for a gown, his well shaved head and slender form. He looked more learned than rugged, not like most Taus men he had encountered. His eyes were hard but without ferocity, and he always bore the same expression. The guard turned and briefly glanced at the other crown-guard at the opposite side of the door, and their eyes made comments in silence. Urgus looked back in their direction, looking past their stoic expressions to the door they guarded, preparing to give advice to those who lacked the wisdom to advise themselves. The door opened and he entered.

"*I called for you over an hour ago. How long must a king wait for his counsel?*" the king spoke with irritation in his voice.

*"I'm sorry your grace, I got here as fast as I could,"* Urgus replied with an almost monotonic delivery. Olius huffed to himself, his eyes staring outside the window and his head replaying his decisions.

*"I've received word the Mhraabs may be planning to betray us. They bait us with the union of marriage and still work to gain allyship with the Locus territory. Do you know anything of this?"* the king requested.

*"Received word from whom?"* Urgus replied with a question, but the king just stared at him with intense eyes. The stormy green eyes that pierced souls. Urgus spoke again, attempting to bring levelness to a rising situation.

*"The Mhraabs are cautious people but they're not foolish. They know the consequences of such a betrayal and I doubt they intend to experience our wrath. I'm sure they only intend to use the threat of allyship to gain more favor and ask for more demands."*

*"More demands? They get a prince out of this. My son!"* He roared.

Urgus paused for a moment, *"Yes, the prince is a high price to pay for access through the mountains. But a price that must be paid still if you desire to get our armies to the Locus regions. We lose that mountain pass and we get cut off by the high mountains. We can go around by sea, but we lose ..."*

*"I know all our options Urgus, you don't have to repeat them to me,"* the king interrupted sharply. He huffed again. His emotions heavy on his face, and his skin highlighting the weariness that plagued him in his late years of sixty. There was much on his mind, though only one took the center seat at present. The agreement with the Mhraabs was a necessity

for his desired plans for the future, but he was not going to be exploited with what he had to give in return.

The chained mountains of Moze, a lined sequence of mountain summits walled off the north like a giant stone guardian. The lands that lay across were bare and ripe, lands that flourished with soil rich in crops, fine minerals, precious stones, and resources of abundance. Natural resources that went to waste on simple-minded natives. The settlements that occupied them were small and insignificant, the only formidability rising from the city of Locus. A boy-child who regarded himself a man.

*"I would advise caution, Sire. Union with the Mhraabs benefit them as much as it does us. Whatever truth there is to these accusations, we still need to tread with care lest we break down months' worth of diplomacy,"* Urgus said, breaking the silence.

The king however didn't break from his, mulling over his options to shut down any potential betrayals with decisiveness. He hated the reality of not being able to send Dions to infiltrate and capture the city like his predecessor did. The idea faced too many hurdles presently.

Firstly, there was a fear that the Mhraabs might replicate actions of the Guyan people years ago, as when their city fell to Thrun, they did the unthinkable and destroyed most of their cherished resources — the Fermelstone mines. Caving in years of solid mining foundation and precious metal ore in a grand act of defiance. A similar destruction to the mountain pass would be catastrophic.

Secondly, a portion of the nation's Dions had been scattered on other assignments and to some of the colonies to mitigate uprisings that had sprung from rebel units. The ones that remained could not be sent away from the main city as by law, there must always be a minimum of six Dions present to protect the stronghold and the royal families.

It was a shame the state couldn't enhance Dion creation, though this reason was mainly attributed to the Dion decree of **358-SP**. A law passed due to the alarming number of fatalities of those sacrificed to the White Rift in exchange for power. Proclaimed loyalists to Thrun who all put their lives in servitude only to be greeted with death.

Many went into the abyss and none came out a Dion. Even Dions who were sent back into the Rift with the hope they would be exempt from its sorcery, and be able to explore more of the depths of its mysteries never returned again.

Any created Dion that ever came back from the Rift, came with no knowledge of what was inside. The mages were at their wits' end on how an unknown mystical power produces unknown results. The randomness of the selection forever a mystery. Still, in an unpopular move by Queen Mius Reis, a decree was signed to stop the action of Dion creation in all forms influenced by the state except for actions taken by individuals of a sound mind, spirit and faith.

By the stated powers of the crown family, I, Mius Reis, Ruler of the Thrun Empire and all its subsets, Server to the faith and the one true god of Sun, Leader of the Sun armies and Queen to all, institute in this decree, henceforth, a complete ban on all Dion creation influenced by the state, forced or unforced. And any and all actions controlled by

**the state in relation to the White Rift and Dion creation. Passage to the Rift will be henceforth under guard and only open to individuals attempting the pass of sound mind, spirit and faith, only under the circumstance they willingly agree to work eternally under the state on the occasion they are granted the powers of a Dion. State attention and resources would be thenceforth focused on the growing and strengthening of our armies into staunch and formidable units in the protection of our ever growing empire. Anyone deemed in violation of this decree, Dion or man will be subject to the charge of treason and face the justice of the high court. This decree shall not be changed or amended except only on authority of unanimity of the tribunal of elders.**

The effect of the ban reduced participants by almost nine tenths. The rest that remained were the terminally ill seeking a last miracle in their dying days, the utterly poor desperately seeking a life of wealth and power under the state, and the gallant and pious claiming that they're the chosen one and had been called with visions from Raja. In about fifty three years since the decree, only sixteen Dions had emerged since, and only fourteen were added under Thrun's rule.

It must be noted that Dions from the Rift have been unable to reproduce. There are rumors of inhumane experiments that have been performed in the search of conceiving Dion offsprings, although none have been confirmed. However, what is widely known is that every instance of a woman Dion becoming pregnant has resulted in a still born, and every instance of a man Dion impregnating a woman without abilities has resulted in the death of the woman and a dead ill-formed offspring in her womb.

It should also be emphasized that after Queen Gyai birthed a Dion, talks reemerged on the new source of Dion creation, but all questions raised were shut down completely by the king so much that any inquiry on the matter was known to send Olius into a state of fury.

Back in the king's quarters, the conversation continued. The echoes from the room escaped through gaps around the giant door. Those who heard the voices, closed their minds to its tune as they have many before. Holding strong to their eternal oath to the crown.

The voices peaked and valleyed; one voice always at peak and the other always at valley. After long, the door opened again and the king's counsel exited, notably with a more peeved expression. He paced faster now, descending down the stairs and through the halls. His mind racing through the complex plans he had in motion and the new threats that formed against them. The plans he had ongoing and the innocent lives he had sacrificed to keep them hidden; ones of men and men made gods. His displeasure pushed a thought in his head, one he had pondered over before.

*How convenient it would be if I could kill all of them. Then only the Taus would remain. Then only I would remain.*

——◆◯◆——

The early parts of midday bore no difference to that of the late morning. The depressing clouds staged protest in the skies, halting any signs of change in weather. Sounds of clashing wood could be heard playing in the open fields west of the Reis estate.

The vast lands that were known to Reis ancestry flowed with a history of blood and iron entrenched in the heart of every child of Reis born unto it. The mansion behind the fields stood strong and fortified, displaying its proud crest boldly and without concern. The sounds of wood sang again until a heavy thud followed. "*Yield!*" a voice proclaimed strongly, and laughter could be heard from the audience of three who sat watching the duel, as the victor stood over the defeated with his long wooden sword still drawn.

"*I Yield,*" the defeated claimed, with such embarrassment it could be felt through his words.

"*How do you lose to your little brother, Copius?*" The boys laughed again, twice as hard this time. The younger brother stretched a hand to help the older with a face which bore layers of regret; it was either mockery of him or the former, and he chose selfishly. Three years younger than his brother but he had a ferocity that could be only attributed to rare talent. His brother on the other hand lacked many, weak in physique and skill, victory was decided before the fight even started, and he purposefully extended the battle to save him grace.

"*Go again. You can't give up, Copius. You're the first son of General Ganius, you shouldn't be losing duels to you little brother,*" one of the boys from the crowd of three said to him, his voice calm and earnest but still with hints of mockery. Copius stood from the ground with a defeated look, threw down his sword and began to walk away. The other boys apologized amid laughs but he paid no mind.

The voice that spoke earlier, spoke again, *"Maybe he needs a little motivation,"* he joked to the laughing crew and added, *"If you leave, I'll fight Jesius myself."* Copius stopped in his steps, the suggestion thrown to him triggered memories he'd rather not have resurfaced.

The hidden meaning to what was proposed was not as innocent as his little brother interpreted. Jesius was clearly elated at the chance to spar with a Dion, a friendly duel with the crown prince known for his remarkable skill and elegant fighting style was going to be a great teaching moment, and his face clearly showed his enthusiasm. He was puzzled when Copius returned to pick up the sword again and wore an expression he couldn't understand.

*"If you lose again, I fight Jesius."* Selius said with a light smirk.

The fight started and Copius launched at his brother, swinging viciously in one slash after the next. His attacks full of power and intent. Jesius defended the best he could, astonished at this sudden display of intensity from his brother. Selius guffawed at the exchange and those who sat by him followed suit.

The duel continued relentlessly.

The younger brother who was filled with a wish to experience battle with a true warrior fought back unyieldingly. He stabbed, jabbed and swung, using all the movements that took down the older so easily earlier, but the one he faced at present was a different person entirely. In a sudden finale, Copius swung hard at his brother, breaking his wooden sword and striking the top of his head.

Blood streamed down Jesius's face as he fell to the ground, the red coloring his eyes and he let out a wail. The wail snapped the older brother out of his ferality. His mind cleared to his handiwork, his ears still filling with the sounds of nonchalant laughter of his audience. Copius's face filled with shame, remorse and apology. He reached out to help his younger brother but Jesius slapped his hand away and ran toward home bleeding.

*"Finally! I knew you had it in you,"* Selius remarked loudly, jumping up to praise him.

*"Let him run, it's just a little blood, it would have been worse if you lost,"* he added, flashing a heavy smile. A rage rose in Copius at the words, but when he raised his eyes to meet the prince's, he cowered, like he had so many times before. Those green eyes had imprinted so much on him throughout the years and he knew the darkness that lurked behind them. Darkness so strong, it swallowed everything it set its eyes on, and in its midst, he treaded as carefully as he could.

Copius saw the splatter of blood on his hands, and the shame he held filled his heart. This wasn't the first time he felt cornered to do something he loathed, but it seemed his life as a royal felt littered with actions he was always opposed to.

*"Responsibilities of a Reis,"* his father would shout at him in that deep vibrating voice, followed by his patented look of disappointment. Copius's thin-almond eyes blinked again to hold his emotions at bay, his shortened dull, blonde hair feeling the breeze that grazed it like wind passing over a neatly cut lawn.

Selius noticed the look on the one he had called a friend for many years and attempted consolement.

*"Jesius will be fine. He will heal with time and anytime he looks at that mark, he will respect you as the eldest son you are. I know how you feel about violence, but you must adopt toughness, brother. In a few weeks, you'll be off to the Mirain colony to represent the crown and you can't wear weakness with your rule."*

Copius nodded to his words, lifting his head and echoing a light smile. It was an uncanny friendship these two had, if you could even call it that.

Among the friends; Kinura Wuhn, Badaius Reis, Figuid Myr and Elaine Trout, Copius knew Selius the longest and knew him the most. He kept his secrets, the ones the prince shared with him and only him, and locked them in the depths of his mind so far down, he wished he would forget.

In a week over a fortnight, he would be leaving to be part of the crown's coalition in the Mirain colony, filling in the seat as the Reis family representation after the predecessor died of old age.

The crown's coalition was a group of five created by the king's advisor Jura Wuhn in the years of King Perolius to represent the crown and its leadership in colonized regions. They were an extension of the royal families and the rule of Thrun. In addition, whatever family of royalty that already existed in a colonized region was to be split and the majority of them relocated to the Thrun capital, settling them among lower families and marrying most off to be integrated into Thrun culture.

The claim for this act was to further the union of cultures, but to the colonized, the truth lay bare — they were being held as hostages in perpetuity.

Copius however took this news of assignment surprisingly well, relishing the idea of being selected for leadership and the chance to leave Cratos and its predicaments. Selius on the other hand wasn't as enthused on the idea of his old friend moving away, and it prompted an unusual sentimentality in him.

"*Okay I'm next,*" one of the other boys from the audience of three claimed. "*I challenge you Badaius,*" he continued.

"*Of Course you choose me, you won't ever challenge Selius,*" Badaius shot back.

"*Why will I willingly challenge a Dion when I can just beat you up instead?*" Figuid replied with a giggle. Badaius fumed and rushed to pick up a wooden sword as the two continued to throw taunts and mockery at each other. Their voices faded into the background as did the tune of their swings. Copius sat down next to Selius watching the reckless duo be even more reckless.

"*You know I'm going to miss you when you leave, you're my most trusted friend,*" Selius engaged.

"*Yeah? You'll still have these fools here to keep you company.*" Copius responded.

Selius chuckled a little, looking at the friends continuing their duel, "*Yeah I guess I will.*"

*"I'm most definitely going to be back for your wedding,"* Copius added teasingly, and they both laughed at the premise.

Selius thought back to the first time he met Copius, a time when his mother was still alarmingly cautious of him playing with other children. The famed general visited the castle in the dead of noon with his young son attached to his hip.

*"I wanted my son to meet the young prince, he must be lonely from being bound inside the castle. Copius will make a great companion for him. Let them grow as young boys and mold each other into great men,"* he proposed, his patented voice pulsating through the air.

Through the years, their relationship grew and Selius found in Copius the closest thing he would get to a brother. He told him everything, a keeper to his secrets and a haven to his thoughts.

He was the only one who knew about the time he sneaked fire ants into the maids' chambers, the commotion it caused and the hilarity of it. The time he pissed from the skies on a group of Taus royals, giggling as they proclaimed it rain.

The time he flew into the drylands and descended into the White Rift about three year-cycles ago, the mysteries he saw inside and the strangeness he felt in himself. The insides of a forest that looked desiccated, broken rocks in the midst of a large crater in the ground, and in its center, a giant carving of stone floating on nothing.

He even told Copius about the foul creatures with Dion abilities that attacked him to almost death, and the thing he returned with, a little wandering beast offspring he saved, one he had nurtured for years.

The day he took Copius to its lair hidden in the depths of the crown's abandoned dungeons, Copius's knees buckled at its sight. A grotesque looking creature as big as a pair of fully grown oxen combined. Its head was wide and sharply narrowed like the malformed head of a rattle viper-snake with four eyes: two glowing on either side of its face, just above its wide flattened nose. The beast yawned from being awoken from slumber, twisting its neck and gaping the width of its mouth. The shrieking growl that escaped through its teeth could paralyze prey.

Copius's heart sank when he saw the many teeth that filled its mouth like the ends of many spears. The strong stench of rotten meat that captured his nose in the moment. The beast noticed Copius and stood from rest, moving out of the darkness and approaching him. Selius had to stop it from going any further.

*"Meet Agui."* Selius said to his friend, beckoning the beast to himself, an action it obeyed, as Selius scratched its head and the beast responded with affection.

Copius stood drenched in fear and mystification. This was no animal he knew of. Its legs and claws were hulking, its tail coiled in a spiral, and its hide was of a darkened brown color shrouding it more in the blackness of the cage.

Copius shivered, his body doing its best to fight the instincts of flight. The closed door behind him would hinder that escape.

The flashes of scattered white that lay on the ground didn't register in his mind immediately, but when it did, he recognized exactly the source of the smell. The bones that lay scattered, and the crushed skulls undevoured.

"*They were just prisoners, they were going to be killed anyway,*" Selius said to his friend as he saw his eyes wander.

"*Oof ... of course. T ... to better use,*" Copius responded, doing his best to hide the tremble in his voice.

The weight of fear that strangled Copius on that day still haunts him even now. A hidden fear that one bad day might get him back in the dungeon on different terms.

"*Yield!*" a voice shouted again, breaking minds from thought.

Finguid looked down at a fallen Badaius, wearing the widest smirk on his face.

"*I win.*"

## Chapter Eight

# DOCK FIFTY-ONE

*"Slow down, you're walking too fast."*

Naemi slowed her steps per her brother's request. The excitement of getting to the ports clouded her thoughts and her legs raced as did her mind. They were still locked in hands as they walked down the road; a young blind boy and girl to the outside world.

Dakai's blindfold still held securely in place.

The dark cloth over his eyes, tied under his dreadlocks. This part of the road was less busy than the former, and they didn't have to suffer the many bumps from nonchalant walkers. They'd been walking for about an hour now, not only because of the enormity of the city, but also due to the numerous wrong turns they took on their way to the ports.

After some questioning to the more knowledgeable, they finally found the right route to their destination.

*"Follow the widest road to the south until you reach the three-junctions, and take the road to whichever port you desire."*

The instructions that were to lead them to the many ships they sought. Instructions that seemed to come with more questions.

*How many ports were there? And was it as easy as walking to a ship to ask for passage home? Would their payment even be enough?*

Naemi's other hand clutched the green bag tighter, everything they had existed in here, and if they were going to get home, its protection was paramount. She whispered quiet thanks to the All-Mother for the extra money and food the sweet woman gave her.

A shame she couldn't tell her the truth of their situation, but it was better no one knew. Telling people they were lost wouldn't always prompt a righteous reaction of help, and they were in no place to gamble with their freedom. Beara's last words rang in her head, *"trust no one,"* and she was right; even the good they'd met throughout their journey couldn't wipe the blacken of the bad, and they had to be much smarter to escape this labyrinth.

They had fallen into tremendous luck meeting the family from before, hopefully a sign of better tidings in their future. They could buy some new clothes, some more food, or even rent a place to rest for the night, *how much does twelve bronze coins afford here?* She looked around the many buildings that flanked the roads for market-sheds and carts, but none resided.

The walls stretched down for every new structure as if a guide to the streets below. The ground bore an unusual cleanness to it, the whole city did. Spotless, down to the brick that lay the roads, only blemished by the stain of the people who walked it.

The houses lining the roads were covered in a light-grain yellow or pale blue with parts of white in certain areas and dark brown roofing; most about two stories tall and others one or three stories. She could see the top of watch towers placed in parts of the city and the movements of watchers atop them.

The people who paraded the streets looked sparse in similarity, from clothing, mannerisms to physical features. She would meet eyes with some who showed emotions of empathy at the sight of her and her brother, others a glance of disdain, and others nothing at all. She continued her walk down the street; much slower in her pacing, fascinated at the experience of a fully developed city, the nuances of the buildings she passed, roads, activities that filled the street corners, and the people. Her pace fluctuating based on what caught her attention.

Dakai complained and she'd apologize and do it again.

"*You're lucky you're not the blinded one,*" he rebutted with annoyance.

"*We are almost there ... I think,*" she answered, while still rattling on about other things she was seeing to her brother. Dakai mumbled an insult to himself. Even through his growing irritation, there was a part of him that relished a return to the status quo in their dynamic. There was much to be happy about; they were free and close to finding a ship back home. *Maybe I shouldn't be soo tense,* he thought.

Naemi yanked him again.

"*Can you stop doing that!*" he blurted out, annoyed once more.

"*We are here,*" she responded with a dazzle in her voice.

They stood at the three junctions, as the forked roads sloped and diverged down the hill to the lake entering the sea, and the hundreds of ships that flooded the ports. It was a remarkable sight that was worthy of the pause Naemi took.

The immensity of the lake, the many boats of varying scale that covered its surface of gray water, the massive walls in the distance and the many people filling the ports with vibrancy. It was loud, buzzing with roaring horns, shouting traders, neighing horses, loud wagons and the steps of multitudes.

"*What is it? Why did you stop?*" Dakai asked, snapping her out of her pause.

"*It is ... incredible. So many people. So many ships. I've never seen some this big, I'm not sure which one we go to,*" Naemi exhaled with admiration.

"*Let's go to the closest ship and start from there,*" he concluded, almost too quickly as he nudged his sister forward.

*Of Course I was going to go to the closest one, I didn't mean it literally,* she thought, but she spared her brother the response and just moved onward. The slope on the middle road was just steep enough for discomfort and she had to hold Dakai firmer lest he lost his foothold. Part of the ground had stairs, another, smooth with rails embedded in the floors and flat carts that traveled up them with some sort of mechanism.

At the bottom, they moved past hurried workers, everyone moving with unknown urgency.

"*Move child!*"

One shouted, almost knocking Naemi off her feet. She jumped to the side, pulling Dakai back, just in time to avoid the man and the cargo he had on his shoulders.

Dakai huffed but spoke no words.

They continued onward, looking for anyone who looked like they were in charge of a ship, or in charge of anything at all. Naemi tried getting the attention of another worker, but he was busy spinning the wheels of a treadwheel-crane and paid more attention to the stack of boxes he hoisted than the new faces that stood beside him.

A couple more paces ahead, to more bridged ships lying at rest, wooden structures started nesting together near the bay full of busied legs. Across the third ship where the chaos was calmer, right next to its bridge connecting ship to shore, she noticed someone who fit a description she searched; a tall plump man with a funny-looking beard dressed in an attire she recognized. She'd seen that red and silver before, throughout their walk in the streets, that same attire and crest-badge spread scattered on different people. They didn't seem to be guards, evident by their lack of weaponry. He held a parchment and directed workers on and off the ship as they loaded more cargo.

"*Sir? Sir?*" Naemi echoed to get his attention.

"*I have no money for you two, move along,*" he spat out after a quick glance.

"*We don't want money sir, we just want to find a ship going to Shore-town.*"

"*Shoretown? Where is that?*"

*"In Primea, the Prim capital?"* Dakai interposed from behind his sister. The man took a long look at the siblings, eyes of deep scrutiny inspecting their being and judging them silently.

When he spoke again, there was a lash behind his voice.

*"I know of Primea, there should be some ships that are going that far north. You will need to go to the trading halls to get more details on what ships are available and which allow for passengers,"* pointing in a direction behind them.

*"You should know most of the ships don't accept labor as a form of payment anymore and the blind one will be expensive; you on the other hand could offer other services. Don't bother going if you don't have any money to pay,"* he ended with a silly expression, his laughable beard dangling on his face like a silly joke only he could understand.

He turned away after, getting back to barking orders to men who were numb to his berating. Naemi thought to ask another question but decided against it, *he's not going to be of any help to us,* and the siblings walked off in the direction of the trading halls.

———◆◆◆———

The halls weren't difficult to reach, the building stood as a monument, shining in ways that won't do any descriptions justice. The marbled floors felt chill on Naemi's soles per her first step and she hesitated for her second. Inside was full of people indulging in various transactions; some more heated than others, red and silver coats everywhere eyes could see.

*Alliants*, they were called; foot workers of the Trading Alliance, responsible for documenting trades, tracking cargo, fielding merchants, and doing anything and everything the Alliance deemed necessary.

The halls were wide in the center with a giant ellipse of sectioned stalls full of Alliants providing services. Divided cages of privacy for the clandestine. The siblings kept on forward, overwhelmed by their present. They looked out of place and people noticed. An empty stall available and quickened steps, they got there just in time for Naemi to meet the gaze of the Alliant woman. A puzzled look flashed her face.

"*Howw can I help ... you?*" she quizzed.

"*We are looking for transport on any ship going to Shoretown in Primea?*" Naemi answered, the woman's gaze lingered briefly and her eyes moved to the papers that lay before her. A moment ensued before she returned her attention to the siblings.

"*There is a silk trading ship set to sail to Shoretown next month,*" the woman reported.

Naemi's eyes widened.

*A month? That's too far, they couldn't stay here for a month,* she thought.

"*Is there nothing closer? Anywhere in Primea? Anywhere close will do.*" Naemi requested, her worried expression covering the majority of her face.

The woman lingered her gaze some more, the urgency written on the face of the girl and half of what she could see from the boy played no parts in her response.

After a second check, she responded, "*There is a ship going to the Prim shore in a fortnight ... and another going to Rune in three days.*"

"*Rune! Yes! We will go to Rune,*" she interjected sharply, a wave of excitement flooding her face. She hugged her brother who was fighting his expressions under his fold.

The woman continued, "*The trader still has space for transport and has priced the service at any value-trade equal to twenty-three gold coins ... per transport.*"

*Forty-six gold coins? We don't have anything equal to Forty-six gold coins*, Naemi thought. The woman stared at them, there was no need asking questions for answers she already knew.

*There is no way these juveniles have enough money to get on a ship; I wouldn't hesitate to call out guards if they did. They bear the stench of thieves. Do they not think I can't see through this charade of blindness and self-pity?*

Naemi looked to the woman and the woman responded with a light smile, "*What would you like to trade as payment?*"

"*We don't have equal value, I could offer labor on the ship as well as whatever value this has for the both of us,*" as she placed the contents from her bag on the wooden extension between them.

"*Sorry the ships don't accep...*" She stopped.

A bulging expression captured the entirety of her face, and her wrinkled forehead echoed more folds on her skin.

"*Where did you get that?*" her eyes fixed on the item placed before her.

*"A friend gave it to us. How much value can we get from it? I will try and get the rest before time,"* Naemi replied, thinking of the family from before. *They offered me work, I can work to get the rest,* she thought.

Dakai listened from behind her, his conclusion not as optimistic as his sister's. The price mentioned was unreachable, he had barely ever seen five gold coins his entire life and now they were supposed to somehow find over forty of them.

The woman fixated on the dull crystalized bracelet.

*That can't be what I think it is? Of Course it's not, how are these delinquents in possession of such a jewel?*

She reached out and grabbed it, inspecting its coarseness and un-smooth edges. The colored glitters that shone inside when held in the shadow of light. It was crafted in exquisite detail, raw and exotic.

There was no doubt this was pure meridian sapphire.

*"A friend gave it to you?"* she asked; she could smell the lie.

*"Yes, how much can we get from it?"* Naemi responded. The woman hadn't moved her eyes off the item once and there was an uncanniness to them.

*Do they not know what they possess asking about worth? They could buy a hundred ships just of its raw value. Should I call the guards? No. That would mean the Alliance would inherit its possession. No.*

She held it for long, almost too long, hoping to find a flaw in it. Something she could point to and render it faux but there was nothing, it was as genuine as when it was dug from the ground. She struggled to return it, her hands fighting her greed and hoping not to raise alarm. Finally she set it back down.

"*It's still not enough to get you on that ship,*" she said to the two teens in a calming voice.

"*However, there is another ship going to Rune tonight, it's already full from our records, but I could talk to the captain to offer you a small space for your value-trade and labor as payment for the both of you,*" she added.

"*There is? We will take it. Any little space will do, thank you, thank you so much. Thank you.*" Naemi praised.

"*No need for thanks darling. Meet me at the Dock fifty-one at the earliest moon with the trade items, and I'll get you on the ship. And remember to keep it safe, the city is being overrun with thievery so much these past few months, better you don't show it to anyone,*" she commented through an appealing smile. Naemi smiled back after returning the contents into her bag, repeating her appreciation. She grabbed her brother's hand, her other hand clutching the bag tightly as they left the stall with faces of exhilaration. The blue eyes that trailed their steps yearned relentlessly for their next meeting, but for them only one thought remained, *we are going home.*

<hr />

The skies flashed in a slow drain of brightness, curtains of a dying gold layered in the far distances of the west. Rays of warmth lost their essence of heat and the cool breeze thrilled at the retirement of its rival. The once blue horizon made its daily evolution from light blue to bright orange and to darkness, influencing others to do the same. The great ball of suspended fire praised for another job well done, flickering parting cinders of warmth as farewell to its gracious host. The end to another day approached for some, but in the spirited city, all that prompted was a change in personnel.

"*Trade never sleeps,*" a saying famous to the city, and its people didn't either, though the context behind trade bore a different meaning.

Merchants and workers who tired from a full day of work desired outlets from their daily torments, a desire so strong that an entire market of targeted pleasures were built on them.

Brothels of every kind; some so sadistic they couldn't even be imagined. Taverns for the drunk, fighting pits for the savage and whatever else could be created as long as there was an equal value-trade for it.

Past the awakening deviances, down the path that was just granted light on torch-stands spaced evenly by the roads, the siblings sat in a boxed corner between two buildings; the only obscure place they could find without a stranger's scolding. It was a hidden section of a smaller alley, slightly dirtied with ragged clothing, a small running gutter of dirtied water, and a stink that almost bordered on discomfort. It was still the best place they had found through their searches however. It was decently lit from stealing light from its surroundings and was well hidden with enough space to house them both, so they made do with what luck had provided.

Dakai finished a flavored rice ball from their food stash, sitting crouched on the ground with Naemi opposite him.

"*Can I take it off? Even for a little while? I feel like I'm going crazy.*"

"*No! Stop asking,*" Naemi blurted in a whisper.

*"I thought you said we were hidden here? C'mon I have been wearing this all day; my head is starting to hurt."*

Naemi looked around to confirm nobody could see them, *"Okay you can loosen it but keep it covered in case someone pops up,"* Naemi suggested. Dakai pulled the entire fold off.

*"Dakai!"* She said in a giant whisper of agitation. He blinked a couple of times, flinching his eyelids to get accustomed to the little light that substituted the dark he was accustomed to.

*"No one can see us, we'll be fine,"* he spoke, and went back to enjoying his rice ball. Naemi stole another look for confirmation. She sat back down and fumed, *we're so close to going home, this idiot better not cause us any problems,* glancing at the boy who was eating like a hound.

*"You know your hair looks a mess, right?"* she commented, drawing his attention.

*"Come, let me fix it,"* she added, and he reluctantly moved over, still prioritizing his food.

*"Naemi?"*

*"Yes?"* Naemi answered.

*"I can't wait to see father again … I miss him so much. I miss home, my friends, the town … my bed. I can't wait to get back,"* his voice coated with a gloom that touched his sister.

*"Me too, I can't wait,"* she responded in a lighter tone, trying to raise Dakai's spirit. After a brief pause, he talked again.

*"I'm afraid, Naemi. I'm afraid of what happens when we return. What if we get back and everything is different? What if father is also*

*out there looking for us and not home? What if everyone blames us for what happened to Raex? What if we are ne...*"

"*Heyy, heyy, it's going to be okay. Stop worrying so much. We are going to get home and father will be there with open arms as well as everyone in the town, okay? Worrying will do nothing for you; we are going to be fine as long as we're together.*" The words came out her lips with tones of inspiration but the heart that said it lacked any. Those were questions that haunted her too, but she couldn't bear the thought of her brother feeling the same.

"*Thank you Naemi, thank you for everything. I don't know what I'll do without you,*" Dakai replied.

"*Ohh, are those compliments I'm getting from my little brother? No more Poison Princess jokes?*" she inquired in a playful tone.

"*There is a time for everything, big sister,*" he said with a smile.

Naemi continued braiding the parts of Dakai's hair that had loosened. A few jokes thrown as time passed and a more uplifted mood grew between the siblings. The skies darkened more and the moon began its reveal from behind the distant clouds.

Time was near and Dock fifty-one would soon be in sight.

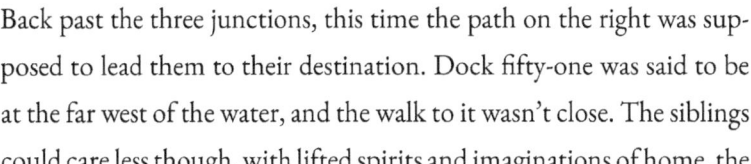

Back past the three junctions, this time the path on the right was supposed to lead them to their destination. Dock fifty-one was said to be at the far west of the water, and the walk to it wasn't close. The siblings could care less though, with lifted spirits and imaginations of home, the trek to the dock was just more time to revel in their enthusiasm. The workers who scattered this time around were barely a handful per ship with some ships having none at all. It was such a contrast from before that it felt like a totally different place.

Most weren't working; some sleeping on bare wood snoring as loud as snarling beasts. Others played board games in groups, loud with their victories and solemn in their defeats. Occasionally, one would make a passing comment at them, one of mockery, concern, or flirtation, and they would quicken their steps, Naemi tugging on Dakai to keep pace. These reduced as did the people as they got closer to fifty-one. Many of the ships near were docked and absent of life only kept company by the gentle water cradling their hulls.

From a distance, she saw a figure waiting next to a barrier. The figure waved to them and called out. The person stood accompanied by another, but her voice put a face to her. She wasn't as tall as Naemi had imagined, only seeing half of her from behind the stall. She was lean with slanted shoulders and wore a dress different from the red and silver. Her hair was mildly long with soft curls, and her face still held the light folds that revealed her age.

The ship she stood next to was dimly lit though there were faint sounds that hovered on the obscured deck. As they got closer, the man who stood next to her came into view. He looked young, younger than any ship captain she had seen. His left eye was lazy, and he had little scars on the top of his forehead traveling up his shaved head. Naemi's eyes couldn't linger on him too long before the woman called her attention.

*"You're here on time; I just finished speaking to the captain and he's agreed to take you,"* she blurted, fanning their excitement.

*"Did you bring your trade items?"* she continued, and Naemi joyously reached into her bag to hand her the gemmed bracelet, and also tried adding the bronze coins, which she refused.

*"Just this is fine,"* she replied with eyes of admiration, fondling over her discovery. Naemi looked to the woman with expectations of what came next, with Dakai standing behind her.

The woman paid them no attention, inspecting the item as if it was a prized valuable.

*"Is that what you wanted?"* The younger man asked, and the woman responded with a wave of a hand. The next things that happened occurred in a quick sequence. A whistle, an emergence of strange men surrounding them, spawning behind boards and darkness, and the sharp sting to the back of her head.

Thoughts didn't even get the chance to form, the darkness hit her almost instantly. She dropped to a thud on the ground, followed by her brother who didn't even get the courtesy of seeing the betrayal. Their bodies lay on the floor with vultures surrounding.

*"Aye! This one will do. But what of the blind one? No one buys blind boys, what do we do with him?"* A voice from the group hissed.

*"Do whatever you want,"* the woman replied, beginning her leave.

And so happened, the price of naivety and innocence paid with their freedom, though this time they were deprived the privilege of enduring through it together.

———————◆◯◆———————

Naemi's eyes opened slowly. Out of focus to what surrounded her and the pain in her head pulsed, the ground was moving, a movement she recognized. She was on a ship.

"*No ... No ... No!*"

The words came out of her with a despair she had felt before. When her sight fully returned, she saw the completeness of her situation, and those she shared them with. Caged with others who looked like her in age. Dirtied, chained, broken. They looked at her in silence, eyes of utter dejection, and she looked at them with same.

"*No ... No ... No!*"

She tried to stand but the chains that bound her held her in place. A face she recognized from before stood outside the cage; the assumed captain, with a smirk on his lips. He spoke words to her, urging compliance in exchange for fair treatment. Flaunting his domain of power and the control he had over his forced subjects. Naemi's head was pulsing harder by the moment.

"*Dakai? Where's my brother? Dakai!*" she shouted, but he wasn't there.

The man laughed, "*We left that worthless shit. Don't worry, these are your new brothers and sisters now,*" he added in a mocking tone.

*No ... No ... No! Not again!*

The thought racing through her mind in repetition. She felt an emotion familiar to her situation — hate, loss, anger, despair. So many emotions coursing through her, she could feel the surge within.

*No ... No ... No! Not again!*

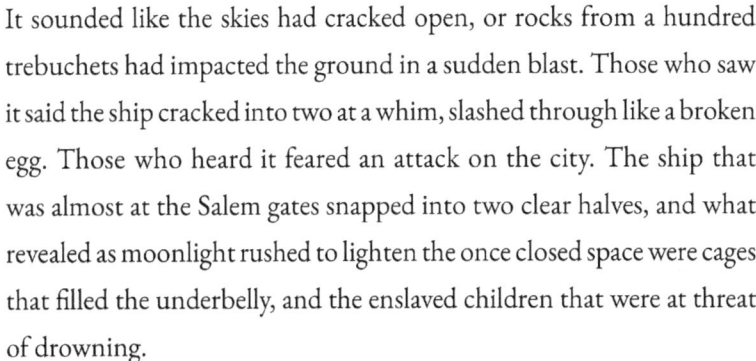

It sounded like the skies had cracked open, or rocks from a hundred trebuchets had impacted the ground in a sudden blast. Those who saw it said the ship cracked into two at a whim, slashed through like a broken egg. Those who heard it feared an attack on the city. The ship that was almost at the Salem gates snapped into two clear halves, and what revealed as moonlight rushed to lighten the once closed space were cages that filled the underbelly, and the enslaved children that were at threat of drowning.

The water rushed quickly, filling its new volume of ownership. The bells rang at the gates and guards at watch scurried into boats to save the drowning. The sea water moved with an urgency and hunger known to sunken ships that are filled in its belly. The guard-boats that converged on time saved the many they could — chained and unchained, stealing the lives owed to the water.

The awe of the split ship didn't last long to be mystified, the sea water swallowed both parts whole before there was a chance to take note, an occurrence that was appreciated by the shadows who were given full account of the incident later on.

In spite of the types of trade that were overlooked for the right price in the city, the Alliance's official stand to the world was the vehement condemnation of the trade of enslaved within their borders, a stand to make the city more appealing to the more advancing nations in the north and east, and their massive mines of gold, rubies and pompous self-righteousness. However, there was a heavy market to be profited from in the trade of the enslaved, and the Alliance played their cards with secrecy.

---

She could feel the descent to the bottom, the pull it had on her, chains stronger than ones she just broke through. She could see the lights dimming, stretching her hand to reach them, but they moved farther away. It was quiet here, calm, the only thing she could feel more was the iciness on her skin, it was soothing for some reason.

*Maybe I should let go. What's the point of all of this? I can just fall and all the misery will end in this quiet place. Is my life pain?* Her mind prompted questions and her mind fought its answers. *What of my brother? What of my father? Can I leave Dakai alone in this place? I told him we would be in this together.*

A thousand questions and a thousand answers all in a fraction of a moment. She could see the two giant masses of wood that inched closer from above, slowly occluding the light.

*I don't want to die ... I don't want to die.* Her last thoughts before she moved again, thrusting her arms and trying to swim away but the forces pulled her down more. She knew what was happening, the same thing that happened in the forest. The tension in her muscles, they felt heavy and light at the same time. Everything she touched was soft as shells. She didn't mean to cause it; she didn't mean to break the ship.

She just struck the floor from anger and misery, and a moment later she was falling through wood into water.

*Are those children going to die because of me?*

The air in her mouth was running out and in her desperation, she thought about the only thing that could calm her mind from the blame, from the pain. She thought of riding through the fields in Soros on Bellie; the air on her face, the flower-flavored scent that filled her lungs. She thought of her mother's smile; the last true thing she could remember of her face. She thought of her father and her brother. She thought of home.

The surface of the water broke just in time for Naemi to gulp a mouthful of air. She had drifted a bit farther from the sunken ship and could see the boats in the distance still searching the waters. A breeze of relief for the saved, but it never vacated the blame. The freeze of the water reached her mind as she broke through its surface, as if a trigger to remind her of her mortality. She hurriedly turned to the lights that brightened the ports, she needed to get back, she needed to find her brother. The sound of bells chimed from behind and others from in front. Without any leads to act on, her only thought was to swim back to shore, back to where it all started. Back to Dock fifty-one.

⚫

Dakai felt the shake that slowly triggered his consciousness, the voice that called out many times. He woke to the darkness, feeling the back of his head where he was hit. There was a wetness there and a cut that stung. The voice that reached out came again, "*You poor thing, what happened to you?*" He hesitated, confused why the voice wasn't his sister's.

"*Leave him Kaise, let's go, who knows what trouble he got himself into, we don't need his problems on our hands. We got him out of the crate, we've done enough, now leave him let's go.*" Another voice asserted through a heavier tone.

"*Naemi? My sister? Where is my sister?*" Were the only words that came out of Dakai's mouth in response. The last thing he remembered was a whistle and then nothing.

"*There's no one else here. We saw drops of blood that led to a covered crate and you were in it. What happened to you?*" The thoughts rushed back to him and the picture felt clearer than before. There was never a ship going to Rune, just another lie.

*For what? To capture us? But they left me, why? Did they take Naemi or leave her bleeding somewhere else as I am?* he thought.

"*Where am I?*" he asked, trying to stand. He wobbled a little, feeling the dizziness that crept in. The frustration of being blindfolded had almost reached its limit. *Damn this fold, I don't care who sees my eyes, I need to find her*, the voice in his head said.

"*You're on Dock forty,*" the gentler voice answered.

"*We have to help him. He's blind,*" the voice continued with a merciful plea.

"*I don't care. We have what we came for. Let's leave before any of the ship's crew returns to catch us around here. Mamuex will be mad if we don't bring what she asked for on time. I knew I shouldn't have brought y…"*

The shockwave sent ripples through the dock. The echoes of the blast rifled past them into the city as well as the distant screams that followed. The view wasn't clear from where they stood but those who could see, saw parts of the ship break. The realization hit Dakai at once, there could be only one cause of that.

"*Where was that?*" Dakai asked, "*Over on the lake. A ship crashed? I think.*" The heavier voice's hostility now turned into concern. The sound of screams came from across the lake, followed by the sound of bells.

"*My sister is there, I need to go help her,*" he moved a step, but felt the weakness in his legs. He thought of taking off his fold but decided against it.

*Would they still help me if they knew I wasn't blind?*

"*How do you know your sister is there?*" the softer voice asked.

"*I just know … they took her. Please … please help me get there,*" he pleaded.

"*No Kaise! We have to leave. Don't get involved in his troubles. The bells are sounding, and guards are going to be crawling everywhere soon. Let's get out of here.*" This second plea fell on deaf ears, for Kaise was already helping Dakai move close to a stray boat that was tied next to a ship.

"*I believe you, I'll help you get to your sister,*" Kaise said to Dakai, and turned to the other person staring at her angrily, "*Are you going to help me or leave me to go alone?*" she quizzed.

"*Who knows all the dangers out there without my brother to protect me?*" she added temptingly. The boy fumed and threw a dramatic tantrum, and in the end reluctantly joined the two in the boat after loosening the rope that anchored it.

He frowned and paddled in silence through the cluster of ships till they were in the open lake. He could see guard-boats in the distance and the sinking ship, and his sense of danger continued to rise.

*Why does she always get us into trouble?*

———————◦———————

Naemi continued her swim to shore. She could feel the exhaustion in her arms, the tiredness creeping in her legs. The shore didn't look to be far away from before, but as much as she swam, she wasn't getting any closer. Salt water burned her eyes and soaked her skin. All she could see were the blurred little orange dots of light beyond, her only sense of perspective.

She still kept on with no desire to quit. Any moment she wasted was one Dakai could be in danger. She continued on, through the piquant taste of rogue water breaching her lips and filling her nose so much her sense of smell dissipated. She could hear voices, but her mind had only one focus.

The voices got louder and louder, finally breaking through her consciousness. She stopped, whipping her head around to find its origin. There was a boat far-off to her left and there were people shouting to get her attention. She couldn't see its occupants and her first thought was to escape from it. She didn't get far in her escape.

*"Heeey ... Heeeeyy, we are only trying to help you. Heyyy ... slow down,"* a voice called from her side. She didn't mean to oblige but her weary body spoke in her place. She turned to see a figure reaching out and two obscured behind her. It was a girl who looked just a year or two older than her with her hand out-stretched. She wore a giant smile that seemed misplaced, and long gold-like hair glimmering in the moonlight. Naemi still hesitated.

*"Come on. The water is cold. Let us help you,"* she claimed. The boat slowly drifted toward her, finally revealing all the occupants.

Two of the occupants looked awfully similar, and the third, *"Dakai?"* Naemi exhaled, *"Dakai!"* she exclaimed.

Her voice came out with a joy laced with sorrow. Dakai removed his fold in disbelief. A thoughtless action for which he cared little, he had found his sister.

An unexpected gift from the universe or a crude jest from omnipotent beings who controlled the fate of mere mortals, the siblings were again united. Naemi hugged the two new strangers with a gladness they couldn't fully understand. Kaise returned the hug with more enthusiasm than her brother.

*"You're not blind?"* he kept repeating with irritation and a hint of confusion, none being greater. Dakai apologized profusely to them both and Kaise accepted willingly.

*"Let's head back Kainu, guard-boats are coming."* Kaise interrupted her brother. Kainu turned the boat back, paddling harder.

*"Oh now you're screaming at me to go back?"*

*"I don't see anyone else in the water and we found his sister, do you want us to wait for the guards to come to us?"* Kaise barked back.

Kainu seeped with anger overflowing, yet he paddled faster, whispering inaudible words to himself.

The quartet reached the shore amidst pursuit from guard-boats far beyond. Blessed with a head-start and a clutter of ships to cover their tracks, they scurried unto land now crawling with more guards.

———◆———

Evasion from the ports wasn't easy, concealing themselves behind one occlusion after another. Kainu knew the ports well and the others followed silently. Through tight corners, dirtied crevices and unwatched spaces, they burrowed through till they got to the streets. Around the corner, turning to make their final dash and a voice halted them, hoarse and boisterous.

The three guards emerged from behind them.

*"Stay right there! Where are you going? Do you not know what the Gate's bells mean?"* The first guard shouted. The group turned, Naemi pulling Dakai behind her as Dakai lowered his head and eyes. Kainu stepped up front, *"Sorry, we wanted to see what was happening. We know we are supposed to be sheltered. We will head back now."*

"*I could throw you all in dungeons for disobeying the laws,*" the third chimed, moving closer to them with a scowl.

"*They're just children Nau, let them have a pass,*" the second reasoned, compelling his companions. The third stared at the group, considering his partner's proposal before noticing the wetness in Naemi's hair and clothes.

"*Why are you wet all over?*" he asked Naemi, his eyes moving from her to her brother behind. Kainu again stepped up to answer, "*She got too close to the wa...*"

"*Did I ask you to speak, boy? Can she not speak for herself?*" The guard roared.

Kainu held his tongue, moving his eyes to meet Naemi's with Kaise standing cowered behind him also; quiet as a mouse.

Naemi looked back to the man in front of her. He wasn't that much taller than her; probably three quarters of a foot taller. He was plump but looked strong with angry hair. His scabbard was on his left and he had his left hand on the hilt.

"*I got too close to the water and slipped.*" Naemi answered, returning his mean gaze. He scanned the group some more with an intense stare and broke into uncontrollable laughter.

"HAHAHAHA. *They look like they're going to shit themselves,*" he said to his partners, and laughed harder.

"*Get out of here back into your houses. If I see you again I will throw you into our deepest dungeons.*" He added as the four hurried to escape his presence.

They continued their escape to shelter, eyes peeking through windows and sometimes full heads of the curious shouting questions. The streets were empty but not quiet.

At a crossroad, Kainu and Kaise took a turn left and when the siblings followed, Kainu turned sharply with a quizzical stare and a sharper tone, *"Why are you still following us? Stop following us."* He barked.

*"Kainu,"* his sister prompted.

*"No! Kaise. No! I told you they were trouble. I told you."* The strains in his voice filled with aggravation. Kaise tried to reason with him as she had before, but her sisterly charm had run out.

*"We helped save his sister, we helped get them out the ports. Now they go their own way. We have enough trouble of our own, we don't need theirs."* His last words had an iciness to it, a quick stagnating silence followed after, and then he was gone. Kaise's leave was slower, so much reluctance, but in the end she disappeared behind the steps of her brother.

Naemi stood there quiet, her mind filled with silence. She meant to say something before, a plea, a sad request for help, some words that could change his mind. The words never formed, or she couldn't think of the right ones.

Maybe she thought it didn't matter what words she chose, and that the outcome would still end the same. A hand grasped hers and she turned to meet her brother's eyes. She wasn't sure what prompted the subtle smile that formed on her lips, an unconscious reaction to seeing a face she thought was lost to her.

There was sadness in Dakai's eyes even when he smiled in response. The siblings retreated from their current path to another in their search for a place to hide. The wet clothes on Naemi felt colder with the chilled breeze, and her mind ignored all the signals of distress her body sent. As their search persevered amidst the heavy patrols that formed, the moon was almost at its peak, brightening its blue light against the black that slithered into alleys and shadows.

The day would be at its end soon and their first chapter in Sailor City would be concluded.

## CHAPTER NINE

# EYES OF A FALLEN EMPIRE

The footsteps grew louder with time, its origins chatty and loud. A city reawakened. The street that was adjacent to them already brimmed with sonority. The full sounds bouncing in the small alley till it reached the boxed corner built into the wall, occluding them from view watched from either side of the alley. It was by mere chance they found this place again.

As they were racing through the streets the night before, a memory flashed in Naemi's mind about something so trivial yet so nuanced.

*I know this area*, she thought.

A recognition that led them to a familiar space of comfort. It lacked warmth, quiet, or any sort of protection from the harshness of outside, but it was a space they could dwell in. The balance of chance — equally good and equally horrifying.

Naemi still barely had any sleep. Falling in and out of consciousness, her body feared the commitment. Her brother sat by her side, though he had no such issues. Through the growing noise, he rarely flinched, lost to dreams of happier days. Naemi retreated back to the solace of her thoughts, thinking of their way forward. They'd lost everything, again. The path ahead was blurred to her. With no money to find another ship and the lingering fear of going back to the trading halls, she questioned herself many times.

Questions without answers. She hated her naivety, the wounds of its consequences still bare. Open scars that taught lessons she would never forget. She needed to adapt to survive, for herself and for Dakai. She needed to leave the gullible girl whose life was of blissful horse rides, warm lakes, and beautiful sunsets. That life was in Soros, and she was far away from there. She continued on her assessment of self, fixating on change with a focus almost eerie. Among all she considered, one option stood in her mind — the Firu market, wherever that was, the third stall on the left of the white sculpture.

There was someone she could go to for help, whatever work she could get she would do it to make as much money as she could. That would be a start, and she would build from there. She turned to look at her brother still lost in slumber; the view calmed her and his agape mouth made her chuckle. She stretched her legs to escape the numbness that formed. The damp clothes made her skin feel tingly; it had a pungent smell and her feet had small sores she hadn't noticed. She needed new clothes and cover for her feet, they both did.

Naemi shook her brother and he jolted awake. She thought of giving him more time to sleep but the day was brightening and soon hunger would start creeping in. Better get to the market now and catch the farmer and his wife bright and early to seek work. Dakai stretched his limbs through a silly yawn, his eyes slowly adjusting to the early day's light.

"*You're already awake?*" he questioned through his yawn. His sister ignored his question, not realizing it was one and spoke of her thoughts to go see the family at the Firu market. Dakai agreed without refute, it was their best option and most likely their only.

"*We also need to find some other clothes, yours smells,*" Naemi commented.

"*Yours too,*" Dakai responded as his sister reached out and ripped part of his sleeve.

"*Put this on,*" she said, extending the cloth to him. Dakai let out a frustrated sigh and took the cloth from his sister. He stared at the wall and then above, taking one last look before covering his eyes.

———◦———

The walk through the streets was full of whispers, some loud and others solemn. Conversations sparking many rumors in faux detail. Many with their own theories for the cause of concern the previous night. Those who loved gossip drowned in its riches. The countless patrolling guards parading the city didn't help either. In such a delicate system of trade, security was paramount, and any threat of an attack prompted an adverse reaction from traders; an effect that wasn't favorable for the Alliance.

For this reason they responded strictly, showing a sign of strength and protection. Armored soldiers combed the city with hawk-like vigilance, searching for the unknown.

The siblings walked the road slowly, ears perked with full attention to soak all they could and asking questions to those who would answer. Sailor City wasn't known for the grandity of its army; in truth, their local population accounted for only three tenths of it, but for what they lacked in size, they made up in wealth and their wealth bought the finest regiments.

The siblings continued on, now with direction in mind they kept to their paces on the road to the Firu market. They stood out but not in a way that compelled notice; the poor are always invisible even when they don't intend to be.

Naemi pondered the endless rumors she heard, none any closer to reality. Most were asinine and full of paranoia. Worries of attacks, conspiracies and stories which had no meaning to her.

*If they only knew the truth, would they even care?*

The thought took her back in time to her second capture, inside the ship and the chains that wrapped her. She felt an uneasiness, the dreadful memories creeping out and her heart beginning to race. She stopped and pulled her hand away from Dakai's hastily.

A tension building in her, fading away the outside and leaving only the feeling of drowning. She fell to her knees, her heart racing more.

"*Naemi?*" Dakai called out. His voice sounded faint to her. Her heartbeat sounding in her eardrums. She needed to get calm and she knew it, the consequences of her last actions still fresh in her mind. Dakai called out again.

"*I'm fine ... I'm fine,*" she responded, steadying her breathing. She escaped to the only tranquility her mind could find and held on to it.

"*I'm fine,*" she repeated, reaching out to grab her brother's hand. The others who walked the road weren't so kind with their words for the two obstructing traffic. Most yelling obscenities and none showing concern. The siblings quickened their steps till they disappeared further into the crowd. She could feel the sting from the cuts on her feet with every step.

Firu market appeared as they reached the end of their directions, wooden stalls stretched plenty, each with its own unique touch. The commodities sold didn't hold such uniqueness, sellers with similar goods grouped in sectioned areas competing with one another. They hailed, hurled, grabbed and pleaded with buyers for an ounce of attention, a negotiation, an argument or surrender to a sale.

Their voices were like many waves clashing against each other. Mixtures of high and low pitches creating a symphony of chaotic voices. The siblings walked through the masses, still invisible to those who sought coin. Naemi searched for the landmark to lead her to the stall she sought, brushing past people and pulling Dakai along. Stepping deeper into the market, as she passed the tall stall that obstructed her view, the glare of light off the tip of the trident's blade flashed her face.

The giant carving of white stone stood about twenty feet tall, shiny and glorious in the middle of the two intersecting roads. The late sunrise magnifying its aura. Naemi stood at its base where the smaller sculptures lay; carvings all round of women fighting for the knight's attention. It was made with such intricate detail that she could see them come alive if she squinted hard enough. It took Dakai's question to get her out of admiration. She turned left then right, noticing the obvious flaw in the directions.

*She said left of the statue. Left from which side?* She thought, ignoring Dakai's follow up question. She moved round the landmark, looking for a familiar face but she saw none.

"*I can't find them,*" she muttered with panic, proceeding to every third stall to inquire. On her second, she noticed a section of sellers were absent. Grouped stalls without anyone available. She moved to the vendor closest by, a younger man with a cart full of oranges.

The man turned to look at the two strangers behind him as he stocked his cart with more produce from the cloth-sack.

"*I give one of you something and you all start coming here. I'm not a charity,*" he said sharply, and grabbed three oranges, shoving them in Naemi's hand. "*One more orange for the blind one and tell the rest of them this is the last of it,*" he ended.

Naemi looked at him confused, "*I'm not here for food, I'm just looking for someone. A farmer and his pregnant wife with a girl-child. They said they would be here to sell berries?*" she questioned.

"*You're looking for Raegu?*" He replied with an inquisitive stare.

"*Yes! Yes that's his name,*" Dakai answered with a weird enthusiasm.

The man looked at him with an awkward stare before returning his eyes to the girl, "*They're gone, all the berry sellers, all of em. Lucky bunch! Didn't even get to set up yesterday before some Dormish-man bought all their sacks for twice the price. Twice! I never get that lucky ... phh. Nobody buys that much oranges. It's always sweet-cane and berries to make shitty wine, who even likes wine?*" The man paused his rant, catching himself from his rattling. The sudden depressed expressions on the girl and boy before him played a heavy part. "*Uh, why you looking for Raegu anyway?*" He inquired gently with dashes of concern.

"*No reason.*" Naemi answered quietly, her disappointment shown in her words. As she turned to walk away, she stopped and turned back to the man, "*Do you need any help selling your oranges? I am a good worker, I can help a lot, and ... and my friend won't be of any bother; we'll take any payment you can give us.*"

The man stared back with eyes that lost their luster and responded, "*I'm sorry kid, I don't have any work to give. I'm barely making a profit on these,*" echoing Naemi's disappointment. He watched as the two children left on to another stall and another, on and on till they vanished behind the swarm of bodies that indulged in their cursed routines.

The rejections kept on until the siblings felt the energy drained from them, some rejections more aggressive than the former. There was no mystical work available for them, nothing to give them enough money for a day's meal let alone passage on a ship. Some sellers asked Naemi to work for no wage, others offered her work on the premise she gave intimate pleasures, and others just laughed in the faces of the siblings.

The ordeal furthered their anguish so much they returned to the only peaceful place they knew, their food for the day being the three oranges they lucked into. Dakai proposed they ration it not knowing where their next meal would come from, an idea that proved helpful the next day. They survived the early parts of the next day on just an orange and a half, water from wherever they could find the cleanest water that could pass as drinkable, and walking the streets hoping for a miracle lest they sleep hungry. But the well of luck had run dry.

Going back to the market on this day, the man denied them more oranges.

"*I told you it would be the last,*" he said with sober eyes.

"*You won't stop coming if I keep giving them to you,*" he added.

They could feel the frailty that grew as their bodies yearned for nourishment.

"*Maybe we should have stayed in the forest.*"

Naemi told Dakai that evening, her heart didn't mean the words, but her hunger did. Sleep was their only solace and they forced slumber till the pain resumed the next day.

In their desperation, they explored other parts of the city. They heard of another market in the west and hoped for better tidings from newer strangers. The day was gloomy and the clouds blanketed the sun at its brightest.

The streets still flowed with gossip and anxiety, and the siblings paced slowly in their quest for better. Passing by a crowded group, Dakai stopped after a few steps anchoring Naemi in place. She turned to look at her brother with perplexity, but he just stood quietly.

"*Dakai? What is it?*" She inquired, but he was silent.

"*That isn't possible. The Kaku are all dead and their empire is nothing but wastelands now, fought over by savages. The Alliance made sure of that. I'd be more worried if you said the Vikinglands of the west.*" A voice said from the gathered group. Five men congregated in heavy dispute though nothing stood out more than the words that were just said. It was the first time they'd heard it since capture and the intrigue froze them.

"*The west have no interests here, it's folly to think they are our enemies,*" a second voice chimed through a faint pitch.

"*They are no allies either! Who knows what those deranged brutes will do,*" the first man shot back. He added, "*We have no enemies worth concerning about. Our Last was crushed into nothingness by the Alliance and all that remains are their shriveled bones in dust. Not even the great Kaku dynasty survived our wrath.*"

A man from the group burst out laughing, another by his side joining him.

"*You take too much credit for the Kaku's demise when the Alliance had nothing to do with it. I've traveled far and heard all the tales. Stories of how they killed each other with their sorcery. The mysterious power they had and how they subdued their own people in cruelty. I heard it all, even how the Alliance cowered at the feet of their King. Don't try to change what has already been written in history,*" his voice carried a strange diction, foreign in nature.

"*History? You know nothing. They were spawns of evil. Their rulers carried the eyes of fiends. You haven't lived long enough to know what immorality they spread in their empire, the bloodlust they carried, even to their own people. The Barbaric rituals in their royal clan. The strange sorcery that shielded their empire. How easy do you think it was for the Alliance to fester the civil war over a quarter-century ago. They fought like animals for the throne, killing off their own family for power. In the end, all that was left was a weakling boy-king who was impaled to death by his own guards. I say good riddance to their extermination.*" The first man spat with vehemence, straining his voice to get every word out clearly. His expressions were nothing short of pure loathing and he wore it proudly.

"*So history should be changed to grace the Alliance as saviors? As the architects of the fall of the Kaku empire?*" the other laughing man responded through giggles. A response which clearly agitated the former.

As tensions rose and tempers ascended to flare, the feeble toned man sought reason, "*Why are we even arguing about dead men? I say some fool left a candle-lamp close to oil barrels on the ship, nothing more. It was no attack.*" Others agreed with him hoping to diffuse the friction that brewed between the two. In the midst of the mild chaos, one noticed Naemi's focused stare at the group.

"And *what are you looking at, girl?*" He shouted, prompting the group to follow his gaze. Naemi pulled Dakai away with quick steps, and the siblings vanished behind buildings. Dakai was still quiet, unresponsive to any of Naemi's queries. The revelation was digested differently on both ends; Naemi soaked it in and let it pass, her mind on the present and not on words of people she had no care for. Dakai on the other had pondered on it to every last detail. To him, this was the genesis to all his troubles, the reason why he was walking on a strange land lost and hungry, the reason why he was taken from his home.

This continued henceforth, a silence that stagnated even till sundown. They sat by each other on the side of the road as many passed, but their minds were leagues apart. Naemi was getting used to the pain; it wasn't hurting as much and felt more of a mild discomfort. The pain was displaced by another emotion — envy. It was a new feeling for her, and she felt the build-up of it looking at the riches that passed her by. People with plentiful not willing to spare even a drop to save them both from destitution. She didn't fully understand this emotion, being something she'd never felt before, and she didn't want to understand it.

Her thoughts battled against each other on the new possibilities this emotion prompted, a battle that lasted through the dawn of the next morning. Dakai was too weak to leave their dwelling today; he kept to himself and spoke little words. She could see the exhaustion in his eyes and it strengthened the resolve in her decision — if they had nothing to live on, they might as well take from others who had plenty.

A sentiment that flared in her through the previous night. Seeing her weakened brother increased her conviction. *They had to do whatever to survive till they got home.* The thought that accompanied her pursuit.

Leaving her brother alone was hard for her, but she saw no other way. They could either stay cramped in this little space and starve to death, or she could use the little energy she had to find food.

"*I'll return soon. Stay here and don't go anywhere. I will find us food. Just stay. I'll be back soon.*"

Dakai nodded lightly; he could feel the lightness in his body and the feebleness he carried. He curled up more in the corner, watching as his sister left, too exhausted to think. He closed his eyes to the blankness in his head and hoped for time to pass. Like being stuck in a dark chamber devoid of any light or sense of change.

He could feel an appreciation for the darkness, the numerous blindfolding had warped his senses and the thing that felt scariest to do was now his solace. He had made his mind wander too far earlier, thinking of extinct people, thinking of his guilt, thinking of his eyes and his future. He had seen too much of the world and he hated what he saw.

*Is this the reason my father shielded me the whole time?*

When he thought of his mother, no picture appeared. He remembered small details like the color of her hair and the color of her eyes, but her face was lost to him. He tried filling in the pieces he missed but the person he created was unknown. He shut his mind down again. Every single thought just flamed into thousands and all he could do to get calm was retreat to his dark chamber.

Today's morning brought little warmth, better than what they experienced the previous night. Dakai didn't realize when he slept again but he woke to a pleasant aroma filling his nose. Naemi held up the roasted pork and corn to him with a giant smile grazing her lips. He rubbed sleep from his eyes hoping to also rub away what he thought were dreams but weren't.

The food was as real as the girl who stood before him beckoning him to eat. He lunged into the meat, like a caged animal freed from capture. The meat was juicy, warm, and tender to his tongue. It tasted as if it was the sweetest thing he'd ever had until he tasted the corn which bested it, an effect of extreme absence. Naemi watched her brother devour the food, patting him on the back to calm him. She took out the skin-bag full of water and offered him a drink which he took to satisfaction.

"*Whe ... Where did you get all this?*" he asked with a mouthful.

"*I got lucky. Don't worry about it, just eat,*" she answered with a smile, watching her brother pounce on more food. She sat by his side taking a bite of some corn laughing at Dakai's unorthodox eating ways and her mind at ease. Only a few words strayed in her thoughts.

*We will be okay ... We will survive.*

## CHAPTER TEN

# LOVE, FURY, CARNAGE

The weeks passed in a promising turn. The changing seasons on the horizon. Soon will come the heavy rains and dark clouds, and the great ball of fire will be pushed back the line of succession.

Two ships to home missed. It'd been over a week since the ship to the Prim shore left; the siblings watched it leave, a little of their hope leaving with it. In eight days, the silk ship to Shoretown will depart and they had to be on it at all cost.

The time that had passed came with much enlightenment about their new region of residence. The anxiety of an attack had withered down somewhat, but security still stood unmoved; a factor that caused a couple of close calls for Naemi, though her good fortune always found her on the side of escape.

Words of protection were spread by the Alliance through their foot soldiers. Sheets of assurance littering the streets with ink and paper.

A home lost and another gained, the siblings were pushed out their beloved corner when lurking eyes pried too intensely. They found their new abode at the top of a three-story building. A little section that was started but never finished turned into their new space of comfort.

A few broken boards to support the erected tent and long heavy cloth for coverage, it became a massive improvement than the former. It had more space, was warmer, harder to notice from prying eyes and had a view of magnificence. The coming heavy rains would thwart the said comfort in the future, but to the siblings that wasn't a future they needed to care for.

———◆◯◆———

Naemi walked the city this early night, some paces behind two staggering drunk men and the women they accompanied. There had been some light showers of rain earlier, and the darkening sky still echoed the aftermath. She had seen one of the men from before, flaunting his riches in his purple linen robe and rich fabric, splurging on trades. She noticed the heavy purse he kept in the slit of his upper breast robe.

The silk green bag with its yellowish lacing. She had pursued him for long, blending behind crowds and buildings to avoid notice, her eyes waiting patiently for a moment in time to engage her target. The past had been good to her, her coffers rising with coins though it still wasn't enough for payment home. About twenty-five gold coins so far, not counting the ones for food and new clothes. Half of what they'll need to pay off passage to the silk trader.

Time was fast passing, and she needed a bigger payoff soon, but a bigger payoff came in proportion with bigger risk, risk that was increased further by the growing vigilance to thievery. Nonetheless, she leaned more on her desperation and luck to overcome the odds, hunting her prey as wild animals do; steady and stealthy.

She moved away from the light.

The ones that stretched through windows brightening sections of the street that were void of light-lamps. Escaping the rays that highlighted parts of her skin and the sleeved tunic shirt she wore.

Her dark pants merging with the shadows and her goat-skinned boots kissing the wet ground softly lest the sound of splattering rainwater give off her presence. The roads were clear but for the four in front of her, a simple grab and dash and she'd be more coins closer to getting home.

Focused and ready, she began her steps to intercept. Four steps in and she felt someone pull her viciously into darkness. Hands that held her from screaming and shading her in cover. Her fear triggered a beginning to her defense system, the one that promised mayhem every time it was summoned.

"*It's a trap, stay quiet.*" The person whispered behind her.

The voices of the loud drunks had disappeared. Slurred speech turned into suspicious silence and then back to loud slurred speech. The steps faded further and curiosity replaced her fears. When the figure revealed itself, his short golden hair, light green eyes and pale white skin couldn't be misidentified.

Kainu wore an awkward smile.

"*Heyyy,*" he said with more awkwardness.

Naemi's curiosity was now a visible annoyance.

"*Sorry I pulled you too hard. Uhh are you okay?*" he continued.

Naemi's response was a stare of irritation, one that lingered longer than she intended. She broke her stare and walked away, an act that prompted Kainu to follow with more questions.

When she reached the limit to his buzzing, she barked at him.

"*Stop following me. Stay away from me.*"

"*I've seen you almost get caught more than once. You're being reckless. You think you know the city well but you don't. They're setting traps everywhere and they will not just throw you in a dungeon, they will do worse, way worse. I know you need money, I know someone who can help. He can help you get a better yield than drunks on the street,*" Kainu replied, one that paused Naemi in her steps.

"*Help? You left us when we needed your help, you didn't want our troubles, remember? And now you offer it freely? For what in exchange? I know it's not out of the goodness of your heart.*" Her eyes stared intently into his as he struggled to find words of response. Before he could speak, she concluded, "*I don't need your help for anything. Stay away from me.*"

The anger flowed with her words leaving Kainu more speechless. He watched as she left, with no more words to utter, a failed attempt at reconciliation. He would think to try again another time, his reasoning not of pure selflessness.

Naemi wandered home with tension. The damp roads still on its recovery to dryness from the light rain that fell earlier. Her disappointment wore heavy on her face. She'd hoped for more coins today, a hope that never turned to reality. Her frustrations and encounter playing back in her head.

*Maybe I should be grateful to him*, she thought.

She could have been captured or caused another incident, one she might not have been fortunate to escape a second time. She did need help. With the ship's departure getting closer, she had to do whatever she could for her and her brother to be passengers, but seeking help from someone untrustworthy was the last thing she would do, her scars bearing witness.

She had gotten this far and she would do anything to get to the end. Regardless, it was going to be much harder to reach the end, a fact which she knew with certainty.

She moved the board that covered the opening to their dwelling, the one that closed the hole in the floor as she climbed up the back-side of the building. It was a tricky climb up, one she had mastered from the many times she had to scale the walls, though there was more stability the higher she climbed. She heard a voice call her name from inside.

*"Yes, it's me,"* she responded.

Dakai emerged into view, stretching a hand out to help his sister.

"*How was work? You're back early,*" he said. Naemi answered with a light grunt and nonchalance, stepping inside and moving toward their make-shift bed. A little candle stood on the hard floor caressing a small flame on its wick. Dakai moved closer to his unresponsive sister.

"*Are you okay?*" he questioned to more silence.

"*Are you feeling the change in your body again? Did anything happen? What happened?*" he pursued.

"*Dakai, stop!*" she yelled at her brother, silencing him.

Dakai retreated from her, stepping outside their enclosure on the thought that she needed some space to herself. Her disgruntlement was visible in her expressions and he worried.

Her frustrations could be from the work she claimed she was doing, work given by the unknown trader who hired her to help with moving goods to market. A job he doubted existed, though all his prying to uncover the truth went nowhere.

She always avoided his questions or replied with vague answers. He pondered if it should matter what work she did as long as they could get money to survive and get passage home, but it did matter; it mattered to him.

———◆———

The dark blue above sparkled with scattered dots of white. The clouds shaded the skies, some with a faint opacity still lingering too long after the rain. Humidity danced with the breeze surrounded by a chilling cloak. Sounds from loud parts of the city disturbed the calm in others, offsetting the balance. It was almost peak of night and Dakai was still sitting outside.

The chill felt more comforting on his skin, and he stayed in its embrace. The day had been eventful in his sister's absence, just as some others had been before. A secret he shared with himself. One spawned from a mixture of boredom and the need to understand the changes he felt in his eyes. The pursuit bore more fruit today, one he wouldn't fully comprehend.

He had been leaving their dwelling against his sister's strict instructions, not into the streets, but onto the flat roofs of buildings close by to see the city more without the need to be blinded.

It started off as an innocent exploration, a simple freedom to see around without the risk of someone noticing his pied eyes, that was until he met her, the girl with the flowered hair. He saw her the first time through her opened window, his eyes invading her privacy, noticing the colored daffodils she kept in her hair and the bliss on her face as she danced in her room.

She was the most beautiful being he'd ever seen, and his gaze lurked long enough to be caught. He ran when he met her eyes, waiting two days before venturing to the same area again. He knew it was wrong to go but his selfish desires trumped logic and he went anyway. He returned to a closed window as he peeked behind the short walls on the adjacent roof.

*"Do you go around staring at girls through windows,"* a voice said from behind him, and he turned to meet her face.

He melted instantly or at least his heart did, fumbling on words to respond.

The colors in her hair brightened her face two-fold. Her white dress stood as a canvas, and even her stern look couldn't hide the elegance she carried. They were of similar age from what he could tell, and she stood holding an oversized stick with both hands ready to swing.

He didn't remember what he said to calm her down, but she calmed, and he kept on till he made her laugh. When she laughed, he felt his body tingle and his mind forget everything that existed.

For once he discovered an emotion far from constant pain and sorrow, and he held onto it with all he had. It'd been about two weeks into their friendship and he'd told her everything. His kidnap from home, his escape, his adventure through the forests and in Sailor City, and his eyes.

A clearly unwise decision made without thought, but in her presence all the decisions he made were without thought. They talked for hours every day, him leaving just in time to make it home before nightfall.

She also told him everything about herself , her two brothers and three sisters, her parents who both worked as sculptors, her love for pottery and fondness of flowers, and her dreams of a giant mangled house-cat chasing her through cornfields.

Their time together was serene, funny, full of joy, a calm through a thundering storm in Dakai's life and he loved every moment of it.

When they talked about his ability and his need to know more about it, she said, "*Try it on me, see what you can learn,*" It was a harmless suggestion that started their activity of him trying to look into her memories, something that failed time and time again, until today.

Today was the first time he intentionally held onto a memory long enough to see it entirely. One of her with a pet bird she had when she was nine.

"*Giwi!*" she exclaimed, smiling from ear to ear as Dakai described the memory. She was ecstatic and in her excitement, kissed him gently on his left cheek. His face glowed with a heavy blush and he felt his breath leave him.

So as he sat under tonight's deep blue, as the skies kept getting darker with their shining sparkles in the far beyond, only one thing captured his entire being, his new found love — Davina.

Naemi turned around another time, looking behind her with hope of capturing hidden figures in pursuit, but there were none, only bustling people who could care less of her existence.

Her irritation hadn't simmered since morning, and as late afternoon approached, it seemed to get no better; Kainu's words still fanning the flames. Another slow day at work for her, and not for the lack of targets. She questioned everything and everyone, too much suspicion causing a sea of paranoia in her head.

*Are any of them more traps? I can't get caught.*

She could tell how the day would go having experienced empty yields before.

Another day without coin, another day full of frustrations. She snapped at Dakai again yesterday, which was the third time in the past week. She hated the exhaustion, depression and anger that came with the expectations. She hated lashing out at the only person who could understand her pain and be there for her, but her fears kept mounting and her will seeped.

She kept on regardless, doing her best to keep together, still searching for luck's golden touch. The southern part of the city was as loud as usual, the streets still as full. It was a personal rule of hers to move consistently through different parts of the city to avoid familiarity from strangers as well as shifting through multiple clothes, though she didn't have many clothes to sift through.

As Naemi struggled to escape familiarity from others, familiarity from herself flashed her eyes.

In the red and silver a few feet from her. She knew those slanted shoulders, that physique, the voice that laughed loud in the midst of friends as her curled brownish hair wobbled to her insouciance.

Naemi stared at the woman deeply, everything fading out of existence and only she remained — the person responsible for her being sold into slavery. The one who led her into chains with smiles and promises of home stood unaware of her outcome. She watched the woman joke and be merry with her group with no regard or regret for the lives she threw in cages, and Naemi's resentment grew.

Naemi could feel the pulsating in her heart seething with insurmountable anger, an anger that had pushed past its peak. She hated her, more than she had ever hated anything in her life.

There was another growing sensation in her, a sudden tension that stood in the depths of her soul, not like the others she'd experienced. It wasn't unbridled or chaotic like the ones she'd known before — no, this stood stagnant and controlled, fitting every part of her body like armor.

Her eyes focused on the woman with a soul full of wrath, but her body didn't move a muscle.

The Alliant woman bid farewell to her group and got on her way, oblivious to the calamity that pursued her. Naemi followed some ways back, her steps neither cracking the land nor lifting her high. She had thought of the woman many times before with a fear she might end up in chains again if they met, but the sight of her today floated emotions she didn't know she had.

Through the crowds, from one stop to another, she followed close and unnoticed, everything else bearing no relevance. Their last stop was far west of the city, a two-level house with roofing made of a light red hue. The door and window casings were of darkened brown wood and more wood moved around the outer walls in an irregular mesh. The rest of the walls were made of lightened gray bricks except for the top of a peaking chimney that was covered in black stone.

Two toddlers came running to greet her with an older male teen behind. She picked the youngest up with a smile, her other hand grasping the bags she brought while the other younger child bickered. Naemi stood out of sight with her eyes still in sight of the house and the shadows that moved by the curtains when they entered. Light turned dark and her eyes never moved off the house. Hours passed and she waited still. She saw the passing shadows and heard the faint voices that seeped out, none wavering her emotions.

Every part of her was numb but for her heart and mind. Soon the darkness came with quiet, a darkness that fed her urges.

---

The window on the top right side of the building was open and she climbed into it, swinging the small doors to get more space to fit into the room. Inside was filled with low breathing that came with asynchrony.

Two small beds at opposite ends with the two little boys in peaceful slumber. Naemi's eyes gazed at them, the flames still burning intensely, she opened the door to a light creak and moved to the next room.

The next was filled with a heavy snore and an older boy lying carelessly stretched on his cotton bed and dreams filling his head. Before Naemi opened the last door she paused, a brief call to sanity which was overshadowed in an instant.

The woman lay quiet in her bed, a table by the corner with a half-melted candle and inked parchments. Her bed was fit in the middle of the room fixed to the wall and left of it was a wooden cabinet full of closed shelves. There was a hanger rack next to the closet, and clothes filled its branches to the brim. Naemi walked to the lady at rest, her peace irritating her more.

Blue light leaked through the closed glass window coloring her skin as she slept. Naemi stood beside the sleeping woman, her face gazing directly down at her prey, and her cast shadow filling her sights with more darkness. Her aura spreading with such intensity, a probable reason why the woman opened her eyes to the menace that stared down at her.

Naemi's hand reached to grab the woman's throat the moment her target's eyes opened, as if instinct kicked in. Something that was so unknown to her now felt so simple.

She could feel it, like a sixth sense, a sensation coursing through her skin. A power that was always full of chaos becoming contained through her fury.

Naemi could feel the life drain as she held her. The woman's eyes were bloodshot, her mouth opened without words and her body was too feeble to move the weight that restrained her. Naemi got closer so the woman could see her face. She wanted to be recognized, it wouldn't be justice if she didn't know who was passing it. She released the pressure in her hands.

"*Do you remember me?*" Naemi spewed in a low whispered tone of vehemence. The woman struggled to catch her breath, water coming from her eyes, nose and mouth.

Naemi echoed again, "*Do you remember me?*"

She saw the transition, from sudden fear to recognition to tearful remorse.

Naemi's hands still massaged her neck slowly, teasing the temptation. The lady nodded, tears wetting her pillows and her skin folding into large ripples.

*"You took us from our family. You killed our friends. You sold us like we were nothing. We just wanted to go home. We didn't deserve any of this. Why did you do this to us?"*

There was great melancholy in her voice, like the woman was the representation of the world, everything that had wronged her and everything she hated.

*"I ... I ... I already sold it ... I'm sss ... sorry. I sold it ... I don't have the m ... money. Ittt ... itss gone ... I'm sorryy."*

Tears flowed hard as the woman spoke, her eyes saying more words than her mouth did.

She continued, *"ppease ... I have children. Pleaas donkill mme. They won't survive witthou me."*

Naemi heard her words and paid little attention to them, her apologies and gibberish did nothing but increase her annoyance. She looked into her eyes more, her scattered thoughts finally converging to a final conclusion.

*"You don't deserve to live."*

And with those words squeezed the neck in her grasp as life began to fade from the struggling body beneath her.

She heard a little creak from behind, so faint it was a surprise it registered to her conscience. She turned to see a boy of three standing by the opened door with a wooden toy boar in hand, gazing at her and the quaking body on the bed. He stood there quietly, the white and blue in his eyes striking through the moon's blue light.

Naemi let go immediately, the realization of what she was doing finally setting in.

The Alliant woman gasped hard for air, coughing repeatedly while shouting at the top of her strained voice for help. In moments, the help she sought came, starting with steps being heard pounding the stairs and voices of concern from outside.

Those who got to the room first would speak to seeing the face of a frenzied woman, with a look only those who have ever experienced the presence of a demon can attest to.

The face of a clueless child concerned about the well-being of its mother.

And shattered window glass from an assailant who had escaped deep into the night.

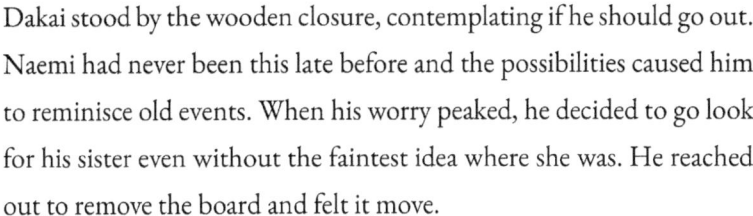

Dakai stood by the wooden closure, contemplating if he should go out. Naemi had never been this late before and the possibilities caused him to reminisce old events. When his worry peaked, he decided to go look for his sister even without the faintest idea where she was. He reached out to remove the board and felt it move.

"*Naemi?*" he shouted and heard his sister's patented response. She pushed the board away quickly, and rushed inside before hurrying to close it. She bolted the make-shift door with her body, her back tight against the board as she sat against it.

She was panting hysterically, and there was complete anxiety on her face. Dakai called out to her another time, confused at her state. She was mumbling words to herself and he noticed the tiny shards of glass in her hair and clothes.

*"Naemi. I'm here. It's okay. I'm here. Tell me what happened?"* he spoke softly, doing his best to calm his sister. Naemi looked at him, her eyes filled with guilt and dejection; she hurtled at her brother, hugging him as tight as she could. The hate that had built up inside her had reached its summit and she poured it all out the only way she knew how. In her brother's embrace — she cried.

———◆○◆———

A full day passed, the siblings stayed in throughout the past day; sleeping, talking, and eating parts of their food reserves. Dried bread and dried cow meat. The swallow was hard on the throat and the chew even harder on the jaws. Water helped a bit. Dakai fantasized it tasting like fresh milk, though he hadn't tasted some in days. A trick that compelled his body into accepting more of the food than he could handle.

Naemi had no such problem, eating without any restrictions. She had told Dakai everything, from the false work she claimed to do, to Kainu's appearance and her descent into iniquity with the force inside her.

The weight on her shoulders fell off as the words left her and her emotions steadied in her heart. Talking to her brother was always a remedy she could count on, and even though it wasn't the easiest to bare her soul, she felt some comfort in having someone to rely on. Dakai was understanding through all their conversations, offering every ounce of support to his sister.

They talked at length as they had many times before, but the conversations were lopsided — the sister exposing her secrets and the brother keeping his to his chest.

Today felt peaceful for Naemi. Two days after her storm, the calm had set in overshadowing her worry, though the worry still existed. She wasn't any closer to fully understanding the power inside her. Dakai drew to her attention the correlations between her heightened emotions and the accompanying trigger it caused. A note she took to mind.

Her other problems still existed, fighting to escape the locked box she kept them in. Regardless, she continued to persevere, emptying her thoughts to the pseudo serenity she created. One that helped relax her spirits and she felt a soothing sensation she hadn't known in a while.

The ground massaged Naemi's body under the heavy cloth that functioned as a bed. Her skin was used to its touch and overlooked the discomfort. Her eyes were closed to force sleep that never came. Her ears searched for sounds when they weren't supposed to. She could barely hear Dakai outside; he had a new habit of sitting silently on the flat roof with his thoughts and the chaotic view of the city.

Naemi still lay in their enclosure, a wobbling tent built inside a smaller uncompleted structure atop the building, covering the rear right quadrant of the flat roof. The smaller structure had three walls erected about six feet tall on the back and sides, and the shorter layer on the front not even tall enough to qualify a fourth wall. The structure had no rooftop and large pieces of cut wood spread everywhere. It was an organized mess and the only solace they could afford, provided they kept themselves invisible to its owners.

Naemi's ears finally caught something worth opening her eyes for. The wooden board that covered their doorway was moving, a rattling sound from someone pushing against its barricade.

Naemi rushed outside the tent and met her brother's eyes hurrying to inspect the source of the sound. They both glanced at each other with worried looks; their only escape from here was a long jump on either end to the adjacent building rooftops, an option Naemi didn't fancy.

"*It's Kaise, please open. I know you're there.*" The siblings shared looks again. No one was supposed to know where they lived. Kaise repeated her words and Dakai felt compelled to remove the bricks that held the board tethered to the floor. Kaise rolled in breathing heavily.

"*I thought I was going to fall,*" she said panting and giggling.

"*What do you want?*" Naemi blurted. Kaise sensed the mismatch in tension and began to apologize. Naemi repeated her demand mid apology, her brown eyes staring into the opposite light green.

"*Mamuex has asked to see you.*" Kaise said.

"*Who?*" Dakai interjected, echoing Naemi's clueless expression.

"*She is the one who saved you from being caught. She cares for all the strayed children in Sailor City, and she has asked to see you,*" Kaise replied, looking at Naemi.

"*What does she want from us? What did you tell her about us?*" Naemi questioned with a hint of agitation.

Kaise still wore her soft expressions, her patterned look of cheer now covered with a layer of dampness.

"*We didn't tell her anything ... not until some days ago. And she wants to see only you. You caught her attention on your own with all your actions. All the gold you've been stealing. She wants to offer you more work.*"

"*I don't want more work from anyone. Your brother came to me with a similar offer to work for some man. Is this some kind of trick? You both left us in the cold when we needed your help and now you show up full of it. We don't want it. Tell whoever it is to leave us alone.*" Naemi responded.

Dakai watched the exchange of words between the girls, reluctant to engage. He was hardly digesting everything his sister had told him before, doing his best to be supportive, and seeing Kaise exposed another layer in their convoluted journey. His feelings toward the twins weren't as strong as his sister's, but their callous desertion did leave a scar.

His concern still lay most with his sister, the burden she carried and the changes that formed before him. He contemplated on them, oblivious to the changes that formed in himself. The lashing out continued, their voices rising, forgetting their presence of invisibility in their rented hideout.

As he stood watching, Dakai attempted something he shouldn't have. Staring at Kaise's yellow flowing hair, her round contoured face with warm eyes and a sharp descending nose shadowing her thinned lips. He stared deeply into her mind, focusing all the senses he learned to cultivate.

His growing hubris in his secret ability. Her mind opened to him, taking him to a location he couldn't control.

A memory of a winter night, her body shivering to the tune of the cold and her ears soothed by a calming song. She sat on the side of the street next to another, both covered in tattered brown sack-cloths for warmth. Her eyes looked to the younger boy beside her, the skin on his face hugging the bone tightly, and his sunken eyes staring back with kindness. His lips moved in a solemn melody; a child's rhyme of a gone mother coming home soon.

*"Mother, it's been too long, the sun is down."*
*"Mother, it's been too long, the night has frowned."*
*"I will be waiting for your return with open arms."*
*"To feel your loving embrace and warming sounds."*
*"Your brave heart will keep me safe."*
*"It will fight all the darkness away."*
*"Till you return I won't close my eyes."*
*"Till you return I will stare into the night.*
*"Mother, it's been too long, the sun is down."*
*"Mother, it's been too long, the night has frowned."*

The song repeated in Dakai's head as the memory faded and before he could stop, another memory pulled him in.

*"You don't understand, she's not asking. She only sent me here to convince you because you didn't listen to Kainu,"* Kaise responded to Naemi in defense.

*"I said leave!"* Naemi reiterated.

As they argued, Dakai dropped to his knees, his mind failing to hold on from the stress he was putting it through. Naemi rushed to him, questioning him constantly.

"*I'm okay, I'm okay,*" he answered trying to regain control of his mind.

Kaise also tried helping, an attempt which was shot down by Naemi. Facing unwavering hostility, Kaise retreated, finally deciding to leave, her last words remaining with the siblings long after she was gone.

"*There are more traps being set to catch robbers. If you keep on, you will end up in the dungeons. Mamuex can protect you.*"

The day of the ship's departure to Shoretown fast approached. Advancing faster than could be appreciated. The preparations of the Zenu siblings were near complete except for what mattered most — payment.

Naemi found the silk trader's ship in Dock five a fortnight back, managing to confirm transport and its availability with the Alliant present in the region. Fifty gold coins was what was demanded, and some extra for his silence on where a young teen gets all that coin from. It had taken too much just to get half of that and finding the rest felt impossible in the growing circumstance.

Naemi paced the Northern part of the city scouting for a potential target. She had wasted too much time dealing with her emotions. The reality that stared back at her was grim and she had to keep on lest they lose opportunity again. She had made it this far, and only a half-step remained.

Twenty-five gold coins then home.

Kaise's words still hovered in her mind. She weighed the risk of capture versus her distrust for the twins and whoever they were endorsing, and the risk of capture won.

*I'm fast enough to escape, and if not, I will use whatever is inside me to free myself,* was the conclusion that settled in her head. She walked through the crowds with her head in the clouds distracted from her primary purpose.

The scent of cinnamon and fresh pie caught her senses, drawing her attention back to existence. She always passed this bakery when she walked this area and her body always had the same reaction.

The scent of the bread out of the oven, the smell of sweet pies and banana cakes held her nose captive and she loved it. It reminded her of her trips to the baker back in Soros and the memories put a smile on her face. She gazed into the bakery's open doors, the people who ventured into it only to come out with prizes of sweet pastry. How she wished she could spend some money on those delicacies. Her face told a story of her mouth-watering urges and she stood there subservient.

*"I hear they sell some of the best almond cakes in the city."*

The voice from behind her was low-toned and mellowed, almost feminine. Naemi turned to face the source, first seeing the woolskin sandals and painted toe-nails, the long greenish robe with graceful white embroidery, the short heavy curled black hair heaped on his head like many tiny circles, the skin on his face whiter than other parts from the beauty powder used.

He had more face paint than most women Naemi had encountered, more colorful ones on his eyelids and his lips distorted by the thinly layered beard that lined the lower part of his cheeks converging on his chin.

"*Do you want some?*" He added as Naemi gazed at him with an expression he was used to.

"*Umm ... Uhh ... no, thank you. I was only looking,*" Naemi apologized.

The man took a small burlap bag from inside the slit of his robe, took out some coin and began to head inside the store.

"*You sure? They smell really good, it'd be a shame to miss out.*" Naemi's eyes widened when she saw the loads of shiny yellow currency the man had, and he was right; the pastries were too good to miss out on.

This was most likely a golden opportunity to get everything she wanted in one fell swoop, so she went along into the bakery, finally in full exposure to the lake of flavor.

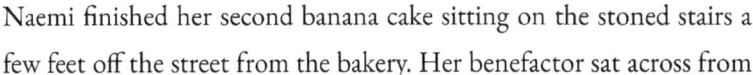

Naemi finished her second banana cake sitting on the stoned stairs a few feet off the street from the bakery. Her benefactor sat across from her, finishing the last piece of his almond cake and showing animated pleasure for the pastry.

The man had a curiosity of her and talked continuously, and she strung him along until she could find opportunity to take what would be hers soon.

*"I forgot how good these tasted. This place hasn't changed at all,"* he said, finishing the last bite to more animation.

*"I see you're saving some for later,"* the man commented, giggling at the sight.

*"So where are your parents?"* he asked.

*"My mother sells clothes at the Firu Market and my father is a guard at the Salem gates. They both left some money for me to buy food but my older sister took all of it and left to be with her friends. I just got really hungry and hoped someone would give me some of their leftover bread,"* Naemi answered through sad sentiment.

*"Older sisters can be very mean. I should know, I had two,"* he said in comfort. The conversation continued for about a half hour full of giggles, advice, and reminiscing.

At the end, Naemi sought her leave with a quick goodbye. As she stepped down the stair, the man remarked,

*"You have very quick hands, I'm actually impressed. I didn't think you could get it."*

Naemi hesitated in her step.

*"There's no need to run, I'm sure I won't be able to catch you ... though I can't promise your brother's safety once you're gone. Dakai is his name right?"*

Naemi's heart skipped a couple of beats at his words, the forewarned capture flashing her eyes as she scrambled her thoughts for an escape.

*"Sorry, that was a tad too rough, an unfortunate habit in my line of work. I can already see the desperation growing in your eyes. Your brother is fine. I'm sure he's exactly where you left him. I only want to talk. I've heard so much about you in a very short amount of time. Kainu and Kaise sing your praises,"* he mentioned with an eerily comforting cheer, and beckoned for Naemi to come sit back down. A gesture she obeyed.

*"You are Mamuex?"* She questioned.

*"That's what my children call me. You are new here, aren't you? And let's be truthful this time."*

The many options Naemi pondered all failed to provide a solid plan for evasion and she concluded on staying put, their conversation taking a swift turn from what it was before. Naemi nodded to the man's question.

*"Someday I'd like to know how you were the only one to escape the ship that caused so much chaos in the city. There are a lot of people who would love to find you, but I can keep that our little secret if you do something for me too. Mmhm?"* he continued with a suggestive look. Naemi nodded again to his request.

*"I have something I need from ... call it a competitor, and your talents fit the kind of skills that I'm looking for. It's a very special item that will mean a lot to me if it was retrieved. It will be a lot of money for your troubles. You won't have to be pilfering on streets anymore and it will also buy my silence of whatever I might know about you. You seem to have a*

*knack for getting out of troublesome situations, so I'm sure you can handle yourself right?"*

Naemi stared at him, realizing the demand that was phrased as a question. She weighed her options carefully, accounting for all she knew and all she thought he would know about her. When she finished, she nodded again to the delight of the man.

A wide smile creased his lips and he stood up to leave.

"Great! *Kainu will come to you tonight. Be prepared. Also think of the money you took as a good-willed advance for your services,"* he concluded, and left strolling through the crowd.

Naemi watched his disappearing trail.

What seemed to be an outcome to her actions of survival had presently caught up to her, and there was a fear of what might lay ahead. Her options were simple. She could run with her brother, find another place to hide or even leave the city for good. Though it didn't seem the man was someone they could hide from for long, and leaving the city meant leaving access to all the ships that could take them home. She could also refuse outright, return the money already taken with an apology, an option that felt doomed from its conception.

The last that remained was to go through with it. A choice that came with heavy risk and heavy reward, one that offered both money and a final end to her afflictions in Sailor City. Once she had the payment, nothing else would matter and no one would be able to control her actions.

Her looming fear did poke at her distrust of everything that was happening and she held faith in her secret advantage. She counted the value of her steal and showed content at the valued twelve new gold coins in her possession. As the late afternoon approached, with nothing left to do than wait for her planned encounter tonight, she set her eyes toward home, eager to discuss the revelation with her brother.

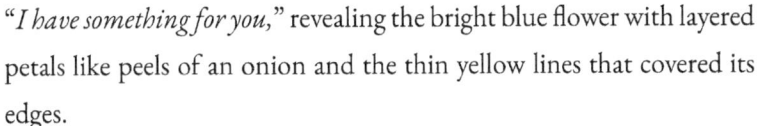

*"I have something for you,"* revealing the bright blue flower with layered petals like peels of an onion and the thin yellow lines that covered its edges.

Its dark green stem holding it up high in exaltation.

*"I saw it early today and it made me think of you,"* Davina spoke with a willful excitement and Dakai echoed her smile. He smelled the gift, the fragrance sharp and tingling his nose.

He sneezed and Davina burst out laughing.

*"Don't smell it that hard,"* she mocked and laughed again. Dakai joined in with contagion as they both laughed as hard as they could.

*"Thank you, it's beautiful ... You're beautiful."*

The compliment made her blush visibly and she tried her best to hide it.

The early evening skies bore witness to the love of youth and its zealous exuberance, dazzling at the sight with blissful cheering.

*"So do you want to try again? I don't want you to get ill like you said happened the last time,"* Davina said with concern.

"*I would like to but I should be heading home now. My sister will be getting home soon,*" Dakai replied, though every part of him wanted to stay longer.

"*Okay, see you tomorrow?*" she asked, and he nodded enthusiastically with a smile.

Before he could get up to leave, Davina leaned in and kissed him on his lips, a quick kiss that felt like an eternity. His eyes lit up like flaming stars and he felt jolts of lightning in his entire body.

He couldn't wipe off the smile that captured his face even long after Davina left, as he skipped excitedly on rooftops, jumping gaps that were wide enough to cause others pause.

His love brimming ever bright as he set his sight toward home.

———◄◊►———

Kainu paced down the wooden stairs toward the open door of the mildly lit room, his steps knocking the boards into sounds of tiny blasts repeating with his descent. When it stopped, he stepped inside to meet the faint light from the light-lamp on the brightened table, shading from glowed yellow to blackened brown, and the three people occupying its surroundings.

Kaise looked up from the work she was doing, relaxing the hair brush in her hands when she met the eyes of her brother.

Mamuex gazed at Kaise's work in the mirror, admiring the new look she wore. She turned to Kainu, "*How do I look?*"

Kainu smiled and replied, "*Perfect.*" A reply she visibly appreciated as she stroked her new hairstyle flaunting it in the mirror.

"*You're too nice, child,*" she commented, and waved it a little more before turning her attention to him.

"*Did you get it?*" she asked.

"*Yes ... I did. I passed it on to him like you asked.*"

"*Perfect,*" Mamuex said with a smile highlighting the cleverness in her response.

"*See why he's my favorite child, he gets things done. Not like you, you grunting bastard,*" she said to the third person in the room, her smile still wide on her face. The recipient of her words grunted in a weird laughter and Mamuex chuckled at the hilarity of it.

"*I met the foreign thief girl today, she is ... Intriguing. She reminds me of myself when I was a young girl.*" The siblings glanced at each other hearing her words.

"*Did she agree to join us? She is tough, very smart and capable. She'd help boost our ranks,*" Kainu remarked with some vibrancy.

"*Yes, she will join you tonight, and yes I agree, she will make a great decoy.*"

"*Decoy?*" Kainu asked, confused. The sound of a dropped brush followed right after. Mamuex turned her eyes to Kaise and back to Kainu.

"*You oppose?*" she questioned.

"*I only think she could be a valuable member of our family instead. We just lost Fremm, we nee...*"

"*Don't mention that traitor!*" she barked with a sudden hoarse change in tone. She inhaled dramatically to calm herself down, exhaling the same. "*It's already done. The wolves are already on her scent. I spent time with her in the open so the Armainers' spies would recognize her. They are already expecting me to make a move; they can chase the wrong tail. All she's good for is to be a decoy; we can find another wretched thief.*"

Kainu felt the urge to challenge but history warned him though his expressions betrayed his silence. Mamuex noticed his look and continued, "*The nobleman from the Trois region in the Lands of Nine asked about Kaise again, a marriage to him would establish her for life. Sure she'd be his seventh wife but who cares if she gets to live lavishly. And of course it will also increase my relations for business, a happy ending for all, won't you say darling?*" She mentioned knowing the sensitivity of the subject. Kaise cowered when Mamuex turned to her, an obvious disapproval to the proposal. Kainu thought to speak again but held his tongue to Mamuex's appreciation; she had succeeded in her goal.

"*You need to go prepare, you know what you need to do and what happens if you fail. And you can go home too Kaise, I need to rest.*"

The siblings left the room at her request, ascending up the stairs and through the pathways till they were clear of the house and the walls that listened. Each contemplating what they heard and what loomed henceforth.

Kainu turned his head around, looking sharply around for any ears that pried, and when he was sure it was just theirs, he whispered to his sister.

"*I'm going to make the deal. Our ship leaves tonight.*"

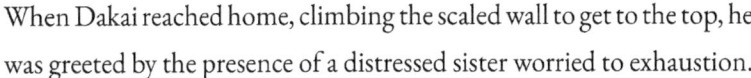

When Dakai reached home, climbing the scaled wall to get to the top, he was greeted by the presence of a distressed sister worried to exhaustion.

"*Dakai! Oh Dakai. Are you okay? Where have you been?*" she exclaimed, running to him, concerned for any harm that might have happened. He brushed off her questions with reassurance that he was okay.

"*He said he wouldn't touch you. I should have never believed him,*" Naemi puffed.

"*Did he hurt you?*" Naemi continued prying.

"*Who said? What are you saying? I went out on my own.*" He replied.

"*What? Why? Where did you go?*" The words came with a change in mood from concern to a clear displeasure.

"*I ... I went to see a friend.*"

Naemi didn't expect the irritation that built up from hearing his response, the casualness at which he spoke the words with such cluelessness of their situation.

"*What!*" She paused with an intense stare.

"*You have friends? How? You're not supposed to go anywhere.*"

"*I was just on the rooftops, I wanted to see the city and I met this girl. Her name is Davina and she is ve...*"

"*How half-witted can you be? And selfish! All you had to do was stay here. All you had to do was wait till I got the money. Did you care about the danger you put us in? What if you got caught again? Did you even care what that would do to me? All you had to do was stay! ... I run through streets taking what's not mine just so we don't starve to death, do you even care? You know how dangerous it is for people to see you and you go out making friends? How foolish can you be? You think you're still a child making friends in Soros? This place isn't home. There are no friends here! Everyone you meet wants to use you or worse, kill you. Have you not learned anything from being locked in a cage? Do you want us to get caught again?"*

The rage in her words shot in the direction of her brother and it pierced him harder than she intended. He already felt guilty for relying solely on his sister without a hand in contribution. Through their stay here, he had felt like a weight forcefully attached to her and the thought saddened him. He found no answers to her scathing words and stared back in a cheerless stare. His happiness before dissipating slowly.

*"End whatever friendship you have. We leave this ill place in two days. We can't have any surprises."*

*"You don't even know her, and you said you didn't think you could get all the money in time,"* Dakai finally spoke up in defense of his love.

*"I don't care to know her. Unless you want to stay for her? I will get all the money soon; I won't spend any more time in this dreadful city,"* Naemi retorted.

The two stood staring off each other with defensive looks till a knock interrupted their exchange. Kainu's voice could be heard outside.

*"I have to go. There is something I need to do. I'll be back later,"* Naemi spoke, moving toward the dwelling's exit.

*"So you can leave whenever you want and I can't?"* Dakai engaged with more defense in his tone. Naemi kept her response to herself, only halting briefly before continuing her steps. She had an unknown task ahead and needed to clear her mind and focus her full attention.

When she descended, she met Kainu with someone else. A bigger kid, tall as a grown man and an exposed fat belly peeking through his unusually shortened blue tunic. His face was smug, and he didn't speak, only grunted responses.

Naemi glanced at him briefly and then at Kainu, the anxiety of her situation growing. Kainu signaled both of them to follow and they walked the streets toward the areas growing with obscenities with the night.

As they got closer, she finally gained courage to seek her purpose in Mamuex's plan. She asked, *"So what am I supposed to steal?"*

------◆◇◆------

Mainers Row was an area known for its repulsiveness, an unfortunate irony due to the sheer volume of activity that transpired in this little section of Sailor City at night. Most people openly declared their distaste for the indecorous area in the presence of day but sang a different tune in the shadow of night.

As one of the famous hubs for night-time indulgences, its streets were lined with establishments that sought to entice every identifiable sense of pleasure that could drain coin from delirious customers; an action it performed to perfection. Even with its existing appeal, it promoted something other areas didn't — anonymity.

"*The many faces of the Sea Siren.*"

Half-faced masques covering the top of one's face to the bottom of their nose concealing the better part of their identity and inversely increasing their desires for indulgence.

Its streets roared with excitement, smelling like a sea of Ale and debauchery. Performers dancing with fire, spitting balls of brightness and engaging in actions of danger. Concealed faces walking in confidence while exposing parts of their body for coin and for pleasure.

Among the establishments in Mainers Row, the most beloved and frequented was the fighting pits. The ferocious enclosure filled with barbarism for people's entertainment, pulled so much attention to all who looked to bear witness to extreme acts of inhumanism — a spectacle that they cheered on gleefully.

Majority of the fighters were enslaved prisoners, sold through underground schemes and made to fight for survival. Those who fought of their own volition, were full of bloodlust and savagery, and seldom fought for the price of coin. This night was no different; the cheers were loud enough to deafen the two men who stood in its center, though they had bigger worries than their sense of sound. It was even more of a shame that the cheers weren't for them but another match planned further in the night.

"*Give us the daughter of death ... Give us the unkillable.*"

Some spat out while others spat in opposition. Their unsealed mouths contrasted by their sealed faces. Their sounds traveled far, seeping into the guarded room at the top floor of the building filled with obscured figures full of smiles from the coin that flooded from their establishments, oblivious to the threats that lay impending.

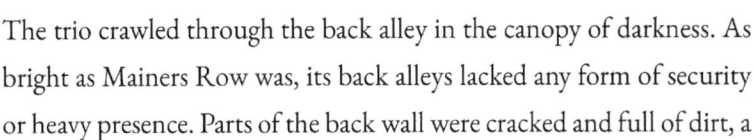

The trio crawled through the back alley in the canopy of darkness. As bright as Mainers Row was, its back alleys lacked any form of security or heavy presence. Parts of the back wall were cracked and full of dirt, a pungent smell stood strong in its territory, full of waste and discarded mess.

Kainu halted in front of the group, pointing to the closed window on the far topmost corner of a three-leveled structure.

"*That's where you'll find it. The room should be lightly guarded. The guards have the keys; you'll need to find a way inside yourself. The windows are reinforced so the only way is through the front door,*" he said, looking at Naemi, and she replied with a concerned expression.

"*I never said it'll be easy. Meet here after and if things get crazy, escape and I'll meet you at your home,*" Kainu added.

"*What will you both be doing?*" Naemi asked, the bigger kid grunted at Kainu and he shot a deadly stare at him.

"*Nothing, we'll wait for you here. Mamuex wants you to do this alone to judge if you're good enough; we will wait till you return,*" he responded.

The idea of venturing into the building alone didn't entice Naemi in the least, but her desperation only saw the money she could earn from this outcome. As she began to leave, Kainu stopped her, paused for a brief second. "*Be careful Naemi,*" he said in a deep cautious tone, and she left without acknowledgment.

The transition from the black alley into the light felt like a splash of cold water to her face, dilating her pupils and stinging her eyes. She emerged from the shadowy lane to the colorfulness of the streets, her first gloried sight being an acrobatic woman standing on a trotting horse and the numerous others who passed her. Colorful masques shading hidden eyes. She paid little focus, heading toward the entrance of the building she sought.

She slipped past the engaged bodies by the door into the heavily vivacious crowds that circled the hollowed center of the building. The inside was bigger than she thought, and it took sometime till she found her bearing. The crowds stood chanting toward the pit in the center obstructing her view and drowning her ears. Women who were nigh naked were walking around with trays of heavy ale and pervy men were throwing money for their attention.

The inside of the building looked like it was built around a giant empty cylinder, starting from the topmost floor to the bottom, giving everyone a clear view of the pit to shout their obscenities. Naemi searched for the stairs, turning her head around until she saw it, climbing past the bodies and the wet floorboards that were wet and sticky with every step.

"*And how much for time with you sweetheart?*"

His voice was rusty, and his mouth pushed a puff of cloud smelling of liquor and rot.

Naemi viciously slapped his hand away and kept on her focus, hearing the profanities he threw on her trail. Other profanities flew past her from those who stood by, *"Kill that bitch,"* though they weren't directed toward her but into the pit. Looming eyes that recognized her from afar waited patiently to catch her in their trap. When she got to the uppermost floor, it was less sizable than the ones below, and less rowdy.

Away from the center, the back rooms weren't as accessible as she'd been informed. Sealed off with walled wooden meshes separating the chaos from the calm, and guarded entrances into the section. She scrambled her mind for a plan, and one came to her in the form of a lazy serving girl engaging intimately with a man by the circle boundary. Her tray of ale was lying unattended. Naemi rushed to grab it, her clothes might not pass for a serving girl but she'd try whatever she could.

For the first time, she stood by the pit and a cheer from the crowd caused her to inadvertently glance inside. There were four people fighting, three of them all looked to be attacking one person. A large lean man stripped of his clothes entirely, bloodied with a shaved head, a heavily scarred back and limping on an injured right leg.

He was fending off the others, retreating backwards after a swing. When one of the smaller men rushed to him, he turned and lunged a shortened knife he had in the man's shoulder leaving him squealing, his turn exposing his breast and private regions. It was no man at all.

The crowd jeered again loudly.

*"The unkillable,"*, *"Kill her for your freedom,"* some shouted, throwing more ale. The sight of the pit disgusted Naemi but there was an intrigue to the woman. Her starved broad shoulders and toned back still

striking through the scars. The woman's leg still bled and she collapsed suddenly on her failed leg, giving an opportunity for the other two to pounce.

They rushed her, pushing her fully to the ground and scrambling for the knife. Her fading strength lost to theirs and with the knife in one of the man's hands, she struggled to break its tip slowly descending on her. It was a surprise she could push one of the two off, the crowd jubilating as the end appeared nigh. The instant one of her attackers got thrown off, her face fully appeared to Naemi, the revelation striking her with such immensity.

"*Beara.*"

Naemi exhaled the words with such compassion and dismay. The woman below was now fighting off two men again as death came descending close. There was no time to think, the thoughts had already been formed before she could realize, and her body moved at a predetermined will.

The sight of someone who had done so much for her, close to death, ignited an action she didn't even think herself possible of.

Once she was powerless, but not anymore.

For her savior, for her friend, for Beara, she leaped off the boundary, falling down from above into the pit.

And what followed next was carnage.

Dakai stood at the base of the two floored building a few feet from
the back doors. He was familiar with seeing this building through the
top window on the left side from an adjacent roof, having done so
numerous times throughout the past weeks, but tonight the change in
perspective waned on him.

His eyes still held the water that produced from his sadness. His
sequence of deep thought producing unstable decisions. The door
opened and Davina slipped out, sleep still in her eyes. She had fallen
asleep not long ago until she heard sounds of little pebbles hitting her
room floor. She peeked through her window and there stood her love,
teary-eyed and pensive. When she rushed down, he mumbled his words
upon questioning.

"*Dakai, what's wrong?*"

"*My sister said we're leaving in two days. I thought we were going to
have more time, I didn't think she could make all the money. I thought
all I wanted was to go home before ... but I don't think I can go without
you.*" He spoke with a deep dolefulness.

Davina's eyes widened at the news, the toll it took on her, hearing the
possibility she always feared materialize.

Her heart sank instantly as did her soul, standing in the witness of the
deep night sky.

"*Come with me,*" Dakai said, so soft it could make the stars cry.
Davina stood speechless. This wasn't how today was supposed to go.
She had gone to sleep earlier with such happiness, and now her peak
had flipped on its head.

Tears filled her eyes as she replied, the words hurting her as it escaped her lips.

"*I can't Dakai ... I can't. I can't leave my family, my parents, my siblings, they're part of my life. I would be lost in Soros even if I have you. My life is in Sailor City, it's all I've ever known.*"

Dakai expected the response, though it did little to dull the pain. For everything he knew about her, he knew how much her family meant to her and he felt a sick guilt for even putting her in the position to choose.

*Why am I even here? Why am I even causing her this much pain? Why do I always cause those I love pain? Would it have been kinder to just leave without a word? Or if we never met and she never knew about me? Yeah, that would have been better than this. Her life would be better if she never knew me.*

His mind questioning his actions, he retreated a step, realizing the finality of the situation and the future they held. Looking into the teary eyes of his first love, he apologized.

"*I'm sorry Davina, I'm so sorry for putting you through this. It would be better if you just forget about me, forget about us. Forget everything.*"

His words poured out his mouth laced with an intention he didn't realize, not knowing what he did even when he did it.

Speaking those words in his state of affliction and internal desires, he unknowingly activated the second ability of his eyes — the cost of his words far greater than he meant it to be. In that moment, as his words compelled the mind of his love to forget everything, he broke her mind, damaging her memories into pieces as many as sands on a desert.

Ripping her identity of everything she'd known and everything she was.

Unaware of what happened, he kept apologizing for breaking her heart, oblivious that he had broken her entire being. His eyes clouded with tears.

Davina dropped to her knees with a heavy thud, slouching to the side with her head hanging backwards in a fall. Her mouth drooled heavy spit and a slow exhale sounded from her throat. Her eyes fell back with her head, lying upside down, staring at the distant blue sky with no idea what it even was. While some of the flowers she kept in her head dropped to the dirtied ground from the sudden thrust.

The dramatic change overwhelmed Dakai in shock, not enough to stop him from leaping toward his fallen love and calling out her name.

As if on cue, the backdoor in front of them opened and the first sight Davina's sister saw was the slumped body of her sister in the arms of a strange boy with demon-colored eyes.

The sight horrified her and the scream that followed horrified him even more. She rushed to her sister, pushing the boy off her.

"*What did you do?*" she shouted repeatedly, the steps from people rushing to her calls getting louder.

Dakai's next action would be something that would scar him for the rest of his life, how quick it happened and the impulse that moved him to do it.

In the presence of the moon and stars who had followed the journey of their love from its blossoming rise to its sudden demise — he ran.

———— ◆◇◆ ————

The fire rose quicker than its creator intended. Flammable messes disposed of without care finally found a purpose.

The creator grunted in heavy laughter, meeting Kainu's eyes as he turned the corner.

Kainu halted.

Finally realizing why Mamuex pushed for him to come with Tilikum. Another distraction or a pure intention of causing chaos to the Armainers.

A countermove to what happened with Fremm maybe.

The endless ploys and games Mamuex played in his ambitions for political power and the enemies he created. Games of which they paid the price, his beloved children used as pawns in moves and counters, bearing all the consequences. This wasn't his first feud and not his second either.

Kainu had seen the collateral of all of them and he hid the part of himself that felt disgust in his role in them, reminding himself that nothing mattered more than him and his twin sister. Mamuex wasn't always like this if it can be believed. There was once a sweet and gentle man who genuinely cared for the lost children he met, being one of them before. But the man he knew now was someone else.


The fire flamed up, catching a stride and traveling up the wall. Tilikum jittered and ran. Kainu did the same in the opposite direction, emerging into the brightened streets.

His guilt for sending Naemi into ambush held him at a crossroad.

The choice between saving the girl he barely knew and getting the item that he was going to trade for escape to a new life.

He put on the masque he hid, entering the three-story building and maneuvering through the crowd to the hidden basement, his choice already made.

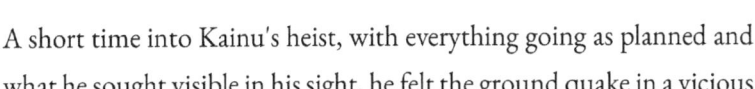

A short time into Kainu's heist, with everything going as planned and what he sought visible in his sight, he felt the ground quake in a vicious vibration preceded by a deafening sound of thunder.

The room shook heavily, its walls pushing away large cabinets, stacked boxes, and anything else lacking a strong footing. A tall lamp-stand frame fell to the floor, hitting the body of the man who lay unconscious. Kainu rose from his fall, hurrying back to the metal lock and box.

He had no idea what had happened but the screams and heavy vibrations that followed meant he had even less time than he did before. He attacked the lock again with his short hook and pick guided only by an ounce of light.

One, two, three and it snapped on the fourth try.

The inside opened to its contents; a record of the Armainers' trade routes, selling history and business transactions. A holy grail exposing almost every deal the Armainers' family did, who they preferred doing it with and the money they kept. Mamuex treasured this above all and so did some other unknown parties.

Parties that would go as far as guarantee secure passage to other realms in exchange for such prized information. The Armainers, however, forethought an attack to be on their gold supplies and kept treasures instead.

Kainu escaped the basement in haste to the main floor only to meet heavy dust, louder screams and fallen wood pillars. He coughed as the dust flooded his lungs and took off the masque to breathe better; there was an intense heat surrounding and people rushing to the exit pushed him in all directions.

He stepped on something soft that almost tripped him, jumping back when he met the eyes of the lifeless body that stared back at him.

Strained voices screamed for help all around but were left to their own whims. Part of the back side of the structure had fallen on itself and the west side of the upper floors were caved in. Kainu stumbled on another body and was aggressively knocked off his footing by a bloodied serving girl running for her life. He landed on a cracked side of the circle boundary holding onto it for support.

The ground in the interior was littered with three bodies and there was a bizarre fold in the ground near the collapsed layers. In the middle, someone knelt near another body, holding its head up and calling out to it. The silhouette held a familiarity to him and the voice all but confirmed who it was — the girl he led to slaughter.

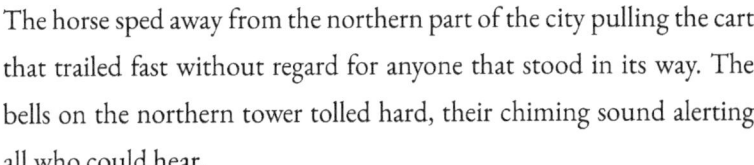

The horse sped away from the northern part of the city pulling the cart that trailed fast without regard for anyone that stood in its way. The bells on the northern tower tolled hard, their chiming sound alerting all who could hear.

From behind, smoke rose into the skies traveling up with black fumes signaling to all the chaos that was at hand. The fire ravaged through the structure, eating as much as it could. Those who were brave enough to venture inside did and those who were saved from its embrace gasped for fresh air.

City-guards who were close converged to the region alerting all fire brigades and all who were needed to control the disaster. Reports of the cause varied from perspective, though there was a growing similarity in most of the stories. Those who heard were slow to believe even with the testimony of the masses.

The horse pounced on, Kainu whipping its reins to move faster. Naemi held on to the side of the cart with one hand and the other held onto a weakened Beara.

She glanced at the smoke in the sky with heavy remorse, the unsettling nature of her creation stared back at her. Not at all what she intended to happen, only wanting to save her friend.

But intention and outcome don't always see eye to eye.

Beara groaned and Naemi reached out, her eyes flashing open and closed slowly. Kainu kept on, almost to his destination.

The memory played back in his head of the woman who pointed shakingly at Naemi, "*You ... it was you!*" The speed at which he hijacked the brigade transport to get Naemi and the enfeebled woman she was attached to away from turning eyes.

The only cause of destruction he could think of was the fire, but the damage that he saw was too severe in such a short time that it made him question his conclusion. To him, this was the second time Naemi was in the middle of disaster, and he wondered what hidden secrets she kept.

Regardless, this night had come with complications he couldn't have foreseen, and midnight was getting closer. Kaise should be on the ship by now waiting for him, and his betrayal of Mamuex will soon come to light.

The horse neighed heavily as it stopped, Naemi's dwelling in sight. Kainu jumped down and moved toward the cart, watching Naemi still holding on to the woman, her helplessness on full display. She was in as much trouble as he was, maybe more. Whoever the woman was and what truly happened was bound to cause commotion that would find her eventually, if Mamuex didn't first. Kainu didn't know what made him ask but he did, perhaps his growing guilt on the many wrongs he had done to her.

"*I'm leaving the city tonight with Kaise, do you want to come with us?*" he asked. Naemi looked back at him, her mind ticking with the many possibilities that branched with time and their outcomes, none of them yielding optimism. Less than two days to home.

Two days to a ship she didn't make the money for. How was she going to survive the days with all the trouble she just caused, and Beara barely holding on to life?

"*Yes. We will come,*" she concluded, all her thoughts converging on a final decision. They needed to escape Sailor City as fast as they could.

"*Can you please get Dakai? Tell him I will explain everything.*"

Beara moaned again painfully, murmuring gibberish through her discomfort. Naemi held her hand tighter, checking the cut on her leg that was bleeding less, though her condition hadn't improved.

Kainu bolted toward their dwelling, scaling the walls and entering inside through the uncovered opening.

The inside of the tents were empty and he had to peek in the outer roof area before he saw the boy crouched on the floor and his head buried in his arms.

"*Dakai?*" he called slowly, perturbed by the steady sobbing sounds that came from him. Dakai sprung up and jolted backward. His mouth opened to speak but closed instantly to no words. His sunken eyes full of tears wetting his lower face. Kainu perplexed at the reaction and started explaining calmly what happened, and what Naemi had requested of him.

"*We need to leave Dakai, we need to leave now.*" Stepping closer to console the boy of whatever ailed him.

"*Stop! Don't come near me!*" Dakai shot out, triggering another compulsion.

Kainu's body stopped responding to his will, paralyzing him in the moment.

His eyes fixed on Dakai who began to panic.

Kainu could feel all of himself and could control none of it, trapped in his consciousness that bent to the will of another, it looked as horrific as it felt. Dakai retreated in hysteria, getting nearer and nearer to the building's edge, "*No ... No ... No ... Not again!*"

The hold broke and Kainu fell to the floor gasping hard for air to fill his lungs. He had never felt as helpless in his life as now, like he was in the grasp of a giant vice. Dakai took another half step back and felt no ground below his feet, turning to see the fall in front of him.

He retreated slightly, looking to the many bright lights in the city and dark smoky clouds that rose like a path into the sky. He had contemplated the fall for long, crying all his pain out but the pain was unending. He thought he was cursed, and his impulse pushed him to take the short path down. All his problems would end, then he wouldn't cause any more pain to anyone.

*I'm sorry Naemi. I'm so sorry.* His last thought being all the people he cared so deeply for.

———◆○◆———

The ride to Dock seven wasn't pleasant. The curses people threw were the least of their worries. Kainu took every shortcut he could think of, navigating through the city as if he'd lived his whole life there. It was a blessing they avoided chase from city-guards. The fire brigade cart played a part in that, as well as the fact that half of Mainers row was on fire.

Naemi held on to Dakai and Beara, anchoring them down. She didn't expect for Kainu to return with her brother hanging over his shoulder unconscious and Dakai with a bump on the side of his head but there was no time to inquire.

"*I had to,*" was the only thing he said and jumped on the horse, galloping with the wind.

The figure that met them, standing next to Kaise, was completely infuriated.

"*This is not what we agreed!*" He yelled in a whisper as Kaise helped the others onto the smaller ship with some of the crew. Dock seven was sparsely populated, not enough to spook attention.

The sounds of bells rang in the distant north, and the smoke clouds contrasted by the midnight sky was such a chilling sight to win focus from. Some ships were already enroute out of the city, the hysterical claiming the city would be burned to a crisp by Dawn.

The irritated figure and Kainu's heated discussion came to a quick end. The man wore a more relaxed face after, shouting to his crew to get ready for sail. Kaise called out to Kainu beckoning him to hurry inside the ship. He looked to his sister and turned toward the city, taking a deep look at the only place he had ever known. He had no friends to say bye to and no family here to miss, but part of him would always be here.

Tonight had pushed him to extremes he could never have imagined and he made decisions he would have never thought himself possible. His sister called out to him again and this time, he retreated inside the ship. Anchors raised and giant ropes that held the ship to shore broke from hold leaving the wood vessel to start its drift on water. Through the lake and waved clear through the giant passageway, they escaped the city that had scarred all of them in its own way, leaving an imprint of lessons they would never forget.

The water carrying them further into the abyss, unto a new destination with more lessons and more tribulations.

## Chapter Eleven

# THE FATHER AND THE SON

The king paced slowly on the wet grass of the royal gardens. The beautified stretch of space on the west lawn of the crown castle was a source of refreshment he visited often to clear his mind.

The skies had cleared from last night's rain though the ground still held its water. It was late morning, and the pond that sat in the middle of the garden had risen to its limit. It was sure to overflow during this wet season, a fact that didn't bother the Black-necked swans that scattered the gardens, but it did bother the Cogno yellow-tailed peacocks that hid at the slightest sign of water.

Other exotic birds filled the area, some bigger than others. The garden was a grande landmark, a staple of the crown castle, remarkable in beauty to anyone blessed enough to lay eyes on it.

There isn't any historical link to which king or queen facilitated its creation, but a lot of old rulers have claimed possession of the title for its origin. The servants of the castle claim differently.

There are stories that have been passed down by older castle workers of its origin being from a child servant who started the garden for her love of nature, and her mother continuing to grow it after her tragic death. They claim that once the gardens grew and its beauty blossomed, a queen claimed it as her own and banished the mother from the castle. It was then given the name; Celestial gardens, denoting its ethereal elegance and stunning magnificence, but among the castle workers it is known as the gardens of Riu.

There's no evidence to back any of these claims of ownership; the first mention of the gardens in historical context appears in **151-SM** and has no assigned creator.

Regardless, the story seeped out through the fences of the crown castle down to the mainland. The common people hold it to be true, citing it as another display of something of worth stolen from those without power.

The royals claim it as faux folklore, saying it's another attempt at commoners making up stories to make themselves seem more relevant than they are to history. Either way, the truth is only known to the god of time, and the doubt of its creator will always exist in the eyes of the people.

Still, every ruler had tried somewhat to improve the monument, and its importance flourished through generations. It had over twenty custodians responsible for its exquisite upkeep and housed some of the most fanciful pieces of nature from even the most remote parts of the world.

Walking through it was like walking through a colorful painting. Every corner triggered a pleasureful aesthetic to the eyes, and the scent that mixed together in bold harmony tasted like rain of scented sugar. Such was the sweetness in the air. Many who got the chance to visit the crown castle always made claims of the striking aroma that doused the breeze in the region, though few were privileged enough to see its source.

Today, Olius moved through the Celestial gardens in his loosened teal tunic and faint brown pants, with a small bucket of seeds he had taken from a custodian. Three crown-guards followed a few paces behind him as he scattered seeds into the grass.

The feed beaconed the birds to him, and they rushed to get some of the delicacies. He watched as the birds scrambled for the food, as well-fed and fattened as they were, they still fought each other for seeds even when there was enough to feed them all.

They quacked and slammed their beaks, beating their feathers against each other in the struggle for what was plentiful, and when a bigger bird came, the smaller ones would cower to it and grant it master-privileges. Thus until another even bigger one would come and uproot the smaller in a continuous cycle, till there wasn't any one bigger than the latter. Then it would call itself king and eat till it granted the rest permission to continue.

Olius refrained from adding more feed and gazed at the behavior of the birds as if he were in a trance. It wasn't something he had never seen before, but for some reason, this particular sight resonated heavily in his mind.

The primal instincts of life that are engrained everywhere, even in actions as simple as birds eating seeds. In his mind, this was a nature of life that would never change.

A simple rule written in the stars and guided by men.

The strong will always dominate the weak.

He had lived by this rule for years, the same one his mother taught him and the same one he taught Selius. He broke from his trance when he started feeling pity for the smaller birds, and threw more seeds into the grass.

He had come here to clear his mind from the issues that plagued it, to breathe in the calming scents and soothe his spirit. He had been bothered of late by a reflection he had seen, a reflection of his life and his rule.

Maybe it was his mortality that was getting to him, even though he was in good health for his old age. Maybe it was the idea that his legacy didn't look to be as strong as he had imagined in his younger years. Maybe it was the growing anger from gossip he heard among the other families from the spies he placed around, or maybe, it was the state's current affairs that plagued him. Like the growing uprisings in some colonized states and rebel activity, the wedding of his son as payment for access north, plus the flurry of other issues he dealt with as king.

His thoughts were bursting.

The burden of a ruler for an entire empire was strenuous and he did all he could to show no weakness. The gray in his hair was more than the black now, and the folds on his skin had increased.

Still, his face looked as distinguished as ever, the morning light cast rays of warmth on the front of his face and it glistened in the light. It was the late fall season and soon the winter would come with heavy cold, but not today. Today boasted warmth after the rains and good humidity in the skies. He beckoned to a custodian tending to some flowers and gave her the bucket with the rest of the seeds.

"*That should be enough now,*" he said to her, and she left with the item. He turned back to one of his crown-guards and asked, "*Where is he?*" with sternness in his voice.

"*I sent word to call for him sire, I'm sure he will be here soon,*" the crown-guard answered. Olius let out a slight grunt of disapproval and turned back to continue his stroll.

The relaxing effect of the garden hadn't taken its toll on him yet. The knot in his mind was too dense to untangle. He had agreed to more demands from the Mhraabs in exchange for his desires. He had spoken to his son and imposed on him a wife he didn't want, all to achieve his ambitions.

There was a part of him that felt saddened by the notion, but he justified the action with the claim that it was a necessity in the advancement of the nation and the crown.

This was a justification he used often; after all, his marriage to Gyai was not made for love but of duty, but he ended up finding immense love in her anyway and she in him, so will happen for his son.

"*A wedding or a war?*" he asked Selius.

"*You're a prince, you're my son. You should know your duty to the crown and the sacrifices you need to bear to advance the state. Soon you too will wear this crown and feel the weight of its choices. Your responsibility to the people and the esteemed families. Soon you'll know what it means to be king,*" Olius affirmed.

Gyai had informed him later about Selius's feelings of neglect from him, treating him only as a dutiful son without the appreciations of the father.

"*You only make demands of him. His duty to this and his duty to that. He doesn't feel seen by you, only bound to service. You send him to make your executions, you force a marriage on him, you scold him for his light transgressions. He wants more than anything to win your approval, but all you present are new hurdles,*" Gyai said.

Olius rebutted the assertion at first, defensive on how his treatment of his son showed nothing but love and trust. His wife's message stayed with him still. Olius had known nothing different himself in his days as a prince. His mother was stern, and his father was unassuming. His parents' relationship was nothing short of tumultuous, and all he knew to do was to be a duteous prince especially in the midst of many siblings.

However, as he kept on thinking over his wife's words, he found some truth in them, and considered change necessary.

A dash of strong breeze blew past him and the curls in his hair swayed in its direction. He heard a sound he was all too familiar with; the sound of thrusting wings descending behind him. He turned to meet the eyes of Selius. His son showed a concerned look and engaged his father as soon as he touched the ground.

"*Father, I came as soon as I was told. Is anything wrong? Is this about the rebel attack in Mirain?*"

"*Somewhat ... But I mostly wanted to see you,*" Olius replied solemnly. Embodying that patented majestic voice of his.

"*Oh.*" The words left Selius with a layer of surprise.

"*Come, walk with me son,*" Olius added, and continued his walk through the gardens.

He continued speaking, "*The attack on the Mirain city was a tragedy. These deviant groups need to be exterminated, and they will be. They seem to be getting bolder. We thought it was just a handful, but it appears there are more. At first, it was disruptions to our transport, stealing weapons and food, and now they organize an attack on the Mirain city. I sent the Dion Astrape to Mirain; I'm sure that will take care of that nuisance. He will stay there through the winter to late spring. Deal a heavy hand once and for all. This isn't the first time we've dealt with a group of outlaws; we will treat them the same as those littered through history.*"

Olius paused and looked at his son, noticing the hint of disapproval that crept up, "*You disapprove of this course of action?*" he asked.

Selius was slow to answer.

"*I don't disapprove, Astrape is a formidable Dion, his gift of lightning is a fearsome ability, but I fear it's a hammer when we're not sure what we are hitting. We aren't even sure of their entire numbers. And there has to be a reason their confidence has increased from robbing transport carts in forests to all out attacks. There's even confusion on how such large explosions were possible without any signs of ample pyro-powder or oil barrels. How are we sure they don't have an unknown Dion on their side? Do they have any empathizers in the state? If we are to rid ourselves of these plagues, we have to be sure they aren't going to infect the other colonies. We should send a portion of the state army to reinforce the area, implement more strict curfews and comb the region to smoke out those in hiding. Winter will soon be here and we can use the harsh cold to our advantage,"* Selius answered.

*"Hmmm,"* Olius let out in a low hum.

*"My son has better counsel than these old idiots who advise me. I will talk more about this with the generals later. You should be present. I need to hear more of your wisdom, son. It seems I've lacked it and focused too much on the claimed wisdom of the old and weary,"* Olius added with a smile.

Selius echoed his smile which lasted longer from the complement he received.

*"Anyway, that's not why I sent for you. I realized I owe you an explanation and an apology. I asked you to honor your duty as a prince and engage in a marriage I'm sure you don't want, but I've failed to honor my duty as a father. I needed to be honest with you and reveal the whole truth instead of cowering behind duty. Do you know why this marriage is important? Why it is important to me?"* Olius questioned his son.

Selius thought for a moment. He knew the answer at the surface but searched for any deeper ones he was missing.

He found none and presented the only one he knew.

"*Because you want access through the mountain pass to continue the expansion?*" Selius answered with a question.

"*I do, but that isn't the entire reason. True, the expansion is entwined in the history of our house. The movement to grow our reach and spread our culture and faith to all the land. Till all is under the Thrun name. Will the mountain pass be worth a prince under different conditions? No. No it won't be, but under this condition it is. You've read all the history scrolls and books the mages gave you. Why do you think the great Perolius Reis started the expansion?*" Olius inquired.

Selius pondered over this question deeply too, thinking of what hidden meanings his father was looking for as an answer. All the reasons stated in the history books were more opinionated than objective.

Nothing was concretely recorded as evidence of why the expansion was started, so Selius answered with his own opinion also, "*The expansion was started because we discovered we could create and harness the power of Dions. Without that discovery we would have never engaged in such an endeavor,*" he concluded.

Olius smiled and nodded, "*That is also true, but that's just one of the reasons and not even the most important. We could have still held steady even after the discovery and only protected our territory, but we didn't. The real reason Perolius started the expansion was because he saw our mortality, the ease at which our existence and significance could be wiped off the world.*"

Olius paused; he had reached a personal favorite area of the garden and took a deep inhale to soak the sweet scent of the flower that littered these parts; its white and blue color soaking in the sun's warmth — the shades of Lynn.

The scent placated his spirits, and he returned his mind to focus.

He continued.

"*After the devastation of the red-pox and Astor's own attempt at colonizing our land, we saw the ease at which we could wilt into inferiority. Our culture, our advancements, our history, all we had built to improve our section of the world, lost to others only because they had more forces than us. So Perolius made a decision to overcome that for generations; Dion creation was just the perfect tool of power to use. The real reason for the expansion was for our sustainability. To grow our reach till we are too big to fall, like a giant sequoia tree with a stem as large as buildings. Our empire needs to grow till we cover all the land. Till all is under the Thrun name.*"

Selius absorbed his father's words and held his attention. His father rarely had conversations such as these with him, and he listened to the parts of his history that couldn't be found in scrolls.

A question formed in his mind however, one that contradicted some of his father's sayings. He held the question at bay for as long as he could, but it was an itch he needed to scratch eventually.

When it got to its peak he asked Olius, "*Is growth the only guarantee we never fall? You speak of history father, but they also contain the tales of empires that fell. Ones that grew too big for their own good, ones that fell to infighting, ones that fell to betrayal, and even ones that fell to massacre.*

*Are we sure our sustainability is maintained even if all the land is under our hand?"*

His father received the question warmly, appreciative of his son's engagement with his teachings.

*"You're right. Growth is not a guarantee of avoiding collapse. So what if we stop growing then? What if I send forces to collapse the pass in the Moze mountains and close off the north to us completely? Would that stop the possibility of infighting, uprisings, betrayal? Our sustainability will always need to be defended because of the nature of people. There will always be new threats we have to face and annihilate to preserve our existence. Our leadership, mine and soon to be yours will determine the future of our nation for generations, just as the ones before us determined for us. We benefit now because Perolius had the foresight to grow and extend our resources, build our influence and our reach. That growth strengthened our power so none challenged us. We grow because we have to. We grow because we need to maintain control over all. The only guarantee with power is power itself."*

Olius moved closer to his son and placed a hand on his shoulder.

He added, *"We are conquerors, son. It runs through our blood and our name. When you become king, you will continue the legacy of our house and mark your name in its history. What kind of king would you want to become? What history would be attached to your name? That will be what you leave to the next generation, your children and those that follow."*

The statement captured Selius's mind, and he prompted to answer the questions that lay in it even though it was asked rhetorically. He had pondered over his future rule for years, for as long as his mind was fully developed enough to know his destiny and the concepts of kingship.

He answered his father with a voice of determination and pride, "*I will be a king who builds on your legacy and pushes our nation to eternal dominance. I want our name to mark fear in every corner of the world. I want history to remember me as a conqueror, as great as you, as great as the visionary Perolius. I will make Thrun one of the greatest empires to exist. Even greater than the famed Kaku empire and the Uzojn dynasty of old. I will do my duty so it becomes so.*"

Olius's eyes gleamed with admiration at hearing his son's words.

The smile that appeared on his face echoed his emotion, showing his well-formed teeth and dignified features.

"*My son!*" he said proudly. "*You'll be a better king than I ever was.*"

Selius smiled back, his heart smiling wider than his lips did. His father's words raised such emotions of happiness and fulfillment in him, an effect that no one else could have as deeply, not even Gyai. He thought to say something back to his father, but the words never came to form, his emotions held control and his smile lasted.

Olius continued with more words. "*I have asked a lot of you, and you have obeyed willfully as any good son would. You've grown to be a remarkable prince and warrior. And I fear I haven't rewarded you enough for it, nor have I shown appreciation. I wanted you to enjoy your youth, more than I had the chance to enjoy mine. Once you don the crown, its weight collapses everything around you, and your focus becomes only for the nation. Even princely duties were overwhelming for me at times, but I shouldn't let my wants overshadow your needs. Your mother told*

*me you desire to join the council of war generals? Are you ready for the*
*responsibility? You won't be able to continue your long disappearances*
*from home without regard anymore. You'll be in charge of gallant men*
*and your words will be their bidding. You'll deal with the internal politics*
*of the five families and taste what it is like to rule. Are you sure you're*
*rea..."*

"*Yes! Yes, I'm ready father.*"

Selius cut into his father's words with zeal.

Olius stared at him in silence, a last opportunity to retract before his words turned final. He could tell his silence was a waste by the joy he saw in his son's eyes.

The desire that filled him.

To him, even with the power he was bestowed at such an early age, responsibility had been a curse he tasted too early. He'd remember his mother's words, "*duty.*" The number of times she'd say that word to him. He never envisioned she'd die at the age she did; he always thought she'd hold onto power even after she was a hundred. It was more of a surprise to him that he was called to rule, put in the center of the politics of retaining the power of the crown.

Even through it all, he did as he was bid, performed his duty to the Reis family and to the state.

The memories of him before the tribunal still reflect on him till this day. Once the crown fell on his head, he was thrust into the legacy and ambition that came with it. Forces that would steer him on until he found his grave, and when that happens, his name will be left to the vices of history to be argued in halls, alleys, and the foulness of people's mouths on whether he was a king to be revered or one to be forgotten.

He stared into the lightness of his son's eyes and hoped he could save his son from its early grip but could tell Selius craved different.

His seed had grown into its own man and its roots craved a taste of true obligation.

"*Then it will be so. You'll be ordained into the council before the earliest sign of winter*," Olius said, breaking his silence. He could see his son try his best to hide his elation, though his expressions betrayed him.

"*You'll join General Ganius in the efforts against the rebels*," Olius added.

Selius responded with the same exuberance he had held before, "*I will not fail you father.*" He replied, and his father nodded in response.

———————◆———————

The warmness that rained from the sun showered blessings on all that stood in its presence. The father and the son basked in its cover through their conversation, at times overlooking its glory.

The symbols of beauty that surrounded them however did not take the sun's majesty as lightly. They stood erect from their bowed positions some hours earlier, and opened their arms and petals to receive more of its splendor. Their thirsts had been filled with water and their skin filled with warmth. They gave back to the world in gifts of sweet aroma as is required in the unwritten laws of equal exchange.

The breeze that passed transported their gifts to all those it could reach, extending their favor through weightlessness till it could be extended no more. The workers in the garden attended to the jewels with careful hands, pruning parts of it that were unsavory and trimming the bushes that held unique shapes. They worked to the best of their ability, doing all they could to not disrupt the fragile ecosystems that grew underneath. Some of the plants required such special care that shed-like structures were built to provide them comfort, ones that looked more pleasant than the homes the workers themselves resided in.

No matter, they did their duty as they were bid to, some with more reverence than others.

Working in such an esteemed location had its way of hypnotizing the mind to create drives of personal significance, though it could be argued that some workers inhabited profound passion for these scattered plants.

The shine of the sun reflected off the crafted armor of the crown-guards who stood in place a few feet from the one they were sworn to protect. The silver metal reflected the rays back like a mirror in the light, the heat it generated however was a problem the guards rarely complained about.

Today boasted a more favorable experience, and they continued their servitude with their mouths closed and eyes vigilant.

"*You can go celebrate with your friends if you desire. I'm sure you want to,*" Olius mentioned to his son. They had stopped near a small willow tree that grew with curly branches, almost like its branches had been swapped with its roots, and Olius admired the gem as he had many times before.

"*There will be time to celebrate, but I'd rather stay here with you. I haven't been to the gardens in weeks.*"

"*I couldn't get you out of these gardens when you were young; you even asked that we build a shed here for you. Bothered your mother and I for weeks. I would have allowed it, but your mother forbade me so strictly. You know how she gets when she turns strict. Widening her eyes and shrinking her mouth.*" Olius laughed through his response and his son laughed at the comment. A laughter that was full of exhilaration, filling the air with the sounds of their royalty.

When the laughter died down, Olius added.

"*You were such an adventurous child, even when you were little. So curious of the world and drawn to its fascinations. So tiny and yet so powerful. Do you know you almost broke your mother's finger when you were only a year old? She was playing with you in your crib and in your excitement you squeezed it too tight.*"

"*She never told me.*" Selius commented in a disappointing expression.

"*I'm sure she didn't. She tends to keep all that away from you. The nurses advised her to stop breastfeeding you for fear you might cause her more harm, but she won't listen. Nothing would come between her and her child,*" Olius remarked.

"*We should have known when he told your mother and I you'd be powerful. We just didn't know how much.*" The king added absentmindedly. He didn't even realize what he had said until moments passed and the silence had grown. When he did, he changed the topic almost instantly, avoiding his son's gaze.

The statement triggered dormant questions that lay in the prince's mind. The questions that form in any child's mind when they're the only known Dion to be born in the realm. Part of him wanted to seek the answer to the question, and part of him didn't. The thought that the answer could challenge the ideas he had of himself, the ideas of specialty and being the chosen one given by Raja himself. Blessed to share the skies with him and fly as high as the sun.

He shook off his desire for answers and willfully bought into his father's diversion.

Their conversation continued as the day continued to form.

They talked more about legacy, history, the politics of the families, their joys and further ambitions. Selius found wisdom in his father's words and soaked all he could from it. They paced through the gardens slowly, occasionally diverting attention to its radiance and the fine large birds that paraded around without care.

The crown-guards followed at a steady pace, the metals in their armor clanging together as they moved, singing a tribute to their presence. The day will continue its form. The sky was full of clear clouds as white patches in the sea of blue. Little dots flowed above showing smaller birds soaring the vastness of the upper space with wings stretched wide.

Life continued on in many parallel instances, every one full of significance and meaning.

From above, the gardens of Riu also showed its significance. The one it had grown through generations. It would be a place that would hold meaning for generations more, though for today the only one it held was that of the father and the son.

## CHAPTER TWELVE

# TALES OF WINTER

Feet stepped out from wood, striking their covered soles unto the palette of sand that surrounded the shore. The salt water glided in over the fine dirt once more, swaying the boat slightly and glided out again in its marked repetition with the tides.

The sands that covered the shore spread long past it, almost like the ends of a desert meeting the sea. Its dull beige color filled the area with soft, granular tiny rocks that sunk into curves when walked on. The sands extended out into little hills and valleys imitating the sea without the need for its recurrent motion.

Signs of life could be witnessed everywhere on the beach but only six people could be seen.

Animals that shared home with the land and sea moved from one unto the other, through the sands and the water. The shore filled with sparkling shells, smooth stones, dead plants, wandering crabs, turtles, and wet seagrass. A chill flowed from the seas, riding the waves of the salt water and crashing into the dirt. The tales of winter would soon arrive, and its songs would fill the air and cause bones to shiver. Till then, those that feared its embrace prepared with haste, animals, and people alike, hoarding food and warming beds before its arrival.

Another zephyr cruised onto shore carrying the smell of the sea with it; salt and seaweed. Four of the boat's occupants were on the ground offloading the last of the bags that filled it while a fifth idled, seated in the sands. When they finished, they pushed the sixth occupant back into the clamping grasps of the water to return to whence he came.

"*It's a quarter day walk to Hanag, you'll make it before sundown if you trek steady,*" he claimed as he rowed backwards in the direction of the main ship that waited. The water pulled him in as he rowed, shrinking his size as the distance lengthened from shore. The ones who stood in the sands stood in silence, four of them gazing at the ship that housed them for over two weeks readying to depart from sight.

The next chapter held promise for some, uncertainty for others and brimming gloom for one.

⬥◯⬥

"*Okay he's gone now,*" Kaise said, turning to Dakai. He ignored her words and kept on his solemn seat.

The dark green fold that covered his eyes sat still with him.

Kainu reached out to take a bag from Beara but she declined, "*I feel fine Kainu, I can carry it, you shouldn't add too much to your load,*" Beara commented, grabbing another bag from the ground.

Naemi walked toward her brother, kneeling on one knee when she got beside him. Her words were slow to come out, a part of her struggled to find the right thing to say.

"*Are you hungry?*" she asked, but he ignored her too, for a moment too long, and he got up from his seat of sand. His shoes were off his feet and he grabbed them, slipped his blindfold down and walked toward the group. Naemi watched as her brother left her, a similar routine to what she had endured the past weeks. He ate little and never spoke a word.

Most of his days were spent silent in the small cabins, broodingly sitting above deck blinded and listening to the song of the sea, as well as helping tend to Beara's wounds.

All these times Naemi did her best to shadow him while staying unseen. She worried as much as she could and tried everything she thought possible to get him to open up but he never did.

Kainu told her everything that happened that night on the building top. The overwhelming sensation that trapped his movements, the deplorable state Dakai was in, his attempt at death, the swing of the wooden board to render him unconscious and the tricky way he had to get him down the building.

Everything that happened in the chaos leading to their escape.

The news flummoxed Naemi at every turn, rendering her distraught. She couldn't understand her brother's actions and she questioned him more to answers of silence. She combed her memories trying to make sense of the cause, and also how possible it was for her brother to have abilities.

Her theories were uncertain, and she lacked evidence to strengthen any claims that formed. It could be argued that focusing on the unknown with her brother helped her take her mind off her own doings and troubles. The blood stains that shone dark red anytime she stared at her hands for too long, and the nightmares that sprung her from sleep.

The past days had been hard on almost everyone, everyone probably except Kaise whose cheerful demeanor somehow found a way to stay alive. Some days Naemi enjoyed it and other days she envied how perky she still was, and how much she could still hold joy and a smile even after everything.

Beara spent most of the time tending to her own wounds and covering up her marks. Her previous state had taken a heavy toll on her and she struggled to adjust to her freedom. Naemi attempted to inquire more on what transpired after they were separated, but she spared little and cared more for Naemi and Dakai's story instead. Kainu spent more time with the ship's captain and the crew, helping around and inquiring more about his destination.

The crew who claimed themselves as smugglers were an odd bunch, extremely jovial and weirdly competitive. Their captain was however still an honest man as ironic as that seemed, though he was very particular about his money and his terms. One time Naemi asked if he was a pirate and he visibly fumed at the premise.

*"A pirate? I am a smuggler, young girl. Don't you dare disrespect my trade by calling me a damn pirate."* He said hoarsely in his brash accent.

*"And what's the difference?"* Naemi asked.

*"Smugglers have integrity,"* he answered with a burst of confidence.

The skies today were as similar as any late morning of late fall. The rains had been scarce the last week. It had rained continuously for three days prior, and the seas reminded the crew of its power and eeriness. Today the sands were dry and looked dry for some leagues more.

The quintet locked the bags in their arms and started their journey. Most of the bags were for the twins, the rest of the three unfortunately didn't have the luxury of packing before their escape. The rest of the items they carried were unfitting clothes they got from the smuggler. Kaise offered to share some of her clothes with Naemi, and Beara got some extra wretched clothing from the men on the ship.

The twins also had coins for their journey though they lost a chunk bargaining for the change in cargo. Naemi offered to pay them off with the money she had. The twelve gold coins she stole from Mamuex. She still had the coin-bag tucked inside her inner pocket and was a miracle she didn't lose it through the turmoil. The rest of her coins lay buried in a wall on a land she hoped never to step foot on ever again.

Their walk continued, steady and purposeful.

Their eyes set on their destination; Hanag, the small city under the Thrun empire. Kainu and Kaise had thought long and hard before deciding on this destination. The city they hoped to start their new life free from the turbulence of a bigger more bustling settlement like

Nuun, Ordiva, Cratos, Yenshu or the moon city of Ishva. In fact Hanag could be regarded as a bigger town rather than a city. A calmer location compared to others, and one under the secure blanket of the growing Thrun empire, an empire known universally for its strength and advancements. One so strong and said to be filled with beings of sorcery in their army, even down to their monarchy.

An empire that could never be threatened. A nice town under such an empire would have the organization and steady rule of law without the proximity to the boisterous, overambitious, greedy, and unruly — a tranquil place to live a good life.

An hour had passed, and they had crossed the white sands and now through the tall grass that grew as long as their knees. The wind was mostly still, and the blades of green strands stood unmoving except for an occasional dance when legs swept through them. Kaise passed dried meat and some water around to the group and they ate to recoup lost energy. Naemi offered to help carry some of Beara's bags but she refused again. Her wounds were not fully healed but her pride was too much to admit she was still weakened. The area of congregated trees ahead was getting closer, and as midday progressed to full form, their journey persisted toward its destination.

The choice to proceed to Hanag wasn't as simple for some on the other hand. After escaping the city of a thousand ports, Naemi and her brother were once again on the open seas. Another opportunity to go home slipping their grasps. If only they could have had one more day in Sailor City, then maybe they would be heading toward Soros by now, or maybe, they would have been caught and thrown into dungeons or worse, killed. Whatever would have happened if they stayed, Naemi felt an ease that she made the right decision in fleeing the city. For all her experience in the world so far, she knew that having people she could trust and feel safe with was to her benefit, and she found solace in that.

The closest major ports that would have ships that might go to Primea according to the smuggler were in Ishva, Krapore and Cratos but the coming winter was going to cause a heavy pause on trading ship movements. The winters here were short but extremely harsh. About two and a half months of frozen water, brutal snow and chilling breezes with only a fraction of calm in between. In about a week or two, the cold will arrive and it will arrive with an icy entourage. Naemi considered her options; the naming of the moon city of Ishva triggered a response of flight in her heart and mind.

She asked the smuggler if he could take her to Primea, *"My father would give you everything he has, please!"*

She pleaded, but he laughed heavily and responded, *"Unless your father is the king of Primea or shits gold, I am not going anywhere north. I'm heading back south, back home to enjoy my wife's embrace and see my little ones. I'm in a good mood however so I can pass by Cratos and leave you off there; I have an old friend I could see too ... kill two birds eh,"* he answered.

Naemi politely declined; heading into another city didn't entice her, a decision solely based on her experience in Sailor City. Heading to Cratos meant she would be separated from the twins and left to endure the winter with her brother and a recovering Beara, having only twelve gold coins to their name. *How long can that even last?* She thought, while she deliberated her shrinking options.

Kaise proposed another solution, one that her brother supported. *"Come with us to Hanag and stay over the winter. We will take you to Cratos in the early spring. It'll just be a couple of days' ride, and we will help you find a ship back home. Beara can fully rest and heal, and you and Dakai will be safe there too."*

The proposal meant more time away from home, and as much as she despised being away, it sounded like the best choice that existed for her and her brother. Having Dakai away from a bigger city also felt safer in her mind, so she agreed to their proposal before she got the chance to acknowledge the new fear that grew inside her. The many twists and turns at every corner of their journey had festered this new fear, breathing life into the flames as it bolstered on fuel that dripped in secret. She had been developing a new fear of the unknown, the malignant idea that everything would go wrong and turn on its head eventually, and this thought in turn negated her urge to take risk in her journey.

<hr>

The sound of hammer hitting nail echoed into their ears. The group walked by a crew of workers who labored on a house by the road. They had walked for hours, resting only near the small settlements they passed and areas of sweet shade and water, Dakai always making sure to keep his standouts from prying eyes. The workers waved greetings, and the group responded kindly.

The town was now in sight. Its layout spread in a graceful organization, though some of the houses settled farther from others. The houses were shorter and much wider, the roads stretched in snake-like curves and the people who passed were warm and full of smiles. The entire town was at the base of a short valley. Walking through the streets reminded Naemi of Soros, although much bigger. The mixed houses with dark wood and dull white brick, the roadside stalls, and the loud vibrant children running reckless without cause. There was a calm in the air, and she took a deep breath to savor it. The town was sizable but still not even a quarter of Sailor City. A fifth of it maybe, though that could be up for debate.

Kainu turned to the group, "*We need to find a place to stay,*" he mentioned, and proceeded toward some locals to question them. Naemi looked around to see more of the town. A drove of donkeys passed by pulling carts of farm tools and food produce. They brayed loudly and deafeningly in irregular intervals to everyone's discomfort. Naemi continued her assessment, looking through the light crowds and the wooden buildings, examining the people and their way of life. They didn't stare back at her with belligerent eyes here, and as she continued, the differences she noticed increased.

One sight that caught her eye was the blue and white armored guards and the strange insignia they bore on their cloaks. There were many of them, a lopsided ratio for such a sized town, and they were all well armored and shielded with spears and swords. It didn't seem an issue for the citizens however; they continued their daily activities and the armored ones paced about with theirs.

Kainu returned with information, and he beckoned the group in a new direction. They followed his lead, everyone still experiencing the newness of the location in their own way. Beara was the only one to attract any stares, and how couldn't she, she was well over six foot with a striking physique, and anytime people saw her, they glanced a second time just to confirm she was a woman. Even with her loss of weight, her arms were still a molded highlight.

Naemi continued her examination of her new location as they walked farther, taking in every detail and noting everything she deemed unique. There were similarities that triggered her nostalgia of home, and differences that snapped her back to the reality of being away.

She continued on her route.

As she walked, she noticed the moderate structure with an aviary built into its side, and its interior full of what looked like messenger-birds. She stopped. She had looked for one of these messaging stations for weeks in Sailor City to no avail. It didn't seem to be a practice used in the city and she searched high and low to no result. She broke from the group and rushed toward the building, what she sought didn't even feel possible to her but her desperation had no mind for common sense.

A young boy sitting distracted was the direct recipient of her eagerness.

*"I want to send a message north ... Can I send a message north?"* The boy looked at her with a concerning look, one that denoted confusion.

After a brief stare, he replied, "*Huh? North where?*" Naemi repeated her desire specifying the location she wanted and it did little to help her case.

"*Uhh, I don't know of there, I can only send to the capital, Astor, Guyan, Du...*"

Naemi cut him off, "*I want to send one north, nowhere else, just north. Is it possible?*" Her voice pitched from what seemed to be irritation or over expectation.

"*Uhhh no. I don't think birds go that far,*" he replied.

The rest of the group entered the structure calling out to Naemi. They had noticed her disappearance just moments ago, and had to retrace their steps to find her. Kainu berated Naemi about leaving the group without notice. Kaise jumped in the scolding also, still holding on to a silent Dakai's hand, and Beara stood some steps away admiring birds in their cages.

The door to the back room opened and an older lady appeared. She wore a long olive kirtle dress and hobbled when she walked. She looked to be in her early fifties, and had unusually long hair, one of faint gold that kissed the edges of her forearms. She inquired from the boy, and he explained what was being sought.

Naemi interjected almost instantly after, her eyes telling a tearful story.

"*Please, is there no way I can send a message as far as Primea?*"

The woman was slow to respond, moving away to shelves by the wall and looking through scrolls.

"*Primea? That's a long way. Even if you could get a messenger-bird there, how would it know where to go?*" she asked Naemi.

The question rendered her speechless. She hadn't thought that far, and that's if she was even thinking logically at all. This little crusade was solely based on hope of the unknown, and even with her developed fear of it, she yearned that the next roll of the dice would be on her side.

"*We had a messaging station in Soros, I just hoped it was possible,*" she answered, lowering her head and turning away to head out as the reality dawned on the possibility of her request.

"*Aah there it is,*" the older lady exclaimed. Her voice still as calm as the tides of a lake. The birds that chirped around weren't as calm however. She walked back to the table with the scroll she found.

"*You are obviously not from around here, this message must be pretty important to you?*" she asked Naemi who had stopped her leave pending curiosity. Others shared a more concerned expression at her statement and she noticed.

"*You don't need to worry here; we welcome everyone with open arms.*" She reassured, and smiled. She looked back at the opened scroll, tracing patterns and lines with her hand.

"*I can't send a message that far myself but I can pass it on to those who can. The mages in the Capital send messages from the Aarcabra to other realms all the time. They share knowledge with other historians, inventors, adventurers and knowledge holds of other nations, even ones far up north. They use migration patterns of certain birds to carry the messages over long distances, and as long as there is a receiving station, the message will be received. These messages can get there fast but not always reliably, and there's only limited messages to send; after all how much can a bird carry,"* she said, laughing visibly at the joke.

Naemi's face lightened and the woman continued, *"Ahh yess,"* she added, pointing to a mark on the map.

*"There is a receiving station near the Prim City in Primea. If it is received there, it is possible to forward it to the town you say. I should remind you that you're relying on a lot of things to turn right for this message to get to its final place. There's a chance it may never reach, but there's also a chance it will."* she ended.

When she concluded, Naemi still stood speechless. It was one thing to hope for it to be possible and another thing to be presented with the possibility. The woman brought out a small paper, a quill and ink beckoning to Naemi to come write her message, but she stood still.

*"Naemi?... Say someth..."* Dakai spoke and stopped mid-sentence.

He was also going through his own set of emotions, first thinking the idea was full of insanity and then being caught in the possibility. Naemi turned at the sound of her brother's words, snapping back into the present and approached the woman. She stared down at the little cut paper three inches in length and almost five inches in width, and in an instant the words came to her in a flood.

The woman etched additional messages and directions on the back of the paper, folded it into a tiny roll and inserted it in a small wooden cylinder tied to a messenger-bird's foot.

She walked outside followed by the group, the messenger-bird secured in the woman's hand, and turned to look at Naemi one last time, *"Are you ready?"* she asked, and Naemi nodded in agreement.

Dakai heard its wings flutter and Naemi saw its black wings beat against the air as it pushed itself into the skies, her hopes flying away with it. She had staged another dance with the unknown and hoped it would be kinder to her this time. She closed her eyes to its trail, calling upon a higher power to guide its path to its true destination.

A prayer left her lips, one she had said before, a prayer to the All-Mother.

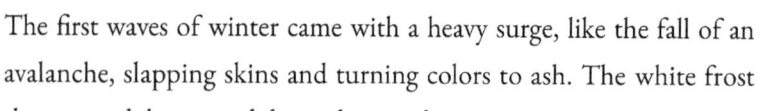

The first waves of winter came with a heavy surge, like the fall of an avalanche, slapping skins and turning colors to ash. The white frost that covered the grounds layered everywhere in its monotone ambience, oppressing all other colors and imposing its will on the lands.

The winds that guided it were even more vicious, turning water to ice in brief moments while chilling skin into wretched discomfort. The first two days of winter were no easy experience, the crew barricaded themselves in the two rooms they had for rent, only coming out at calmer intervals. They had been in Hanag for over two weeks, preparing themselves for the jolt of cold, gathering heavier clothes and getting as much food as they could store. The gatherings weren't cheap and even for a town that lacked the vigor of a bigger city, money still flowed fast.

The taxes were the most surprising to the twins; Sailor City never had such heavy taxes for daily spending, such was reserved for the traders and their loads, but here, the crown's tax was strictly enforced.

Kainu saw it best to look for work as early as he could. An ironsmith had a few openings for apprentices, maintaining weaponry and fixing chinks in metal. He had no experience in iron work; most of the people who were chosen didn't either, they were hired anyway for the scarcity of applicants.

Beara offered to hunt citing her mastery at the skill though the group requested she rest and gain more of her strength first. Kaise also tried to get work and got offered a job at the guard stables, but she rejected the offer due to her fear of being close to horses.

"*I always feel like they're going to kick me,*" she said to them, and everyone laughed at her words.

Naemi spent her time lazing around not interested in any work. The job in the stables was the only one she expressed interest in, but once another boy was given the duty, she regressed back to being useless. She did talk a lot however, trying to pass her time by engaging in conversation with Beara, the twins and her brother. Never giving solitary to her thoughts and herself, and if she was ignored, she would go to her corner-bed and sleep the time off.

Dakai was a total contrast to his sister though it can be noted that he was making visible progress toward the positive end of the spectrum. A first step to healing — a long and slow step. He talked more now, still a boy of few words, wearing his silence as his cloak. He kept on with Beara's treatment as her progress lengthened and her strength gradually returned to her. He still observed his long bouts of silence and self-thought. Naemi gave him his space, ending the continuous questions and hoping he would come to her when he was ready.

Dakai's trauma still held him captive.

The flashbacks he had of Davina and the blame he held bound his mind like chains of heavy metal, and he couldn't find the strength to release himself from them. His suicidal tendencies had worn off at least. His sister's words and worry still mattered to him, and in hindsight, he regretted the idea of deserting his sister. These clearer thoughts came with the clarity that only time could provide. He wasn't this way days after they left Sailor City; his actions then were still borderline erratic and the thoughts that swarmed his mind were still full of self-harm. He had locked himself in one of the lower cabins once, knife in hand, its sharp edge just an inch away from his left eye.

*If this is the source of my curse, I should truly blind myself, I'm already having to live without my eyes*, he thought.

His hand shivered as he drew it close, seeing the knife's tip start to blur in his sights, his hand shivered more, so much that he exhaled violently and dropped the knife. Even with the mountain of blame he carried, his fear still trumped all. In that moment, he was still a boy of thirteen thrust into a world he was not ready for, a world too cruel for his innocence, and he drowned in its abyss. He cried again that day till his tears ran empty, leaving only his sunken eyes.

Kainu was one of the people to approach him during this time, a surprise to Dakai considering their last encounter. He came to apologize for the strike to his head, and inquired about his health. Dakai's expressions spoke instead of his words and Kainu understood the caution.

What Kainu had experienced that night was something he would never forget. He had heard of people with strange abilities and wizardry in other realms of the world and always thought it was a myth made up by sailors to make themselves seem more interesting than they were.

*Is that why he covers his eyes? Does his sister have the same ability? Is that how she's capable of all these strange happenings?* Kainu thought.

He shared his findings with Kaise that night and she received the news with bewilderment.

Back inside the room of Beara and the Zenu siblings, the door opened and Naemi entered with Kaise holding logs of wood for the fire. Their boots invited trails of snow as they entered, and they shook off the buzz that came with a sudden change from cold to warm. The fireplace waited patiently for its fodder and the silence in the room disappeared with the entrance of talkative people.

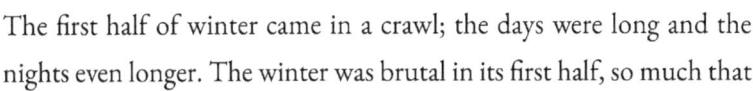

The first half of winter came in a crawl; the days were long and the nights even longer. The winter was brutal in its first half, so much that most nights, the five of them shared the same room to conserve heat.

The fire ran through its feed fast as it fought the seeping chills that passed through cracks and tiny spaces between closures. Clothing needed more layers for reinforcement, and personal cleansing was done with raw snow for some and melted ice for others.

Either way, the toughest of the battles were almost passed and the crew continued strong on their victory quest. Beara had gotten a lot better; her strength was almost near its peak and her hair grew more with time. She could move more smoothly now, evident by the giant logs she hacked into pieces for the fire with the new axe Kainu made. She had expressed heavy discontent on idling the days away, proceeding to ignore cautionary advice from her young healer after a while.

*"I can hunt; I will be of better use working than lying around waiting for my body to fully heal,"* she retorted. Kainu got a bow and some arrows for her, then on one morning, she set out into the woods with Naemi following eagerly.

They were gone for hours, long enough to incite worry until they returned later midday with Beara carrying a giant black hog on her shoulders, and a small group of townsfolk following her. Naemi followed among the townsfolk, while carrying three hares hanging on a stick.

The unknown group bargained among themselves, each proclaiming a price for a piece of the fresh meat. Wild meat like this was scarce during the winter time and people offered good money and trade exchanges for the chance to taste a piece. Beara sold parts of the hog and one hare for a few silver coins and grain.

That night turned out to be the most joyous time they all had experienced in a long while, a night where their bellies were too full bordering on discomfort, and their lips shone with grease and warm pork.

They joked, ate as much as they could, and there was still more left over for the coming days.

They laughed hard and drank, Beara doing most of the drinking though everyone took a turn.

Even Dakai felt loose enough to take some sips of Beara's strong ale, and he didn't last long to take a third; drowsiness overcame him, forcing him to slumber. The rest continued on, Beara being the most vocal. So vocal that her words turned into songs, her low toned voice echoing melody that her companions couldn't understand. They just laughed merrily, trying to follow her rhythm. She was obviously heavily drunk and joyous, evident by the huge smile she wore and her pleasing expressions. She rarely wore her emotions on her face, only on the rare occasion she was ecstatic or enraged.

"*This reminds me of my time back home, my family would have feasts for as big as a hundred people, we would slaughter full grown oxen, goats, chickens, pigs ... oh soo much meat. And we would eat till our fill and sleep under the open sky. My father would start a song and we'd sing with our hearts, shaking the skies with our voices.*" Beara commented out of the blue, she paused, a deep sigh exited her and her eyes held stories of reminisce.

"*I miss those days, I miss my family.*" she exhaled.

The four who sat around her went quiet listening to her words. Beara was never known to talk about herself in any way, and always ignored questions that pried at her history.

"*Where is home? Why don't you go back?*" Kaise asked. Beara continued her stare into the fire, its orange flames reflecting in her pure hazel eyes as if holding her in a trance. Her shortened brownish hair waved in the colored hues of the light's reach, and her white skin glowed with the intermittent flow of the fire.

"*I can't ... I can never go back,*" she spoke, her gaze unbroken from the gaze of the fire.

The door rattled slightly, another knock from the evening winds that sped as fast as a gazelle. The group kept their gaze on her with full attention.

"*Why?*" Kainu asked, the only one with the courage to inquire further. Beara took a long sip from her cup, emptying out everything the cup had, excess ale running down her lips and chin in nonchalance. When she finished, she slammed the cup to the ground in a slower tap. She turned to Kainu, her face almost detailing her emotion.

"*I did what was right,*" her words were almost inaudible.

"*I saved a friend from the jaws of an animal, but when the story was told, the serpent's status, his power and his lies swayed the hearts of men and my words of defense did nothing more than become a nuisance. They judged me for having the strength to oppose their power; I saw it the very moment I stepped in the midst of their courts. Not even my father's words or my brothers' could convince them to reason. And when I had hoped my friend would provide witness, she ...*" Beara paused and inhaled deeply, and then let it go, the rest of the words struggled to form but her face held its steadiness.

"*She took his side and threw me to the wolves. He told everyone I was jealous she loved him instead of me, so I attacked him with intent to kill him so I could steal her for myself. Such cowardice! But in their eyes, I had broken many sacred Viking laws and I was exiled from the land, exiled away from my family."*

The room was quiet after her words, except for the sounds of the wind and Dakai's untimely snores. Beara was staring back into the fire; there was a calmness inside it for her and she grappled to feel its warmth.

The feeling made her continue her unraveling, telling her tale to her small audience.

*"I left my home and was pushed into the world after they branded me sinner and murderer, marking my skin and my name foul. I sailed to many parts, selling the only skill I had, my way with the sword, just to survive. My skill though was always needed by the degenerate, the unworthy, because they are somehow always the ones with enough money to pay for such skills. So I would work for them, everyday questioning myself and my morals till I again decided to do what was right. And when I did, I made more enemies. Even when I tried to go under worthy causes, it always failed. My life seems to be marked with a lot of tragedy, and a lot of failure ... But I've never once regretted any of those decisions I made. They always felt true to me and I did them regardless of the consequences."*

Beara then turned to Naemi with an apologetic stare, *"I'm sorry for the part I played in you and Dakai's abduction. I know my atonement will be to get you back home, and I'll do everything to make that possible,"* she said to Naemi.

Naemi stared back with no ill will toward her friend. She only smiled lightly and nodded in response.

When Beara's stare returned to her place of comfort, she heard Naemi's voice reach her ear, *"What's your true name?"* Naemi asked.

She looked back at Naemi, her eyes relaxed to the words, *"Brynhild ... Brynhild Thorsten."*

———— ◆◇◆ ————

More mornings passed and the harsh cold days showed signs of losing its stronghold. The hunts weren't always as fruitful as the first, though there were lucky occasions in between. Naemi and Beara still went on the hunts nonetheless, hoping each hunting day was a chance to catch good meat and make even better money selling portions. After a while Kaise opted to join the duo, citing that it was boring to be left alone with Dakai who kept to himself and his own devices.

The three would explore the forests, and the unskilled did their best to learn as much as they could from the adept.

Everyone seemed to benefit in their own way with the exposure to the raw beauty of nature mixed with its imposing season of cold and white. Kaise delighted in the experience of the forest region. All her life in a dense city had denied her the beauties of a wild landscape, its giant trees and crafted mountains that peaked in the horizon. She had been known to exit Sailor City on occasion but never far enough to matter. Beara enjoyed her freedom and a remembrance of her childhood. After living a time so close to death while fighting in pits as entertainment for the depraved, there was a shift in her appreciation for her freedom. She inhaled fresh air and felt the white covered sands on the ground, enjoying the taste of self-agency.

Naemi also relished a similar taste, thinking back to her trips with Ozai and how the world felt much smaller and more secure during those days. She would give a lot to go back to being that naive, though weirdly enough a tiny part of her saw her naivety as weakness. Her journey was molding her in many ways, molding her mind and her soul into something without innocence.

Even now that she felt an ounce of calm and safety with friends, she always expected the possibility for change and braced herself for the stochasticity of the world and its endeavors. In her mind, her ultimate protection for herself and her brother were her powered abilities, and she worked secretly on herself to have more control over them.

During times where they would split to cover more ground and set hunting traps, or days where the weather spoke more favorably, she would engage her ability in seclusion, working to know more about herself and what lay inside of her. There was a fascination to it, an entirely new sense that she could bend to her will.

She could almost summon it now, with her mind at ease.

Whatever it was she didn't know but what she knew were its effects. The power was making her heavier and lighter at will. Like tensing a muscle to make it tighter and letting it go to loosen. She could feel the forces of the ground that pulled and pushed on her as her weight morphed to her will. The limit to how much she could morph was relatively unknown, as any muscle gets stronger with practice. For now, her short extent was still a thrilling revelation.

When she made herself heavier, her movement slowed somewhat but that came with an absurd amount of strength. She once lifted a boulder off the ground with such ease, it felt like a leaf snapped off a branch. When she touched anything, the slightest pressure made it crumble in her hands and the ground sometimes felt like beach sand. When she loosened herself to the opposite, she could feel the lightness that carried her, sometimes lifting her feet off the ground till she began to lose her balance and float. Her fear of being whisked away would kick in, and she would reverse her intent just to fall back down on instinct. She went as high as four feet one time and forgot to control her fall back down. She fell flat on her face, her reaction after getting back up was uncontrollable laughter.

It was an exhilarating experience for her in truth, and she did her best to not get caught. The fascination of her abilities occupied her mind and the intrigue of her brother's added company. These thoughts of their strange abilities filled her, and the nightmares of its consequences pushed further back inside the dungeons of her mind. She couldn't wait till she was able to talk to her brother about it.


Today, she walked in the direction of the curved yellowish maple tree back toward the town. Another hunting day without any game, the third day in a row. She was supposed to meet Beara and Kaise near the tree, the three had split to check traps and cover a larger area, though she and Beara were the only ones with bows and arrows.

The revelation that she was also good at archery was a surprise for Beara, and even she herself didn't think she retained such precision of the skill after months of treacherous ordeal. She moved through the soft snow at a slow pace, her right hand clutching the string of the bow that was hooked over her arm.

The arrows rested calmly in the quiver over her back, her white stained boots took one step and another, its dried animal skin layers doing its best to keep in warmth. The breeze stood still, an occurrence that was appreciated compared to much windy days when the breeze slapped faces and froze cheeks with its cold hands. Midday was almost gone but its light hadn't been altered much. Naemi continued her slow pace to the rendezvous. She was frustrated about the possibility of another day without a hunting prize.

*I hope Beara and Kaise had better luck*, she thought. At this rate she was looking at a dinner of rolled corn dough and mushroom soup — she hated mushrooms.

A movement caught the side of her left eye, a light dashing that was happening some ways beyond the occluding tree stems that stood in unison. Naemi stopped, moving swiftly to hide behind a tree. Her target moved again, dragging its presence into view. It was a young deer, about three feet in height, though if its growing horns were accounted for, it would be well above four.

It was a light brown color edging whiteness with its legs of a darker hue. The animal slowed down to a stop and looked around to certify its safety. Its black nose and voided dark eyes scouted its area confirming its privacy. Its horns swayed on its head like a giant crown of majesty moving up over its head and curving into two forks. The deer moved toward a shrub at the base of a tree seeing some wild berries.

Naemi placed the arrow on the string slowly, shifting herself from the tree and adjusting her stance. She moved her body into a line of sight, her steps sinking into the snow as gently as a hand enters water. She steadied the bow, her hand drawing on the string to extension.

The cold kissed her fingers but it mattered little. The point of her arrow gazed at her opponent; its majestic stand silhouetted by the colored background of winter trees and a snowy landscape looked even more beautiful. The deer raised its head at a faint sound, its eyes meeting hers briefly. She steadied her breathing, her hands calm, her mind free and her heart clear as a summer day; she let go.

The squeal that came from the dying animal was high. The arrow that pierced its lower front shoulder drained its life slowly. The pain anchored it in place, the arrow had found its mark in its lower lung and its breath faded even through its loud pleas. It lay there as blood from its body turning white into red.

Its eyes frozen to a single frame. Its ears heard the steps that approached it until its last sight came into view. It stared at the face of its killer with a sorrowful plea, and she looked back with a blank stare. Her knife in hand. Its pleas said to the wind, but the still wind carried it nowhere. The knife pierced its heart in moments, its cold touch chilling its pulses as it took its final breath.

Naemi lifted her head hearing Beara's voice call to her. She responded to give direction to her location. Beara came into sight a short time after with Kaise behind her and a bag of mushrooms in hand.

The duo showed visible elation at the hunted prize, and hurried toward her to help transport the prey. Naemi smiled at their joy, echoing hers in return.

*"We are having deer soup tonight."*

————————◄○►————————

Dakai lay in his patented staidness on the flat cotton bed being the only occupant of the room. The room wasn't dark, the window pair on the far end of the wall tilted at an angle to allow the flow of the day's light. The chill also flowed inside uninvited, though today presented to be one of the warmer days of the winter. The chilly reign was showing increasing signs of an end, and the streets started to fill again. Naemi and Kaise had left to go see Kainu at his workplace, Beara was snoring loudly in the other room and here was the only place he could have some quiet.

Over two months had passed already since they'd been here, months that went slower for him in his sights of darkness. Majority of his time had been spent inside with sparse occasions where he'd sit outside the house to feel the air and fresh breeze. He would sit outside while the interruptions of Beara hacking wood played in the background, or the warmer days when Kaise would force him to go on a walk with her.

He wore his fold more times than he didn't, even at times when he was alone or just with the crew. At first, they tried to encourage him to use it less once they got their own area of privacy, but Dakai rarely listened. The two rooms they rented were on land bordering the outskirts of the town, land that was owned by an older couple. The man was once a builder, though these days he had neither the strength nor the will to get back to his profession, and his wife still dabbled in her passion for pottery. They were a sweet couple, their house was a bit off from the rented space, and Kainu and Kaise frequently went over to help with chores or share a good hunt.

Dakai continued his gaze on the wood boards that filled the ceiling, the silence in the room was appreciated, but if he strained his ears hard enough he could still hear the echoes from Beara's loud exhales. He breathed out, and switched positions to search for more comfort. The bed he lay on was closer to stiffness than softness and gave him all the comfort it had to give. The comfort he searched for however was in his mind. He had made long strides in healing over the past weeks, his thoughts of self-harm were caged in the dungeons of his head, and he looked forward to a promising journey back home.

Naemi had detailed the contents of her message to him, informing their father where they were and where they would go on their way back home, as well as their projected durations.

Dakai had tuned his thoughts to optimism as hard as that was to do. He had gone through a sort of mental disconnect from his ability, fighting the occasional flashes of memories that came to him on distorted days. Memories from his friends that he never meant to trigger. He had already experienced the emotions of self-hate and its deadly effects, and hoped to free himself of bad thoughts. His friendships that grew — especially with Kaise who seemed to transmit her positivity to him like a flavored radiance — helped save his soul from a continuous spiral.

Overall, time had been good to him and the calmness of Hanag also played a bigger role. The process was still far from complete. He still had dreams of Davina, dreams of her face and her fall. The sound of her dropping to the ground played in his ears like a reverberation of his past, and his sins reminded him of their proximity. He spent a lot of time in his head; his life and history were like a puzzle he needed to solve.

His eyes had a story that was lost to him, and he needed to know more about his power. He couldn't envision the rest of his life with little sight and little words, the possibility of hurting another person shadowed him every time he opened his mouth. His words were now restricted to short sentences, never ones that carried a demand. He nodded more and resorted to using his hands as direction in tandem with his words. He yearned so much to tell his sister what happened, but the more time passed, the more he avoided reliving that dreadful day.

Nevertheless, he looked forward to going back home and seeing his father.

Early spring would be here in the coming weeks and their tenure of peace in Hanag would end. They had been through so much already, but there was a renewed hope for a better journey home.

# Chapter Thirteen

# SHADES OF SPRING

Shades of spring came in tiny rippled waves creeping in against the battalion of cold. Its early days saw unfortunate losses, but as time passed and its hold grew stronger, the gentle waves grew into giant tides, blossoming into the skies like an army of Astonian Ingrid butterflies, and the overwhelmed cold started its retreat into irrelevance.

The east had its own history of the seasons, their ebbs and flows, their strong rise into imperiums and their subsequent fall into unimportance. So was the doomed cycle cursed to repeat in unending continuance. The people who occupied the lands did their best to live through it still. They knew not any different, and they will never know any either.

Their whole lives had been filled with these timed changes they couldn't control, powerless in the face of the true god of the world, one their acclaimed gods could never measure up to.

A god that had set laws in stone that could never be broken, and the new season abided by the laws without question.

The messenger-birds flew in from the capital, passing their messages sent from the mages in the Aarcabra. The time-keepers had marked the start of the new season and the time of spring had officially begun.

Spring came with a freshness that could be sensed in the pulse of the air, a freshness that cleansed the lungs and caressed the insides of all who were fortunate to inhale its breeze. The scents that laced outside were of blooming flowers, sweet trees, warming lakes and growing fruit. Nature splashed into the skies and painted the lands with its color. Its many hues could be seen all over, its green dominating its portrait.

A warmth flowed with the change. A glorified incandescence that swept over the realm, melting snow and softening ice. The skies stood brighter, the sounds that filled the air felt more pleasant. The entirety of the Thrun region and beyond welcomed the spring with open arms. The streets of Hanag also showed joy for the new season. Those who hid in the warmth of their homes flooded outside to enjoy the change, flushing it with more sound.

Kainu drove the nail into the wood another time. Two more hits of the hammer and the wood piece held stiff and secure. He shook the leg of the table to confirm its stability and stood from the ground when he was pleased with his work.

*"You have the hands of a workman! Thank you for your help son, my knees don't bend the way they used to anymore,"* the old man commented to Kainu. His wife came into the room quickly after with a tray of food in hand and added further praise to Kainu's work.

The broken table had been an issue the man had hoped to fix for the past couple of days, but the growing pain in his knees played hindrance to those plans. Kainu offered to fix the table on today's visit; he hadn't been by in over two days and noticed the fallen pieces when he entered the house.

There were also a few other errands he helped the couple with during his visit; picking up supplies for the woman's pottery, getting meat from the butcher, buying extra grain, and sending over a box of wooden utensils and clayed pots to the market to give to the couple's daughter to sell.

The old man had a unique skill with wood craftsmanship, though he did less of it in his old age. Their daughter was as sweet as they were. She was slightly shorter than normal, plump with such smooth dark skin, and always wore a radiant smile that highlighted the slight gap in her teeth. There is gossip that they had two more sons who passed to disease, but Kainu never found the courage or necessity to ask.

The woman offered Kainu the food she brought in as she does almost every time he visited, and Kainu went through the routine of denying it twice before reluctantly accepting it even though he was hungry. He stayed there for a bit longer, engaging in conversation and answering questions that were thrown at him.

The couple were a curious bunch, a notable attribute common among older people. Nevertheless, he answered their questions and told them his stories. The one of how he left his family of fifteen who lived in the outskirts of the Guyan region to move closer to Astor and the capital. The story of his friends who were going further into the capital to visit their older brother and his wife, and their aunt who was guiding them.

The couple empathized with his stories and offered help however they could. The man had once claimed to help Kainu build a house in the early summer and Kainu felt such a wave of joy at the possibility of owning his own house that his eyes showed traces of water. The man mentioned it again today during their conversation.

*"Summer is the time for building strong houses. There's a lot of land to buy, the bricks dry fast and the trees turn ripe and tough for good wood,"* he added.

Kainu acknowledged his words with a flash of happiness in his heart and eyes, his mouth though still full of food. As he finished his visit and bid the couple goodbye, his heart still carried the joy that had sprung. He walked back to the area he resided with a smile on his face. His stay in Hanag had been everything he had hoped for. A far cry from the tumultuous life he had under a faux caretaker.

A life characterized by manipulation, moral blindness and a sinking sense of self-worth.

The history of who he used to be was a page he hoped never to go back to, and his desire for a new life was one filled with simplicity. A simple life with simple dreams, a house to call his own, friends he could trust and share moments with, and a family he could adore. He wanted this for himself and he wanted this for Kaise, and so far Hanag felt like the best decision he ever made. He had friends at home and at work, he had the resources to live a quality life, and soon he would journey to the capital to see more of this great land.

He pushed away the thoughts of consequences however, the consequences that seemed like impossibilities to him. He was far away from Sailor City and there was no way Mamuex would find him here. His betrayal and his theft would fade away into amnesia, or so he hoped.

He continued his walk home, a quick stop to get some rest and head back to work. The spring-time came with more work so he did his best to get as much rest as he could, when he could.

Spending hours in the forge was no joke, but his skill was growing rapidly and soon he would be able to forge quality metal work without guidance. His walk continued as the day blossomed, the sky still littered with its shades of spring.

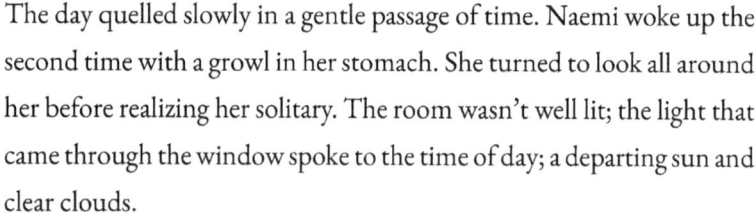

The day quelled slowly in a gentle passage of time. Naemi woke up the second time with a growl in her stomach. She turned to look all around her before realizing her solitary. The room wasn't well lit; the light that came through the window spoke to the time of day; a departing sun and clear clouds.

There was a sweetness in the air, a trail of a sugary scent that hinted to a prize of tastiness at its source. She sniffed the air like a wolf searching for its prey. Her hair tousled from the rapid movements in her sleep and the strings that bound her hair in tidy buns were missing from service.

Her face wore a sort of twisted frown, not because of her emotions but solely due to the distortion she had from heavy slumber. She rubbed her eyes casually and sniffed the air some more, the scent got stronger and she broke into a pleasing smile. She brushed over her tummy and stood up from the bed, fit her feet into some sandals and dashed outside.

The sight that met her was all she had hoped for and more. The simmering stew pot on the fire and the loaves of bread that lay to the side. A second small fire flamed some inches away from the first, and had cobbed corn roasting over a wiry metal mesh.

Naemi fell to her knees and let out an animated exhale of pleasure before rushing to get some of the food.

"*The stew is not fully done yet!*" Kaise's voice sounded from the side. Naemi didn't even notice Kaise and Dakai sitting by the side of the wall.

She let out another animated exhale, this time of frustration.

"*Is it lamb? I know it's lamb. Who made it? Dakai, did you make it?*" she asked.

"*Nope. Not me,*" Dakai answered, pointing his finger at Kaise. He was crouched down looking intently on Kaise's outstretched leg and Kaise wore a sad grimace on her face.

Naemi stared at them briefly and nonchalantly said, "*So you made the stew? Ugh?*" with an uncertain stare.

"*What do you mean by that? Are you not even going to ask me what happened? You almost slept all day,*" Kaise said defensively, still fighting through the pain she was in.

*"Mmm your last stew wasn't uhhhh the best ... but this one looks and smells good,"* she said rubbing her hands together pleasantly.

*"And I can guess you went near the flowers again and finally got stung,"* Naemi added while making a mocking face.

Kaise let out another yell when Dakai applied pressure to the stung area. Her eyes felt the water that gathered behind it and she didn't have enough resolve to push back heavily on the negative comments about her cooking.

*"Dakai and Kainu said they liked it."* She shot back, but Naemi paid her no mind, her only focus on the warm loaves of bread that sat by the fire.

Kaise continued, *"I just wanted to add some Beal leaves to the stew after I finished. I didn't even see where it came from. It stings so bad."* Kaise added and let out another yell.

Dakai noticed his sister's desperation for food and directed her to the roasted corn, *"There is some honey in the other pot too,"* he mentioned, pointing to the pot. *"You can have it with the bread or the corn. If you want. Aguera brought it earlier, her parents wanted to give us a farewell gift before we left for Cratos,"* he added, referring to the sweet couple and their daughter.

*"Arn theey too days eerly for that?"* Naemi commented with a mouthful of food. Dakai just shrugged in response.

A silence of words ensued for about a tenth of an hour and Naemi engaged Dakai again.

*"Have you eaten yet?"* She asked.

"*'I'm not that hungry. I'll have some of the bread and lamb stew when it's done. Did you enjoy your sleep princess?'*"

Naemi giggled at the comment and smiled. It was not a secret how long she liked to sleep, but giggled more at her brother's attempt at mockery. He had been more relaxed the last couple of days, an effect of the change in seasons or the proximity of their departure to Cratos. The journey ahead felt clearer. Everything they had experienced so far prepared them for their return.

They weren't alone this time; they had earned more coins through the winter and through their friends. The period through the winter had cleansed them, washing their bodies and minds in a pool of healing and releasing them back into the world. Some stains were harder to clean however, stains that embed themselves so deep they become part of the whole.

Still, there was a lot to look forward to, the journey back to Primea was going to be a long one with extended time at sea, but that was a worry for another day. Most of what needed to be packed was already done and all that was left was the anxiety of continuing on their journey. As surprising as it was, Hanag had a silent hold on them, and the realization brought forth intriguing emotions.

Regardless, they were ready to keep on.

The need to get back home was paramount and nothing could deviate them from their goal. Naemi finished her second honey-dipped cobbed-corn with bread-loaf, thinking of going in for her third, but she hesitated, *I need to leave room for the main meal*, she thought and stopped. Dakai was stirring the contents of the pot while Kaise relaxed on a chair, her affected leg left to the exposure of the air after Dakai finished treating it.

"*Where is Beara?*" Naemi asked?

"*Last I saw her, she was up in the fields near the shaded tree,*" Kaise answered.

Naemi got up to go in that direction and Kaise added, "*You should take some food to her too, haven't seen her eat all day.*"

And so she obliged, Naemi's last words before she disappeared being a plea to her brother to come get her when the stew was finally ready.

———◦———

The area where the crew lived extended past their section into a sort of open field with trees that lay sporadic. The land around here wasn't owned entirely by the couple that housed them, just a section of it. There weren't many people who lived in this area. It was nigh quiet and the closest houses scattered some ways away. It wasn't a long walk to the town however, which was much louder with people who lived in heavier clusters.

The place where the crew lived was only a two-roomed building, a passion project started by the old man about eight years ago when his middle son finally showed interest in being a builder. It was a very late change in desire, but he had felt so much joy at one of his sons finally showing interest in his line of work. Mobed; his middle son had left the family a year prior, going as far as the Zaire region and the southern realms of Igeria and Nhad with a hope to live his dreams. Insatiable dreams of a young man who saw the world as a canvas and wanted to have his imprint on it.

Unfortunately his journey was short and he returned with disappointment. The world he met was cruel and unjust, being a man of no great name and no money, he found himself starved and unhoused, plundering through streets just to have a day's meal.

At its worst, he set his sights back home, stowing away on a ship till he made it to Cratos, and then journeying to Hanag on foot. He survived the almost four day walk on moldy bread and water. His return though brought immense joy to his family, and his decision to join his father's trade made it exponential. His father had started feeling the effects of his age and the reality that he could pass on his skill to his son was elating. He got all his tools and found a section about three hundred feet away from their main house to work on a startup build; a two roomed house, one to get his son's feet wet and show him all the tricks of the trade. His hope was to complete the build together and work on a bigger house closer to their main house, one that would last generations.

His hope never saw fruition.

Halfway into their build, on a random morning, Mobed got bit by a black mamba. Its lethal venom sealed his fate in mere moments. All they could do was watch his decline to death, the antidote never got there in time.

There weren't enough tears to cry, not enough potions to heal a shredded heart, not enough words to describe the pain. The hurt of losing a child was a tragedy to wish on no one. Eyes bled after its water ran dry, and voices disappeared from burdened throats.

Massi and his wife, Dauna, mourned their middle child through the seasons. It took long before he found the courage to finish what was started, finishing the building through his aches and old age in the memory of his beloved son.

The couple decided five years ago to rent the space to weary travelers and people seeking shelter in order to put the house to good use. It would be a shame to see the place collect dust, an occurrence which triggered emotions that were too hard to bear.

The heartbreak that was felt never healed, the pain lingered in their hearts like a fractured scar for long, only for them to suffer another tragedy four years after.

------◄○►------

Naemi walked up the gentle slope with both hands occupied with food. The sun was almost out of sight, but there was still light in the skies. The clouds hadn't parted much; they lazed above without worry, their eternal service always unnoticed and unappreciated.

Naemi finally saw Beara standing behind the shaded tree; she had a long stick in the grasp of her hands, the one she had carved to replicate a sword, and was swinging it around with intention. She had been doing this for a few weeks and some parts of the calmer winter. She claimed she was losing her edge and needed to regain her skill with the longsword, a thought that started her long hours of training in the quietness of the fields. Beara would spend most of her free time here by herself. Naemi noticed her desire to sometimes be on her own and with her own thoughts, and at times struggled with the balance of when to leave her to her whims and when to provide company.

Beara saw Naemi approach and broke into a wide smile seeing the gifts she bore.

*"Just when I was feeling hungry,"* she spoke with a pleased desire. She dropped the wooden sword and walked to meet Naemi with her eyes focused on the honeyed bread and corn. Naemi giggled at her intensity. Beara split the food into two and offered half to Naemi but she declined, mentioning that she was partly full and waiting for the main meal to fill the rest of her hunger. Beara wore a more pleasing look hearing that all the food was hers, and retreated to the base of the tree to enjoy her delicacy.

Naemi moved toward the wooden sword she had dropped and tried to raise it from the ground. She tried the first time and failed due to the weight and tried again, lifting it the second time with ease, swinging it around with only one hand.

Metal swords were not common to citizens here; they were mostly carried by guards, warriors, or anyone who could provide reasonable reason to the state for their possession. Beara hoped to avoid any unwanted interactions with guards and opted for a wooden sword even when Kainu mentioned he could sneak one out of work for her. She denied his proposal and carved one out of fine heavy wood, wood that could replicate the weight of the sword as close as she could get it. She paused from eating, staring at Naemi with the sword in hand.

*"How are you able to raise that?"* she said with genuine intrigue. The wood had been heavier than she herself anticipated, and even with her training, she felt the weight of it in her swings and needed both hands to grip it firmly.

There had been unexplainable things that had happened with Naemi dating back to their escape from Sailor City. Questions she had that were never voiced. Pieces of a puzzle seemed missing, and she had been sensing a difference in Naemi and her brother. Naemi dropped the sword. She unconsciously used her ability to pick it up the second time and stood silent at the revelation.

Beara stared back and asked a question she had held back for a long while, *"How did you find me? In Sailor City ... How did you save me from the pits?"* The memories in her head didn't tell a compelling story.

Fractions of it seemed out of sorts and she could never make sense if it was real or imaginary.

*"I saw death call to me, then I saw something ... someone, someone falling from the sky. I felt the ground shake beneath my body, and everything collapse around me. Then I heard your voice from afar calling my name. I thought you were dead, I thought you and Dakai never made it."* Her voice resonated with such sincerity and softness.

Naemi stood still without talking, she had kept so much to herself that there was a difficulty in pushing the words out.

Nevertheless, the words came out eventually, slow, and then in a rush. Beara's emotions rose and fell in waves as she listened to Naemi's journey. The turmoil they went through and how they found each other again.

It was nothing short of fate; invisible strings that tie the paths of people together.

She saw the scars in Naemi's eyes, ones she wasn't sure will ever heal properly. The news of mystical abilities opened a dimension of thoughts she couldn't fully process in the moment.

She had heard many stories on her travels, but had never encountered one.

The exposed missing pieces of the puzzle fit in place, and the entire picture revealed itself.

*"Thank you ... for saving me. I was sure that was it. My entire life. Even when I was fighting, I felt the will to live drain from me. I owe you my life, Naemi."*

*"No, you don't. I owe you mine,"* Naemi interjected. *"I wouldn't be here without you,"* she added.

*"No you wouldn't. I should have freed you long before. You could have been home now. I was just ..."* she exhaled, *"I only cared about myself and my own desires."*

*"You cared enough when I needed it. That's all that matters to me,"* Naemi replied.

Beara's face wore heavy despondency and Naemi felt regret for the burden she had placed on her friend. She could see the blame Beara carried on her face and tried her best to cheer her up.

They talked more, exposing their thoughts and fears to each other. Talking through the growing darkness until Dakai showed up abruptly. The main meal was ready, and their remaining hunger forced conversations to end. The day progressed rapidly to a close and the date for their departure would soon be here with renewed spirits and motivations.

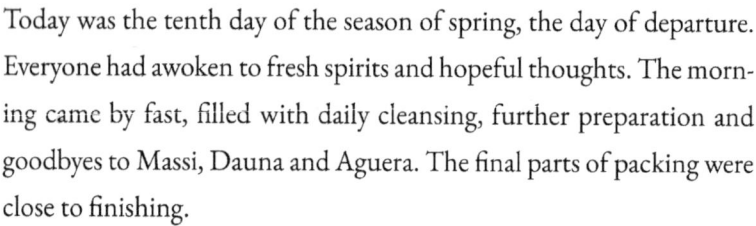

Today was the tenth day of the season of spring, the day of departure. Everyone had awoken to fresh spirits and hopeful thoughts. The morning came by fast, filled with daily cleansing, further preparation and goodbyes to Massi, Dauna and Aguera. The final parts of packing were close to finishing.

The bags they carried were much less than the ones they entered the town with months ago. It still had most of the essentials they needed, although Kainu and Kaise contributed more to it being less since they needed only the items for their travel to the capital and back. The rest still needed all they had for the journey ahead. It would have been a blessing to have horses for the journey, but their finances had spread thin due to the expected price of transport on a return ship, and three heads meant three loads of coins that needed to be saved. The hunting prizes helped greatly in building their coffers as well as Kainu's contribution from his apprenticeship wages.

Everything they needed to plan for had been planned for. The crew also got a donkey from Massi to help with their load. The old man offered it as transport claiming the donkey was lazy and it would be in its favor to do some work rather than to eat and shit all day. The animal didn't show any appreciation for being thrust back to work. It was loud at odd times and stubborn to move, so stubborn the crew drew straws to select whose responsibility it would be to move the beast.

Unfortunately, Naemi drew the shortest and was not very pleased at this association. For as much as she loved horses, she never extended that love to their shorter cousins. The feeling was mutual for both, and the rest of the crew laughed continuously at the bickering of the two.

The quintet started their journey close to midday; the major road to the capital was past the town square, a little north to their present location. The road was a vast organized network that smoothened transport from the capital to all notable regions of the Thrun kingdom.

Dubbed the roads of llores; named after the Queen Llores, wife of Alius Reis, who saw the need for developing quality roads as an essential need for an active economy and pioneered its development. An action that has been fostered long after she left the world though her name is forever entrenched in the love and appreciation for its creation.

The town square was decently populated, the markets close by normally reached peak density around late midday and the people who passed went along engaging in their daily routines. The crew continued along with Naemi a few steps back. The donkey would occasionally slow its pace and the duo would engage in a back and forth of leash tugging until the animal gave in again.

The road was in sight now, occupied with people leaving the town and others arriving in a near even exchange. Horses, wagons, trade transport and travelers all around. Kaise called out to Naemi to quicken her steps and she did, only for the donkey to slow down again. Naemi tugged on its rope and it brayed loudly in rejection. She threw curses at it and tried to pull it harder to little result. Eyes turned to her failure and people chuckled in passing.

The rest of the crew stopped their movement, and Kainu retreated back with Beara to help her while Kaise stood with Dakai. Naemi stopped tugging in frustration, still throwing curses at the animal who wouldn't budge. She heard someone call her name and raised her eyes to meet its source.

"*Naemi?*" The voice said again, its origin gentle and despaired.

She almost couldn't recognize the face that looked back at her in the instant, the hair that grew out of the face was tangly and disheveled all over, the cloak was rugged, stained and torn in some places, the boots were muddied with heavy brown plasters and the eyes, his eyes, carried disbelief. Like what he was seeing was an illusion in his mind and he waited for a response to consider it reality. The brown in his eyes looked back at her, his steps slow and his mouth agape.

"*Naemi!*" he said again in such deep melancholic relief. His voice, so distinct that the sound of it triggered the nerves in her being to shout words she couldn't find the control to do herself. The longing he had in his voice, the mixture of great sadness and great joy mixed in a mesh of conflicting emotions.

Naemi's eyes were frozen to the man who walked closer to her, her mind blank to everything else as he approached. His eyes, his voice, the face that looked changed with scars of his journey, his change in weight and the tattered clothes couldn't deny who it was in her mind. It was him. Her mouth finally opened and all she said was,

"*Father!*"

## CHAPTER FOURTEEN

# I WILL SCOUR THE WORLD TILL I FIND YOU

His embrace felt crushing. His arms wrapped around her in a loop and his eyes blurred from the tears that showed his gratefulness. The tightness of his squeeze, the words he formed in incomplete sentences, the wetness that soaked his face from the depths of joy that only a man who had experienced the darkest pits of misery could achieve.

Naemi hugged him back even tighter, tight enough to hold him in place lest he disappeared if she let go. Her heart cried as did her eyes; tears of longing. She could feel his emotions through their embrace, the tension in his soul, his dried and weary skin, the smell of his clothes, everything about him told tales of a journey into an abyss that had wrestled with him in so many ways.

Ozai saw his son through watered eyes, "*Dakai? Son?*" Dakai stood some feet away with Kaise oblivious to what was happening. He inquired from Kaise on why they were still waiting for Naemi, and before Kaise could describe the scene to him, he heard Ozai call his name.

The darkness that covered his eyes interfered with his perception at that moment. He didn't get the privilege of perceiving his father as Ozai approached him; maybe if he had, his reaction would have been different.

When the voice hit his ears, his body halted its movement, but his mind raced a thousand leagues in an instant. The voice triggered a shock that rippled down the corners of his being, and before he could fully process the reality, he felt arms wrap around him and cries of appreciation fill his space.

He stood speechless and motionless. Disbelief held him in a trance for too long.

"*Fa ... Father?*" he finally asked, his cracked voice starting to reveal emotion.

"*It's me son ... it's me. I'm so sorry ... I'm so sorry for what you've been through,*" Ozai responded with cracks of his own. Ozai touched the fold on his son's face and felt more sadness for Dakai's harsh exposure to the truth, the truth he hid from Dakai all his life.

Dakai still restrained himself from belief, the weight of emotion that would prompt was something he wasn't sure he could handle. His father continued to speak to him and Dakai just stood there.

*I've had dreams like this before. I'll wake up soon, I'll wake up to another quiet morning and disappointment,* Dakai thought.

He fought reality with denial, but the cracks of truth began to show. He could feel him, the coarseness of his father's hands on his face, his unique voice; so tender and coarse, the vise-like embrace that pressed them together in union. As the truth got closer, Dakai attempted to take off his fold to strengthen his perception but Ozai stopped him.

A tear fell from Dakai's left eye, wetting the cloth on his face. The denial he had was fading gradually, the truth in front of him was real and indisputable, and as the dam burst, his emotions flooded him.

The rest of the crew stood gazing at the revelation and subsequent fallout. The emotions that hovered were heavy and they shared glances with each other oblivious to what to do or say.

The people who passed shared brief interest in the spectation, a quick look and subtle intrigue, but ultimately turned their heads to their daily business and desires.

As the entire upheaved world of the Zenu family corrected, it barely registered as a blip in the lives of others. An unfortunate truth but still a real one, the threaded lives of people are only as significant as the threads they share. Some threads as close as they get in proximity are ultimately uber-leagues apart in destiny.

Naemi walked to her father and brother, and joined them in embrace. Dakai had broken down in tears and Ozai consoled him repeatedly. The three shared their moment for as long as time went on. They had been apart for so long, the emotions that had been hoarded had been full and overflowing.

The words they kept had grown so long that they would sound like gibberish if formed into sentences. They cared not about how long they spent on that road, for it wouldn't even account for a fraction of the loss they felt. Kaise walked up to Beara and Kainu, they all looked at each other with shared emotion.

"*So what do we do now? Do we still leave?*" Kaise asked. It was a valid question; to leave or to continue with their journey this day. They discussed it among themselves, highlighting reasons for each and eventually settling to postpone the journey. Today was too weighted to start the voyage to the Cratos capital.

The shift in energy had been drastic and they needed time to recuperate and reorganize. Beara approached the family and informed them of the suggestion.

"*We think it's better we stay here for some more days. It'll be good to spend some time together with your father before we set off again. We have a cozy home here to rest and more supplies to restock. If we leave now, we will be bound to life on the road until we get to the capital.*" Naemi nodded at the recommendation and spoke to her father and brother.

She beckoned Kaise and Kainu to come closer and introduced them to Ozai as her friends, "*Father, these are our friends, they're the reason we are still alive and well. We wouldn't have made it here without them.*"

Ozai thanked all of them with endless appreciation,

"*Me and my children owe you everything, I can't thank you enough,*" he said.

His soft expressions and kind eyes spoke to the indebted gratitude he felt, and the crew felt the weight of his words. The family of three started their return back to the house in Hanag, and the rest of the crew followed.

Kainu walked behind the group pulling the reins of the donkey, now being designated as its master. He pulled, tugged, and shouted curses as the animal fought back, moving at a snail's pace. Naemi turned her head to the scene and a wide smile plastered her face. She turned back and kept on walking, the flames of a boundless joy brightening her heart more.

They arrived at the house around half of an hour later; their walk back was filled with layered multitudes of heartfulness. Emotions spoke louder than words and they soaked themselves in the high of ignited euphoria.

Kainu and Kaise parted to the main house to give reason to their sudden return, and Beara left to isolate herself in the fields to give space to the Zenu family. Dakai finally found the privacy to give sight to his eyes, finally seeing his father who was lost to him. The traces of water in his eyes stayed even through his happiness and his elation knew no bounds.

A thought crossed Naemi's mind, one that drained her mood almost instantaneously. She thought of what she missed from the past, and its horrors traveled with her memories.

"*Raex?... Di ... Did he?*" Her face showed her change in emotion and her question rippled the same change in the rest of the two.

The room got silent, Ozai shared a somber look with his daughter and shook his head slowly in response.

"*And Rema?*", Naemi added through melancholy. Ozai exhaled heavily to brace for the weight the topic carried. His face looked more aged from his months of stress. He had strange cuts on his face, scars that looked old and others that were freshly healed on his lower neck, upper left chin and higher forehead area.

The gray in his hair had doubled, although the amount of hair he normally kept had doubled similarly.

He held the hands of his children and spoke.

"*Rema left to stay with her children in the Prim capital after Raex died, ten days after you were taken. The loss of her son broke her in many ways ... it broke all of us. I arrived from Shoretown the following night after you were captured and was met with wails and anguish. Part of the house had been burned black, and the rest was filled with ruin. The bodies had been moved by then, but I could still see the stain of blood that littered the soil. My heart sank when I saw it, I feared the worst.*" He paused to gather himself more and continued with heaviness in his voice, "*They showed me the body of the dead outsider, they told me they had searched the deep forest for hours, and about the tracks of horses that disappeared through the rocks directed to the southeast of the region. We sent word to surrounding towns of what had happened, asking people to lookout for similar outsiders and to return word of any sightings. I wrestled with restlessness every hour you were gone. My children ... Oh my sweet children, what darkness you must have gone through.*" Ozai wiped a trace of a tear from his son's eyes and a smile of appreciation brushed Dakai's face.

*"I left Soros in search of your trail. Chasing whatever news I could to find you. I sailed to many parts of the high seas, scavenging cities and towns with nothing but the slightest clue from sources that were far away from certainty. I could see the hopelessness at points through my voyage, the thoughts whether you were even still ali..."* Silence captured his throat briefly. *"But I never gave up. I couldn't. I wouldn't. I promised your mother I would take care of you, and I failed her. I failed you both. I prayed to the All-Mother to keep you safe, wherever you were in the world. I spent months traveling everywhere I could reach, some places not as forgiving as others. As my despair grew, my internal struggle conflicted between going back to Soros in hopes you had somehow returned, or move farther across the lands to places I hoped I would never see again. I had been away for months and the thought you made it home only to have me away was a feeling I couldn't overcome. I returned home after weeks of travel with a faint hope of a miracle, only to meet another face of disappointment. The house was empty and growing with stray vines. Everything was covered in dust and the only thing that disturbed their silence was my feet hitting the boards on the floor. My hope turned to shame; I felt shame to stand in the walls we once shared without you both in it. I knelt by your mother's grave and promised her, I'll scour the world till I find you, I will travel to the ends of the seas if it meant I could see you again."* His children looked at him intently, hearing his words and soaking his journey.

He continued, *"Before I could set off again, I was notified of a message that had arrived some days earlier, a message from you."* Ozai's eyes echoed the jubilance he had when he heard his children were still alive. Like a brightened light at the end of a dark tunnel, its rays gleamed with joy. *"I couldn't believe the possibility and when I read it, I couldn't wait through the spring to see you again, I couldn't take the chance when I finally knew where you were in the world. So I did whatever I could to find passage to this region and get to you, and I'm so glad I did ... my beloved children, I'm so glad to see you again."*

The light in the room pulled from one source and stretched its rays to every corner of the walls. Tides of emotion filled the cornered space as well as embers of solace. The inside of the room was clean and organized from its expectation of solitude, though plans had changed drastically.

Dakai's voice broke the silence next with the sound of earnest apology.

*"I'm sorry too, father. All this, everything that happened was because of me. It's my fault we were taken. I went against your wishes even when you told me to always stay in Soros. If I had listened, this would never have come on our family. I'm sorry, I'm so sorry."* His apology traveled deep from his soul and was visible even in his gestures. Ozai wore guilt in return.

*"Oh son. Nothing that happened was ever your fault. You could never do any wrong in my eyes. I am the one who failed you both. I couldn't fight my own fear and cowardice, and kept truth from you. I didn't know it would come to this, not after so many years. I thought we were safe now. Even when I restricted you to Soros, I did so in caution, I thought harm was far away. Me and Shaye always hoped to tell you together once you had grown older since you were the only one who had the eyes, but as time went on, I grew false feelings of security. I didn't want to taint your view of*

*the world, especially after your mother had died so suddenly. Our history is ..."*

He stopped mid-sentence and glanced at his children with shame in his eyes.

*"I ... I didn't want to change your view of us."*

*"What ... who are the Kaku?"* Dakai asked.

It was a question he could hold inside no longer. His entire life had been turned over because of his assumed association with a group he knew nothing of, and now that he had the chance to find answers he couldn't wait any further.

Ozai felt the sting of the question.

The slight miss of a heartbeat when something you dreaded finally arrives. He expected questions the moment he saw his son with a fold over his eyes. Whatever experience his children had fought through had unmasked topics he needed to speak on.

He took a deep breath.

*"The Kaku are your mother's kin ... your kin. They were the monarchs of the lands of Zaire in the south, and led the dynasty that controlled the entirety of the south for generations."* Ozai tried to add more words to his sentence but relented, the sounds seem to fall back into his throat and the words with them.

*"Why am I being hunted for my eyes?"* Dakai questioned again. He could feel the reluctance to answer his questions and it fed more into his desire for answers.

Ozai stared at both of his children and could feel their eagerness to hear his response. The truth behind the veil was a burden he had hoped never to place on his children, but hiding it helped no better.

*"Your eyes identify you as a child of Kaku lineage, and the Kaku are demonized."* A part of him resented the truth he had to share and the consequences it would create, but as his children looked back at him intently, showing the shallow traces of hardening they had adapted through their journey, he realized exposure was necessary.

*"I wish I could say the reasons are unjust or people are wrong. I wish I could tell you your ancestors were beloved and history has been reversed to paint them as evil, but I can't, because they were not. Great as they were, most of the Kaku clan were full of malevolence and depravity. They ruled the lands with fists of iron and people hated them for it. They conquered nations and annihilated bloodlines they saw as threats. Massacred, enslaved, and imprisoned people from defeated lands to maintain their dominance. The people under their rule lived under restriction, and if they ever formed an intention to rebel, their plans would fail before it even started. The people were forced to worship their ruler and the clan was to be revered as gods amongst men."*

*"You are being hunted for your eyes because your eyes are the mark of their rulers, and the only way you can be identified as Kaku. Your mother called it the trait of the emperor, colored eyes that she said granted the user certain mystical attributes, one that the clan had used in secret for generations to sustain their power. It was a rare trait that was passed down through the bloodline, though there were never more than five at a time. Your mother and I never thought any of our children would get*

*it, and when you did, we tried all we could to protect you from the life that awaited. Soros was small and isolated, far away from news of the south. We had already been there for years so we were sure you could have a life there. Still, we wanted to maintain your innocence for as long as we could, so I restricted your life and I'm sorry for that. I held the truth from you for so long and I was wrong for it. We didn't want your childhood to be burdened with fearful thoughts. Your mother wanted only the best for both of you, and no matter what the truth is of her family, remember her as the sweet and gentle woman she was, because that is who she was. She was too good for her family, she was too good for this world. That is why we ran away."*

Silence ensued for moments after Ozai finished his speech. The weight of his utterances closed their mouths but opened their minds to the gravity of their reality, and the history that shadowed them for as long as they would live. Dakai sunk deeper into his mind, connecting dots and making sense of more pieces of the puzzle, though many questions still remained.

Naemi looked at her brother and then at her father; she could see the patented look her brother had when he isolated himself in deep thought. Her father on the other hand wore an expression of shame she had never seen before.

She had always adored her father's poise and control through varied circumstances; she had seen him bear so many emotions before, but shame was never one of them. She reached out to grab his hand and attempted consolement.

*"You did what you thought was right. I know you and mother wanted the best for us, I will always know that, and nothing I ever learn will change that."* Her words lightened his expression and a light smile drew on his face.

The room had gotten slightly darker, and she stood up to go start a fire in the fireplace. The warmth that hovered still stayed and the gloom from outside went unnoticed. Time had been going fast though it was still quiet outside.

No one from the crew had returned and Naemi made a passing remark of it as she set up the fire. She grabbed water from one of her packed bags and offered it to anyone thirsty, her father being the only one to accept the offer. Dakai was still quiet and Ozai struggled to find the right thing to say.

*"You said the eyes came with attributes? What attributes?"* Dakai engaged suddenly.

Ozai obliged his request and replied, *"Your mother mentioned they had the power to see through minds and control actions. To reach into someone's memories and see their past lives as if the user was directly living it. To speak commands and control the actions of people just through their words. The eyes could hypnotize and compel all except those of similar Kaku bloodline even if they lacked the colored eyes. Activating the eyes was done when the users were young children, and mastering it took years to achieve. The mind is a delicate organ and compelling it the right way is even more delicate. Fortunately yours never, even when we lost your mother. She was very strict about how I treat you in the event of her death, and is the sole reason you never saw her die or her body after. We couldn't risk the possibility of what that sudden pain would cause to you."*

Ozai worried about how much he was telling his children in such a short time.

*Could they handle all this information? Is it right to tell them everything at once?* He thought.

He had always envisioned doing this with Shaye, and when he lost her, he had hoped he never had to do it. He moved his eyes from his son to his daughter, noticing a changed look on Naemi's face.

*"Activated? But it ..."* Naemi paused her comment and stared at her brother.

*"Dakai?"* she called to her brother, and he looked at her with the glowing in his eyes.

She had connected some dots of her own, and the conclusion she came to filled her with unease. She already knew Dakai had activated his abilities, but the realization that her own death may have caused it triggered self-blame in her, and she felt responsible for everything that had happened thereafter.

She heard her father call to her asking what was wrong. She hoped so much to tell him everything but feared the repercussion. Opening her journey to him also meant revealing her sins to him. Revealing the pain that the world had caused her and the ones she had caused the world.

*Will he still see me as his innocent little girl or see me as something else? Something changed by the world?* She thought.

She opened her mouth to speak and before the words could leave her lips Dakai spoke, *"I ... I killed her, I destroyed her mind."*

---

Kainu and Kaise saw Beara sitting by the roots of the shaded tree with her back resting on its wide trunk. They thought she was asleep but as they got closer, her eyes opened to meet their gaze.

The sun had disappeared long ago, even through midday, and the glumness of the sky had lasted long afterwards continuing to approach the early evening.

"*You went back to training?*" Kainu commented, seeing Beara's long wooden sword resting a couple of feet away on the ground.

"*I got bored and needed to clear my head,*" she responded. Kaise set the basket in her hand to the ground and Beara smelled the aroma that came from it.

"*Are you hungry?*" Kaise asked.

"*Starving!*" she growled as she lunged toward the basket.

"*Careful! Not all, it's not for just you,*" Kaise remarked.

Kainu giggled at her aggression and turned his attention to the darkening sky and its floating white fogs. There was a sweetness in the air even besides the food's aroma, and he inhaled a deep gulp to refresh his lungs. He turned his focus to the longsword that lay forgotten on the ground, attempting to pick it up with both hands. He strained as he raised it a few inches off the ground. It was heavier than he expected, the long blade affecting how much force he had to hold the hilt with.

"*Why is it so heavy? Isn't this a training sword?*" he mentioned. Beara never left her attention from the pork pie-cake in her hands and answered him after she finished swallowing the food in her mouth.

"*Should a training sword be worse? We train to get better, no?*" And went back to her food.

Kaise covered the basket with the rest of the food and sat next to Beara. She and Kainu had spent the last six hours with the old couple, informing them of why they had to postpone their trip to the capital, as well as helping them cook food for their lunch and subsequent dinner. Time had passed quickly through their discussions, making the twins stay longer to give privacy to the reunited family.

"*Do you think it's fine to go back now? I bet they haven't eaten since we left.*" Kaise rose and asked the group.

"*I was starving, I'm sure they are too.*" Beara seconded.

"*There should be some snacks for the journey in their bags, but yeah I agree we should go back. This is better food anyway,*" Kainu finalized.

Beara finished her last pie-cake and walked toward her training sword lying where Kainu left it. She wrapped it in a dry cloth and shoved it into a hole near the tree roots. The group gathered themselves and began their return to their housing. The sound of Kaise's voice could still be heard through the wind as she kept talking en route. Darkness continued its formation as the time for its stronghold increased, late evening would soon arrive and throw its blanket of black all over.

A knock was heard on the door, then a voice inside the room replied to the outside request to come in. Beara opened the door and met the eyes of Naemi and her father. They sat with their backs leaning on the wall and Naemi's head resting on her father's right shoulder. Dakai was sleeping, curled up on the ground with his head on his father's lap. The room was warm and its source of light glowed from the fireplace.

"*We brought you some food,*" Beara whispered to them revealing the basket as she widened the door. She set it gently to the side and its aroma escaped into the noses of the room's occupants. They thanked Beara gracefully and she replied with a smile.

"*I'll sleep with the twins tonight, your father should sleep here,*" Beara commented, and Naemi nodded to her suggestion.

The door closed back again as she excused herself, and the room returned to its previous state barring the fresh scent of pie-cakes introduced. It had been about two hours since they ended their serious conversation, their voices had run dry, their water reserves had emptied through their eyes, and their bodies were weakened from the turmoil of emotions that rose and fell like the tides of war.

How much is too much? How much emotional drain can one take in a day until their bodies give out and their minds wander in extreme fatigue?

Whatever threshold there was to it, the Zenu family breached it today.

Ozai had listened to his children's journey with a sunken heart and a stagnant pain. The pain of a parent hearing their child's crisis knowing they weren't there to be their savior. It was a pain that stung the heart and itched the nerves. One he could feel in the deepest parts of himself that he wasn't even aware of. Things he heard of their journey arose so many different waves of emotion in him.

Anguish, sorrow, bewilderment, more anguish.

The world had stolen his children from him and when it gave them back, it had broken their spirits and reformed their souls into something else, something he wasn't even sure he knew at the moment. Ozai balanced between gratefulness and anger at the higher power that treated their lives as mere tools to satisfy its boredom.

His heart ached for his children.

Throughout their lives, he had done everything he could to protect their innocence, protect their joys and wide smiles as any parent would. He had experienced the world in all its cruelty, his history and his participation in it was still undisclosed to his children. He turned his head to his sleeping son and brushed his hair. The flaming embers of his resolve grew stronger nonetheless. Whatever they had been through, whatever they had done, they were still his children, and nothing would ever change that.

He thought of his wife, *I wish you were still here Shaye, you always knew how to make everything better.* And he closed his eyes to meet his happier memories of her.

*"You should eat,"* Naemi said, stealing his attention.

The words pulled Ozai away from his thoughts and triggered the feeling of hunger in his belly. He hadn't eaten since last night when he was wandering the streets of Hanag with purpose though without destination. Surviving on his last salted fish and water. He had bigger worries at that time than a good meal; he would have gone hungry for weeks if that was the payment he had to make to see his children, but luck had found its grace on him, and hunger was now a priority.

The mention of hunger released his senses to reveal his starvation; the scent of the food didn't help either. He had no choice but to agree with his daughter.

"*You also need to go clean yourself, your clothes stink.*" Naemi added. Ozai took a second glance at himself and smelled his clothes, the truth was clear and he giggled slightly at the reality of his daughter telling him to go clean when it had been the other way round for years.

"*Yeah I should. I haven't had a full bath in days.*" He responded in defeat.

"*I will ask Kainu if Massi could spare a few clothes to help. We can eat when you finish,*" Naemi concluded, and her father agreed.

The rest of the evening went as planned. Fresh clothes, clean bodies, filled bellies and growing spirits. Energies had depleted so much that they looked forward to sleep and the rejuvenation it would bring. The night danced to a slow song of passing time and darkness while eyes closed to slumber. For the first time in a long time, the Zenu family slept under one roof once again.

⎯⎯⎯◆O◆⎯⎯⎯

Naemi jolted upright from sleep and looked around the room frantically. The seeping light of dawn gave sight to her eyes, and her nerves calmed when she saw the two resting bodies sleeping scattered on their beds. It was the second time she had done that in mere hours, flinching from sleep as if to escape from another realm. Her mind calmed when she saw her family, and her heart slowed its racing.

She feared she would wake to a different reality, opening her eyes to realize everything she had just experienced the night was faux and the truth that remained was only the grim actuality of the world. She exhaled a sigh of relief and fell back on her bed. Sleep had left her and all that was left was a recovering sense of health and a dreading sensation she couldn't pinpoint. She listened to the quiet sounds of breathing from the other occupants in the room; she always envied how silently they both could sleep. It was as if they were sleeping on a bed of soft feathers. It was simultaneously irritating and charming.

She moved her jealous focus off her father and brother; no matter her feelings she could acknowledge the need for good sleep especially in these moments. She retreated to the confines of her mind as she stared at the above, looking at the darkened ceiling and light that gradually changed its hue as the day took to form.

She longed to go back home with her family. Back to her life and routines, everything was simpler then. She thought of her old friend Bellie and how much she missed that silly horse. She thought of her friend Raex, the long conversations they used to have, the ones about their ambitions, their goals and what they searched for in life. Raex would talk at length about his desires to be a warrior, climb the ranks and become one of the greatest fighters in all of Primea, great enough to be knighted by the queen.

*"I will be the first Knight from Soros, you wait and see,"* The passion he had was so visible in his expressions, layers of pure unfiltered joy of a young boy. She would mock him a little about his wild dreams and after, fill him with lots of encouragement. So was their dynamic.

*"What is your dream Nae?"* He asked her once, and she couldn't find an answer for him.

*"I don't think I know yet. I have things I love, but I'm not sure what I desire for my life. I'm happy here, I'm happy with my family so I guess whatever it is, I want to be happy doing it."* She answered.

*"Maybe you'll take care of horses forever,"* Raex teased.

*"You know what? I'll love that too,"* Naemi laughed in response.

She fought off her darker memories with lighter ones when they tried to invade her recollection. She'd like to think in another life Raex got his dreams of becoming a knight, and rode through the streets of Soros with people shouting his name with laudation. She stayed in the comfort of her mind for long not realizing she had drifted back to sleep again.

———◆———

Dakai awoke to sounds in the room. Morning had arrived close to three hours past, and the day had already taken on its full form. He extended his body in a full stretch, straining the pleasant feeling until it turned unpleasant. His sights were hazy and he blinked many times to recalibrate himself. He had slept for long, after pouring out his heart and his secrets; he emptied himself of a weight that anchored his spirits since its inception.

The weight he held on to left but the lessons he learned didn't, lessons and scars he would bear forever.

A lesson as simple as knowing himself and the danger he could be if he wasn't cautious of his actions.

A lesson with an unbearable cost.

For those imbued with immense power bear the responsibility of its uses, and their actions will be judged by their own conscience.

"*Who's the sleepy potato now?*" He heard someone say, then heard his father giggle at the person's comment.

"*Did you sleep well son? There's food, you should come and eat,*" Ozai added. Dakai rubbed the blurriness from his eyes, his consciousness still out of sorts. He felt the rubble in his stomach that affirmed his father's concerns and obliged his request.

The porridge was warm and the taste of honey and crushed walnut added an extra spice to it. It washed his throat clean and gave his nerves the spark of lightning they needed. His face though still lacked any pleasant expressions as he drank.

The sounds of his sister and father conversing still continued and abruptly he commented, "*I want to go home ... I'm tired of being here. I miss Soros, I miss my friends and our home. Can we go back soon? I want to go back.*"

There was a brief silence, then his father affirmed, "*You're right son. You've been away for too long, we all have. How about we leave tomorrow? We will head back to the ports and find a trading ship going back north.*"

*I will promise them all the money I can give when we get back home; and I'll work as part of the crew in addition to paying for transport. You both won't h..."*

"*You don't have to. We already have money for transport for three and you can take Beara's seat since we won't need company anymore,*" Dakai interjected with an enthusiastic expression.

"*You do?*" Ozai asked, puzzled.

"*Yes! Naemi and Beara sold hunted meat during the winter, and Kainu and Kaise gave us some of their coins too.*" Dakai added. Ozai looked at his daughter.

"*You hunted?*" he commented, and he turned back to his son, "*Are you sure Beara won't mind?*"

"*No I don't think she will,*" Dakai added again with enthusiasm, "*I can go ask her, and then tell the others we are leaving tomorrow.*" He continued, and before his father could say anything, he whizzed outside and disappeared behind the door. Ozai's later words never formed enough to reach him.

"*Seems sleep gave him too much energy,*" he said and turned his focus back to his daughter.

"*You don't approve? You have that look you give me when you don't approve of my decisions. You get it from your mother,*" Ozai remarked with a lightened smile.

"*Do we have to leave this soon? We just got you back. And you're not even fully rested. The journey back home will be long, and you'll need as much rest as you can have. We can stay here for as long as we can till you're ready, we don't need to go tomorrow,*" Naemi responded with a plea in her tone; she wasn't in support of the quick departure especially after everything that had happened, and she hoped her father would see the same.

*"I understand. I know it may be too quick for me to set back out, but I will be fine. I got favored beyond my greatest desire; the All Mother smiled on me and led me to you two. You and your brother have been on strange lands for far too long, it's time we all went back home. Don't worry about me; let me carry all the worry for you and Dakai. These old legs are still strong as stone."*

Naemi agreed to her father's rebuttal reluctantly; she'd already sensed the steady desires of her father and brother, and the odds weren't in her favor. She gave up her quest to focus on other endeavors. If they were to leave tomorrow, she needed to go make preparations; feeding the donkey, checking their food supplies and confirming to the others of changed plans.

She stood to mark her leave, but before she left, she grabbed a small knife from the inside of one of the packed bags and handed it over to her father.

*"Your hair looks a mess,"* she said, and Ozai replied with an affirming chuckle.

The rest of the day went by in a slow cycle. Some of the group stuck to their repeated routines, others idled about with nothing to do, and the rest helped prepare for the journey ahead.

The rescheduled departure date brought direction to their plans, and those who had to repack did so diligently. Still, more conversations were had about altered plans and changed destinations. Beara was more than willing to give up her seat to Naemi and Dakai's father. It was nothing short of miraculous that they were able to meet their father at the right time before their initial departure, and his presence meant her duties as guardian would be coming to an end.

Her emotions swelled at the thought, but she held them at bay until their final goodbyes in the capital. Naemi tried to convince her to come along still, but she declined.

There wasn't enough money for all of them, and she didn't wish to keep them away from home any longer.

"*Where will you go?*" Naemi asked her. Her mind had no answers to the question.

"*I don't know yet. I think I might come back here with the twins after and stay for a while until I find my next destination.*" Beara replied.

"*You should come see Soros sometime; we have the most beautiful mountains there. They stretch for long and give the best views during sunrise. We could go horse riding through the stretched fields too. You'll love it,*" Naemi added.

The realization that they would be parting ways soon prompted emotions that were heavier than they both imagined. Beara smiled at Naemi's request and promised to come visit Soros in the near future. Ozai also shared more endless thanks to Beara and the twins. He was forever indebted to these strangers he had only known for less than a day, and he knew not the words to express his eternal gratitude, not that there were any.

The rest of the day continued in ordinary fashion, a sunrise progressing to a sunset. The suspended ball of fire retired to its chambers after the day had ended and darkness gladly took its place.

The Zenu family also retired to their chambers, passing time and engaging in sparse conversation.

"*I'm making you the best rabbit stew I've ever done when we get back home. I know you must have eaten a whole lot of strange foods throughout your journey. I will feed you both so much you'll turn plump with fat.*" Ozai remarked.

His children looked back at him with brightened smiles and cheerful faces.

"*We could go on more hunting trips now that you've picked up the skill. Dakai you sure you still don't want to learn?*" Ozai questioned.

Dakai pondered on it briefly and answered, "*I think I can start some lessons.*" Ozai wore a big grin upon hearing the answer; his smile rippled his skin on both sides of his mouth and his son could feel the joy that emanated from him. He had cut off most of the hair on his face and on his head, returning to a look his children were all too familiar with.

"*I'm glad to hear that son. Your mother loved to hunt and I just want you both to share more of her desires. I see her every time I look at you both, her imprint is as clear as day on your faces. She would be so excited to see you both enjoy her passions.*" Ozai shared a pleasing look, his eyes showing the reminiscing that went through his mind.

"*Father? You never told us how you met mother,*" Dakai asked, breaking him out of his daze. The question caught Ozai by surprise though it still held true; he had never mentioned how he and Shaye met. As much as they talked as a family before Shaye's passing and as much as he talked about her after, he never revealed how they came together.

Maybe it's because he thought the conversation would lead to topics of her history and he did everything he could to avoid that. He took a calm breath before engaging, his voice still as warm and spirited as ever.

"*I never told you because I feared revealing your mother's history, but I reckon I also feared revealing some of mine too. I grew up an orphan, left on the doorsteps of a local orphanage to a caregiver who was the only mother I ever knew in this world. I lived my life in the slums of the Meor city with other children I called brothers and sisters, striving our way through the hardships of the Great Meor cityscape. When I think back at that time, all I can remember is the grimness of the slums. The strong smell of the gutters, the scorn on peoples' faces, and the greed that shaped our minds and filled our bellies. Kindness was a rarity in such a place, and we developed scales in exchange for the best parts of ourselves. When I got older, my choices got smaller. As bad as the orphanage was, at least I could depend on it for meals to survive. But once we were older and newer children filled our space, there was no space for children our age, so we were thrust into the streets as it had happened to many before us. Our options were dwindled. We had to decide whether to find an apprenticeship, resort to pilfering or join the Kaku army. Apprenticeships were hard to find and even harder to maintain. 'Orphan-scum' they called us. The name had a bad reputation and people seldom gave us jobs, and would rarely pay a*

*good wage even if they did. Some of the others resorted to robbery, but the price for stealing was steep; a severed hand as well as months in the fire pits or Charia mines. The Kaku army was where most of us ended up, volunteering to be sent to wars in exchange for steady meals and quality roofs to lay our heads under. It wasn't such a bad idea at that time, three years under the army then we would be eligible for a repost. The choice to stay in the army or the chance to join the Meor city guards, region scouts and other units. The dream was to join the Meor city guards along with many of my peers. It was the most attainable and its benefits were all I could hope for. Enjoying the privileges of the city with the backed power of the monarchy. My year under the army regiment was one of the hardest I ever endured; I looked to the future with hope, and that's mostly what held me together during that time. I charged into battle with my spear and shield and fought under the Kaku name; I slayed and I was almost slain many times. I committed many sins under the name of my master, sins that stain my hands till this day. I can claim I didn't have a choice in my doings, only doing what I was told, but that would be a lie. Whatever orders I was given, it was still my own hands that carried my actions."*
Ozai paused, inhaling deeply and steadying his heart.

*"In my second year, I saved a noble knight from certain death, an action that changed the path of my life for eternity. He was so grateful that he offered my name as part of the selected few to join the royal guard units as repayment. A rarity for a second year guard. My life blossomed in such a short moment, I was still on the bottom tier of the royal guards, but the youngest royal guards were still living leagues better than any other regiment. I trained under them for another quarter year before I*

*was assigned to a group of three guards protecting a member of the Kaku family, a young woman with hair black and shiny like the stars that sparkle in the night sky. I questioned my oath the first time I laid eyes on her. I fell in love with your mother before she even knew my name, and I loved her more even after she did. The love that grew between us was forbidden and she gave up everything so we could share a life together. I chose love over duty and never regretted it, not even for a passing moment. We ran as far as we could, as far north to avoid her family's reach, and two years later we heard news of their collapse."*

Ozai's story seeped deep into the ears of his children and the result showed with their mostly blank expressions. They had learned so much about their history in such a short time that even though they soaked their father's words, dissolving his tales would take much longer than they would realize in the moment. Naemi was the next to speak.

*"What caused their fall?"* she asked.

Her father answered with uncertainty.

*"I don't know, and your mother didn't either. I only heard gossip from travelers on my trips to Shoretown, gossip that was far removed from reality."*

*"Do you think any of them are still alive?"* Dakai interposed.

Ozai hadn't considered that possibility in years. There was a chance there still were surviving Kaku living in parts of the world, maybe some with their own offsprings who inherited the eyes of the emperor, but the idea was not something he had focused on for long.

Nevertheless he didn't want any growing intentions spawning in his son's head and answered confidently, "*No son. I don't think any are still alive.*"

Dakai heard his father's response and could feel a low wave of disappointment pass through him. It surprised him that he felt that way. Everything he had heard about these strange people was full of distaste, but the idea that a part of his ancestry were all erased floated a layer of sadness inside him.

"*I'm glad you met mother. I'm glad to have you both as my parents.*" Naemi commented.

"*Me too,*" Dakai added. Ozai couldn't contain the smile that formed in appreciation. Exposing his past to his children and that of their mother's was a difficult thing for him to do. He had always kept his flaws from his children, though now through everything they had all been through, he owed them the truth.

They deserved the truth.

He reached out and pulled his children into his arms and hugged them as tight as he could. Even if he couldn't fully experience what they had been through, the battles they had lost and won through their journey, and the strange changes they had all developed in themselves. He would always know one thing — they were his children, and he would do anything in the world for them.

Kaise called out to signal to everyone that the time for departure had reached. It was early morning and some still slumped their feet as they exited their rooms. The group had planned to leave earlier this time, though that came at the cost of waking up earlier to prepare. The lack of extended sleep wasn't fully appreciated, and its effects were visible on some faces. Kaise tried her best to cheer them up, stretching out her gleeful demeanor to see if anyone might catch its contagion.

It failed.

Kainu got back to the house just in time, pulling the stubborn donkey behind him. He had as much luck with it as he had had before. Naemi saw the animal and shook her head violently, "*Nope ... nope. I won't be the one in charge of it this time. I don't care which straw I pick. It hates me.*" She claimed boldly.

"*I think it hates everyone,*" Beara added. Kainu tied the reins to a pole almost out of breath.

"*Well it won't be me either. We can just leave it here so everyone carries their own bags for the journey. Unless someone wants to volunteer?*" Kainu engaged.

"*Don't look at me, I'm blind.*" Dakai mentioned, and turned his focus back to folding the cloth he was to use as a fold for his eyes. Kaise looked back at the faces that turned to her and wore a dumbfounded stare.

"*Surely you don't think I can tame that damn thing?*" she questioned.

Ozai broke the standoff and volunteered his services.

"*I will lead the animal. I'm sure you all just misunderstand it. Donkeys are slow to warm to new faces, but when they do, they are very dutiful. How tough can this one be? I'm sure I can handle it.*"

Everyone agreed quickly to his volunteering and made no rebuttals. The bags were loaded on the animal and the journey started soon after.

The crew had said their second goodbyes to the old couple the night prior in preparation for their early leave today. They walked through the town to the tune of sparse bodies and yawning guards. As they got closer to the border, onto the roads of Ilores, Naemi turned back to look at the town with one last look of appreciation before she left for good.

She held her brother's hand firmly as he still paced forward and she took one last breath of the air of the town. Naemi had formed a certain peace here, and had created memories with such significance that she never expected to have in a place like this. She heard a donkey bray and turned her eyes to meet Ozai struggling to get the animal to follow him.

Dakai heard the struggle and giggled at the funniness of it. He asked Naemi, "*Should we go help him?*"

Naemi giggled back and answered, "*No, I don't think we should. I'm sure he can handle it.*"

The journey from Hanag started on the twelfth day of spring of the Thrun year **412-SG**. The group traveled for days, resting when they could and taking shelter in the nights at places of convenience.

Some days, they would be lucky enough to find a room to rent in village settlements or smaller towns that littered along the path to the Cratos capital. Other times, they would be left to the exposure of nature and the cover of trees, sleeping with nothing but covers for warmth and open sky. Nonetheless the journey continued with more delight than not.

The roads were safe and the people who passed showed kindness except for a few bad apples.

The landscape was always a highlight however. From green fields full of herded Tengee buffalo, layered steep hills with stunning views of the blue horned mountain goats, ravines with rushing clear water bordered by creeping plants that brightened greener than gemmed emeralds. There was always something to stop and gaze at in intervals of the journey, and those who were departing enjoyed the view for one last time.

The roads widened and narrowed; they'd pass other travelers going in opposite directions and join others going in the same direction. Ozai had found a bush with wild raspberries and used it as bribery for the donkey to quell its stubbornness. His children laughed and threw jokes at each other, all of them full of the joy that came with returning home. Their minds were so occupied with the present that their uncanny senses hibernated in dormancy with no sense of danger.

They reached Astor on the early morning of the fifteenth day of spring, those who had never been there marveled at its beauty. It was reminiscent of the scale and grandiose of Sailor City, but its design was of significant difference. The crew felt fascinated on its distinction and marvels.

The city boasted a lot of red colors, presumably tied to the religion that was so ingrained in the entire Thrun region.

Similar to Hanag, this entire region worshiped only the Sun-god, an enforcement so strict that it was against the law to worship anything else. There was even a temple here dedicated to him, and talk of an even bigger one in the capital. The crew toured the city, engaging in sightseeing till their thirst was satisfied.

On the sixteenth day of spring, they started their trip to the capital. Another day closer to the ports, another day closer to home.

## Chapter Fifteen

# THE STENCH OF DEFIANCE

The stairs that ascended to the temple stretched high till it reached its climax. Elevated with a steepness that challenged many of whom sought its climb today. About a hundred feet of soaring steps curved wide over twice the climb, the gray concrete slabs tested the many guests who sought passage on this blessed day.

The loud sounds that surrounded the area shouted laudation from behind their barricades, sending a wealth of praises to the presence of high royalty and opulence. Kingsmen pushed and tugged the fencing that separated the cardinal from the undistinguished. The second and third guard reserves were all armored and active for the event, parading places of importance.

The closed streets leading to the Sun-god's temple only opened to guests of the royal wedding. The base of the stairs filled with converging guests drenched in the riches of high society.

A myriad of crushed blue halite rocks layered the grounds, coating it with protection from evil and spirits of malignancy. Those who lacked the strength for ascension made up for it with their status, noted by the many palanquins that traveled up and its muscled bearers that moved with it.

The view from the eyes of the crowd was a palette of splendor; the ocean of fine designs, textiles, colors, and jewelry rose envy in the hearts of men and festered dreams for some that would never come to fruition. The fancy robes the women wore, the smooth lacing and stitching with precious stones and colored metal. The men, with their graceful linens and sharp garments smelling of sweet fragrances of nature, contrasted by their glorified weaponry that rested calmly on their waist, inspiring more grace.

All the guests marked with bright faces, the ones known to plump cheeks from fatty foods and filling juices. Whitened smiles and whitened eyes from never knowing the smell of hunger. They conversed and laughed without regard, still with an internal desire to outdo one another and steal a glimpse of the spotlight.

Behind them, the enormous sanctum shadowed everyone. Completed a shy over a century ago, known universally as one of the most ambitious scales of architecture, the Sun-god's temple was breath-taking in all forms. Built with over six thousand and seven hundred laborers, painters, stonecutters, artists and the power of the Dion Makora, it was the first time the abilities of Dions were used in matters other than war.

On this late morning, the temple still stood even more majestic with extra layers of glamor that denoted the taste of a royal wedding. The lightened blue and scattered clouds that filled the sky awaiting the obscured sun did little to affect its glory. The faint red that cloaked the majority of the building gleamed with pride, the yellow engravings that marked the sacred words of Raja, the white that coated the stone pillars that surrounded the base of the temple, the silver and black covering the steel doors.

The walls of the building rose to varied peaks all around, rising high but still belittled by the center. The high ceiling that converged into a sort of twisted long cone with the Sun-god emerging out of it, his left hand reaching out into the skies. It is a common occurrence that if you're in the right place at the right time in the day, you can see the sun in Raja's hand as it was always intended to be. The shimmering god in all his glory.

More of the temple coated with beauty, long floral garlands stringing over doors and walkways. Scattered petals plucked from the graces of the Celestial gardens added their own spice of magnificence to the venue. Every additional touch of enhancement that could be done was done, the scales not seen since the wedding of King Olius to the Lady Gyai.

The new wedding of the future crown leaders was as glamorous as it was supposed to be.

It was an occasion for the ages, a spectacle that was needed to jolt the capital into the start of the new year. The scents of spring flourished with its new engagements, the ones people had raved about all through the winter. The harsh cold had come and gone, once again defeated with the skills of patience and preparation. What followed came with gifts of delight, clearer skies, and warmer days, its greatest gift being today, the sixteenth day of spring, of the year **412-SG**.

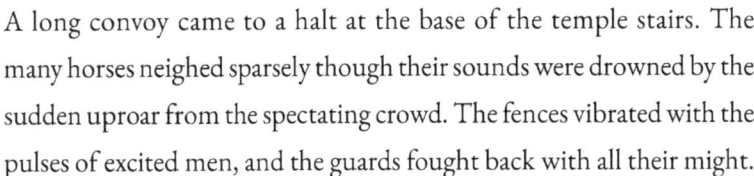

A long convoy came to a halt at the base of the temple stairs. The many horses neighed sparsely though their sounds were drowned by the sudden uproar from the spectating crowd. The fences vibrated with the pulses of excited men, and the guards fought back with all their might.

The crowd spread like a vast lake, their heads poking up to get a glimpse and their mouths full of loud words. The king alighted from the carriage with smiles, waving to the people of his kingdom. His imperial robe was white as a clear day's cloud with a golden cape sweeping behind him, and his crown sat gently on the black and gray on his head. He cheered back at the people, further igniting their love as he walked between his crown-guards. The queen followed beside with glamor, brightening as a star along him.

A body escaped through the crevice of guards holding the people at bay. A lanky man of average height and partially missing teeth rushed toward the queen with a mouthful of praise. He got unusually close until the giant arms of first commander Jerroin Aryee of the crown-guard latched onto him and slammed him down in a forced thrust.

The queen heard his bones crack, a sound even louder than the yell that followed from him. He was whisked away by guards quickly after, not that any of this even caused a pause in the cheering crowds. Selius got down from his carriage next, a little later than his mother. He was visibly fuming from being required to ride with the crown carriage.

He hated carriages and horseback riding.

"*Why ride when I can fly,*" he would say, but Olius mandated it for the ceremony and he obliged. Selius forced a smile back to the eager eyes that called to him and waved back to their hails.

Dressed in full ceremonial garment. The fitted heavy blue and golden yellow tunic with the embroidery of the house of Reis and its accolades, drenched in finery and recherche.

The sword with the blue meridian sapphire hilt dangling in its black leather sheath matching his glossy boots, he walked to the carriage behind his as its occupant descended from it. Her ravishing gown flaunted unto the ground preceding her steps.

Selius stretched his hand out to help her down and she grabbed him gently. The other occupants in the carriages that trailed had all descended, and a few women rushed to help the princess Morlain off her carriage. She ignored their help, focusing only on that of her future husband. They helped regardless, picking parts of the overly stretched dress that kissed the floors as she walked. Morlain smiled to the crowd, spying the faces that looked at her with cheers and those with distrust.

The white dress of native descent she wore still sparked interest in their eyes, no matter the feelings behind them. It was strangely woven with unique flows and ridges to those who lacked the knowledge of its origin. It covered her body as beautifully as armor covers a knight, and she beaconed to eyes all around.

Her hair was of a dark cinnamon hue, long past her shoulders and the ends were covered in little round stone pebbles that rattled when they swayed. Her face was flat and rounded, with features uncommon to the Thrun people. Her rounded eyes, flattened nose and small lips echoed with all the Mhraabian people that trailed her; notably her mother and uncle. The Mhraabian king was not present for the event, as well as none of the Mhraabian army, only a sizable group of guards, a small portion of additional family, and excess servants.

When all converged behind the king and queen at the base of the stairs, they began their walk of ascension, climbing past all the halted bodies that bowed to the peak of royalty. Their lowered faces hid their emotions though their eyes still wandered showing spite to the new intruders to their blessed nation. Intruders who flaunted their depraved culture in the presence of the holy temple.

*Such insult, such abomination.*

More distaste grew for Olius's allowance of this disrespect, though you couldn't tell behind their smiles.

The remaining crowd followed the lead of the crown, bounded on both sides by men with armor and unceremonial weaponry. Through the walkway of colored walls, extruding sculptures, historical paintings, and into the large rounded center filled with organized seating and elevated podiums.

The seats all formed around the staired podium in the center about six feet off the ground. Four walkways sectioned the seats into four quadrants, intersected in the middle by the podium and the towering ceiling. When the king and his wife finally seated, everyone followed accordingly in loud response.

Most of the seats were filled with every prominent person known to the five royal families and beyond, none expecting to miss such a historical occurrence in almost a half century.

The only notable faces unavailable were Bymba Myr; head of house Myr said to be on one of his luxurious voyages. Atacie Coor; the renowned fashionista and designer for the royal families who hadn't been seen for some days. Urgus Taus; the advisor to the king, said to be on a mission in the colonies, and Lama Wuhn; the famous starred Mage who claimed she had better things to do than attend a wedding.

Four men in red robes and shaved heads walked behind the Sun-priest down the walkway adjacent to the third and fourth quadrants. They climbed to the top of the podium staring at all amidst the silence and started reciting the song of sun — the royal wedding had begun.

---

Two guards walked down Jura street looking through alleys and emptied roads for any signs of trespassing civilians. The road was nigh empty except for a royal carriage that just whisked past them with the rider shouting curses that they get out of the way.

They mugged and cussed in whispered responses.

They were some distance off from the ceremony, though part of the backside of the temple could still be seen from their higher ground;

mostly the midsection and the top. They had no view of the spread crowds and flamboyant dresses even on their high ground, but the shouts of glory that rang from afar still swung by their way through the wind.

They were part of the third reserves called upon to provide more security for the event; however their lazed bodies and ill reputation relegated them to the final outskirts of the secure area.

They both galavanted the area with their tightened armor plates too tight for their rounded bodies. Naate, the shortest and less stout of the two, slid his hand behind the brick that shadowed the little curved hole in the ground and brought out the liquor bottle he was forced to hide some moments ago.

"*Let me have a piece, you've almost drunk everything.*"

Wezel grunted at him, and snatched the bottle. Naate fought back but the taller outmuscled him and gulped down a few heavy swallows. Naate readjusted his helmet as the force tilted it on his head and he fumed, an agitated look covering his face.

"*This is why I hate working with you, so fucking greedy,*" he mentioned with distaste and shoved his partner.

Wezel laughed and swung the bottle back to his friend with a heavy belch and more laughter.

The bottle was almost empty now and Naate cursed repeatedly at his friend as he tried to drink what was left down to its last drop. Wezel continued laughing until two strange traveling lights in the sky caught his eye. He squinted his eyes as if that would make whatever he was seeing clearer.

The skies weren't as transparent as they used to be about an hour ago and more whitened clouds shaded its depths, but a second look confirmed what his initial assumption was.

"*Ey ey Naate? Is that not a fire arrow?*" He beckoned to his friend, shaking him violently. Naate slapped his hand off with more agitation and moved his focus from the liquor bottle to what his companion was pointing to, just in time to catch the second arrow descending on the base of the temple ceiling.

A small ignited fire flared into a low bright spark and disappeared behind parts of the roof.

Naate unconsciously let out a faint yell of shock and the two guards looked at each other with mouths agape with the same thought in mind. They started to run toward the temple yelling to attract attention, but as Wezel took his fourth step, he felt a scorching pain go through his neck, and his chest felt as if it had been pierced with flames. He fell to the ground in a heavy thud unable to scream, his body wiggling irregularly and his life withering away with the blood that marked the brown road red.

Naate turned his head still running only to see his fallen friend; his short legs did not take him far before he also met his fate from the three arrows that pierced him in almost lightning-fast succession. Arrows with tips of Fermelstone punctured through his armor with ease leaving both their impaled bodies forever tethered to the ground.

———————◆O◆———————

Selius stood at the altar with Morlain as she read her pledge of eternal union, reciting it after the Sun-priest; the sanctified spokesman of the Sun-god. The prince stared into her eyes with a faint smile painting his lips, gazing at the woman who would be his future with almost no knowledge of who she was.

She looked back at him with a bigger smile, speaking the words with a genuine profoundness to them, her lips moving to its tune and the whole auditorium listened with attention.

Selius felt a strange rush of sensation jolt through him; his senses began feeling an eeriness he wasn't used to, like a sting in his veins alerting him to danger.

A warning that came too late.

The blast was loud and the ceiling rumbled viciously. The vibrations rippled the interiors and the boom sent a shockwave through the walls. An eruption of screams followed, then a shortened silence. As if their minds were denying the reality of what was happening in the moment.

The next blast shook them to their core. The mixture of sounds that filled the insides were deafening, blinding the ears and filling bodies with dread. Their fear grew more in proportion with the elongating cracks that extended on the stone ceiling like a slow moving flash of lightning.

Pieces of sand and small rock freed from the breaks that formed above and hurled toward the floor and those who occupied it. The entire ceiling looked to bend downwards slowly, and the breaks in the rock traveled fast. The peak of the commotion reached when the bigger rocks started to fall, those still in denial of the direness of their situation, started to feel its cold touch on their hearts.

Once the broken rocks were in the hands of gravity, it showed the hundreds below no mercy. The first giant rock landed near the end of the first quadrant section. The sound of rock crushing bone was chilling. A quick crunching sound followed by a splatter of blood bursting from their flattened bodies to all around. Their existence deleted in mere moments. The people who saw it happen screamed with all they had, but in the presence of louder screams their voices were overshadowed by the masses.

All were on their feet with many rushing to the visible exit of the internal chamber. The converging of hundreds to one opening forced a stampede through the doors, crushing those who lacked the prowess or the luck to make it through.

They clawed, pushed, and scratched one another just to get an inch of space. Their bodies pressed together, suffocating in the presence of colored air, their only tell for direction being the light that shone through the doors. Their senses drowned in the midst of oversaturation, the only sense that remained was their sense for survival.

Another large rock descended, then another followed, raining down death to those below. The dust that filled the air colored everywhere gray, occluding sight. The once colorful insides of the internal chamber of the temple now only held one color of prominence as everyone screamed and ran.

The six crown-guards present surrounded the king and queen with swords drawn, protecting both from any attacks that may be intended to sneak by. They punched, kicked and shoved those who dared run in their direction, moving steadily toward the secret exits that only they knew. More pieces of the ceiling rained down. The next large slab of rock broke off, rushing down toward the six men surrounding the crown.

Their attempts to save the ruling royals was almost destined to be futile until the Dion prince dashed above his parents in a quick charge, breaking the fall with his hands and unnatural strength. His wings though struggled to maintain his flight in his twisted motion and he threw the rock away to rid himself of its weight. The rock crashed into a wall on the side, cracking it and smashing the bodies of the people that cowered there in hiding, hoping to escape the stampede.

The screams of many flooded into the outside. The people who successfully squeezed past bodies to get through the doors hurried down the high stairs and into the open only to meet more commotion.

The outside was also filled with more screams as people looked up to the impending doom that seemed imminent.

The crowds ran helter skelter.

The common people ran as fast as they could to flee the area with their eyes pointed above. The giant statue of Raja that stood on the top of the Sun-god temple was tilting slowly after its base had been ruptured. The ceiling inside the temple was bent like that of an inverted concave and the long exposed cracks showed bare with its continued spillage of little rocks and dust that filled people's noses.

Chaos was everywhere.

Astonishingly, amidst the huge blasts the famed temple had suffered, the breaks that had formed in its crown, and the vibrations that still continued from panic-struck high-borns trying to escape its confines, the bending stopped.

The rain of large rock halted except for a few falling smaller chunks and light grains. Those who were vulnerable to its destruction though cared little for anything other than escape. The explosion that had ruptured the building couldn't complete its cycle and the braces that held the ceiling bent but never broke.

From outside, the embodiment of the Sun-god tilted toward the ground but still stood strong and unstable, glaring back menacingly at those who wanted its doom.

Unfortunately, the attackers didn't enjoy the luxury of analyzing the effects of their assault, the screams of two fools had alerted the right people and they had lost their cover of surprise.

They zipped through streets and alleys, taking advantage of the mayhem and splitting themselves as the hounds and armed men chased their tail.

Pandemonium rang as hard as the bells everywhere in the city. Chaos and questions laced with fear floated with the breeze.

Puzzlement on who was brave enough to attack the stronghold of their great empire, getting so close as to annihilating most of their royal families in one swoop. The chatter was loud and reverberating, and as it spread, a foul smell trailed strongly through the wind with it. One that challenged their self-proclaimed superiority and importance. It crept into their homes under cabinets and through woodwork filling their noses with its odor.

A stench that will become known in their histories and one that will be passed down as the worst one of all — a stench of defiance.

## Chapter Sixteen

# THE PRIZE OF REBELLION

The skies filled with the release of dozens of messenger-birds into its vastness. They spread their colored wings wide, gliding into the breeze and fluttering their wings till they could feel their hollowed bones floating upon nothingness.

At first they looked like a colored cloud released above the Aarcabra, but as they dispersed, they all took to their own destinations, fading the stain in the sky back to its original hue. Their job was an important one, delivering a message with the seal of the crown to all Thrun forces in the entire region; Dions, ruling councils of colonies, and extended legions.

Every extension of the crown's power was to receive one message. A message to ignite a cause that will ripple through the land and forcefully uproot threats that have been otherwise treated too gently.

Threats that had grown the strongest audacity of striking at the head of ultimate power.

The message detailed what had happened, and all that was to be done in the coming days to begin the removal of the malign from the benign. Concrete instructions on the path that lay ahead, and at the end of the message four words engraved in isolation. Words that will change futures and deform the trajectories of lives.

Four words that will spark the beginning of all.

**"ALL REBELS MUST DIE"**

---

It had been three hours since the attack. A cold, somber layer blanketed the entire Cratos city. The only dominant sound that rose was the marching of infantries through the streets. Their heavy boots slapping the ground with thunderous effect as they moved through the city.

The entire city was under lockdown.

The ports had been shut, markets, taverns, everything that needed to close down was closed. The imposed curfew affected everyone who didn't work directly under the state; highborn or low. The citizens kept themselves inside their homes with doors and windows shut.

The tensions that laced the city were high and people stayed in the safety of their houses for fear of being accused as a rebel if found wandering the streets without cause. Still, some found ways to escape without notice, others also found it crucial to send messages to the beyond to inform the world of the heavy hit the renowned empire had suffered.

The wedding had brought many foreign eyes to the capital, and they extended their ears after the fallout to search for information that might benefit them, while making their own personal moves on the grande gameboard. It was a few hours till sunset, but the sun seemed to still linger high in the sky.

The devout were full of grief, their faces ridden in tears at the experience of absolute blasphemy to their god. They prayed and shouted in the confines of their rooms for atonement, and took the lingering sun as a sign of Raja heeding their cries.

The Sun-god temple still stood as it had been. The leaning statue and bent ceiling were a heavy concern, though they hadn't shown any signs of it moving any farther. The bodies that lay inside the temple continued to lay at rest. About sixty confirmed dead out of the three hundred and twenty guests, and many more sent to the mage-healers with bruises, cuts, and broken bones.

The bodies of the dead shown visible after the dust settled.

Their faces filled with varied emotions as they met their end, their glamorous silk clothing and fine jewelry with precious stones, now stained with the color of settled sand and darkened blood. Their eyes looked to the above only to see the cause of their doom. There hadn't been so many highborn deaths since the red-pox, their mixture of young and old lives diminished to soulless flesh.

The Dion Kweku was sent into the temple to inspect its integrity along with taking account of the dead with his abilities of self-replication. The other Dions present in the capital were tasked with security, some returning to their respective royal houses to offer protection as the five families retreated to their strongholds, and the rest were tasked with protection of the state. The king had been guided back to the crown castle in haste; he was lucky enough to avoid any serious injuries, but Gyai hadn't experienced the same luck.

In their rush to escape through the hidden tunnels, she fell and struck her head, her old age not used to quick evasions. Half her face was bloodied as the crown-guard Jerroin carried her in his arms speeding into a carriage and heading toward the crown castle. What followed after were the outraged instructions of a king riled with immense fury, instructions that led to a message sent to every corner of the Thrun empire.

---

In the insides of a dungeon in the capital, a voice screamed in immeasurable agony. The sounds echoed throughout the inside space, bouncing on the jagged stone walls and by the guards that stood unmoving until it disappeared into nonchalance. The scream came again, as it had been going for over a half hour.

The type of screaming a man does when all his pain receptors are being fired at once. The victim was so loud that the strains in his throat could be felt through the pulses in the air, but as much as the people inside heard his pain, none moved an inch to help him.

General Ganius descended down the stairs to the depths of the dungeon. His mind was clouded by the news he had just received moments ago.

A mixture of heavy sadness and unbridled anger filled his heart.

He had wished his son Copius had made it out unscathed. He had searched for him throughout the tumult in the temple, as rock rained down death on them.

One moment he was next to him and the next moment gone. He searched for him for long after, even after he was called to duty. And when he was summoned by the king, he tasked one of his subordinates to continue the search — a search that had finally concluded.

A burn formed in his heart from the pain of losing a son, a first son. No matter how fractured the relationship with his eldest son was, he still loved him greatly in his own unique way.

*A son should never die before the father*, he thought.

Water formed into tears but his hardened eyes would not let them through. Eight members of the Reis family had all been confirmed dead, and more still lay critically injured.

Sons, daughters, mothers, fathers, all killed by the actions of savages. Savages who attacked a weakness they didn't foresee, striking at them with such precision that they would have all been rendered extinct without the luck of their god. They were so close to death, he felt it as the rocks began to fall and chaos ensued. In the presence of a force he couldn't fight head on with his sword, he felt true fear for the second time in his life.

Seeing the possibility of himself, all his family and children being wiped from existence in one fell swoop. His face hardened more as he walked through the dungeon to the screams that came from ahead. His mind replayed all the decisions he had taken in pursuit of quelling these rebels. He had underestimated their ambition, their resolve, and he blamed himself for its consequences.

The flames from the torches that hung on the dungeon walls highlighted his crisp jaws, the three scarred slashes on his right cheek and his determined expression. He walked from light to dark to light again, switching through the frames of color as he got closer to his destination.

The guards saw his approach and opened the cell door he headed toward, revealing the source of the screaming.

The inside of the cell was brighter than it was outside. Three torches flamed inside the cell and the victim was strapped tightly to a bolted chair with his hands and feet bound. An older woman turned to meet Ganius from inside the room as he walked in.

"*Is he ready to talk?*" The general spat vehemently.

"*Hesss almost there general ... Thiss one has a strength about him, but he can't resist for long. Hiss insidesss should feel like they're boiling. Every sensssation of pain he can feel is being triggered as we sspeak.*" The woman replied with a slow stretching of her words.

Her voice was straining and slithery, overshadowed by the groans of agony of her victim.

The general stared at the man with nothing but hate in his eyes, "*Where are the rest of them? Speak and I will give you a quick death. Or else you will continue to suffer a pain beyond your wildest imagination.*"

The general growled at him with intensity, reaching for his neck and squeezing till the red in the man's eyes darkened.

"*General, you will kill him and losssee the anssswers you ssseek. Let me work and find you the truth. Ressolve is like an onion, after you peel all the layers you're left with nothing but the core of the man. And in that core you will find truth.*" The woman intervened. Her disheveled hair and stained hands were visible in the light.

She mixed together potions on a table away from the two men and returned her focus to the general after.

It took everything in Ganius to remove his hands off the throat of the man, though his eyes still stayed its focus. He gazed intently into his soul, noticing the low jet-black hair on his head, the extension of full hair that covered the side and lower regions of his face. His orange skin and broader nose, all features similar to the Guyan people.

Ganius scoffed to himself in disgust.

They had been lucky to capture at least one of the rebels to interrogate, but had lost the rest to the wind. Their numbers weren't fully confirmed but to the best of their knowledge, there were either five or six in total.

The idea that such a small group could cause such damage troubled him greatly, and he yearned to discover answers. The chaos after the explosion had given them cover in their escape, and they knew not whether they were still in the capital or had gotten a head-start out of the city.

Regardless, there were searches underway, ones throughout the entire city and others sweeping through the forests and into the mountains. The rest will soon be found one way or the other, and their heads will be separated from their bodies as the prizes of their rebellion.

Ganius scoffed again; he couldn't stand the sight of the low-life and turned to leave the cell, but as he did, he heard the man force a laugh through his groaning.

"*We did it, we rid the world of most of you demons.*" He strained his voice to get every word out, still holding back screams.

Ganius turned back to meet his reddened eyes and forced smirk.

"*Don't you want to know how we did it?*" He added, his body was still shaking as a result of the potions that coursed through his blood, but the determination in his heart fueled his words.

"*We placed them at night, while you slept in your precious castles. The climb was high, but the price was worth it. How great it was to see you all drown under the temple of your false god ... Drown under stone. How many died? Is your king dead? Tell me and maybe I will give you some answers.*"

The man fought through his pain with every fiber of himself to say those words to the general. To him, his work was done and he would hold strong until his inevitable death came.

The general looked back at him with an abhorrence that seemed to rise with time. He took a step toward the bound man and had to hold himself from reaching out and draining the very existence out of him. It was the man's smirk that annoyed him the most. The face that looked at him with defiance and mirrored disdain. He forced a calm on his heart and leveled his mind as any greatly disciplined man was supposed to.

He leaned toward the man and spoke as gently as his roaring voice could manage.

*"You think you succeeded? You merely showed us a blind-spot that will never be open again. Your attacks barely caused a scar. We built our buildings with the greatest minds and strongest Dions and you thought you could bring it down with a few blasts. Yes, the building shook and a few stones fell, and what? About fifteen people died? No, about ten rather, all people of unimportance. Our god still stands high, those who got as much as flesh wounds will heal, and all that will be remembered will be tiny scars. This attack will be wiped from history and your efforts won't be remembered in time, but what will happen after will be. We will ravage the region you hold so dear, the men, the women and children. It seems we have been too lenient with your people and they need a firmer hand in their lives. We will find anyone who shares any relation with you and sentence them to execution. Your partners will share the same fate with you soon. But you ... I will keep you for some time. Let you rot here and strip all your layers till your own mind betrays you. Then you will beg me for your own death."*

Ganius retreated back a few steps then turned to the older woman. *"I need answers before sunset,"* he said, and left the cell trailed by yells and curses from the bound man.

The woman looked to the bound man and smiled.

*"You're holding ssstrong againsst the pain. I will admit, I am impresssed, and I don't get impresssed often. No matter, thisss one here might be too much for your heart, but it will certainly loosssen your tongue. Don't worry. You won't die. You can't. The general won't like that,"* she affirmed.

Her stained teeth reflected in the yellow flame light, and she gently unsealed the potion she held in her hands.

Time continued on as it always does, and the events of the world continued with it. In the Thrun region, the sun still lingered, about three hours more till it reached its time to set.

———◆◇◆———

Selius sat by his mother's bedside, glancing at the stitches that covered the upper right side of her face. Part of her hair had been shaved to make room for the healers to clean her wounds.

That part of her whitened skin was discolored red and the blue paste that was supposed to prevent infections discolored it more. She hadn't regained consciousness for over four hours and her breaths were slow. He had been sitting there for close to two hours, substituting for the king who had to leave to the throne room and meet with his other generals to deal with the aftermath.

He refused to go, even with her steadied state and available healers at her call. He could hear her voice in his mind, the one that would scold him for sitting with her when he could be in the generals' meeting planning their response to this attack.

"*I'm fine, go be with your father and generals*," she would have said, and he still wouldn't have listened. She lay there gracefully as she always was. Her brown and gray curled hair rested calmly on the pillows, the rest of her face with a sincere sage-like embodiment. Her skin was at peace and shining in reverence. Selius smiled at her serenity.

*She'd hate that scar so much*, he thought.

He had never truly wrestled with the idea of losing a parent, and today, when he faced the possibility, he felt his soul succumb to emotions. He blamed himself for not flying her out of the temple. He thought his parents would have been safer going through the tunnels and he didn't follow due to his loathing of being underground.

He had saved those he could, redirecting the fall of large rocks and flying out people of importance. He had even saved his bride and parts of her family, but never foresaw this. Not her injury, and not such a devastating attack on the state. He had been confident that his methods in the rebel regions had proven fruitful when the attacks subdued significantly throughout the winter. His plans had even facilitated the capture of some of the rebel groups.

All the reports through the winter had been positive, and he had reveled in his victories.

He blamed himself for the tragedies as he stared upon his mother, and the burning anger that seeped in him continued its boil.

A knock was heard on the door, and the heavy brown wood was pushed open after.

A crown-guard appeared from behind it. *"The king has requested your presence, crown prince,"* the man with gingered hair said.

Selius replied with silence for a moment then answered. *"Tell him I'm with my mother, I will come when she's awake."*

*"He insisted, crown prince. They have found the locations of the rebels."*

The comment grasped him almost instantly and he stood to his feet. He took one last glance at his mother, kissing her forehead gently and left with the crown-guard.

Olius's voice could be heard quaking the halls even before they reached the interior of the throne room. His furious eyes hadn't changed one bit with time. Six war generals sat surrounding the stone table in the middle, two crown-guards stood behind the king, and a few second commanders stood close to the walls of the room.

"*How is she?*" Olius asked his son softly when he entered the throne room.

Selius shook his head slowly and he could see the tenderness leave his father's eyes at his response. He exhaled forcefully and his sternness returned to him. He turned his focus to General Ganius and prompted him to speak.

The general rose up and addressed the king.

"*We have extracted three locations. Places they were supposed to meet in case they were divided after their escape. We know they are armed with an unknown explosive and weapons of Fermelstone. We have already sent parties to two, but the last, Riqua, is a small settlement about three hours from here. It is possible they had such a head-start after they escaped. We sent word to our closest outpost nearby, but it only has a unit of about a dozen soldiers, and they have been told to only surveil from afar and not engage. We need to use one of our Dions to get there quickly. We need someone fast and powerful to end these savages once and for all. For all the lives they have taken in such cowardice. For the life of my eldest son and all those who have been grieved."*

Selius's eyes widened.

"*Copius is dead?*" he asked in a broken tone.

General Ganius softened his expression, realizing he hadn't employed any sensitivity in breaking the news to his son's closest friend.

"*I'm sorry son,*" he said to the prince.

"*Send the Dion Gaan,*" the king commanded abruptly.

Everyone turned in surprise. "*Sire? Gaan would get there fast but I'm afraid he lacks the strength to overcome any surprises. I would advise we send Sel...*" General Mathuid Myr spoke but the king interjected with a rambunctious demeanor.

"*You'd rather I send MY SON?*" Olius bellowed.

The room fell silent.

"*Father? I will not stand by while these barbarians escape from our grasp. We have underestimated their will for too long. I will do what must be done to terminate this disease from our empire. You gave me charge of this; let me bring them to justice,*" Selius verbalized.

Olius was slow to answer. He was never one to doubt his son's power but the possibility that he could lose a son and a wife on the same day was one he struggled to get over. He looked into his son's eyes and it was a mirror of his own.

The determination, the anger, the drive that lay behind it. He nodded reluctantly to give his son permission and as Selius was about to leave, he called to him.

*"Son! Bring me their heads!"*

## Chapter Seventeen

# THE BEGINNING

"*I see it. I see it. Look, over there.*" Kaise called back to the crew.

She stood some feet ahead of the group and pointed to an area to the left of her. The part of the road they were on snaked up a low hill and descended into more slithered curves beyond.

Kaise stood at its peak, feeling the early brushes of the warm wind that kissed her golden hair and waved her dress in gentle flaps. Her eyes gazed in the direction a little turn away from the roads of llores, a small settlement area situated a visible distance from the main roads. It didn't look as big as a town or as old as a village, just a cluster of houses covering a minimal section.

She could see about twenty houses all together, if not accounting for the smaller sheds that lay sparse. As low as the hill was, it still gave a good view of the lands that lay ahead. The rest of the area looked similar to ones they had walked past for hours. The beauty of the landscape had been a consistency that never altered. They had met more people on the roads a few hours after leaving Astor.

Those settlements were an hour or two away and evenly spaced, but as they got farther, the roads got lonelier.

The only company they had were the naturally distributed trees and vegetation. The ones of different shapes and heights that painted the land with its many hues of green.

The new spring had bolstered their leaves and stems, giving them a surreal sense of elevation. And in response, they danced with the clear winds, rustling their branches and adding to the tunes of nature. This area had much flatter lands compared to the others. The lands here rose to little peaks and fell to smaller valleys, some smooth, some sharp and others full of irregularities.

The last settlement the crew had passed was over an hour and half away, and slightly bigger than this one. They had rested there for some time and learned why the roads had been way less populated than usual.

Ozai had mentioned throughout the entire journey of how scarce the roads looked compared to when he traveled it. He hadn't taken many stops on his initial trip to Hanag, and claimed he met more travelers on his way there. When their curiosity peaked, they asked a local at the last settlement and he informed them about a royal wedding that was happening today, puzzled at how they weren't aware.

"*The lord prince is getting wed to the most beautiful woman in all the known realms. You don't know? The roads have been full these last days with people going to see. I hear the capital is full of people from all realms attending. I'm sure the roads will be full again with people returning in the next days,*" the man said with excitement.

The news was a pleasant revelation for the group.

People from all realms meant more ships and more opportunities to get transport back to Soros. The possibility that plenty of ships from Primea would be available was sweet news to Ozai and his children.

They continued their journey with shortened rest hoping to cut the time in their journey, but after another exhaustive walk through stretched leagues of land, their fatigue grew even more and their food reserves reduced. They decided to get some rest at the next stop for travelers, the small settlement about three hours away from the capital by horse ride.

Riqua, they were told it was called, and they hurried to make it there before sunset.

They hoped to rest there for a while, restock some supplies of water and light snacks, and head back on the road to make it to the capital before nightfall.

Beara was the next to reach Kaise, and Dakai followed some feet behind. He had loosened his eye cover and walked on his own volition when they were sure the roads were lonely.

Kaise stayed ahead mainly to alert him of oncoming travelers, and also because she was the only one with more energy to spare, maybe because of her heavy contribution to the reduction of the food reserves. Ozai was close behind them. He hadn't faced any more issues with his transport since the discovery of the delicacies for bribery. The animal followed him obediently, waiting for its sweet reward every few leagues.

Naemi and Kainu were the last ones behind, both of them engaging in talks about history and how the present had been kind to them. They walked slowly without even noticing their reduction in pace. Their words though still had hidden layers of goodbye. They had met in the strangest of circumstances, and their journey together had grown under heavy turbulence, but they were glad to be settled on leveled ground now. Kaise called to them, breaking them out of conversation.

The sun had begun its path to set.

The golden light waves in the west showed bright with part of the sun sunk into the landscape.

The complexion of the sky spread in a beautiful coloration — the light blue, meshing with scattered white, fading into a light yellow then a reddish-orange spread. It was a repeated tune that would never lose its luster, like the songs of old that great bards play to soften the hearts of men and bring them to tears.

The extended forest area beyond the Riqua settlement looked to extend as far as the horizon from their point of view. The forest area looked dense, and the top of the trees tried their best to touch the skies, though they failed continuously in their inutile attempts.

Dakai covered his eyes back again before they began their walk back to the settlement, his hands holding Beara's hands. It wasn't a long walk from the main road. They reached the settlement not long after.

There were only about twenty people seen outside, the wooden buildings looked simple and unimpressive; not like the last settlement. There was a stable ahead, past the six buildings on their left, and a couple of horses poked their heads to look more into the dullness.

The second building from Kainu's right looked like a tavern, or it tried to be. The doors were crooked and the building's wood looked rusty. There were sounds of laughter from inside the tavern, and a man burst outside through the doors and yelled curses at whoever he was walking away from.

The crew stood at what looked like the edge of the settlement, taking in all that existed. There were three market-sheds spread on either side of the walking path, but only one had a seller present and she was fast asleep. There were two water wells ahead, one by the stable and another further ahead.

The people who saw the group paid them no mind, continuing with their own lives and their own concerns.

"*I will go check if they have any food in the tavern; it'd be nice to get something warm to eat or some ale to soothe my throat,*" Beara said with some enthusiasm.

"*I want to sit and rest, can I come with you?*" Dakai asked, showing interest.

"*Yeah I'm coming with you too,*" Kainu added.

"*Me too, I'd love some soup,*" Kaise stated, but her brother stopped her in her tracks.

"*Not until you go buy back the food to refill all the ones you ate. There's a food seller right there. We won't have enough for the journey because of you. You can use some of the extra coins. And you can take Naemi with you, since it was both of you doing the hoarding.*" Kainu asserted to his sister.

She frowned at his words and he replied with a condescending smile.

"*I didn't eat that much, why do I have to go? My legs need to rest too,*" Naemi pleaded.

"*I'll trade you for taking the donkey to the stable,*" Ozai proposed. He had the last bag of raspberries in hand and fed one to the donkey. "*She's well behaved now; she won't give you any trouble.*" Ozai added.

Naemi gave it a quick thought and accepted; she'd seen some fine thoroughbreds in the stables and wanted to get a better look at them anyway.

Someone tapped Ozai from behind; he turned to the stretched hands of a boy-child about five years of age. He had slimy short black hair, a runny nose and dirtied hands from playing in the dirt.

Ozai traced his hands to what the child was pointing to, the raspberries he was feeding the donkey.

"*Oh child, these aren't good for you. These are wild berries,*" he explained, though the child paid no attention to his words and persisted.

"*Marcely! I told you to stop begging from strangers,*" a voice shouted. The boy ran in fear to the shed close by and the lone seller who was now awake.

"*I'm sorry, I hope he wasn't bothering you,*" the woman interceded. Ozai brushed it off as a child's natural curiosity; he passed the bag to Naemi and proceeded with Kaise to inquire about the food items being sold.

The rest of the crew went their previously stated ways. Naemi had no issues leading the donkey to the stable even though her anxiety expected the animal to revert to its previous behavior. She directed it into an empty stall in the stable and changed her focus toward the seven horses that rested there.

The inside of the stable was sizable, like that of a rectangular house. The interior had been sectioned into many smaller stalls at both ends, and a walkway in the middle.

The stalls near the entrance were open to the outside for the three horses that reared their heads. The rest in the interior stayed quietly sheltered. Two of the four inside were sleeping, and the other two just gazed at her quietly. They were both on her right, standing at the far end of the stable surrounded by other unoccupied spaces.

The closest one was a dark black horse, perfectly monotone and blending into the darker parts of the stable that formed as light departed with the sunset. The farthest was of a light gray color, two shades below white with a brown spot spread above its nose and under its eyes.

The resemblance wouldn't be exact to most people, but to her the similarity was unmistakable.

To her, it looked just like her long lost Bellie. She walked toward the horse and reached out to brush the bridge of its nose and it responded willingly. She laughed as she looked into its eyes. It stood there calmly with its broad shoulders and muscled legs. She opened the door to its stall and went inside to get a better look at it.

The brown wasn't splattered on him as was on Bellie; its brown spots appeared to be more of concentrated dots.

Regardless, he was a fine horse and she brushed the hair on his skin in acknowledgment as she walked around him inside his stall.

Her feet hit something hard on the floor and its contents rattled. It was a big item wrapped in heavy cloth. There were others wrapped the same way and positioned by the rear corner of the stall. She tried to place it back where it initially rested, but something had torn through part of the cloth, an arrow with a reddened tip and black shaft.

The whole item seemed to be full of it.

She placed the item back quickly and stood to depart, and that's when she heard voices near the stable entrance.

*"We should leave now. We failed our attempt and waiting for the others is risky. Who knows what happened to them. If they got caught we could be in danger,"* a voice stated.

*"None of them would betray us. They would die for the cause before letting a word slip out their mouths. We will wait for another hour before we leave. We can't just abandon the rest,"* a deeper voice affirmed.

*"We are not abandoning them. They knew the risk when they chose to come. They will find their own way back to the mountains if they escaped. They could be waiting out the chaos at other hideouts. But what if they're caught? Those animals will drain the truth out of them no matter their loyalties. We need to go. If they send any of their warriors here, we will be at a severe disadvantage. You should head back to the camp, our people can't lose you, we can't lose our leader,"* the first voice expressed passionately.

A brief silence ensued.

*"You know I'm right. I know you don't want to leave them but we have to. Everyone back at the camp is depending on your leadership. Staying here is a risk,"* the first voice added.

Another silence ensued, a longer one than the first.

*"Okay. Get the horses and weapons; I will go tell Quame and Bassa we are leaving,"* the second voice concluded.

Naemi stayed quiet in the stall without an idea of what to do. She hoped to politely explain her intrusion and walk away quickly if she was caught. Steps could be heard toward other horses who neighed in response to the stranger's engagement, and finally a face revealed at the edge of her stall.

A man's face looked back at her. He slid the stall door open gently when he noticed the girl hiding in the stall.

He looked to be in his mid-thirties, and wore a brown cloak that hid most of his garment. His deep blue pants still exposed beneath it, with his boots which were more brown than black from faded dirt.

His hair was mostly shaved and black. His eyes were focused and deep brown, complimenting a sort of triangular face with carved jaws and full lips. He had a puzzled expression on his face at the sight of Naemi, and opened his mouth to speak.

"*What are you doing in here girl?*"

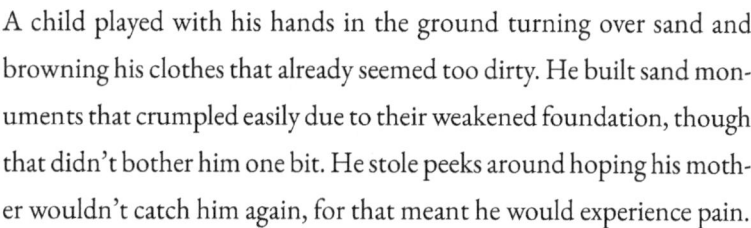

A child played with his hands in the ground turning over sand and browning his clothes that already seemed too dirty. He built sand monuments that crumpled easily due to their weakened foundation, though that didn't bother him one bit. He stole peeks around hoping his mother wouldn't catch him again, for that meant he would experience pain.

He looked quickly around him to verify his abandonment, looking all over his surroundings. His eyes however caught an abnormality when his head glanced past the skies.

An irregularity that broke concepts of the world he knew, the ones that existed ever since he had the ability to know his own consciousness.

There was a person standing in the skies.

Its body looked unusual. One of its arms looked longer than the other and there were strange extensions on its back that swayed in a repeated motion. The sun which was almost out of view cast embers of its last light on the being, and it reflected white in the sky.

The sound of galloping horses caught his ear and he turned to a sight he could understand. The sight of more than a dozen soldiers riding into their settlement with swords bare. He got up from his play area, running as fast as his little legs could carry him toward his mother with a heart full of fear.

Selius hovered above, looking down on the miniaturized lives of the people below, his eyes seeing everything. His body covered entirely in his replenished armor. The white and gold metal drenched over him like a fitted cloak and the hardened leather covering his wings with its extended sharp tips.

His helmet sat gracefully on his head, focusing his eyes to his cause, and he held his long weapon firmly in his left hand. He had arrived only a moment ago and waited till the soldiers from the outpost reached the area.

There weren't any signs of escape from his godly view, the area was mostly open except for the forest region about two-tenths of a league from the settlement. If the rebels were here, that would most likely be their escape route. He steadied his heart from the immense anger that filled his insides, the thirst for vengeance that rose to its peak.

He cleared his mind to his only purpose and descended in a rapid fall.

His feet hit the ground with a boom.

The sound rippled throughout the area and the force vibrated the sands pushing dust into the air and coloring the air brown. When the color settled and his visibility stood unobscured, all who saw him froze instantly.

The fifteen soldiers who rode into the settlement plagued into homes and buildings with weapons drawn. They broke down doors and slammed bodies, pushing everyone they could see into the open, into the presence of the crown. Selius searched through the faces that gathered around him marking their features and the ones that stood out to him as treacherous.

The faces that looked back at him saw the embodiment of a myth. Their eyes brought to reality stories they had heard through time.

The stories that changed people's view about the possibilities in the world and their own insignificance in it. The stories about supreme beings who walked among men with abilities they could never fathom. The stories of a crown prince who touched the sky at will and drank the blood of his enemies. The revelation broke the minds of those who had known nothing in their lives but normalcy.

They stared with widened eyes and mouths shut in fear.

Selius stared back at the people who surrounded him as his mind churned. There were about eighty people excluding his soldiers. He saw the varied expressions that looked at him, the dominant one being one he was used to. He searched their eyes for signs of disdain; an easy give-away for the depraved souls with hate for the crown.

The bodies that stood around him all looked petrified. His mind churned more, eliminating the weak and the young till all that was left were twenty-two possible suspects.

Then, he finally spoke, his voice chilling, his demands absolute.

*"There are people hiding amongst you. Murderous lunatics who have committed the worst of sins against the state. They have disguised themselves as travelers, lurking within your homes to escape the judgment they deserve. You have a choice. You can help bring these vicious creatures to justice, or you can all share in their fate."*

His words reached many ears and turned their faces with more fright than they originally wore.

The confusion, the uneasiness that ran through their bodies. Their mouths wired shut, their voices stuck to the bottom of their bellies like the weight of a stone sinking deeply through the depths of the sea. They turned their heads to one another, hoping to avoid being the first to speak.

The only sound that rained through their midst was that of soldiers shouting commands, and the drumming of beating hearts. Courage ran skelter in most, but for a few it lingered and rose.

For a few, this was a chance to deal a heavy blow to the crown. A golden opportunity to make up for not burying the heads of the Thrun empire in stone, and not felling their sun deity to the ground.

The successor to Thrun's impure colonization stood in front of them, the next generation of their evil rule. One who himself had attributed to the deaths of many of their brothers and sisters in arms. A symbol of Thrun's strength and greatness.

*How great it would be to take him down.*

They searched for an opportunity to attack, a chance to go retrieve their weapons and put their lives on the line. Courage is a burning fire that blinds men to the rain clouds above. Their undying resolve strengthened and they waited for what came next.

Selius's focus remained vigilant, all his senses firing with peak awareness and his eyes scouting through the grains. His mind had contemplated the situation. He had no certainty the rebels were here, but he also had no certainty they weren't. The risk of the rebels escaping through disguise was unallowable, and he would do whatever he needed to, to make sure that such a future was avoided.

"*You!*" Selius barked, pointing the edge of his weapon toward two people who stood in the front, though there were three who stood together.

A younger man a dash below six feet with a medium, strong frame and shortened golden hair. He stood next to a freakishly imposing woman holding the hands of a disabled boy. People gasped in drowned voices, but their legs wouldn't move from fear of being branded guilty. There was nowhere to run in the presence of one who could reach all.

Two soldiers rushed toward the two, pushing the boy to the ground and wrestling to pull the woman into the prince's presence.

One soldier managed to subdue the younger man but his counterpart failed with the woman and two more soldiers joined him. They drew their swords toward her and forced both her and the man onto the ground in the middle of the people as the prince approached them slowly.

"*You think I can't see through your ill-fated disguises,*" Selius shouted. He let the tip of his weapon kiss the ground, dragging through the sands as he approached them.

"*Your desperate attempts to flee judgment after you were bold enough to attack the crown. Tell me where the rest of your aiders are?*" The prince demanded.

The voices of the accused sounded denial to the accusations, denial that mattered little to him. In truth, all he had were his suspicions, but he cared neither about their lives.

His itching for retribution couldn't be contained any longer and he intended to send a message to all who watched, a message that would motivate them to push out the guilty.

"*They are not who you seek,*" someone shouted from beyond Selius's view.

He turned to see an older man step into the inner opening.

"*They are only simple travelers helping me and my children to find our way back home. We have done nobody any harm, and we mean no harm to the crown. We are not who you seek.*"

Selius looked at the man intently, approaching him till he stood about two feet away from him.

He was tall, strong looking even through his age, and wore scars on his face and neck area that spoke to his battles of defiance. Surely they didn't think he would fall for this ruse, this phony trickery concocted to grant them escape from his wrath.

He looked back at the man and spoke with a tone of unbridled vehemence, "*You're exactly who I seek.*"

His strike after was swift.

Piercing the man's torso till the red Fermelstone blade could be seen through his back. Blood dripped down effortlessly, some of the insides of the man's body dripping with it as Selius retracted his blade from him.

The body hit the ground as fast as gravity could pull it down.

Screams rose all around him though there was no sound greater than the shrieking sound that came from a building beyond — the building that held the horses.

The cry turned heads from how loud and haunting it sounded. Like a high-pitched release of internal pain that causes bones to shiver and eyes to bleed.

A man ran out from the stable with a panicked expression at what was inside. He held an arrow and bow in his hand. Selius dashed to the front of the stable to break the man's escape, gleeful as he had discovered another of the rebels, and stood in front of him with his partizan dripping blood.

His senses called to him abruptly.

There was a vibration beneath his feet. Something was running toward him fast, something big enough to quake the ground and send ripples through it. He turned in confusion only to meet a hand reaching out toward his face. He evaded some, but he had turned too slowly in his assumed safety and the force that touched his helmet knocked him off his feet, crushing him through buildings.

The people who saw could not believe what they were witnessing. There was a girl chasing after the crown prince in a state of absolute fury, and her words were clear for all to hear.

*"I will kill you ... I will kill you!"*

The soldiers who were present didn't get enough time to believe what they were seeing either. The imposing woman who had been brought to the middle pounced on one, attacking him and taking his sword. The fourteen soldiers left prepared to attack her, and before they could, others from the crowd joined in attacking them.

The rest was chaos.

The weak and afraid ran helter-skelter by no fault of their own, they cherished their survival and did what they could to maintain it. Swords clashed swords and the sounds of battle began. Those who fought against a common cause united without even knowing the names of one another.

Some distance away, the two calamities fought; the sky and the ground colliding with rage upon rage, fury upon fury.

Dakai heard his father speak and then screams all around him. In his blindness, everything felt so disorienting.

First, he was pushed to the ground and felt Beara pulled from him. Then he heard Kainu and Beara's voices speaking to someone, and a moment later heard his father's, followed by something hitting the ground, then an excruciating yell.

All happening in quick progression, never giving him enough time to process anything. He thought against removing his fold, knowing the commotion that would bring. He got off the floor and then felt the rush of people running. They pushed him to the ground and ran over him in their escape.

His dilemma heightened; to take the eye fold off or not. Hands grabbed him and a voice he recognized followed. The hands snatched the eye fold off his face and called to him again.

The rush of light was blinding for an instant, then he saw Kaise's face.

"*Dakai! He's dying!*" she mentioned with a shaky tone.

The sounds of swords clashing filled his ears. He saw Kainu fighting a soldier and Beara doing the same.

Kaise shook him back to focus and repeated herself.

"*What? Who?*" Dakai asked, still getting his bearings.

She pulled him toward the direction of the body that lay in the sands, and then he understood.

⚬

The blood had spread throughout and Ozai lay there still. Ozai's body had felt the chill of the cold blade through him and the sting of his body hitting the ground. It was painful, a pain that ruptured his body and his soul. He forced himself to breathe, but his body was rapidly failing him.

Everything around him felt quiet.

He could see the darkening sky; it felt so close for some reason. His fingers felt cold, his throat felt dry, and he couldn't feel his toes. He breathed through his mouth, a sound that was quiet to him but to anyone else would sound like the exhale of a dying animal.

That light-pitch pulsed groaning that came with every breath.

Time passed slowly with his extended view of the skies. He saw people run over him and then saw a girl call to him. A girl he recognized but couldn't remember her name or where he knew her from. She left hurriedly and moments later returned with another face he knew, one he could never forget.

"*Son.*"

He said with the little sound he could muster.

He didn't hear his own words, or the ones Dakai spoke to him. He could see the grief on his son's face, the tears that rolled down uncontrollably.

"*You took my eyes instead of your mother's.*" Ozai said with a smile. He could feel the last embers of life that remained in him and held off the tears that lurked.

*"Forgive me Dakai, tell your sister to forgive me for leaving you both too soon too."* He took another forced breath, the wheezing in his chest louder than before.

*"I'm going to go be with your mother now. Take care of your sister, she'll need you now more than ..."* The breath left him as did the last sound.

Dakai stared at his father's body quietly.

He was knelt in a pool of blood-sand, his hands and parts of his clothes were bloodied all over from attempting to clot the gaping hole in his father's body. He couldn't find the voice to scream, or any voice at all.

He felt the awakening of the power inside him with the rise of his emotions, and feared to speak lest he endangered Kaise next to him. He raised his father's head into his arms and cradled his dead body.

The tears that flowed filled his eyes and flooded his face. There was a burning in his heart that filled his entire chest, one he felt he needed to scream to get out but he never did.

In the midst of despair, some turn to rage and others only fall deeper into the abyss of pain.

———————◆O◆———————

Selius felt his body fly through buildings, breaking through wood till he finally slammed into the ground. He could feel the vibrations in the land still; whatever had hit him wasn't relenting. He felt the ringing in his ear, the dizziness that tried to capture his head, and shook out of it.

He rose from the floor slowly.

His armor was stained with the color of the ground. There was wetness on his lips, in his nose, and a heavy pain on the side of his jaw. He reached to feel his lips under his helmet and noticed part of it had broken off. About a quarter of it, from the lower left side of his face extending to the side of his left ear and below his eye. The rest of his helmet was cracked and the lines drew through the metal like the long roots of a pine tree.

He touched the wetness right under his nose and saw blood. His eyes widened. He hadn't seen his own blood in years; not one from a battle.

His mind fired like flashes of stars in the night sky at the possibilities.

*How do they have a Dion? There was no mention of that in the attack?* He thought.

He didn't have any time to diagnose his situation, the vibrations got louder, and this time, he was fully focused. Naemi lunged at him again, drenched in the extremes of such a primal rage that it could be argued that what was attacking was not her at all. Selius zipped back and to the side, now fully alert and engaged with the disaster that was in front of him.

The hit he had taken earlier focused him to what was at stake and the danger that potentially loomed. He tightened his fist and felt nothing in it. He had lost his favored weapon when he was being thrust through buildings. The calamity in front of him attacked again without break, and he evaded, he needed to find his weapon to have any way of damaging her. She was screaming at him with repeated words that were incomprehensible to him.

He studied his attacker, a girl of darker skin and fiery hair. She wore a sea-green tunic, and her pants were dirt brown. Her eyes had a light in them that screamed of fire, and Selius focused his mind more unto her.

He thought of what ability she possessed.

He had fought many Dions of varied ability and his skill always reigned supreme. She would be no different. Her power was most likely related to force, the heaviness in her steps that made the ground tremble. She was strong but not as fast as him, not even close. She attacked again and he avoided her swing. She didn't seem to have any fighting skill of her own, all her attacks were rushed and without precision.

She was fighting out of pure anger and he saw right through it. He saw an opening after she lunged at him again and he countered with a heavy kick to the side of her shoulder. His right leg hit straight into her and the shock reverted back through his armor.

She never moved.

He dashed backward to avoid her next attack and saw clearly the dent on the greave on his right leg.

*How strong can she be?* He thought.

He contemplated his next move; he needed to find his partizan, thinking that the Fermelstone blade would definitely be able to damage her. He dashed away from her, heading back to where it all started to search for his weapon.

His senses alerted him to something dashing toward him fast.

*It can't be her, she's not that fast*, he thought. He wasn't taking any chances however and zipped away from the path of whatever was behind him.

Two rocks whizzed past him with force. He looked back and the unknown Dion was throwing projectiles toward him. She wasn't fast, but she was resourceful. Breaking the land and hurling giant rocks toward him with such force. He eluded them with speed, moving through the air like a boundless fluid; like air itself.

Selius caught a flash of the red Fermelstone shine of his blade. It shone bright in the midst of the growing darkness, as the sun had left and the day descended rapidly toward the dark. It lay near some wood debris of a building that had been ruptured. He rushed toward it, seeing his attacker rush toward him.

He descended toward his weapon and readied in an attacking stance.

He knew what was going to happen next, a scene he had seen a thousand times. His attacker will launch an attack and he will counter with a strike of death ending the battle.

And so happened, the Dion sprung toward him and he spun away from her. He turned to her exposed back and struck with all his might with his blade, and nothing happened, just a loud clanging sound like when steel hits steel and stone hits stone. The Dion turned back swiftly at him, as bewilderment filled his face and his expression was of confusion.

*How strong can she be?* He thought again.

The distraction cost him. This time she had an opening of her own and sent a fist into his chest. He couldn't evade it in time and tried to block with the shaft of his weapon though he still took damage, and was sent flying again.

The land bore witness to the duel as the two disasters fought each other. The fractures that formed in the ground, the parts of nature that fell as collateral to their battle, the scars that will be etched in stone forever.

Those who saw it from afar did all they could to evade it. Some just stood and watched, seeing the extremes of rage and the uproar it would cause when stricken. Others watched in sorrow seeing friends lose themselves to the underside of emotions.

Regardless, no one dared interrupt. The sun was nowhere to be found now. There was little light in the sky, the light gray hue turning slowly to dark.

Selius rose from his second fall to see the steel shaft of his partizan broken. It had taken most of the damage from her strike, but the dent on his armor breastplate was still glaring. His chest hurt, the bruise hidden behind the fractured metal armor. He held both sides of his weapon still, standing from the ground and retreating into the air.

As dangerous as she was, she hadn't shown signs of jumping high or flight. The Dion reverted to throwing projectiles at him once more and he evaded them. He rid himself of the piece of his weapon without the blade, though his mind still contemplated its usefulness.

The part of his weapon that remained was only as long as a sword, and even though he preferred longer weapons to shorter ones, he made do with what he had. He focused his eyes on his enemy, still thinking on how he could defeat someone he couldn't damage.

She had proven to be extremely formidable and he wondered why the rebels didn't use her in their attack.

*Did they have another plan to use her then? Why use explosions when they had her?* He contemplated.

He pondered more and couldn't find any meaningful justification. Nevertheless it didn't matter now; he needed to kill her today. She was a threat to their state and leaving someone this powerful was unallowable. He gazed at her from above and she did from below, still in her state of fury.

He noticed her breathing had gotten heavier. She had been on an unrelenting rage for close to half of a half hour now, and her body couldn't handle the immense state it was being put through for long. Selius also noticed the change in the reducing number of stones she threw toward him.

A plan formed in his mind, and a sick smile grew with it.

He clenched his fist with his shortened weapon in it, and dashed toward her.

Naemi watched as the demon in the sky descended, approaching her. Her mind was broken as much as her heart was. Her insides felt like they were being scorched in flames, a scorching pain rising high till she could feel nothing anymore. Her heart filled with something else, an overbearing desire that filled every part of her, a desire to see the thing with wings crushed in her hands.

To rip out its parts till there was nothing left but blood and bone.

The desire consumed her ever since she saw that scene, ever since she saw the blade go through her father. The sight of it turned her eyes red and raised a wrath so bad her consciousness lost possession of her own body. She had stayed in the stable out of fear when she heard the soldiers come in and the winged man descend suddenly from the skies.

She had wanted to go be with her family and her friends, but the man who caught her in the stable cited it was dangerous. She stayed there, confused at what was happening till she saw Beara and Kainu being forced to the middle. She had planned to go help, hoping to summon her ability to save her friends.

Then she saw her father, and the sudden strike from the demon that killed him instantly. The emotions that captured her were sudden and intense. The cry that left her lips was inaudible to her own ears, and the wrath that followed took over her entire soul.

Presently, her focused eyes cared only about one thing without care for the consequences that grew. Her wrath had taken her body to its peak without the strength to keep on maintaining her ability.

Her lack of knowledge of her ability, her ignorance about the effects of such a rapid rise, and the subsequent effects of not having a trained body and mind to maintain it.

The copious amount of energy she was exerting at the time, and the unwritten laws of equal exchange. She didn't know any of it, and in truth, she wouldn't care even if she did. She braced for another attack on the winged demon and thrust toward him again, lunging, darting, throwing fists and everything she could to try and hurt him.

All he did was evade her. He never tried to strike any longer and only got close enough to make her surge, then he would evade. He kept on in his annoying attempts until they were back near buildings.

He zipped around one building and reappeared with a long rope in his hand. Naemi continued attacking him unremittingly, but he kept eluding her until he had tied a piece around her, and then he pulled hard.

She fell to the floor with the strength of his pull.

Her power had been waning away fast, the water that ran from the well was finite and she was close to bleeding it dry. She hadn't trained her power to overcome its shortened limits yet and the demon took advantage.

He pulled her into the skies; she could feel the rush of the wind as her consciousness slowly pushed out her wrath. Her hands struggled to grasp onto anything but air.

She saw herself depart from the land, moving high above as everything shrunk in size. She flailed about recklessly, trying her best to gain control of herself and the force that dragged her through the winds, but it was all for naught.

There was an abrupt pause in her motion, like the world had stopped momentarily, and she could see the entire sky in the far beyond.

Then suddenly, she felt herself being pulled toward the ground in a violent rush, and then, everything went quiet.

The strike to the ground sounded like two combined strikes of heavy thunder sounding at once. It pushed sand in all directions followed by a force of wind that could move mountains.

The ground broke and showed the body that laid at its mercy, the body in the center of the carving in the ground, bones broken and silent. Its eyes were still open, and its breath was almost non-existent.

Selius came down from above with his shortened weapon in his hand. He looked at the girl who could barely move. He had lost his helmet a while ago from her incessant chasing.

His hair was full of dirt and his face dirtied more with the traces of sand that occupied his face with the dried blood. He walked in front of her and gazed at her fallen body with a smirk on his face.

"*You don't understand your own power, do you? Such a waste. You could have been a great weapon to the empire, but now you have to die,*" he said to the defeated.

He extended the tip of the blade to touch the skin on her arm and it cut her easily, pouring blood from the small cut he made.

He smiled more and raised his weapon for a final strike.

He heard the whiff of what approached and swung to deflect the three arrows that came to him in lightning quick succession. He fumed at the interruption and attempted to kill the girl under him again, but three more arrows followed.

The dust that colored the area after the impact was settling, and he could see the source of the arrow from afar. The shooter shot two more and he avoided them.

*Such a nuisance.*

He took a quick glance at the girl to confirm she couldn't move, stepping hard on her fingers to feel her reaction, but all she did was groan silently. Convinced she wasn't going anywhere, he flew off the ground, moving toward the archer to rid himself of his annoyance.

The man ran behind some buildings, and he chased him. When he finally caught up to the archer, four people sprung from the insides of broken buildings to surround him with weapons drawn. He saw their faces and recognized some. He laughed aloud out of the blue, the kind of laugh that comes from the belly and fills the heart with pride. He saw the imposing woman he first intended to kill and the others he had suspected.

He laughed louder and spoke in her direction.

"*I knew it. I knew you were one of them. So these are your friends? Where is the other one? Is he lurking around too? Hoping to jump out of the shadows soon? I knew it. I was going to kill you all anyway, but I'm glad I was right,*" he joked.

"*Thrun is a stain to these lands. You and your depraved state are nothing but vultures, vile scourges, taking what's not yours and forcing the true owners into servitude. You force them to worship your false gods while you drain resources from our lands. You deserve to atone for your sins, the sins of your fathers and forefathers,*" the middle-aged man on his farthest right said in anger.

He was a tad below average height but had a brawny build. He wore black pants and a dark-green oversized long cloak reaching just below his knees. His hair was a wavy mess and he had no hair on his lower face.

He held a long whip in his left hand with a sheathed blade on the right of his waist, and his expression was of animosity and determination.

Selius laughed again at his words.

*"And you will fix that? You will bring down Thrun? You will kill me? YOU?"* He continued to laugh.

*"These lands are now and will forever be under Thrun rule. We won it in battle. We won it because your ancestors cowered when they heard our name and felt our power. Your silly ideas of liberation bore me. You can win it back like we did or die like you're about to. Your attack on our state was cowardly, just like your ancestors. Now fight me and die, I have been asked to bring your heads."*

Selius readied himself for their attack, searching through those that surrounded him to see who would attack first.

The archer shot at him again and he deflected the arrows with his shortened weapon. He zipped toward the archer, but rope from a whip wrapped around his neck and two people flanked him; the bald man and the imposing woman. He tugged hard on the choking whip. The brawny man held strong on its hold, pulling back hard along with another of the assailants. The bald man swung at him with his long sword, and Selius responded with a swing of his own.

The swords clashed with the sound of kissing metals. Selius forced the momentum of the man's sword into the ground, stepped on the sword with his armor and slashed the bald man across his exposed body. The prince's weapon split through the attacker, drawing an opening on his skin from the man's belly to the base of his neck.

The insides of the man spilled unencumbered, draining from him as gravity got hold of it. Selius kicked his body away, still tugging on the rope that hindered his movement. He thought to fly up, but his head was exposed and he had no visibility of the archer, so he obstructed the view of his head with his wing.

*His arrows are tipped with a light layer of Fermelstone. It won't be enough to break through my armor, but I have to protect my head.* Selius thought.

The imposing woman gave him no time to think further and swung her sword in the direction of his head. Selius deflected the sword with his right gauntlet. He swung a kick at her and she lowered herself to evade, but when she came back up he returned his kick backwards and hit the woman in the side so hard that she flew through a building, disappearing out of sight.

Selius used the blades on his wings to slash through the whip, tearing its choking hold from him. The corner of his eyes glimpsed the archer's location and the next arrows that targeted his head.

The arrows shot straight at him and he bashed them away as he had before with his weapon. His vigilance peaking to its extremes, he was aware of everything around him. Compared to the disaster he just fought, these fighters were mere nuisances to him and he focused every strike with precision to make quick work of them.

The next assailant attacked him; this man was the tallest of them all, even taller than the imposing woman. The man attacked Selius with a morningstar, swinging the weapon with all his might at the prince. Selius evaded his weapon then gyrated his extended wings in the process.

The knives on his wing armor sliced clean through the man's head, and his body dropped in a thud. Another set of arrows shot at Selius and he dashed away from them quickly, visibly annoyed at the pest for still shooting them. He zipped toward the archer, preparing to end his life with one swing and was blocked by a sword of pure Fermelstone. He looked at the one who swung it, the man who spoke back in proclamations. The man pushed his sword away and swung at him again but Selius jumped back.

Then, the man barked orders to the archer,

"*Go! Now. You know what to do.*"

Selius looked at the archer as he tried to escape behind buildings. He thought to stop him at first but the futility of whatever he planned to do bothered him little.

"So you are the one giving orders? ... *A pure Fermelstone sword? ... Are you Guyan royalty? You look too brutish to be Guyan.*" Selius questioned, but the man stood quiet and in a fighting stance with his eyes intently focused.

"*Doesn't matter. I will kill you first and kill him too. He won't get far. Everything you plan to do will fail. Your attack on our state failed. You'll die here today, and your head will be used as a symbol of deterrence to all who would dare rise against us.*" Selius claimed boldly.

The man dashed in Selius's direction and struck, the prince blocked his strike and gyrated again but the man evaded it and countered, a move the prince had to visibly avoid, considering his exposed head and the

Fermelstone blade the man held. The man attacked again, his shorter frame gave Selius some issue, as well as the loss of his favored weapon.

Regardless, he was a capable fighter, capable enough to contend against him and not die immediately. He held a stare of utter focus against the prince, his brawny frame didn't hinder his speed but only bolstered his strength, and his precision was worrying.

Selius felt the hint of weariness from the Dion who had chased him all around. His movements had slowed too but there was no way he would lose to such a man, not even if he himself was just a man.

The man swung at him again and he deflected, swinging his left wing with the edged blades toward him, a swing which the man predictably avoided. But as the man countered, the prince swung his wing back as if he was making another strike, and instead lowered swiftly to his knees and thrust his weapon into the middle of the man's chest as the man attempted to elude his attack.

The man groaned deeply, the shock of the pain loosened the Fermelstone blade from the man's grip onto the ground.

Selius's blade pierced his chest like a knife pierces bread. Blood poured out onto the ground as well as pieces of light green stones from his oversized cloak.

Before the prince could take notice of what it was, he reached out and held the prince in a hug, an act that pushed the blade more into his body. Selius looked at him puzzled, puzzled at his actions and even more puzzled at the huge smile he wore as he headed to his death.

*"Is this how you die? Like a crazed child? Don't spoil a good fight with such a pitiful death."* Selius claimed.

Selius felt the movement of an arrow, and he was on alert, but the two fire arrows weren't toward him and shot right into the man's back. He looked at the beyond to see the archer's face staring at him.

Something felt wrong.

"*Do you know about fulminate crystals?*" The man said in a crazed laugh.

"*What crys...*"

Boom!

━━━━◄◊►━━━━

Sekoile shot the arrows into Presus with a heaviness in his heart. His fingers struggled to let go of the arrow even when he knew what was at stake. He had no time to grieve after he had shot them, no time to grieve the person he had known all his life — his leader, his brother-in-arms, his friend.

He had seen his friends die right before his eyes, dropped quickly like swatted flies, and his heart struggled to maintain sanity. The plan they had was risky with high margins for failure, but it was the only one they could muster to achieve their goals.

Their entire escape had been thwarted by the sudden appearance of the Thrun prince. The strange girl he met in the stable had turned out to be a raging Dion, and the muscled woman and younger man who joined them in fighting the soldiers claimed to be friends of hers.

They all watched and heard the sounds of her rage as she pursued the prince, her wrath causing the land to shake. He saw the body of the man the prince killed, the one her friends claimed to be her father, and the boy who held it in his arms with despair on his face. The boy with the eyes of the famed Kaku demons. Sekoile had retreated at the sight of him. He had heard the tales of the Kaku, heard of the brutality they carried, and he raised his bow in fear.

Presus had calmed the tensions that rose, focusing the group back to a common cause.

"*We have to save the girl,*" he told Sekoile, "*With such power she can help us defeat Thrun, help us destroy their empire.*" Presus added.

Their plan was made in haste and quickened by the sudden strike to the ground that concluded the battle between Dions. He had done his part and now he needed to escape in case the prince wasn't dead, for he would surely die then as well as all those he was escaping with. He ran quickly, headed in the direction of the three horses that waited.

Two horses were tied to a cart with four people inside and an additional one person on the front-seat holding the reins. The third horse had nothing tied to it, but the rider was the woman he fought along with. She called out to him, stretching her hand and he grasped it. She whipped the reins and triggered the horse, commencing their escape.

Darkness grew bold with the rise of the evening. The horses galloped through the sands and vegetation toward the forests. Beara could still feel the heavy pain in her sides.

She knew parts of her ribs were broken, but her focus mattered more on their escape. Kainu was ahead of her with the two horses and cart. Inside were Kaise, the unconscious body of Naemi, Dakai, and the dead body of Ozai.

Beara kept stealing glances at the sky hoping the winged man wasn't in pursuit. The sound of running horses spread through the quiet all around, their hooves inching closer and closer to the cluster of trees ahead.

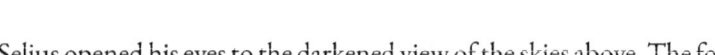

Selius opened his eyes to the darkened view of the skies above. The force of the blast had thrust him into the ground some feet away.

The idea of the man wearing an explosive came to him late, and he had tried to dart backward but never got far enough. He had protected part of his face with the armor on his right wing but he could feel the burns on his lower neck and cheek.

His armor was painted with the colors of intense battle.

Part of his hair was burned and there was blood all over him, majority of which wasn't his. His body felt an ache he wasn't used to. Ones he had never experienced even through his years of intense training. He groaned as he stood up slowly from the ground. He had endured three of the hardest hits he had ever felt in his entire life, and he felt the toll of them.

He looked to the source of the blast — to the scattered insides of the man.

The spread blood over the sands and broken wood, the torn flesh, shattered bones, and stained brown all around. He huffed quietly to himself, picked up his shortened weapon and the Fermelstone sword the man used that lay in his sights. He spread out his wings and took to the skies, his eyes searching from above for the archer.

Selius searched and searched but the archer was gone. His eyes found nothing of note, only dead bodies and hiding commoners. The body of the Dion girl was also gone.

A revelation that made him scream in anger at his failure, a loud sound that traveled through the air till it depleted into the void.

The evening cared little for his frustrations, the darkness continued on its reign as the evening strengthened. The endeavors of the world traveled on as they always do, regardless of individual inconveniences.

However, a sound played some leagues away — a slow sad song only audible to those who grieved. It played as a dirge, a melody to the fallen and a guide to their souls as they left to the ever-beyond. It filled hearts with comfort but still flamed their inner plights for vengeance.

Maybe it was a ballad that played through the winds, or the hidden sounds of the world that sang to all those who had suffered pain today. Nevertheless, to those who heard it, it was somber and clear.

It was a song of requiem, a requiem of revenge.

# EPILOGUE

When people talk about the histories of the world, about the stories of the great lands of the known world and the lore that is woven in the sands like browned fabric, they speak as if they have all the knowledge. As if the books and scrolls have all the truth, as if the songs of legends paint the entire picture, as if the tales they hear are indisputable. It can be argued that in the eyes of the future, the truth of the past is whatever the present say it is, for they are the current keyholders of history and ultimately control what will be remembered henceforth. So has it been since time immemorial, and so will it be till time's end.

When people talk about the woman land-breaker who broke the world, they tend to forget the truth behind the girl she once was — the sister, the daughter, the friend. The truth of her being, the love she held in her soul for her family and her companions. They forget she was once a person, and her story morphs so much into a legend that the truth of her fades away into just a shadow. A shadow though that still lingers. However much the light may try to chase it away, it stays true to its nature, attached to the body no matter what. For the truth can never be really forgotten, there are some who will always remember, there are some who will always be brave enough to tell the world.

"Dreams without goals are just dreams, and ultimately they fuel disappointment. On the road to achieving your dreams, you must apply discipline, but more importantly, consistency. Because without commitment you'll never start, but without consistency, you'll never finish." Denzel Washington.

# ABOUT THE AUTHOR

Kiki Yaw Sarpong was born in Accra, Ghana in the year 1996. He went to St. Peter's Senior High School in Ghana, and moved to the United States after graduating. He pursued a Bachelor of Science degree in Mechatronics Engineering at Pennsylvania Western University, and continued to pursue a Masters in Robotics at New York University. Presently, Kiki works as an Engineer and Novelist. Kiki has always had a deep passion and appreciation for storytelling, his favorites being mostly biased toward Sci-fi and Fantasy. In Kiki's free time, he likes to watch long video essays about beloved movies and tv shows, or go biking in beautiful scenery.

**Follow my socials:**

https://linktr.ee/kikisarpong

www.ingramcontent.com/pod-product-compliance
Lightning Source LLC
Chambersburg PA
CBHW072335020726
47506CB00004B/893